HEAVENS
ON EARTH

—

Carmen Boullosa

TRANSLATED FROM THE SPANISH BY
SHELBY VINCENT

DEEP VELLUM PUBLISHING

DALLAS, TEXAS

Deep Vellum Publishing
3000 Commerce St., Dallas, Texas 75226
deepvellum.org · @deepvellum

Deep Vellum Publishing is a 501c3
nonprofit literary arts organization founded in 2013.

ISBN: 978-1-941920-44-2 (paperback) · 978-1-941920-45-9 (ebook)
LIBRARY OF CONGRESS CONTROL NUMBER: 2016959429

—

Cover design & typesetting by Anna Zylicz · annazylicz.com

Text set in Bembo, a typeface modeled on typefaces cut by Francesco Griffo
for Aldo Manuzio's printing of *De Aetna* in 1495 in Venice.

Distributed by Consortium Book Sales & Distribution.

Printed in the United States of America on acid-free paper.

Praise for Carmen Boullosa's Novels

"In its first English translation, *Before* offers a perfect introduction to Boullosa's fluid and powerful writing...Beneath the events Boullosa presents in often comic terms—playing childhood games with her half-sisters, visits to her grandmother, the shock of coming into womanhood at the time of her mother's death, her savage dreams—is a powerfully rendered sense of loss and separation." —JANE CIABATTARI, *BBC Culture*

"Utterly entertaining—a comic tour de force. I loved [*Texas: The Great Theft*] and think it deserves a very wide readership." —PHILLIP LOPATE, author of *A Mother's Tale*

"Brutal, poetic, hilarious and humane...a masterly crafted tale." —SJÓN, author of *Moonstone: The Boy Who Never Was*, on *Texas: The Great Theft*

"Boullosa's *Texas: The Great Theft*, is evidence that our ideas about postmodern cowpoke tales have been woefully premature...What is outstanding in Boullosa's work is the deep sympathy expressed for every human encountered." —ROBERTO ONTIVEROS, *Dallas Morning News*

"*Before* is a small gem that brings to mind two other gems of Mexican literature: Juan Rulfo's *Pedro Páramo* and Carlos Fuentes's *Aura*. This comparison is not overstated. Like its predecessors, death is a central theme in Boullosa's novella. *Before* differs, however, in the playful, sometimes irreverent way in which the protagonist confronts this macabre topos." —GEORGE HENSON, *World Literature Today*

"This first novel [*Before*] is raw and unadorned, like a vein opened up on the page." —AARON BADY, *Literary Hub*

"A luminous writer...Boullosa is a masterful spinner of the fantastic." —*Miami Herald*

"I don't think there's a writer with more variety in themes and focuses in his or her writing...The style and range of Carmen Boullosa is unique for its versatility and its enormous courage." —JUAN VILLORO, author of *The Guilty*

"What is both moving and also lucid about Boullosa's prose, though, is her ability to take one in and out of a scene fraught with disorder and violence, and place one back in the rich spirit of humility encountering sublime beauty." — MATT PINCUS, *Bookslut*

"Like Eimear McBride's *A Girl is a Half-Formed Thing*, Carmen Boullosa's peculiarly spooky novella uses formal experimentation and an uncompromising emotional honesty to explore the formation of a young woman's identity. Only a writer as fearless as Boullosa could so perfectly capture the unease of youth with such Angela Carter-like weirdness." —GARY PERRY, on *Before*, bookseller, Foyle's, London

"The return to childhood that Carmen Boullosa has given us feels unlike any other book that I have read. I can't say enough about Boullosa's incandescent writing, which glows from within, radiating possibilities, contradictions, ambiguities." —TERRY PITTS, *Vertigo*

Dear Reader:

This novel is not written by an author, but rather by *authors* plural. There are three characters who claim to confess within its pages, and two who claim to have written it. If I have any authority over this book, I will say that the true authorship does not belong to any of those indicated above, but rather to the beat of a destructive violence I have sensed in the air, in the air of my city and in other places: an atmospheric throbbing, so to speak.

There is such a thing as a violence that avoids the corrupt paths that have led nowhere and then runs into Sleeping Beauty centuries later. It is a noble and heroic violence, one that is princely and all hugs and kisses. Unfortunately, Mother Nature is not like that in this book. This violence is one that erupts but does not lead to discovery; bursts forth, leaving nothing in return; and ultimately, destroys. I plucked it from the air because I did not know how to avoid it. From it, and with it, I moved forward with the non-traditional and complex form of *Heavens on Earth*. Each line is aware of the destruction behind it.

Take this book, reader, and give it the warmth I was unable to find for it along the way. Let it be reborn in you; may it be yours.

Fondly,
CARMEN BOULLOSA

Indies of the world, heavens
on earth

BERNARDO DE BALBUENA

I wonder how you have managed
to overcome the daily use
of time and death

ÁLVARO MUTIS

This book is composed of three different narratives. For reasons that I do not understand, it was given to me to turn into a novel. But it is not a novel, nor is it three, but rather two that are super-imposed on each other: Lear's, which occurs in the future, and Don Hernando de Rivas's, which took place in the past. Estela condemned her own narrative to a supporting role: that of the translator who translated into Spanish the memories of the Indian, who, in sixteenth-century Tlatelolco, wrote them in Latin.

Perhaps if Estela had known how to represent herself in the following pages, the book might have become a novel, while at the same time being three novels. Tradition has permitted, on other occasions, for one to become one and still be three. But the two are condemned to separation. In exchange, the gods have given the number two the gift of dialogue. At the end of the book, these two separate novels embark on a dialogue—one that excludes the author and that allows Estela to reveal herself, a dialogue that occurs elsewhere, one that does not exist in these pages.

A novel is dialogue and unity. This text, on the other hand, is nothing but the proclamation of the heavens on earth. Heaven comes to earth in literature. Man, warrior by nature, becomes, in the din of a warlike inferno, what he perceives. What angel, imper-ceptible to human senses, endowed the universe with language? For man, everything evokes the war he yearns for.

Intercontinental war has erupted. If the powers that be do not arrive at an expeditious agreement, if they do not resolve the internal struggles over the territories that were once nations, only a few months are left to man and perhaps to the natural world.

JUAN NEPOMUCENO RODRÍGUEZ ÁLVAREZ

EKFLOROS KESTON DE LEARO

Today my name is Lear. Unfortunate circumstances forced me to abandon the one I was using before. The people of my community call each other by number. But I can't even conceive of myself without a name. I even baptized everyone else in L'Atlàntide— Italia, Evelina, Salomé, Ulises, Jeremías...

I don't know who my parents were because I was conceived in a test tube and raised in The Conformación (the first stage is The Cradle and the second is The Image Receptor). I can't explain my existence in the same way men did in the time of History— *for even though dust you are, Lear, to dust you will not return.* But I found a connection to the ashes of earlier times through my work as an archeologist. I'm the only one in my community who does this kind of work, not to mention the only one among the living who stops to think about the mother and father she doesn't have. Through my work, I connect with, and try to recreate, our ancestors. But this gets me into serious trouble because everybody else in L'Atlàntide wants to deny that we are descendants of the men from the time of History.

I work in the Center for Research because, even though memory and remembering are currently disdained in our community, this institution preserves memory. Whenever I find something I want to keep safe, I leave it here in the hopes that one day it will recover its original form. I also do my writing here in order to safeguard it. Instead of using papyrus or paper, a quill, fountain pen, pencil, ballpoint pen, typewriter, computer, or chisel and stone, I use the writing instrument of my people and my thoughts glide through space without leaving a physical trace of the rhythm, sound, or shape of the words. But my thoughts won't be inscribed in books, as they would have been in the time of Time, in the time of History. Instead of being written in ink on pages that turn and are bound by thread or glue, my words will assume their truest, most accurate form. No light will touch them, nor will ink or heat stain any surface. Stripped of physical form, they will keep watch over the Center for Research. And despite their advanced form, their subject runs backward, in a counterclockwise direction—in direct opposition to the normal order of things. While I bow to the past, the rest of L'Atlàntide stands on tiptoe reaching for and trying to hold onto the perpetual present in the hopes of recreating the sublime Natural world that the men from the time of History destroyed. I, on the other hand, remember them, talk to them, and describe our world for them.

We live suspended in the upper atmosphere of the Earth, far enough away to avoid the radiation, the ruins and destruction, and the sandstorms and toxic storm clouds that cover the surface. I like to think we established L'Atlàntide here, in this way, for aesthetic reasons—beauty rules our colony, and, to my constant delight, our rooms are transparent. We've learned to appreciate the beauty of the light and dark, the clouds, the moon, and the stars. Given the abundance of waste and rubbish that covers the surface of the Earth, we have, by consensus, decided not to add anything to the cemetery of things.

As lords and masters of the air, we've achieved more control over this element than the men from the time of History ever did. Although they figured out how to endow a disembodied piece of plastic with a relative degree of intelligence, we've been able to use the components of the atmosphere to build our houses and guarantee our survival. Our dwellings are made of air—air that impedes the entrance of air and never lets in either heat or cold. Solid air—an invisible material without substance or physical form—that tempers and attenuates the strength of the winds. Even our clothes are made of air—we wrap ourselves in it whenever we leave the transparent walls of L'Atlàntide. Our tools are made of air. Everything here is made of air. Even the Center that safeguards my writing is made of air (or you could say it's made out of a transparent material like glass, except that it's not hard).

In our world, air is the element that propels us, supports us, elevates us, and protects us. In our creation myth air conquered the sun—air ripped off man's overcoat, stripped him bare, and mastered him. Air—the wild element that we domesticated in our environment—flows in a filthy current over the surface of the Earth. Whirlwinds, hurricanes, cyclones, and tornados—often so dense with dust and rubbish that the sun can't get through to touch the ground or the water—unleash an uncontrollable rage over the empty planet. There, too, the wind conquered the sun—this is the Age of Air. Enveloped in a whirlwind, the Earth wears a tattered outfit that no longer has a skirt, bodice, stockings, or hat to go with it. The torn dress is adorned with the rubbish that the wicked weather has bestowed on it.

Our home, however, is an Earthly Paradise (like the one

inhabited by the first man and woman in the Bible legend), but a paradise without vegetation, suspended in the middle of the sky. We live in an enormous, transparent, flattened sphere that doesn't have visible walls or floors and was built without mortar, cement, stone, or brick. It's the exact opposite of a house, castle, or cave. We don't have things, nor do we use or make things. All we have is water.

Even though I study the past and I write in order to be faithful to the past, my connection to the past doesn't mean I'm disconnected from the present. The fact that I do historical research doesn't mean that I collect unnecessary or dangerous material and it doesn't mean that I don't dream about the future. Most people in L'Atlàntide think we should only be concerned with the present and the future. In fact, they think we have to forget the past completely because it was merely a lesson in errors—a lesson on how to destroy the Natural World. If it's true, as they say, that we only need to focus on the present and the future—and if we erase the past completely like they want us to do—Time, or what we know as such, would dissolve. We would float in an amorphous mass where there isn't a place for Time. The proposed reform— calling for total oblivion—means that we would lose conscious awareness, we would lose everything it means to be human. But what if we didn't lose consciousness? What if consciousness left us instead and closed the doorway to the imagination? What kind of future would we have? Do we have another door to the future? To be able to imagine we have to remember, we have to listen to the voice of memory. That's what I think anyway.

We've managed to overcome sickness and old age and it's been a long time since any of us has known death. But memory must play the same role for us as it did for the Ancients, our predecessors—the men from the time of History who once inhabited the Earth. If we forget everything, we would lose the thread of life. The clouds would no longer strike us as beautiful; neither the light of the sun, nor the play of the shadows in winter, nor the beauty of the flower would have any weapons that could touch us. But our thinning hair couldn't even reach our ears and there would be no way for us to convincingly imitate beasts because Mother Nature couldn't protect us.

This belief that I profess like a proselytizing preacher is not shared by anyone else in L'Atlàntide. They say we should break all ties with the time of men. But didn't we baptize our colony "L'Atlàntide" in honor of those we've condemned to oblivion? The name itself invokes the time of History. Of course, now nobody ever even mentions the origin of our colony's name. Nobody remembers the continent submerged under the sea with its grove of golden oranges and orichalcum (the red mineral that Atlantis dragged down when it disappeared). Nobody ever talks about those who dreamed of Atlantis, those who described it, or those who swore to have seen it. The people of L'Atlàntide want to bury the memory of those who preceded us and justify this desire by saying that all their knowledge and actions only brought destruction, and that we, the survivors, must run from it. However, everything we do is somehow related to the civilization that existed in the time of History. The survivors don't care anymore that the name of our colony, "L'Atlàntide," retains both the Catalan accent and the French ending. It doesn't matter to them that words are gradually losing meaning because they're busy inventing a communication code that won't use words. I try to tell them that any code will allude to the past, to History. The disadvantage of a new code is that it will be limited, imperfect and, thus, useless from the beginning. Not only will this wordless new code limit our ability to imagine, it will also reduce the number of our imaginings. I'll admit that language was imperfect too—as my favorite poet, Álvaro Mutis, wrote: "Words are, already, in and of themselves tricks—traps that mask, conceal, and bury the framework of our dreams and truths—all marked by the sign of the incommunicable." But at least language had the power to invoke the memory of other times and imaginings, and all that was, by the arbitrary law of reality, impossible.

Anyway, back to our bond with the men from the time of History, didn't we leave their waste on the Earth so that we *wouldn't* forget? Except for what was necessary to recreate the gardens, we haven't removed any of their trash or debris. Instead, we've preserved them as a monument to foolishness and misman-agement. But why should we hold onto their mistakes and deny ourselves their greatest treasure? If we do, then we'll forget the symbolism behind the junkyard of trash and debris and imagine that the Earth was never any different than it is today.

Right now the community is only interested in forgetting the past and imposing a communication code that will nullify lan-guage. But eventually things will get better. One day we'll under-stand that to remember is to survive. Then language will regain its proper place and the memorious will be the soul of L'Atlàn-tide. Once again we'll hear the laughter and fear the darkness. Then, my ethereal "writings" will turn into books. And I won't change my name anymore. I won't call myself Lear today and then Clelia or El Príncipe tomorrow. Then, I won't be able to maintain this blindness that can't distinguish the wolf from the lamb.

For now, I'll write even though there isn't anyone who can read what I've written unless they're willing to travel back in time to learn the language—back to the time of History when humans lived in nontransparent houses cemented to the ground, surrounded by things. This will happen only when L'Atlàntide surrenders to the power of Nemesis.

I respect the past because I remember. But I don't do so blindly; remembering the men from the time of History doesn't mean singing their praises, lamenting their demise, or exalting ourselves. I remember them by writing for them, even though they don't know it because they destroyed themselves. Remembering doesn't make me a doe-eyed optimist or a slave to the past. I remember in order to stir my imagination and sharpen fantasy's penetrating point.

My archeological work involves the recovery of books and manuscripts. I'm not interested in salvaging other objects—I don't look for memories in things anymore—and it's been centuries now since I've recovered anything other than a book. The works of art that had any value on Earth remain intact under an air-bubble connected to the surface that we call *Das Menschen Museum*, or the Museum of Man. But I don't think anyone ever visits it. Sometimes when I remember the atmosphere burning, I think I feel what they used to call "melancholy." But I've had enough of the sad, cadaverous footprints of things—dirtying the bottoms of the seas and lakes, the water of the rivers, and the surface of the Earth— dancing a macabre dance in cyclones full of man-made things.

So why books? I work with books because they survive across time. From the moment a book is written, it begins to interact with the past and the future. Books have always been the memory of other times—those that have been, those that will be, those that couldn't be, or can't be, or that should have been. L'Atlàntide, on the other hand, survives because the community is determined to hold tight to an isolated moment floating in stagnant waters that repel death.

I'm writing these notes before I begin to paleograph and annotate my most recent discovery, a manuscript I found in the Library of the College of Mexico. It's not that I'm particularly interested in Mexico. I don't "believe in you," Mexico, as a hair-gelled poet once regrettably sang out. No, I don't believe in you. On the other hand, I don't see any reason to attack a place, ripping it up as if it weren't a part of the Earth. I might not believe in you, Mexico, but I do love you in the way Ramón López Velarde, our divine national poet, wrote: "not the myth / but your communion bread of truth / as I love the young girl who leans over the rails / blouse buttoned up to her ears / skirt touching her delicate ankles."

This is not the first time I've discovered material for my work at this site, but I've also searched many other places. Excluding Seville (with which I have a history that I've promised myself not to write about here because if I start, there's no stopping me), I've found important texts in the British Library, in the national libraries of Madrid, Bogotá, Paris, Mexico, and in the John Carter Brown Library; not to mention those of the Arab world, Russia, China, India, and Tibet. I rarely work at the Library of Congress in Washington, however, because they left all their material in the form of microfilm (MF) inside a closed capsule that survived the chains of explosions. I don't work with MF because it's not my field of expertise. Those who work with MF work with intact objects. As an archeologist, I work with dust and extremely small particles, with the memory hidden in the material. In my work, I use particle magnetizers that I won't describe here because they're invisible like the memories they recover, and also because this is not the place to explain the science or the knowledge of my colony. Our science can't really be communicated in words anyway.

The only memory of the past L'Atlàntide wants to preserve is that the men from the time of History destroyed the Natural World and caused their own extinction. The people in charge of MF have let themselves be convinced that all the teachings of the past are destructive and so now nobody works with microfilm anymore. Fortunately, before they adopted this position, they translated the MF into our reading code, the result of which is a basic universal library of two thousand volumes. According to those in charge, the men from the time of History selected these two thousand titles themselves, so even though the people in charge of MF are complete idiots, it's not fair to blame them for the barbaric selection criteria. The Bible and the Koran were at the top of the list, followed by fifteen encyclopediae considered to be essential and some twenty scientific books, including Newton's *Philosophiæ Naturalis Principia Mathematica*, Goethe's *Theory of Colors*, and Leonardo da Vinci's papers on the behavior of water in which he asserts that the surface of the moon and the center of the earth are made of water. Next come the classics, among which we do not find Quevedo, Plato's *Dialogues, The Iliad*, or

The Odyssey; but instead *Gone with the Wind, Uncle Tom's Cabin*, and an atrocity titled *Jonathan Livingston Seagull*. These are followed by another three hundred similar horrors, but no Faulkner or Rubén Darío. There are two frivolous, sentimental novels by Clauren, but nothing by Chekhov. On the list we find everything (even to the last word) written by Madame de Staël, but not a single word by Chateaubriand, Voltaire, or Rousseau. Having mentioned all these, I shouldn't feel the need to add anything else, but I don't want omit other examples. They didn't save any part of *One Thousand and One Nights* other than some frankly horrific versions of a single story incorporated into tawdry anthologies, such as *The One Hundred Best Erotic Stories* and *Adultery and Misogyny in Literature*. The selection doesn't have a leg to stand on; the entire list is vile and plain nonsense. Nothing can be said in its defense; it speaks for itself. But, there's no reason for me to speak badly of it. After all, I dedicated myself to archeology because of my contact with this list. An annotated translation of Juvenal led me to Quevedo and Boccaccio took me to Homer, though sometimes I walked hand in hand with less reliable tutors, such as an insignificant little writer who led me to Octavio Paz.

I've recreated countless texts and transcribed them here in the Center for Advanced Research. In the process, I've learned how to appreciate the beauty of books, to recognize the incomparable craftsmanship of a few volumes, and to distinguish between one edition and another. Although they're considered to be objects, books are not things. We survivors don't want anything to do with things. The relationship man had with the things he made or altered only resulted in one mistake after another. In fact, every morning when I leave L'Atlàntide and descend, by way of the Punto Calpe (which is the name of the staircase made of solid air that we constructed to connect L'Atlàntide to the Earth), I'm confronted with the artificial mountain we made when we were establishing our colony. This mountain—a macabre monument to man's love of things—is made of pieces of plastic, disposable diapers, bags, packaging, electronic equipment and appliances, furniture, clothing, etcetera. Because I very rarely descend any other way, I'm faced with this reminder almost every day. If that weren't enough to make me despise the love of things, this fact certainly is: when I reach the surface of the Earth I can't admire the branch of a tree, a flower, or even a single leaf because in the places where the rubble might conceal these treasures, there are none left. We survivors have cultivated some gardens with the seeds or the memory of the remains that we salvaged from the destruction, but I almost never visit them. This is something else that the other survivors don't understand—they say it's foolish and unnecessary to dirty my feet among the ruins since we've created an earthly paradise in an artificial enclosure that replicates the natural world and is "untouched by the hand of man." It's as if they believe that they've succeeded in replicating the garden where still-innocent Eves and Adams stroll because they haven't recreated the serpent.

Okay, enough. No more beating about the bush and avoiding gardens. On to the manuscript…I was coming from the Central Library of the city of Bogota, where I had just restored a beautiful herbarium from the Fondo Mutis, which I discovered by accident—a mistake I can always be proud of. Confused by the name "Fondo Mutis," I came upon this lovely text that was hidden behind some work by the other Mutis (his relative and my poet) as I was pursuing such verses as these:

> Each poem a bird that flees
> from the site marked by the plague.
> Each poem a suit of death
> over streets and beaches flooded
> with the lethal wax of the defeated.
> Each poem a step toward death,
> counterfeit ransom money,
> target practice in the middle of the night,
> riddles the bridges over the river,
> whose sleeping waters travel
> from the old city to the fields
> where the day prepares its bonfires.

But as luck would have it, in confusing one Mutis for the other, I came across a beautifully hand-illustrated herbarium that actually had nothing to do with my poet, but is more closely related to poetry than the two authors were by blood. The scientist is also a poet, both pursue the same mystery. Unfortunately, the people of L'Atlàntide weren't concerned with mystery when they constructed the gardens. For them the gardens were an end in and of themselves. They didn't understand that the hand of a god (to give it a name) was on the vegetation or that an unfathomable mystery arose from that touch. The people of L'Atlàntide believe that the gardens belong to them, but in reality the gardens are *foreign* to them; they belong to the other, to the unknown enigma. And we can never approach this unknown mystery without words. Their foolish plan to eradicate all traces of memory will distance us further and further from the spirit their gardens need in order to be truly real.

As I was saying, I was coming from the National Library of Colombia, in Bogotá, after restoring the Herbarium Mutis (and then sending it to our good government in order to request its inclusion in the Menschen Museum), when I decided to continue my search in Mexico for the verses of the other Mutis, my poet. I chose to go to Mexico because in the course of my research I found confirmation—in the form of an issue of a Bogotá newspaper adhered to the back of the herbarium—that my Mutis was quite popular in Mexico. So why not look for some of his books there? Until then, I had believed that Mexicans didn't read, period. The proportion of books destroyed per kilometer in Mexico (something I had previously researched) is frankly absurd. Not that there weren't books; in fact, there were thousands and thousands of the most absurd titles stacked up in bodegas. I thought then that my appraisal of the reading habits of Mexicans was unjust, that they probably just read the books they found in the libraries. On the other hand, why not read in the cozy shelter and silence of a bodega? Given their atrocious living conditions, why wouldn't they prefer to read standing uncomfortably in humid, semi-dark bodegas, ruining their eyes and damaging their lungs by breathing the unbreathable air? The notion that they read in bodegas makes more sense than the idea of their books squeezed together, uselessly decaying, for no reason at all. Moreover, why would they have printed so many books if they didn't read? And anyway, even though it might seem to me that it would be uncomfortable to read in a foul, humid bodega, maybe it wasn't for them. Perhaps it was better than being exposed on their hostile streets or crowded together in noisy rooms listening to the blaring television. Or maybe, like us, they were more interested in silence than comfort. Anyway, it was only because of my Mutis that I made my way to the Library of Mexico. And since I was there, poking around, I decided to translate a manuscript with a Mexican theme—but I repeat, not because I have any special interest in Mexico. In "The Death of Capitan Cook," my Mutis wrote:

> When they asked him what Greece was like, he spoke of a long line of convalescent homes built on the shore of a sea whose poisoned waters advanced, as slowly as waves of oil, over shallow sharply pebbled beaches.
>
> When they asked him what France was like, he recalled a short passageway between two public offices in which some scabby guards were searching a woman who was smiling ashamedly and where splashing cables of water rose from the courtyard.
>
> When they asked him what Rome was like, he described a fresh scar on his groin that he said was a wound he received while trying to break the windows of a streetcar abandoned on the outskirts of the city in which some women were embalming their dead.
>
> When they asked him if he had seen the desert, he explained in detail the erotic customs and migratory pattern of the insects that nest in the porous pits of marble eaten away by the saltpeter in the inlets and worn down by the handling of the coastal traders.

But like I said, I don't fantasize about the existence of nations. Anyway, I found this manuscript in the Library of the College of Mexico, which is located in the Pedregal de San Ángel in the southeastern section of Mexico City, where new endemic flora and fauna emerged after the area was covered in lava with the eruption of Xitle in 600 B.C. The Pedregal de San Ángel was ultimately consumed by the city; but even as recently as 1972, someone saw a puma around the Ajusco volcano and somebody else saw a lynx running in the Iztaccíhuatl mountains. But now the city has completely devoured its own beauty. My poet once lovingly described this region:

> Upon my arrival in Mexico in October 1956, the generous hospitality of the painter Fernando Botero and his then wife, Gloria Zea, allowed me to live in their warm company during my first few months in exile. We lived at Kansas 7, apt. 2, in the Nápoles district. My first views of the city were unforgettable, and today I remember them with an incurable nostalgia.
>
> When the evening light made it impossible for him to continue painting, Fernando and I used to stroll down the lushly tree-lined Insurgentes until we arrived at Reforma, where we would either go to into the forest or go see El Caballito. At that hour, a clear opalescent sky radiated a subdued violet light, the likes of which I have never seen in any other part of the world. A good number of fin de siècle French-style homes were preserved on Reforma, which lent the Paseo a gentle, peaceful feeling. Everything was enveloped in that incomparable light, in that purity of air that made the trees, the houses, and the people stand out with a precise and miraculous force.
>
> Spellbound by the beauty of the city surrounded by green hills and watched over by the intense whiteness of the volcanoes, Botero said to me: "You need to stay and make this your home."
>
> I took Botero's advice and here I am. But now nothing is left of the city that dazzled and bewitched me so much that I made her my second home. Even worse, we have

succeeded in turning her into a hideous overcrowding of architectural horrors and a nightmare of lethal fumes that are killing us in a suicidal vertigo.

What have we done to deserve this punishment? Each person has his own answer. Speaking for myself, I would say that I didn't know how to be faithful; I didn't know how to maintain the exquisiteness of the city that I remember as the most beautiful in America.

Oversight and lack of consideration like that must be paid for with the highest price conceivable: life.

Once upon a time, the Pedregal de San Ángel was inhabited by coyotes, raccoons, cacomistles, badgers, hares and rabbits, arthropods and butterflies, as well countless birds of all kinds, including falcons, eagles, and hummingbirds. In 1902, Mexican novelist Federico Gamboa described this region in his novel *Santa:*

> Still unexplored by what is assumed to be more than half, it is volcanic and immense, dotted with shrubs, colossal monoliths, and such sheer rocky inclines that not even goats can stand on. It has incredibly clear, serpentine streams of unknown origins that disappear into the ground only to reappear at a distance, or noiselessly fade away into cavities and clearings that seem to be maliciously concealed by grass. There are deep, black caverns and grottos full of mysterious brambly bushes with deformed leaves that are almost heraldic in shape. Fantastically twisted cacti adhere to the side walls of these profoundly deep abysses whose deadly interiors are so deep that a thrown stone causes corpulent, sinister birds to take flight but never touches the verdant and florid bottom...

> It is covered with a thicket that tears at the clothing and the threat of a tarantula or a rattlesnake strike is ever-present. And whatever might be lurking in the distance is even worse: mountain lions, jaguars, and death… Legends of vagabonds abound, stories of apparitions, and lost souls who wander these lands as soon as the sun goes down. It is full of enchanted places with traditional names: Nest of Sparrowhawks, The Fountain of the Lovers, The Skull, The Stag…

If any of the other survivors in L'Atlàntide had snooped around in my archives, they would've discovered that I often stroll through the gardens I come across in my research.

The manuscript has two alternating (rather than consecutive) parts, one of which was written by Don Hernando de Rivas, alumnus of the Colegio de Santa Cruz de Santiago Tlatelolco. However, I didn't discover his version in the original language, which was Latin, but rather in the translation done by the author of the second part of the manuscript, Estela Ruiz, who will introduce herself in the following pages. Just to be perfectly clear: I would have preferred to paleograph a more literary text than hers. This manuscript is not a work of fiction; or at least, fabrication doesn't appear to have been the intent of either of the two authors. I came across the manuscript by chance and I brought it here myself, but I'm not going to pass judgment on it because "There is only one form of reasoning other than geometry: that of facts."

I will proceed to read the manuscript and will begin with my transcription of the two epigraphs Estela uses to introduce the text:

I thank God there are no free schools
nor printing, and I hope we shall not have them these
hundred years, for learning has
brought disobedience and heresy and sects
into the world and printing has divulged them
and libels against the best government.
God keep us from both.

The first epigraph was attributed to the Governor of Virginia, Sir William Berkeley. I greatly object to her use of this because these lines are not relevant to the text she translated, despite the fact that it was written in the past, in the unchanging flow of the time of History. But I've transcribed it here anyway so that the echo of the joke might some day reach the ear of another member of our colony, as it has mine.

On the other hand, I have no objection whatsoever to the second epigraph:

Would that Mexico be a shared homeland and inn;
Treasury of Spain, center of the great world;
Sicily in its crops, and in pleasant
Mild summer its temperate region.
Venice in plan; in high
architecture Greece; a second
Corinth in jewels; in profound knowledge,
Paris, and Rome in sacred religion.
Another New Cairo in grandeur;
curious China, in trade; in medicine
Alexandria; in rights, Zaragoza.

Imitate many in mortal beauty;
and be unique, immortal wanderer
Smyrna; that Homer might enjoy
in Balbuena.

This was signed by Don Lorenzo Ugarte de los Ríos, Chief Constable of the Inquisition in Nueva España. It seems to me that one might divine a black humor in this selection.

The next page of the manuscript, following the epigraphs, begins with a sort of confession by Estela, which is then followed by the words of Hernando de Rivas. I'll divide the manuscript into *cestos*, respecting the order begun by Estela. Each voice will have its own *cesto* and I'll close each when it's the next one's turn, whether it be Estela, Hernando, or myself. As is my custom, I'll open and close each *cesto* with a phrase in Esperanto, my "Open Sesame" for the Center for Research.

These clarifications made, I'll begin transcribing Estela's text and then continue with the text written by the Indian, Hernando de Rivas.

I'll now close this section from the colony of survivors called L'Atlàntide, in this luminous year without name or number, more than one hundred years after the disappearance of natural life on earth (no one knows whether it's exactly 213 or some other number because we're not allowed to count).

Slosos keston de Learo

EKFLOROS KESTON DE ESTELINO

In order to explain my relationship to the text, I'm including a preface or introduction, in my own words, to my translation of the sixteenth-century manuscript signed by Hernando de Rivas, alumnus of the Real Colegio de Santa Cruz de Tlatelolco. I want to explain why in the hell something that came to me by chance is so important and why I set out to re-write it. I'm doing this for myself, no one else. It is so important to me because in a way it's mine—it's part of my history, part of my being, part of my birthright. It belongs as much to my present as to my past. I'm not sure how to best put it. It's important to me because…I'm afraid that before I begin translating, I'm going to have to explain a few things.

But first, as a preamble to my explanation as to why Hernando's manuscript is so important to me, I'm going to describe a sequence of images I've spliced together in what might be considered a sort of video clip in the form of a disjointed series of images commonly seen in today's television and bad movies.

The video clip begins with a scene that actually happened in my childhood; however, now I'm viewing it as a spectator, as if I weren't part of it. The protagonists are a grandmother and granddaughter. First, I'll describe the location of the scene because, rather than taking place in a typical household setting, like the kitchen or living room, this scene takes place in the natural herbal essence laboratory for the pharmaceutical industry owned by the grandmother.

The home-based laboratory is of domestic proportions, about the size of a house. You enter the laboratory through a wide, dark passageway, both sides of which are lined with cardboard drums that contain dried herbs and powders, shiny metal canisters of alcohol, and all the raw materials used to make the pharmaceutical products she sold. A floor-to-ceiling wooden bookshelf, full of large glass demijohns containing transparent, translucent, and dark-brown liquids is in the middle of the laboratory. (The smell of the lab is indescribable. Rather than being unpleasant, it was more like an overly intense freshness that could quickly become sickening. Not for me though because I always loved being with my grandmother and would happily spend all the time possible helping her with her work. I used to help her filter the substances in the laboratory, or fill tamales, or make chocolate by hand in the kitchen for the family, or count crochet stitches. This is not part of the video clip, but remembering the laboratory reminded me of it. No other place smells like it—it was a mixture of valerian root, fresh herbs, and alcohol. I can still smell it to this day).

Facing her liquid library (the wall that was full of large demijohns) and at the foot of the tall windows that look out into the courtyard where sacks of herbs lay, there are metal drums that contain the liquid preparations that are filtered drop by drop into the mouths of the demijohns that are always dying of thirst because the drops fall ever so slowly. A large iron table covered with a single piece of granite stands in the center of the laboratory and a set of scales and a hand-pump (that's used to empty the large demijohns) sit at the foot of the table.

The grandmother and granddaughter talk while the former removes a paper filter from the funnel, over which the tap of one of the metallic drums drips, and replaces it with a new one. Earlier in the scene, as they do every month, the grandmother and the granddaughter had worked together to fold the large sheets of white filter paper into pleated fans, which they first cut with a knife into perfectly sized squares. The grandmother places these paper fans into the funnels; the former molding themselves to the shape of the latter as the filtered substances drip from the taps of the metal drums into large demijohns like the ones on the bookshelf. When the demijohns are full, the grandmother labels them with the name of the extract contained within.

My young life was marked by all the things inside my grand-mother's laboratory, Velásquez Canseco, which takes its name from the two last names of my grandfather who's been dead almost twenty years now. I can still clearly see the labels, pens, bills of sale, and the old typewriter on which she typed them, as well as the paper filters and large glass demijohns that held the secrets made in the laboratory. And I remember my seemingly innate attraction to the mysteries of the substances that were made using seeds, almonds, and hazelnuts, as well as all types of herbs, including chamomile and alfalfa. As I recall, the herbs occasionally arrived full of slimy snails that we grandchildren loved to play with and that our grandmother valiantly battled against in order to keep them away from her rose bushes.

In the scene I've been describing, the grandmother and grand-daughter are talking in the laboratory while the grandmother works with the filters and large demijohns when the subject of a hand cream that just arrived on the the market comes up. It's called *Nivea* and it comes in a blue tin with the name written in white letters across the lid that looks like the tin of the *Crema Teatrical* the grandmother has used since time immemorial.

"You shouldn't use *Nivea*," the grandmother says disapprovingly to the granddaughter. "Never."

"It makes your hands soft, Abue."

"It might make them soft, but it has glycerin and glycerin darkens the skin. Your hands will turn brown."

It darkens them? Turns them brown? I didn't understand what she was getting at. "It darkens them, it darkens them," I kept repeating to myself. I didn't see the problem. When we actually had this conversation, many years before, we children were on school vacation. It was two days after we had arrived, toasted and black as night after having spent three weeks in Acapulco. What did it matter if glycerin darkened our hands since we had already "darkened" our entire bodies with the exception of our bottoms and a strip across our chests, two ridiculous white patches of skin that were visible only under the spray of the shower?

As a child I never dared talk back to my grandmother when she used that severe, judgmental tone. Nor could I have understood that her comment—unjustifiable in any situation—was a bad habit left over from her own childhood. My grandmother was born and raised close to Comalcalco, Tabasco, and many of her relatives lived in Chiapas. I didn't know the Chiapas relatives, but as a child I tasted many of the foods they used to send from one of their ranches in Pichucalco. I remember fondly the cheese from Chiapas, which was delicious when she mixed it into her *fideo* soup. By itself, however, the flavor was too strong for my taste even though my grandmother used it to make quesadillas in her special way, putting them on the comal at low heat so they were crisp and crunchy like *tostadillas*. One of these days I'll be brave enough to make them myself and see how they taste. Now you can buy the Chiapas cheese almost anywhere, but when I was young it would arrive in Mexico City almost like contraband. Back then, you couldn't find it at the grocer's or in the supermarket, and you could only occasionally find it at one of the weekly mercados. It was shaped like the Dutch cheese ball (which is what we used to call aged Gouda when I was a child) that the cousins from Chetumal used to send to my grandmother. Those of us who live in the capital like to say that Chiapas is as far away from Mexico City as Holland is. But even though now you can easily find the Chiapas cheese locally, I never buy it. I prefer to keep it safe in my memory—a precious relic of my childhood—as if it were a part of my grandmother and therefore untouchable. I think the only time I was brave enough to buy some of the ingredients that she would use in her kitchen (for celebrations under any pretext) was a few months ago at the Villahermosa market where I bought a large, smoked freshwater gar; pickled oysters in diamond-shaped glass bottles; and something called mameyes. But these mameyes were different from the mameye fruit that is hard, round as a ball with a rough rind, an enormous bumpy pit, and hard, firm flesh. It's an incomparably delicious fruit whose flavor evokes the taste of peach, a bit of mango, a tiny bit of piñon, and another tiny bit of pear. I also bought fresh nances and sweetened cocoplums. The latter are black and so cloyingly sweet that you only want to eat one and really just to get to the center of the pit for the rosy, round almond that is crunchy and hollow, and whose taste is both unusual and incredibly delicious. A friend who went to Cumaná, Venezuela, for a conference told me that the Venezuelans make a kind of cocoplum nougat in which the seeds and flesh are mixed together. But I didn't find any because it wasn't the right season.

From Villahermosa I also brought back a couple of kilos of *chinines* (a huge fruit that is a distant cousin to the avocado, but has a white fibrous flesh that's a bit too sweet) and three dozen live crabs tied together with the fibers of a banana leaf and packed in a cardboard box that I carried by its corded handle and put at my feet on the plane. Crabs are so stinky that it's no exaggeration to say that the stench is unbearable. When the flight attendant was trying to figure out what the hell smelled so bad—or which inconsiderate mother was carrying a dirty diaper in her purse— she passed by and didn't suspect me with my wouldn't-hurt-a-fly look. In order to maintain my feigned innocence vis-à-vis the "stinky diaper," I kept my reading glasses on and didn't take my eyes off my book the entire trip, except when the flight attendant passed by I would briefly raise my eyes from what I was reading, smile at her, and—hypocrite that I was—wave my hand in front of my nose so that she'd know that the inconsiderate person's crime was bothering me too (even though we were one and the same). As soon as I got home, I threw the crabs into the bathtub of water I had left to rest so the chlorine would evaporate. The following weekend I invited a few friends to share in the delights of my gastronomic purchases. We prepared an unforgettable feast even though for me it was also bittersweet because nothing tasted the same without my grandmother. The one thing that was the same, however, was the sound of the crabs clawing the inside of the large metal *tamalera* as they were trying to escape while they were being steamed alive.

Cooking crabs is a cruel process. The first thing you do is to throw the live animals into the pot and then you have to rope someone into preparing them. Whoever has the job of pulling the flesh out of the thin legs and then stuffing the "head" of the animal with the leg meat will suffer almost as much as the crab did. The flesh attached to the cartilage of the crab's thin legs has a more delicate flavor than the fat claws (known as the teeth or grinders). The grinders are eaten separately and are not braised, but simply boiled in salted water. If the crab is fresh, the boiled grinders are deliciously aromatic and don't need any seasoning. You shouldn't have to add any herbs or even a squeeze of lemon before eating them. In fact, lemon on the claw of the fresh crab is a gastronomic crime.

Before being stuffed into the head, the flesh taken from the thin legs is sautéed with onion, garlic, capers, aromatic herbs, pepper, and the juice of the liquid used to clean the heads after the innards are removed. So where does the cruelty come in? That which pertains to the crabs is perfectly clear—they're cooked alive. And the person who prepares them suffers with the work involved in extracting the flesh from the thin legs, which requires a rolling pin and patience. The thin legs first have to be cracked with a rolling pin and then the pieces of shell have to be painstakingly removed from the flesh until it's free of any remnants. Additional suffering comes by way of the olfactory sense—the smell is awful.

This makes the entire process laborious because everyone involved has to endure that stench for hours. The finished dish, however, is exquisite and it seems that the odor of the live crab, which is renewed by the crushing, remains in the shell once the dish is completed.

Back to the video clip: the grandmother, in the white coat she wore to work in the laboratory, and the granddaughter, in pants and a shirt, are talking, faithfully replaying a scene from my childhood. Suddenly, an enormous blue tin with *Nivea Cream* in white letters falls between them. It becomes a blue strip that divides and splatters them with huge blue splotches. On the grandmother's side the blue splatters turn white; on the granddaughter's side, they turn dark brown. The white splashes on the grandmother's side transform into parasols under which fair-skinned women walk, most of whom are dressed in fitted, embroidered silks and brocades. Some wear veils over their faces and bright white gloves to protect their skin. Thus, white from head-to-toe, the women are even more dazzlingly beautiful.

The camera angle widens as the enormous blue jar suddenly falls, allowing us to see the houses next to the sidewalks that are elevated almost half a meter above street level. Children chase each other around and young men in hats pass by. Older women, dressed in deep mourning, sit in their rocking chairs next to the doors of their houses, embroidering or crocheting as the afternoon fades. From time to time they acknowledge the passersby, greet the young people, nod their heads to some of the young men, and talk among themselves in a leisurely, unhurried manner. None of the women in the rocking chairs are Indian, and none of the Indians walk on the sidewalk with the men and women described above. The Indians walk on the street, which is not paved with asphalt or stone, but is rather just a dirt road, made of a "brown" mud the same color as those who walk on it.

A heavy rain, or tropical storm, suddenly lets loose. To say it's pouring rain is not an exaggeration or a cliché, but rather describes the situation perfectly. The streets are flooded with rain. The women, their rocking chairs, and the children quickly go inside the houses. The Indians lift the white passersby onto their shoulders so that the elegant people won't get their feet wet, so they won't get covered with the muddy water that runs like a river through the streets. In the midst of running through the rain under their burdens, the Indians transform into mules; as the torrent of water becomes even heavier, they turn into enormous, almost monstrous, animals better equipped than mules to carry their loads; and then, as the water streaming by the houses becomes a wide, roaring, brown river, they morph into functional machines that transport smiling and elegantly dressed passengers. The beautiful white women maintain their composure and keep hold of their little veiled hats, gloves, and white woolen spats; likewise, the white men hold onto their hats, and their linen suits and silky smooth cotton cravats remain unwrinkled.

The camera angle widens further and the screen is once again split in two—the grandmother on one side and the granddaughter on the other are still involved in their conversation. On the granddaughter's side, the brown splatters of cream take the form of semi-nude sunbathers, toasted brown and dancing around a bonfire on the beach. Some of them are blonde, some are brunette, and others have black or white hair, but both the men and women wear their hair long so those who have shirts on could pass for either gender. Because their bodies are almost androgynous, burnt by the sun, turned leathery by the wind, and hardened by exercise, they're free of any gender distinction whatsoever. The black foam of the waves that break on the beach is as dark as the night. Suddenly, out of nowhere, the waves join in the dance of the "savage" naked men and women who wear feathers on their arms, heads, and ankles and whose skin is painted with brilliantly colored stripes. Meanwhile, on the grandmother's side, under a harsh rain, the white people continue riding on the backs of the Indian-machines above the tempestuous river that the street has turned into, smiling cheerfully as if everything were peace and joy across the face of the earth.

The juxtaposed images change abruptly. The grandmother's side now advertises *Crema Teatrical* in enormous letters superimposed over a beautiful, rosy-pink female face, which itself is superimposed over the subdued light of the sun rising over the Iztaccíhuatl volcano, known as the White Woman. The granddaughter's side advertises *Nivea* in similar letters superimposed over the blue of the bonfire that becomes even bluer as it melts into the sleek, brilliant blue of the lid.

This is where the succession of images ends. Perhaps it isn't necessary to explain, but my grandmother's remark (which I hadn't thought about in decades and must have been locked away in my unconscious) was wrapped up with an unsettling feeling. I believe that when my grandmother expressed her opinion about glycerin's effect on the skin, the black liquid substances being filtered through the funnels formed into angry whirlpools inside the large demijohns in the laboratory. I think these substances remembered the people who picked the herbs she extracted, the ones who knew them as herbs in the fields, who carried them in bags to the market, and who carried them from the market to my grandmother's car. The substances inside the large demijohns roiled with anger out of loyalty to the Indians. And I know that if my grandmother had seen their anger, she would have been ashamed of her comments. The dark light of the extracts, shining from inside the demijohns, would have enlightened her and opened her eyes, it would have made her understand that the old order was pure perversion, that it defiled the collective soul and hung like a rope around the neck of our land.

In her lab, my grandmother lived a life she couldn't have even dreamed of as a child. Time and again she would tell me how her father used to beat her for disobeying the rules. Because she was female, she wasn't allowed to jump rope or play with a ball. But one morning, thinking she was alone in the inner courtyard of my great-grandfather's plantation, she couldn't resist the temptation to try to jump rope. It was just her bad luck that my grandfather passed by at that moment and whipped her—"for lack of respect"—with the very rope she was jumping, until the servants brought him his riding crop so he could continue beating her. Then he locked her in her room for a week. He wouldn't even let her out to eat or to empty her chamber pot. So, she ate and drank locked up in that room, living with her own shit and shedding bitter tears, all the while being consumed by the punishment inflicted on her by others.

The Indian workers lived near, but not on, the plantation. The young men grazed the livestock owned by the whites and the women picked coffee on the land owned by the whites. Only the huge domestic staff—made up of mestizos—lived on the plantation.

As an aside, I'll just add that my great-grandmother took in newborn babies who had been abandoned. The first one she took in was left on the ground under the arch that led into the courtyard, right where the venomous *nauyacas*, which are palm-pit vipers, could have eaten the baby. The enormous *nauyacas* that lived in the area ate the baby chicks of the hens and the turkeys. They would also devour the newborns of the women who left their babies unattended in hammocks while they picked coffee beans. My grandmother used to tell me that a *nauyaca* could slither silently up a tree, along a branch, down the rope of the hammock, and swallow a baby whole without a peep, before anyone even noticed. But she never had any stories about men who could slay these hideous monsters and rescue the children from the serpents' hellish lairs. The dragon might have had his Saint George but the *nauyaca* of Tabasco never met her match.

Because everyone knew that my great-grandmother took in abandoned children, she ended up adopting eight (or eight survived, I'm not sure which) over the years. These eight then should be added to my grandmother's five "natural" siblings, who were all raised by the nursemaids my great-grandmother brought in from Comalcalco or Pichucalco. I'm not sure if any of the adopted ones were Indian, mestizo, or mulatto, or if they were all white, but I'm guessing they must have all been white. I never asked my grandmother because she would have been offended by the question and would never have accepted any accusation of racism, which was something very ugly. As far as racism goes that was the horrific crime of the Germans. However, everyone knew that the Chinese were dirty petty thieves, the Blacks were lazy and smelly, and the Indians didn't have any sense or reason. And everyone knew that the reason the Indians didn't work inside the plantation house was because they were dirty and stinky and they lied, but not because they were Indian. That just wouldn't have been acceptable.

The Revolution broke out when my grandmother was a young girl living on the plantation near Comalcalco with her parents, her thirteen siblings, and a legion of servants. I don't know which was the worst of the tragedies that that crazy, beloved Revolution brought upon them: the loss of their lands or my great-grandfather's death in a shoot-out between the revolutionaries and the *federales*. According to family lore, they looked for a doctor who would treat my wounded great-grandfather and the only one they found refused to save him out of fear for his own life. And guess who that doctor was? The father of Pellicer, one of our most important modernist poets.

The *federales* took everything: livestock, clothing, furniture, and even the crops. The servants joined the revolutionaries. Left with nothing, my great-grandmother had no choice but to leave the eight adopted children, along with the few coins she had managed to hide, with a neighbor woman. My great-grandmother had promised to send the woman some more money as soon as she could to help feed all the little ones. We have no idea what happened to those children because the *federales* later beat the poor woman to death. So, there's no telling where my grandmother's adopted siblings—the ones taken in by her mother's generosity, only to be lost in the revolutionary hurricane—ended up.

On seeing the family's misfortune, my grandmother's godmother offered to take care of my grandmother, who was eleven years old at the time. But once she had my grandmother under her control in Villahermosa, she treated her like a servant. I never asked my grandmother exactly what she was forced to do, but I'm sure she had to mop because she didn't despise anything more than the mere thought of mopping. One day, when I told her I didn't know how to mop, she replied, "Good Lord! Why would you want to know how to mop? Neither my daughters nor my granddaughters were born to mop. Nor was I, but with what happened to us…" And then she was lost in her thoughts and I didn't dare say anything else, but her silence conjured the image of my grandmother on her hands and knees scrubbing the floor.

My grandmother, bless her heart, was finally able to return to her mother when she was a bit older. She didn't manage to get back to her mother earlier either because she hadn't wanted to be a burden or because she hadn't been able to escape from her godmother's control. And since she was older, she was able to help out with expenses by sewing for others.

According to family lore, her brothers got rich because they worked hard and were organized and enterprising. I don't doubt they were (clearly, they had to be), but in all honesty, I'm sure they also took advantage of their race. They were all as white as jasmine, most of them had *ojos claros* (the blue or green eyes so prized by elite white society), and they were known to have come from a "good family."

My grandmother married a military doctor who, before he received his degree from the Military Medical School in the capital, was a child-hero. The story seems pretty far-fetched to me, but…my grandfather's father, who was in the military, was in Perote when the federal army took the fort and he was taken prisoner along with his son (my grandfather). The boy jumped through the window of the jail and ran to notify the troops, who were fighting against Díaz in Xalapa, that his father was imprisoned in Perote. The troops arrived just in time to retake the fort and save my great-grandfather's life. Even though I've heard the story a thousand times, I really don't know whether or not it's true. But I do know that after the Revolution he went back to Oaxaca where his mother's family was from. The Cansecos had cochineal farms, among other things. While he was in Oaxaca, he was commissioned to Tabasco, where he met my grandmother. They married and remained in Villahermosa, where they became friends with Tomás Garrido Canabal. They worked with him as he rose to the position of Governor of the State of Tabasco, and my grandfather became Minister of Health under him. My grandfather successfully eradicated malaria from Tabasco, where a school was later named for him. My grandparents left Tabasco with Garrido Canabal and they all headed to Mexico City together.

I've only recently learned about the school from my mother's brother. He also told me that my grandmother had been invited to the inauguration of the school not long after my grandfather's death, but that she refused to go because "those government people are all a bunch of thieves." But I doubt that was the real reason.

I think it was probably because my grandmother and my grandfather's relationship was always a pretty difficult one, even in memory, and she just didn't seem to have any desire to honor him. Not that she wanted to erase everything either. I remember a photo of him in the office that continued to be his, even though it was she who used it until the day she died.

Even though the relationship between my grandmother and grandfather was difficult and quite bitter at times, it wasn't a loveless marriage. For years I was my grandmother's favorite and she never tired of telling me, during those favored years, that I was the spitting image of my grandfather, which I ceased to be when I quit being her favorite. I lost her favor when I committed the sin of growing up (a mistake I've always regretted, but for which there was, and is, no remedy), even though my face didn't change much—I still have the same lemur face I had as a child, a face with a little of the Indian inherited from my grandfather Canseco.

My grandfather died very young, suddenly, without anyone knowing what was wrong with him, despite the fact that my grandmother exhausted herself searching for the best doctors to treat him. In a final attempt to save him, she traveled with him to a hospital in San Antonio, Texas. The doctors there examined him but didn't find anything wrong. He wasn't ill with anything specific, he was simply on the verge of death. The same thing happened to my mom—she died as young, and as suddenly, as my grandfather. But she didn't go to San Antonio. She just went to the Spanish Hospital because I don't think anyone realized she was so close to death. I hope it's not my fate to die young. But my fear of dying at the same age as my mom or grandfather is another story;

and anyway I'm older now than either of them were when they died, so I might as well let go of that stupid, useless fear.

When my grandfather Enrique was alive, my grandmother worked so much that it was only after she was widowed that she noticed she was living in the city and not in the forest with snakes, revolutionaries (or even worse, *federales*), and wicked godmothers; and that even though she was a woman living alone, she would jump the rope of her work and play with the balls of her orders and her payments. Her life wasn't too bad.

The home-style chemistry of her laboratory lasted only one generation. Time passed too swiftly and synthetic products soon replaced natural extracts in the markets. In a way, she was the intellectual accomplice to the end of her fabulous laboratory. I remember her telling me countless times that I didn't know the horrors of living in the middle of the forest in an era without running water, electricity, or even proper streets. When my grandmother made that comment she clearly wasn't thinking about the Indians who still live like that in the forest and are, in fact, even worse off because they don't even have a small stretch of farmable land, much less a plantation like she did. They wouldn't even dream of the right to education, food, or good health. Condemned to misery and poverty, they wander around in what remains of the tropical forest, the same forest in which, according to the chronicles of the Conquest, they sought refuge in order to escape abuse at the hands of the conquistadors who invaded their land hundreds of years ago. Unfortunately, the years have shown that escaping into the forest didn't protect them from abuse. In my grandmother's eyes, nature was harsh, dangerous, and repulsive. There's nothing like a civilized courtyard with a nice, clean cement floor. She never thought man would be able to tame the forest, much less be capable of destroying it, or that in doing so he'd put all life on the planet in danger. But we weren't talking about that.

In recalling the past, I was indirectly trying to explain why the manuscript I'm going to translate is so important to me. Even though I live in modern-day Mexico City and share in the fantasy of a post-revolutionary mestizo country, I hold my grandmother—her life and experiences—very close. She lived a different past, but one that, to a certain degree, remains alive today.

I haven't said a peep about my other grandmother. That side of the family was so accustomed to marrying among themselves—in order to protect the "quality" of the family—that the last names repeat like images in a hall of mirrors. Every two or three generations, one of the women would marry a foreigner "from a good family" to bring in some new blood, and thus ensure that there wouldn't be a drop of Indian blood. My grandmother was one of those, she married a Galician. Each time a relative was about to get married, the family first asked the last name of the future spouse, and if it wasn't one of the very few "well-regarded" names they lamented: "Too bad. Another one marries a nobody. What will become of us?" According to my grandmother, they were all marrying nobodies, but I don't remember a single cousin marrying an Indian or anyone who didn't belong to the group of whities. I wouldn't dare contradict my grandmother, but all the cousins' spouses appeared to be "quite decent." One cousin married a man who was Secretary of the Treasury during the previous administration, another married the sister of the current

Secretary of Commerce, another married a former Secretary of the Treasury, another the director of a bank, and all the others married the owners of one thing or another. And, of course, a couple of them married foreigners. This is why I'm not married yet, and won't marry anytime soon. So, unless the Oaxacan painter Francisco Toledo asks for my hand, I won't marry. In addition to the advantage of being Indian, Toledo is endowed with the gifts of beauty, intelligence, imagination, creativity, an artistic sensibility, and generosity. But unfortunately, he's married. So for now, since I haven't found a more suitable suitor, just to be contrary, I have my Hernando—a dead Indian priest.

As you can imagine, my relationship with this second grandmother was never a close one. But she is second only in the order of affections since she was born in the last year of the last century and so was actually older than my other grandmother. And just as she is my second grandmother, I was always a granddaughter of the second order for her. My father, blinded by love, married a commoner from Tabasco. A bad move, because it meant I wasn't born with *ojos claros*. And despite my mom's efforts—religiously washing my hair with chamomile to keep the blond highlights—my hair was brown before I was nine years old. And anyway, I was barely out of infancy when my eyebrows turned very dark, suspiciously black, which firmly established me as a granddaughter of the second order. But I wasn't written off entirely because everyone who saw me not only believed I could improve my lineage by marrying the right person, but also had an opinion about whom I should marry.

When one of my aunts saw my dad walking with my mom in the city center and he introduced her as "my fiancée," she ran to tell my grandfather that my father was engaged to a "*fea.*"

The connotation of *fea* was quite clear and didn't have to do with her looks: it meant "common," "low class." The truth is that my mother wasn't particularly ugly or particularly pretty. However, over the years they all acknowledged that she had at least one good feature—she had extraordinary skin.

The same night my aunt discovered the relationship between the two young people, my grandfather gave my dad an ultimatum: "Quit seeing that *fea* or leave this house. We have high expectations for you and first you have to finish your degree and then you have to marry well." My dad left them alone with their expectations and ran off with my mom.

My grandfather had three objections to my mom, whom he didn't even know. First, she was common; second, she was from Tabasco and everyone knows that "Tabascans are very bad people"; and third, my father hadn't finished his degree. Many years later, seven to be exact, the young couple saw my grandfather on the street and my dad ran to kiss his father's hand. The old man said he'd like him to come to the house, but without my mom. At that point, seething with rage, my dad (who was as quick-tempered as his dad) walked away from my grandfather without another word, sure that one day his parents would realize what fools they had been. I can easily imagine my grandfather's eyes as he observed my mother's lack of "class," which only reaffirmed for him that he'd been right in rejecting her. My dad was extremely handsome, and I'm sure that at some point in my grandfather's heart of hearts he had wondered whether it might all come down to the fact that my aunt, perhaps secretly in love with my dad, accused my mom of being common in order to keep him to herself.

The next morning, my mom wrote a note to my grandfather. She explained that my dad had not only already finished his degree, but he had even completed post-graduate studies abroad and had a good job. She added that she knew very well that she was common and that was something she couldn't cover up with "makeup." In addition, she said that she wouldn't know if the people from Tabasco were good or bad since she left there when she was two years old and knew very little about the place. And finally, she suggested that he should welcome my dad without prohibiting her to set foot in the house because that would be unacceptable to my dad since "the two of them were one flesh" (and at the same time she promised my grandfather that she would not set foot in that house). Although my grandfather was a fool, he wasn't a monster and so he invited both of them, along with their daughter (me, of course) to come to the house.

I was five years old and I remember that first visit perfectly. They fed us some awful breaded, cooked carrots that weren't hot or cold or crisp or mushy. In fact, I was so fixated on those disgusting carrots that I can't even remember the rest of the menu, except that there wasn't any dessert and the lemonade wasn't sweetened at all. It was so different from my other grandmother's house, where every meal was a feast and her desserts were legendary. I'm not sure which one was my favorite—maybe the *copa nevada*, which was a type of custard (made with just eggs and sugar, not a single spoonful of flour, and time; and it had to be stirred continuously over low heat with a wooden spoon so that it wouldn't stick and burn on the bottom of the pan, or it would have a smoky, burnt taste) that she served in little cups and topped with some nougat that she dropped by the spoonful into boiling water so that it would solidify and then on the top she sprinkled some cinnamon, which was ground at home because, as my grandmother used to say about the bottled stuff they sold in the supermarket, "who knows what kind of nasty things they put in it, and besides, it doesn't have any flavor."

Anyway, to get back on track I'm going to recount how the manuscript fell into my hands. But in order to do that, I have to mention two more things about my life. One is that I know Latin very well. I not only read and write in Latin, but I can also converse in Latin. I know this is a bit strange in Mexico today, especially for a woman, but it's because when I was a little girl, I told my father that when I grew up I wanted to be a priest. He explained to me that I couldn't be a priest because I was a girl, to which I replied: "No problem, then when I grow up I want to be a man." He laughed and told me that wasn't going to happen, but the first thing I would have to do—in case the Church changed the rules—was to learn Latin. So, guess how I interpreted that? Ignoring, or not understanding, the real meaning of his laughter, I believed that I *could* be a man when I grew up. That's certainly what I wanted. In fact, I imagined myself thousands of times giving mass as a mustached priest, adored by my parishioners. I saw myself as a bishop giving mass in the cathedral. I wasn't interested in anything else that had to do with being a man; just the priest's cassock, which is, to some degree, the representation of his "purity," his virginization. As a little girl I simply wanted to wear a priest's robes.

Back to my dad (but not my mistaken interpretation), I know from some psychotherapy sessions and a few more in psychoanalysis (although I don't think I ever talked specifically about it with any of my four therapists) that he arranged Latin lessons for me in order to help out a friend. This friend was a deacon who for some reason (which I suspect to be carnal) never managed to get himself ordained as a priest. The truth is I think my dad really used my Latin lessons as a pretext to keep his friend from starving to death. The deacon friend embraced us both: my father out of affection and for the few pesos that he earned for each class and me for my illusion that one day I would be able to consecrate the host dressed in gold in front of an altar. It wasn't a bad dream—to wrap my body in glittered finery worked by the hands of the *castas*, and then use my own hands to conjure the mystery of the sacred. In other words, use the work of others (those who gave us the gift of beauty) to produce something that can't be seen—the mystery—something that the erotic act invokes, emulates, and on rare occasions achieves, if you're lucky. Although, truth be told, I write the latter without much conviction. Anyway, these days the mere thought of going to mass turns my stomach. And now I really could be a priest if I wanted to because the Anglican Church ordains women. But the truth is I'm not that crazy.

So, when the manuscript came into my hands by way of a chair (it actually did come out of a chair)—ripping through the fabric of time—I could read it because I was a diligent student of Latin and because I had studied the paleography of colonial texts for two years.

Unfortunately, the manuscript is in pretty bad shape. Some passages are illegible because of stains on the paper, while others have completely disappeared or fell apart in my hands as I tried to read them. I know I should have taken it to a restorer or conservator immediately, but I didn't want to. I decided it was mine as soon as I considered working with it. So, I restored what was missing in my own way.

I should probably explain how it came into my hands in the first place. Given that it's a manuscript from the sixteenth century, it would make sense to assume that I found it in the Archives of the Franciscan Foundation housed in the Museum of the Institute of Anthropology where I work (I've been a researcher there for the past seventeen years. Currently my subject is Indian and Spanish women of the sixteenth century.) But that's not how it happened.

My parents and I (this is the second, and last, thing I'll explain about myself) lived in an Indian pueblo for a year. My mom was pregnant for the second time with another child who would be stillborn (I was the only live birth). We went there as a "missionary family" to catechize the Indians of the pueblo. To be clear, the catechizing was pretty relative. I was seven years old and my job was to help show the short films. Every time the "ping" sounded on the *Mambo: The Child Martyr* record, I would turn the knob on the projector that changed the image; it was as easy as winding a clock. Fray Jacobo de Testera (or Tastera), the inventor of audiovisual catechism, could never have imagined that with the subtleties of modern technology his method would allow an ignorant little girl to catechize simply with the turn of a knob, without the help of an Indian translator or a human voice (even her own).

There were always young people in the house who came to stay with us for a few weeks. One or another of them would be in charge of setting up the screen on which the illustrated drawings of the lives of the saints would be projected, another of turning on the record player and the speakers, and I was in charge of advancing the filmstrip at the sound of the "ping"—a little bell that rang at various points during the story—indicating when it was time to change the illustration. Dad drove a Jeep that more than once ended up stuck in an overflowing little arroyo. I clearly remember the time we spent the night halfway across a flooded creek, stranded in the middle of a stream that roared at our feet, or rather, below our tires, while we were plunged into utter darkness, surrounded by the impenetrable thicket of the forest. There was no way to get the Jeep out of the mud in the dark. I didn't shut my eyes the entire night; I just stayed awake praying for daylight. There wasn't a moon that night, and in the darkness I was terrified of the noises in the forest and the roaring arroyo. I was afraid the water level would rise and wash us away, I thought wild animals would come and eat us, or that scary men would come down from the hills and take everything we had. I imagined thousands of horrific endings. So, I waited for the first rays of dawn before I fell asleep. Working together, the adults—who, along with their children, had seen a couple of the little filmstrips about the lives of the saints, heard the words of the priest, and perhaps received some sort of vaccination or medicine (penicillin, for example, or a cough syrup, both of which were given out indiscriminately) that would cure them of one illness or another—quickly got us out of the predicament.

Some of the children came from communities that were so remote and inaccessible that we would have to choose between showing the filmstrips, handing out dry goods, and giving vaccinations. Another of my responsibilities, as a member of a missionary family, was to delouse the Indians. Without asking their permission, we would shave their heads and apply Flit lice killer with a hand pump. This was a DDT pesticide that must have been harmful to their health in every way, but it would kill any lice that were alive or dormant once and for all. However, when a louse and his friends came to live in my long tresses, they didn't shave my head, but instead took me to Mexico City. My grandmother made an appointment for me at a beauty salon and they applied a liquid that smelled to high heaven, but didn't damage my hair or leave any nits or live bugs behind. Now that I think about it, we never used any masks when we were applying the Flit, so, if I suddenly die of some kind of cancer, it'll probably be because of that bug killer. If so, we could be martyrs too, in our own way.

At that time the highway didn't go to the place my parents chose for their Catholicizing work. The only way to get there was via a mud path or rough dirt track, which was impassable during the rainy season when it turned into a muddy river. At its worst, it became a full-blown river, and then it was impossible to identify the path of the road, let alone travel on it. The Indians of the pueblo spoke their native Otomí instead of Spanish, even in church, where the priest, who was the parish hero, gave the homily in the local language. When the Vatican decreed by sealed order that the mass had to be said in Latin, he took the benches out of the church and talked to them in Otomí. He was an honest man who had a fighting spirit and was devoted to his cause. It burns my tongue to say it—because time (and my education) has turned me into priest-burner—but he was, and still is, an exceptional man. He's now the Archbishop of the Isthmus of Tehuantepec. I respect and admire him so much that I would stick my hand in fire for him.

It's almost as if somehow that pueblo has moved closer to Mexico City because the distance that separates the two seems so much shorter now that you can get there on the highway. It's no longer necessary to go Tampico first (even though in Mexico all roads lead to Tampico) and then travel the road for at least eight hours before you reach that impassable gap or pass, or get on the teeny-tiny plane that my parents somehow managed to acquire and kept on a ranch near Tampico. Since there was nothing remotely resembling an airport, that little plane used to land in empty fields surrounded by crops, frightening the few cows that were wandering around. The bare earth of the ranch that served as our landing strip constantly changed depending on which piece of land was fallow at any given time. The ranch had some mounds on it that, according to the owner, who was an engineer, were pyramids covered with earth. But, he always said, "don't tell anybody, because if this gets out they'll seize my ranch to excavate and not give me a single peso in exchange. And then, after they take my land, they won't even excavate." "*¡Gobierno Ratero!*" If there were pyramids on his ranch the engineer could hardly have made them disappear. If he had the money, he should have built a mansion using the rocks from the pyramids. And if he had any aesthetic or historical sensibility, he would have left the pre-Hispanic carvings visible, like the architect Parra did with the houses he built from the ruins of colonial buildings. If, as I suspect, the engineer destroyed the pyramids to protect his ranch from the "*gobierno ratero,*" he would have kept alive a tradition in our country based on the belief that it's better to self-deprecate rather than to constantly fear being raided. Brilliant!

This extraordinarily profound and exquisite concept of the government that routinely steals from its own citizens—our *"gobierno ratero"*—has come up more than once in my lifetime. When I was a little girl, nobody in my neighborhood voted, or nobody took voting seriously anyway, yet everyone complained about the lack of democracy. And although it makes sense that there would have been center-right *panistas* in my neighborhood, I don't remember any. So, to the fact that I deloused the Indians, you can add this to my list of sins: I used to stick up blue and white decals touting the slogan "Christianity yes, Communism no."

I heard the following conversation more than once:

—Who did you vote for?

—Me? I voted for Cantinflas, everyone's favorite comedian.

Things have changed in Mexico in this regard as well. I remember very clearly my mom telling me about how her father, my grandfather, fought against ballot box theft during the 1946 elections (which of course seemed like ancient history when I was a kid). The story about my grandfather and the ballot boxes happened when Ezequiel Padilla was running for president. My grandfather knew Padilla through Doctor Demetrio Mayoral, who was the dean of the Military Medical School and my grandfather's friend at Father Carlito's school in Oaxaca. They had known each other forever and professed an enormous affection for each other. Their affection was so great that when my grandfather died, Doctor Mayoral was the first one to come to the house carrying an enormous bouquet of gladiolas, which he arranged in vases with his own hands while he wiped away his tears.

When my parents married, Doctor Mayoral and his wife Celia

were their *padrinos de velación*—they sponsored the young couple by paying for the ceremony and standing up for them in church. Doctor Mayoral walked my mother down the aisle and gave her away because my grandfather was already dead by then. My Uncle Gustavo told me that when my mom called to ask him to be her *padrino*, Doctor Mayoral asked, "What should I wear? I don't have any elegant clothes, tell me what to wear," to which she replied, "Wear whatever you like, Doctor. It doesn't matter to me what you wear, I just want you to walk me down the aisle." The doctor arrived wearing those pinstriped pants and a black double-breasted jacket that the older generation used to wear. He was quite refined and upright in the old-fashioned sense and, at the same time, very loving with his old friend's family.

Anyway, Doctor Mayoral introduced my grandfather to Ezequiel Padilla, who had been the public prosecutor at the trial of José de León Toral when the young religious militant was accused of assassinating president elect Álvaro Obregón on July 17, 1928. It was in his capacity as Secretary of Foreign Relations that Padilla attended the international conference in San Francisco, California where the United Nations was founded in 1945.

The election of '46 was not without irregularities, and there was certainly no such thing as an electoral register. As the story goes, my grandfather arrived at a polling station just as deputy Fernando Amilpa, a thug of PRI Senator Fidel Velázquez Sánchez, showed up to steal the ballot boxes. My grandfather lost his composure and—so that the Revolution would not have been in vain—pulled out his gun, stuck the pistol in Amilpa's back, and said: "leave that, you *hijo de la fregada*, or you die. They might kill me for it, but you'll go first."

Amilpa and his accomplices dropped the ballot boxes and left. PRI candidate Miguel Alemán won that election. The story they used to tell about Alemán, when I was a little girl, was that he ordered Lake Texcoco to be dredged so that he could look for Moctezuma's Treasure. They didn't find any treasure, but the outcome was the same in the end because his family made a huge fortune (one of the many fortunes of the Alemáns) when they partitioned and sold the lake land.

Back to the Indian pueblo of my childhood where we lived as a missionary family. I won't mention its name here because the place looks nothing like it used to. And it's not really an Indian pueblo anymore, but is more a conglomeration of people crammed together, living in chaos, imitating the worst aspects of the Western lifestyle, and all the while maintaining the distance required and imposed by poverty. It's changed so much in the last two decades that you could say it has vanished into the mist and that a phony pueblo of the same name has sprung up in its place.

When I was a child living in that pueblo, the people of all the nearby villages used to come into town on Sundays to buy and sell merchandise, and then the modest weekday plaza would turn into a huge, bustling mercado. We lived in a big house at the foot of the mountain next to the three or four other non-Indian families who spoke Spanish, had money, and were trying to escape the *gobierno ratero*.

When I dream of our time there—that is to say that when the muddy pueblo of my childhood enters my dream world—it has been transformed into a dusty Roman village where Catholics and Pagans fight violently over souls and temples. I've dreamt about it in so many ways and so much has happened in my imaginary village that it no longer has anything to do with my real childhood experience. Using the intangible substance dreams are made of, my dreamworld provides all the material necessary for the saga to continue. Once upon a time those dreams were connected to my childhood memories, but that ended a long time ago and now the saga follows its own story line.

The protagonist of my dreams is Saint Adrian, or better yet, simply Adrian. He probably shouldn't be called "Saint," because in my dreams he appears as a healthy young man from a wealthy family, long before his beatification. Adrian is a young army general who belongs to an old family from the area that has worshiped the gods since time immemorial. The gods themselves honor the lush, natural world that borders the town—the river and its rapids, the ravines exploding with green, the countryside with its trees and caves. In one of these caves—here Adrian's Roman village coincides with a legend popular in the Indian pueblo where we lived that year—lives an enormous serpent who wears a magnificent crown on her head. Surrounded by her subjects (serpents like herself, but smaller in size), she guards a chest full of gold and emeralds that once belonged to the ancient kings. The coincidence is imaginary, of course, because I never saw the cave in the Indian village nor have I actually ever seen it in my dreams. Adrian betrays the family gods when he "hears" the call of the one God and fights in His name against tradition, provoking with his "illumination" a gut-wrenching conflict that ultimately destroys the pueblo.

The saga has been running through my dreams for years. And though I might not dream about my Adrian for weeks at a time, he always returns, and always with new adventures, so to speak. They never repeat, and since they're dreams they often contradict each other—contradiction is, of course, permitted in the dream world—and sometimes an adventure even contradicts itself. Adrian is the only constant. In the last dream-episode, or chapter, two eagles flew in circles above Adrian's house. The entire pueblo crowded together to see the enormous birds. In this dream, I'm a little girl dressed in a long white gown that trails on the ground and I'm in love with Adrian, an unmarried young man who still lives with his parents.

In these dreams I'm always somebody else and I always play different roles. In fact, I play so many roles in the nighttime saga of Adrian that sometimes at the beginning of the adventure I don't recognize myself, I don't know which role the night has assigned me. But I'm always female and always in love with him—or could be in love with him if it weren't for the prohibition against incest or the taboo of age—but my love is never reciprocated. At best, I might be his spiritual lover. The closest we've ever been physically is a chaste kiss on the cheek or a friendly hug. And sometimes I don't see myself because I don't know which role I'm playing. There are dreams in which several women love Adrian and I can't recognize myself as any one of them in particular; I might be several at the same time, or at one moment I might be this one, and the next another. But my identity always revolves around being in love with my Adrian.

For some reason, in this chapter of the saga, I'm living in his house, which is why I could see the eagles' arrival up close. Adrian is still asleep because it's very early and the only ones in the house who are awake are the old people and the children. But then the noise made by villagers of all ages who are looking at the eagles wakes him up.

"Adrian," I say as soon as I see him, "what are those eagles doing?" My voice provokes frightful shrieks from the eagles and hastens their descent. They raise as much dust as helicopters when they land. They alight at the foot of the steps to the house, settle, and then, before our eyes, slowly turn into stone. From there, the dream follows the usual pattern of religious conversion followed by destruction typical of these dreams.

I sometimes wonder where the dust of my Roman dream village comes from since it originated with the Indian pueblo of my childhood, which was surrounded by lush countryside. Occasionally, my dreams foretell the arrival of the one God who prohibits the continued worship of the ancient gods and in retaliation turns the area around the pueblo into desert. I've been told that the dust is now a reality in the pueblo because it's been so many years since it's rained that even the trees have dried up. This ecological disaster has exacerbated the poverty in the pueblo to an unimaginable degree. In fact, somebody told me that she recently passed by the pueblo on the new highway and that there was a line, kilometers long, of people begging on the side of the road, each with a hand extended toward the cars. It's hard to understand why each one of these hundreds of beggars would extend their hands to people flying by at incredibly high speeds on that magnificent new highway. They couldn't possibly expect anyone to save them; if anything, most people would be afraid of all of that neediness standing upright only by the grace of God. Perhaps they were simply stretching out their hands to feel the cold spine of death in an attempt to make its arrival slightly less bitter.

All these dreams end the same way—destruction arrives as soon as Saint Adrian triumphs and successfully forces his one God on the entire village. Although the way it happens varies. I've seen wars, witnessed fires, and have even watched the entire village completely disappear before my very eyes for no apparent reason at all. Sometimes things exit the dream-space as if shot out of a cannon, spinning out of sight. Everything goes—the houses, the furniture, the people, the sky—and is hurled outward, toward emptiness, leaving nothing.

Anyway, back to the subject at hand. Where did Hernando's manuscript come from? As it happens, an old school friend—from the year I studied in the Indian pueblo where we lived as a missionary family in the seventies—came to the Institute to look for me. She had asked the people of the pueblo who had some relation to my family—nannies, cooks, chauffeurs, women who did the cleaning, etcetera—where I was. These were the typical "peer" relationships ("Who's there?" asks a woman's voice. "Nobody, señora, just me," answers the domestic worker) engendered by Mexican generosity. She knew that I read Latin better than I read Spanish because I was constantly showing off with the missal, a breviary, and a Vulgate that my father had given me for one of my birthdays.

We weren't close friends. I don't think anyone in that school was close friends with anyone else because the nuns who were in charge of the girls' education created such a hostile environment that neither fostered friendships nor was conducive to the learning of addition and subtraction. Or maybe it wasn't the nuns who were to blame, but rather the uniform—we wore cherry red jumpers made of a coarse fabric and white blouses with sleeves to the elbow—which was suffocating in the extreme heat of the Huasteca region. I remember that when we couldn't bear the heat anymore, we girls would raise our skirts and fan ourselves with them. The nuns scolded us for this, but despite all their shouting, we kept right on doing it. The uniform was absurd given the heat and humidity in that region. And now that I'm thinking about the school, I have to tell a story about the onions we used to eat just outside the school. I don't remember if it was before or after we tucked up our skirts to cool our feet in the river, but we used to stop at a little store where, for a nickel, we could buy a slice of pickled onion that was sprinkled with a pinch of salt and wrapped in a little triangle of brown paper. It was delicious. It didn't taste like any I've ever made myself and I've tried to make them countless times in a variety of different ways. One time I even bought a glass pickling-jar—like they had at that little store—to pickle some onions, along with some large green chiles and carrots. I think the key is probably the vinegar. The fact is that however much I've tried, I've never managed to replicate the taste of those mythic onions.

I also remember the festival tamales. They were so big that if I were to lie down next to them, they would have been bigger than me. They didn't taste too bad either. The pastries, on the other hand, were repulsive. The worst ones were the bright-Mexican-pink sugary balls of pastry that not even a child would want to eat; in fact, they would have been too sickly sweet even for a stone.

The call from this childhood companion not only surprised me, I was also ashamed because at first I didn't know who she was, even after she told me her name. She brought me an extremely old manuscript that was in pretty bad shape. She explained that her family had found it in a chair they had preserved and kept safe—as if it were made of gold—in their big old house since time immemorial. They were abiding by the firmly held belief, passed down for generations, that they had to preserve that chair at all costs. And so, for generations they had been sticking little wedges here and there, adjusting a leg with a hammer, putting a little glue in the joints…One day, despite their efforts to prolong its life, the chair fell apart. They discovered that the chair had a false bottom and found this manuscript, written in Latin, hidden inside. My former schoolmate asked me to read it and tell her what it was about. A few days later, after examining it, I explained to her that, although it was in bad shape, I would like to paleograph and translate it, and that if she wanted, we might be able to sell it to a library for more than a few pesos. Instead of giving me a definite "yes" or "no" answer, she made me dizzy with the charming verbal gymnastics typical of the Indians ("How was the fiesta?" "It was nice, señora." "Was it fun?" "Well, somewhat."). She never returned for the manuscript, and it took her a long time to call me back. When she finally did call, she said they'd thought about it, discussed it a couple of times, and decided that they weren't really interested in the manuscript. They had hoped it would tell them where the treasures—in which they had believed for generations—were and since that wasn't the case, they didn't want any more to do with it. They decided I should keep it for myself, that I should accept it as a gift from their family to mine, since they owed us so very much (although I can't imagine what the hell for). I reminded her that they could sell it, but she didn't seem to believe that was really possible. She hung up the phone after saying good-bye very quickly, but very kindly, while I promised her I would try to find some people who might be interested in it and that I would let her know how much they would pay.

I have the manuscript here with me and somehow I consider it to be mine. Even if it's not my property, it's my *fiancé*—I've committed myself to it. Because my grandmother used *Crema Teatrical* and wouldn't let me use *Nivea*. Because my other grandmother, to her genealogical shame, recited the same last name five times for every twenty. Because I'm Mexican and I live as all Mexicans live—respectful of a random, yet rigid, game of social castes, despite our oft-cited Revolution, Benito Juárez, and political rhetoric praising our Indian ancestors. And because I believe our history would have been different if the Colegio de la Santa Cruz Tlatelolco hadn't had the sad fate it did. The manuscript is important to me on a personal level. Maybe I feel partially responsible for the sin my parents committed when they went to infest an Indian pueblo with the one God, a pueblo that until then had preserved some small bit of sanity. Or because my grandmother and her relatives from Comalcalco, Pichucalco, Tuxtla, and surrounding districts considered it normal, until recently, for Indians to carry them so they wouldn't get their shoes muddy. And because her family always married among themselves so that they wouldn't contaminate themselves with Indian blood. Of course, we actually committed this sin on both sides of my family, so if I seem half crazy, I have a good reason; if I'm weird, it's because of the curse of incest. And because my other grandmother—blonde and ditzy, quick to chat, gossip, and smile, playful like her brother, and very beautiful even as an old woman—secured her position by marrying a handsome, educated, but very stingy and mean Galician (his stinginess and meanness are another story and don't come into play here).

As rudimentary as my paleography skills might be, I don't want to give up the manuscript because I've established such a profound connection to it. I've approached my work with it as both a very personal matter and as a trivial matter, like a game. Trivial is the only label I want to give it, because it matters so much to me that I don't want anyone else to have it. I'll use my sabbatical year to work on it in the Library of the College of Mexico. This is my favorite place to work because from the window I can see trees and the gardener sweeping the leaves with his traditional twig broom; because the books here are in order and there are more than sufficient resources for my research; and because they sell very good coffee in the cafeteria (I go to the students' cafeteria instead of going to the researchers' cafeteria). Fortunately, the coffee hasn't been affected by the attack on the people that seems to be the modus operandi of most of the public services in the city. So, as long as they don't attack the coffee and decide to reserve the real stuff for the privileged, leaving us with the Nescafé, I'll happily continue working in the College library (even if the telephones at the entrance don't work).

Since I'm treating this work as a game, it's important to respect its ludic nature. And since it must be trivial, I won't show it to anyone. This game has rules, and one of those is to conceal the manuscript without destroying it, storing it where it has the best chance of surviving. So I asked the carpenter who is fixing my bookshelves at home (I'm running out of space for my books) to make a three-part housing for the manuscript with the measurements I gave him. Now I can easily move it without calling attention to it. He also made me some wedges to support it. I'm going to cover one of the private reading tables in the library from top to bottom and keep the translation locked in there until I finish. I'll make a false bottom for the table and deposit my version of Hernando's text, along with my own writing, inside.

As I've said, the original manuscript is in pretty bad shape. As much as possible (which is not much), I've tried to reconstruct what is illegible. What I refuse to do, however, is to write a single line that doesn't interest me, that isn't important to me, even if that means skipping entire passages written in my Indian's shaky hand. When I suspect that the incomprehensible fragments allude to times before the arrival of the Spaniards, I've turned to the original sources, to documents transcribed by Icazbalceta (instead of the better-known Sahagún). When the fragments refer to colonial life, I've done the same thing and turned to Torquemada, Motolinía, Mendieta, Mariano Cuevas' *Documentos para la historia de México,* the *Códice Mendieta*, the *Franciscan*, and of course Icazbalceta (who was even more useful in this case than in the former), along with some other sources I've been scavenging from the shelves of my beloved library. I've even taken the liberty of recreating—out of my own imagination—any illegible parts that allude to the Indian himself. I've decided that's the best way to do it. Why not? It's *my* personal reading of a manuscript that belongs to *me*, that speaks to *me* from the sixteenth century and explains *my* present. Nobody else will get their hands on it (for the moment anyway), unless there's something I didn't account for, other than the passage of time, which might lead to its discovery inside the table. Although it came from a chair, I'll hide it in a table because I've noticed that the library chairs don't last very long; since they're not made of wood they're always breaking. When they repair or replace the tables, the manuscript will appear. At that point nobody will recognize my name or signature, but the name of the narrator is traceable. I found it on the list of students of the Colegio de Santa Cruz Tlatelolco. It's his story that matters anyway.

Since this "introduction" ended up being more of a personal justification for my translation, the reader can simply ignore it. I didn't think of you, reader, when I wrote it. I did it only for myself—and for the table, for the inert wood that will serve as its tomb until the time comes for it to be discovered. Then the reader will only need to rip out the pages I've written and listen to the confession that begins on the next page.

(Final parenthesis—I have to add a quote by José Emilio Pacheco: "Mexico dreamed of being modern and modernizing; she wanted to enter the unimaginable twenty-first century without first resolving the problems of the sixteenth century... The Chac Mool still lives in Filiberto's basement, as well as our own. For him, we're the ghosts").

Estela Ruiz. Mexican. Age 40.

Slosos keston de Estelino

EKFLOROS KESTON DE HERNANDO

Though I am a person who lacks even a glimmer of faith, I am going to tell you a frightful story—even at the risk of writing nonsense—that I believe I must get down on paper before it dissolves into oblivion or chaos. The frightfulness of this story stems from the unbridled power of vileness and envy. And although my account runs the risk of being as unbelievable as, if not more so than, false memories—which, in order to achieve an appearance of truth, spin quite a charming farce—I will not spin lies or tell tall tales.

Fray Andrés de Olmos convinced Viceroy Mendoza that he had found the toe bones of a giant's foot in the Viceroy's own palace. Based on that spurious discovery, they deduced that giants had once inhabited these lands. There are even some who say they remember that some enormous bones and teeth were once presented to the old Viceroy Velasco. Others talk about a real giant who walked in the Corpus Christi procession. I am not going to write about giants or any other type of fantastic tricks or deceptions. *Let's not ask him if he ever saw any monsters; monsters were no longer news. There is never a scarcity of terrifying creatures.* I will recount only what I saw with my own eyes or heard with my own ears and believed to be true. I will write down only the things I witnessed and those that were told to me by someone who witnessed them.

There will not be any freakish monsters other than the ones that actually exist or any nonsense other than that resulting from my own clumsiness. I will not invoke the seductive veil of lies or the light of any faith. Instead I will rely on events and make use of whatever I can that will help me tell the story.

I will not scatter the stale and sterile seeds of a magical reality across these lands. Nor will I speculate, like an open-mouthed and dim-witted gullible fool, on the reasons or causes for the "strange properties" of these lands, or wonder if the criollo sons of the Iberians have a different quality of wit, or whether it is true that they do not live as long as those born in Europe, or why they gray early…

I am going to tell you the most detailed story my old memory will allow me to tell and I will, as much as I can, anticipate any questions.

I am not afraid of offending anyone with my story, as it will be several hundred years before anyone will lay eyes on these pages I am writing in Latin because it is the language in which I know how best to do it and because I know it is a language that will continue to live in the future, since it has resisted the passage of time. I will hide my writings so as to bequeath them to other times. Since I have already spent many hours remembering what I am recounting here in order to provide it with a shape in the form of words, I do not see any reason to run the risk of angering anyone with the truth, and thus shortening the number of days left to me before I see heaven. The innocent truth, stated without the shadow of malice, could possibly irritate somebody. The spirits reveal themselves. I can give more than one example of how the written word has caused problems in these lands. But instead I will offer just one example that took three men—Fray Pérez Ramírez, González de Eslava, and Francisco de Terrazas—down in one fell swoop for irritating Viceroy Enríquez Almanza and resulted in their imprisonment.

It all began with a *pasquín* that was circulating during the festivities surrounding the investiture of Inquisitor Moya de Contreras. On the 5th of December 1574, the day Moya de Contreras was consecrated as Archbishop, Fray Pérez Ramírez presented a short pastoral comedy, titled *Desposorio*. Then on the 8th of December, the day the second ceremony was held to confer the archiepiscopal pallium on the new bishop, Fray Pérez Ramírez presented the *Third Colloquy* of Fernán González de Eslava. During the entr'actes, two farcical interludes were performed that apparently offended the viceroy. One because it was assumed that the bearded man alluded to the viceroy himself and the other, titled *El Alcabalero*, was considered to be rude and inopportune because the viceroy was having difficulties enforcing the new law that imposed the collection of excise taxes ("I might have excused all the other interludes, but this turned my stomach. Nobody could have approved of this because the consecration and placing of the pallium is not a farce"). All it took was for the viceroy to add the *pasquín* to the interludes presented during the festivities for these two situations to be combined to produce three victims. Two of them—Pérez de Ramírez and González de Eslava—I understand. But Francisco de Terrazas? Does my memory fail me or did they suggest that he was the author of one of the two interludes? Does old age now affect even my memory? I cannot believe it. I can trust my memory to any caprice—even to recite the lines González de Eslava gave to the character of New Spain in the colloquy: *The being who love inflames / cold does not mortify / love will fortify / and the virtue of those who love / renews and vivifies.*[1] It was undoubt-

---

1   In Spanish in the manuscript. Estela's note.

edly ignorance that caused Francisco de Terrazas, the son of the conquistador, to be taken into captivity (if only for a few hours) and attribute to him the authorship of the work that had irritated the viceroy. He is not only a man of quality and a gentleman of the people, but he could not have been the author of *El Alcabalero* because it was written in a distant land by Lope de Rueda.

The *pasquín,* or "libel," as they called it, was posted on the cathedral door on Saturday the eighteenth. The criminal court judges considered it disrespectful and greatly offensive to His Majesty King Felipe and His Royal Justice.

The three men named above were imprisoned. One of them, González de Eslava, wrote a letter to the archbishop. One of the copies (of which he made several) fell into my hands and said something along these lines:

"On December 20,[2] I was peacefully and quietly living my life when Doctor Horozco, court judge for the Council of Castile, came to my house with constables and other people. He barged into my bedroom and opened a chest from which he took my writings and other papers. On the same day, Your Illustrious Lordship's public prosecutor also came to my home with two court bailiffs, a minister of justice, blacks, and others. They took me into custody with a great deal of noise and fuss and put me in the archiepiscopal jail. The following day, Antequera, the deputy of the criminal court and other men came and walked me along the street and across the plaza that separate the archiepiscopal jail from the Royal Palace. As it was the feast day of Saint Thomas the Apostle, there were many people on the street and in the plaza

---

2   In Spanish in the original from this point. Estela's note.

who were startled and scandalized at the sight. Most of those who witnessed this knew me, had conversed with me over the past sixteen years that I have lived here, and were moved to the greatest compassion for me because they were certain of my innocence. That is how I was escorted to the room where they torture those who commit horrible and atrocious crimes. That is where the wooden burro they use to torture wrongdoers is kept and by which only God knows the anguish and tribulation I suffered. The above-named gentlemen asked me if I had written or ordered the libel against Don Martín Enríquez, Your Majesty's Viceroy in New Spain. I replied that it was not my habit to commit wickedness of such enormity or any kind of abominable and horrible actions. I, Sir, was imprisoned for seventeen days."[3]

As for me, I do not want to miss seeing the sun for a single day. Even without any intention to offend, the raw unvarnished truth (which is what I want to write here) would pierce the chests of some arrogant people like an arrow. I will not have to use a sword to nail the truth to the Cathedral door; it would not be necessary to wield a weapon or draw a bow in order for the truth to pierce their chests. Death will come for me soon enough and though I might still want to live even if I had my face to a wall and could no longer see the sky, it would not be long before Mother Nature would satisfy me and fulfill my foolish appetite. When death arrives I will no longer see anything illuminated by the light of the sun. I do not want to quicken this difficult, but unavoidable, ending. I am alive and my eyes are open. I want the sun to at least touch the nape of my old neck before we say goodbye to each other forever.

---

3   The Spanish ends here and returns to the Latin. Estela's note.

I write this as I revisit my memories, seated in the courtyard of the Colegio de Santa Cruz, next to the convent of San Francisco in the village of Tlatelolco, the neighboring city of Tenochtitlan-Mexico, which some say is part of the original city because there is no separation between their houses and the low wall that divided them in earlier times is almost gone.

It has been a year since my legs gave up. They no longer perform their duty as legs. They no longer carry me. Now I carry them. They hang inconveniently from my body and occasionally bother me with pains that are their way of reminding me that they used to serve me, that they used to carry me from here to there. Their remorse at not complying, even poorly as they have done in recent years—slow, heavy, and unsure; stumbling through their basic, though indispensable, work as legs—manifests in the stabbing pains they torment me with. Ah legs! You should have played dead in silence! I am so ashamed when the boys carry me here every morning from my cell and back to my cell every evening; sometimes I have even wet myself like a stupid dog. I am a legless dog lying in the sun remembering; my feet lie beside me. From time to time they remember me and get up to kick me, angry because they have been cut off. But this old dog did not chop off his own legs. As a dog I do not know how to use an ax. A cruel being cut them off, slowly and calmly severing each band of ligaments while observing me mockingly with his ax brandished, considering what he will cut off next.

That cruel being is Time. The years of my life, the ax. The dog's legs are my legs, they hang inertly next to me. I am the dog. I bask in the sun and am grateful to feel it on my skin. That bright star almost overcomes (but cannot completely dispel) the cold because nothing can warm the blood of the dog that walks so slowly that the poor body freezes in its tracks.

My blood no longer rushes in my veins. It knows that everything must end in death.

I sit here, tethered to the chair by the rope of old age. The chair was carved ex profeso[4] for me by former students of Fray Pedro de Gante in the school of San José, situated next to the chapel of the same name, adjacent to Mexico City's church and monastery of San Francisco. Now no one has the skill to embroider the inexpensive, but neat and colorful, ecclesiastical adornments. The exquisite manner in which these adornments were embroidered made the students famous. It was a skill they learned from the maestro, Fray Daniel, an innocent cherub who was Italian by birth but who took the habit in the province of Santiago and wore an iron chainmail against his skin for more than fifty years. Ah Fray Daniel! When he walked, he embroidered the floor with a zigzag pattern. Now nobody knows how to embroider in the same way (I do not mean on the floor, that step is easy to learn). The grandchildren of the students of Gante's school, who learned how to embroider fabric from the students of the refined and sensitive Fray Daniel, do not have the mastery of their masters. Evil has infiltrated and destroyed all the very best this land has to offer. The last time I heard the choir of the Church of San Francisco, their horrific mistakes hurt my eardrums. It would seem that they can no longer read music, nor have they learned the rules by ear. In my time, the same choir was the wonder of the Tyrians and Trojans.

---

4   Like this in the original. Estela's note.

That choir perfectly emulated the fluttering wings of the angels and the brilliance of the staircase to the heavens. All of this—their cultured voices warmed by the light of the soul and the stars; the adornments with which they dressed the altars, embroidered in the gold of wisdom with a needle and thread; and not to mention the lessons in Latin, the trivium and the quadrivium that they no longer teach—all of this, like my legs, has died. Some things remain unchanged—they still practice these arts, but now they are more like magpies or crows than artists.

I would be lying if I were to say that the very air has been contaminated with the weight of evil and hatred. I would be lying, though I almost dared to do so. I feel that the air is sick, tainted by so many mistakes. It is dirty with the wet sand of vileness and folly. But I do not notice it when the air touches my face and the wind carries the song of the cicada and the laughter of the children to me seemingly unaffected by the evil of envy.

Here I am, tethered to the chair made by Gante's students, writing on the pages bound by the students of this school. Beneath the seat of my chair—the throne of the legless one— the students made a hidden compartment for me to keep the book in which I write every day. When I die, if anyone wants to see it, he will have to wait until time destroys the hard wood the chair is made from, which was extracted from the closed forests that cover the steep hills, where some of the Indians hid in order to escape the violence of the Spaniards, where it is not possible to live in order and harmony, where there is no human law, and where many wild beasts live in the dense vegetation.

How long would someone who wants to look at my writing have to wait? One hundred years? Two hundred? Three hundred? According to those who work with them, the trees of those forests never die and their hard wood is as indestructible as they are. Hidden, the pages will await the passage of time. No light from the sun, no air, no water will penetrate this wooden fortress. Nobody will be able to read these pages until a more noble time arrives and somebody might be disposed to read my story.

I will begin with the beginning of my own story, I will not return to the age of Anáhuac. As I have already said, I will recount only that which I saw with my own eyes and I could not have witnessed those times. I will not go back to when[5]

—

If the son of a nobleman was a gambler and sold his father's things, or sold some land, he would be secretly drowned.

If someone stole a canoe, he would have to pay its worth in mantles; if he did not have the mantles, he was enslaved.

It was law that a person who practiced witchcraft, and brought evil upon a city, would be sacrificed by having his chest split open.

Anyone who killed with potions, drugged a household in order to more easily steal from them, or was a highwayman, would be hung.

Any man who enslaved an underage girl who subsequently died, was either himself enslaved, or made to pay the priest in goods or property.

5   A new page, written in Spanish in the original, begins here. Estela's note.

Anyone who stole in the street market was stoned to death.

If a father sinned with his daughter, they were both drowned with ropes around their necks.

In some places, a man who lay with his wife after he had betrayed her was punished.

Male prostitutes, sodomists, and young men who put on or wore women's clothing, were hung.

Women who committed adultery were stoned to death along with the men with whom they had sinned.

Taking a ration of food from another during wartime was punishable by death.

Traitors who talked to or notified enemies of plans during war had their property taken away and torn asunder and all of their relatives were enslaved.

A thief, who had not used what he had stolen, was enslaved; if what he had stolen was of value and he had used it, he was put to death.

There was a rigorously enforced law that a person who sold a lost child as a slave was himself enslaved and his hacienda was divided into two parts, one of which was given to the child and the other was given to the person who was going to buy the child. If there was more than one seller, they were all enslaved.

Judges who unjustly sentenced someone and people who made false testimony to the chief judge in a legal dispute were subject to the pain of death.

Fathers scalped, beat, and pierced the ears, thighs, and arms of their young sons and daughters when they were wicked, disobedient, or naughty. Sons of lords or rich men entered the temples in the service of the idols at seven years of age where they swept, made the fire, and lit incense. If they were negligent, naughty, or disobedient, their hands and feet were tied and their thighs, arms, and chests were pierced with pointed sticks and they were pushed down the steps of the small temples.[6]

—

The reason I was listing some of the laws of the ancient Nahuas in Spanish is only to make it clear that I do not want to be clear—*because someone was spying over my shoulder.* Fortunately, my hearing is good and I could hear the footsteps of a student approaching. Apparently, his curiosity was piqued when he noticed me writing here—in the middle of the courtyard of the Colegio Imperial de la Santa Cruz de Tlatelolco, on this poor plank of wood that the boys placed between the arms of the chair for me to use as a writing surface—in the blank book they bound for me in the workshop, using the remnants of paper left over from our printing press. The student patiently began reading, following with his eyes what I was writing in a clear hand (though perhaps no longer as beautifully as I once did) in the Italian cancelleresca script as dictated by Vicentino in the volume entitled *Il modo et regola de scrivere littera corsiva over Cancellarescha* (a text that disappeared from our library without even bidding us goodbye, like so many other volumes, including those that Miguel made us learn when we were young students in this school).

The boy who was spying over my shoulder will believe that I have gone mad and will make fun of me, thinking that if Sahagún,

---

6 The original text in Spanish ends here. Estela's note.

surrounded by scribes and informants his entire life, could never train his Calepino, I, a legless old invalid (in every way except my mind) had to be sick in the head to spend my time writing down idiotic ancient practices while sitting in the sun in order to conserve the little bit of warmth left in my body.

Now that the busybody has left, bored with reading all the laws I managed to write down while he was spying, I will get back to work. The laws were those I remembered hearing the elders talk about, the ones Sahagún and Olmos brought in as informants. These laws never applied to me because I was not of their time, nor was my mother an adulterer, nor my father a traitor, thief, or false judge. I know more laws than these—as well as the wisdom and stories of the ancients—that I could use as a shield should the need arise, but I do not believe it will be necessary because my graceless body does not call attention to itself. This old man does not have any grace, he is only repugnant; even worse, the poor old paralytic is doubly poor because he lives like a member of the mendicant order. This has been my humble destiny.

I pick up my pen again, but not for the purpose of fooling innocent students. I want to tell the story from beginning to end and in order to do that I have to say where, when, and how I was born, adding a little bit about my early years to explain how I became part of the history I want to recount. I will begin with my birth, move forward as quickly as possible, and will not stop until I reach the end. It is true that from time to time my vision clouds and I see only black, as if I were already a guest of the De Profundis. But even if my vision gets cloudy, my imagination and my brain do not. For example, when I refer to the

De Profundis, there are several things I am sure of and others I can imagine. One is that the De Profundis will not be my final resting place because interred there, in an old room of the convent of San Francisco, are only friars and benefactors such as Doña Beatriz de Andrada, in a marked tomb, and her husband Francisco de Velasco (she, because she paid for the construction of the De Profundis with her own money and he in order to keep her company). It is understood that Hernando will definitely not sleep there among such famous people because he is just an Indian. At the end of times I will not be in the De Profundis when I see an angel coming down from heaven holding the key of the bottomless pit and a great chain in his hand, and lay hold of the dragon, that old serpent that is sin, to bind him for a thousand years. When the heavens rip open and the time of judgment arrives, will I wake up? Will it have been in vain that I was not born a warrior who, after dying in a glorious battle, transforms into a fluttering hummingbird? Will I just be bone and dust forever? Will I be made to pay for my faults by torture? When the hour of vengeance arrives ("For these are the days of vengeance, that all things may be fulfilled, that are written," wrote Saint Luke), when the seas cover the earth and the earth covers the sea, and the dead, just and unjust, awake, will I be made *to sit*, reliving my life in my sad chair? Supposing this will be the case, it would be best not to go where conjectures and fears gnaw at the brain, leaving the mind wasted, as happened after Francisco Vazquez de Coronado's long, fruitless, and failed expedition to Cíbola in search of gold in 1540. If this is where the inevitable end were to lead me, I will return to where they will bury me without any fanfare.

However, before going back there, and since I have just said what I know, I will now say in a trice what I imagine. Since the aforementioned De Profundis will not be home to the bones and dust into which death will convert me, every time my vision clouds I make a game of walking through its darkness, rehearsing an end that will not be mine. Because even if my vision is dark right now, my plebeian bones will be buried in the graveyard of the pueblo where a streak of light will sneak through. The brutal sun beats mercilessly on the barren hillsides where I will end up without any fanfare to accompany me to my final resting place. The light of the sun does not respect the bones of the commoners, known as *macehuales*, and I imagine light leaping among them, scoffing like a little Lucifer at their forced repose, celebrating the false triumph of darkness.

But my days on this earth did not begin like that. I was born a male child, seventy-one years ago, on 14 October of the year 1526 in Texcoco. There was a great celebration with glorious music and a lavish array of delicious foods. Many respectable people were invited from Mexico City, five leagues away, for the celebration. As presents, they brought many jewels and a lot of wine—the jewel that made everyone most joyful. There was no incense or myrrh (I must stick to the facts of the story), but gold, precious gems, clothing, home furnishings, and even two horses were brought as gifts.

After the mass everyone went to the palace of the noble lord, where, following dinner, as was customary at that time, there was a grand party attended by a thousand or two thousand Indians. On the day of my birth, 14 October of the year 1526, they all danced until vespers. Indians, whites, and a few blacks—all a little inebriated, bellies full of delicacies—celebrated on the blessed day that my mother gave birth to the poor, legless dog I am today.

It would be a generation before the grandeur of that fiesta would be forgotten, but not even an hour passed (I have to say it, even if it does not flatter me), before they forgot my birth. My mother and I were left alone, lying on a miserable mat, while everyone else, nobles and commoners alike, enjoyed the celebration of the first Indian marriage in New Spain.

The truth does not flatter me, but even if it does not, it is the truth and I must tell it here. The celebration was not for us, but since we were there, I will recount it as mine. Let us say that I have set aside my pledge to honor the truth and that the celebration was for me. On the one hand, I can claim it as ours without feeling any remorse whatsoever and without diminishing the celebration of those who were being honored because that Indian marriage was not the first celebrated in these lands. I have heard that there was another one before this one, but it was not commemorated.

On the day mentioned above, Don Hernando Pimentel, brother of King Cacama of Tezcoco, married and, incidentally, so did seven of his friends, all of whom were brought up together in the house of God, and that is why they came from Mexico City, as I have already said, along with many others such as the conquistadors Alonso de Ávila and Pedro Sánchez Farfán—the former was the first auditor of New Spain and the latter was the majordomo of the municipal council—both of whom had accompanied Cortés in the taking of Tenochtitlan seven years before.

They very solemnly watched the blessing of the rings and the *arras*, which was the bridegroom's traditional gift of thirteen coins to the bride. There were *padrinos*, and after the dance and vespers, the noble lords and their relatives offered the newlyweds home furnishings and clothing as gifts, and thus the bridal chamber was nicely furnished. Even Hernán Cortes, the Marqués del Valle—who was at that time was preparing to leave these lands to take presents to the Emperor—sent a servant to offer an impressive number of gifts.

But for me, nothing. Nothing for Mama either. Nothing special for either of us on the celebrated day of my birth, no fanfare or celebratory foods. The third member of our story—my father—was swimming, his legs kicking toward the sun, as he tried to distance himself from the ship in which he had hidden and that had set sail six days hence. Nobody knows if he reached the coast, or if a serpent ate him, or if an alligator ended his life with the thrash of his tail, or if an enormous fish swallowed him, as happened to Jeremiah. If by some miracle he had reached the shore, he could hardly have said, "I am Temilotzin, one of the noblemen of Tlatelolco," because he had sealed his own fate when he threw himself into the sea.

Coincidentally, his end began with a fiesta to which the people of Acallan invited Quauhtemoc, the sovereign ruler of Tlatelolco; Couanacoch, sovereign of Tezcoco; Tetlepanquetzal, sovereign of Tlacopan; and Eca and Temilo, both nobles from Tlatelolco, the latter being my father. They traveled to the celebration under a canopy of fans made of quetzal feathers and decorated with gold, under which they carried a splendid array of royal mantles, beautiful sandals, and jewels including gold pendants, jade necklaces and bracelets, and beautifully carved emeralds. As soon as they entered

Acallan they were given the hot, thick, sweetened cornflour drink known as *atole* and the sweet roasted blue cornflour drink called *pinole*. After they finished eating, they presented the gifts.

At the sound of the *teponachtli* drum, everyone sang and danced while they played with quetzal-feather balls. Meanwhile, the short man with the fat calves who was chosen by the Spaniards to supplant the lord of Tenochtitlan was jealously listening to the festivities from Malintzin and Cortés' camp and he was angry because he had not been invited to the party. He called to Malintzin and said: "Do you hear how your false friends celebrate the inspection of the troops? They have decided to attack us in the morning. I know this for a fact because we heard them discuss it during the night. I am only concerned that they will kill Lady Malintzin and Captain Cortés."

As the sun set over Acallan, the lords ate again and then left. In Uaymollen, without knowing that they had been accused of conspiracy by the false and lying lord Cozte Mexi, they submitted without resistance to the soldiers who waited for them in ambush because they had no idea what was about to happen to them. As soon as they had the noble lords in their hands, the soldiers insulted them and beat them—doing things to their bodies that I do not want to describe here. Then they hoisted them up the Pochote tree and cruelly tortured them. Quauhtemoc, Couanecoch, and Tetlepanquetzal were lynched without the formality of an interrogation.

The other two lords invited to the fiesta, Eca and Temilo, had spent the night in Acallan. Their men woke them up to tell them that the sovereign and his noble friends had been killed. Seeing that dawn was upon them and realizing that escaping without being seen would be almost impossible, they boarded a Castilian ship on the advice of, and with the help, of their men. They went into the boat's stable, raised one of the planks of the floorboard inside, and hid themselves underneath. Their men put the plank back in place and Eca and Temilo hid, with water and bread made of corn as provisions, where it would never occur to the Spaniards to look for them. Unfortunately, the ship set out to sea before night fell the following day when the cover of darkness might have helped them escape.

After they had been sailing five days, having overcome the first waves of seasickness and on the verge of more seasickness, dying of hunger and thirst since they had already drunk all their water, Temilo lost his senses and began shouting madly. As much as Eca tried to silence him, Temilo screamed, howled, and cried saying: "What is going to become of us? I left my wife alone to give birth to our first child. I sent her to live with her kinswoman in Tezcoco because I couldn't continue living in my village. How will they treat her? Will they treat her like the princess she is? Will they treat her like a slave? How will they treat her? And what about us? Will there be a sky above the land we are going to? What will the home of these terrible men be like?"

The neighing of a horse traveling with them initially hid Temilo's howls, but when the howls grew louder than the neighing, the men were discovered and removed from their hiding place and given food and water. When they gave their names they were treated honorably in consideration of their noble status and the Marqués was immediately notified: "We have discovered Ecatzin (the man who won the flag) and Temilotzin Tlacatécatl hidden onboard."

Malintzin approached and tried to frighten them: "The lord says that we are going over there, to Castile, to see the supreme sovereign. There, perhaps, you will be drawn and quartered. They will treat you horribly. How many of the sovereign's soldiers have you killed?"

How many had they killed? Neither of them knew how to respond, but their hearts were filled with terror.

When Cortés saw them he treated them like great lords. He invited them to sit at his side and said in formal Castilian:

—Now you are great sovereigns. Please do have a seat.[7]

Temilo lost all composure. Too many things had happened in one week. Without any apparent reason, Cortés had ordered Quauhtemoc to be assassinated for treason; he and Eca had hidden in a boat that had set sail before they expected; for five days they had pretended to be planks between the planks, drinking a sip of water every time thirst burned their throats; meanwhile, in their hearts they wondered what the land, where these dogs raised enormous horses, would be like. Would there be a sky and stars? What kind of dirty customs did they have? What would their buildings, houses, temples, and roads be like? What kinds of trees and plants would be there? Temilo imagined monstrous things and cruel two-headed beings and white feather-winged chargers. He also thought he might see three hideous women sharing a single eye; a giant waving his trident at the sea as if it were a piece of cloth; naked women with white skin and blond hair coming up out of the water, being born out of enormous oysters; and enormous smoke-

---

7   This sentence was in Spanish in the original. Estela's note.

and-fire-spewing dragons and serpents walking across the ocean; and he imagined specters and demons waiting to meet the boat. Ultimately, the fear of the voyage was greater than the fear of being discovered or dying. It is not surprising that their situation might make him howl and betray their hiding place. Nobody would think that it was out of cowardice that Temilo said to Eca—in front of the Marqués, Malintzin, the noblemen who accompanied Cortés, and the sailors—and still crying loudly:

—Oh sovereign Eca! Where can we go if the boat has already been sailing for five days?

Thus, caught unawares, Cortés and his men could do nothing when Temilo ran toward the stern of the boat howling like an injured animal and threw himself into the water.

I was born amid music and a celebration that was not for me, on the same day my father, Temilo, one of the noble lords of Tlatelolco, jumped off the boat, kicked his legs toward the sun, and directly toward his death, if he was lucky.

Eca visited La Sacra and Cesárea, His Catholic Majesty Carlos V received him with honors, and he returned to New Spain on the same ship that was carrying Fray Bernardino de Sahagún. Upon returning to these lands, he served as governor of Tlatelolco under the Spaniards for three years.

This was the first story I heard told of my father. But there was a second one, in which I have no faith at all, but must recount anyway. According to this one, after my father threw himself off the boat he was rescued by a rope, which he grasped and was obliged to climb up when one of Cortés's men tied it around him while he was in the water. He arrived in Castile and met Carlos V who favored him and on whose generosity he lived for many years. He learned to read and write, and later as an old man, he wrote in his own hand, the "Memorial de la casa de Moctezuma sobre la pretension de la grandeza de España al señor rey Felipe II," which was given to me by the person who told me the second version of the story of my father. But, as I have already said, I do not believe this second version because if it is true that he could read and write, why did he never write to my mother or to me? Why did he not use his letters to bring us to him, or to protect us in these cruel lands, or to take care of us in some way?

I will quote an excerpt from the letter anyway:

"Count Don Diego Luis de Moctezuma, son of Don Pedro de Moctezuma, and grandson of the Emperor of Mexico, the ninth and final Moctezuma, claims that: obeying the Royal Order of H.M., he has come from Mexico and today finds himself sitting at the royal feet of H.M., and he hopes that distance will not hinder the generous influence of your royal presence—for only the relationship of grandson and legitimate heir of such a celebrated monarch, though the Crown or violence or rights of other princes might have taken it from him, in case such an unforeseeable and unfortunate event that might unexpectedly occur—he might take refuge in Spain and benefit from the royal protection of H.M. fashioned out of the benevolence of such an august spirit, to preserve some of the luster respective to his lost throne, of which H.M. each day provides magnificent examples, enriching with revenue and honoring with high positions many who, fallen from lesser heights, gain considerable prosperity from their fall, with no more merits than the favor of H.M., which they quickly experience, for as much as the efforts of the Crown and the royal palace demand.

The discoverers and conquistadors of New Spain are resplendent with dignity and *grandezas* and noble Courts, acquiring for their descendants regular favors with which they increase the splendor of their houses. The supplicant, then, should not find himself before H.M. and his Court with less brilliance, having the royal blood of that emperor still so fresh in his veins, and so recently being in that incomparable service..."[8]

The Crown might have been very generous with my father, but his masters were not; that which is written in such an elegant manner is not what it seems if it was by chance his hand that authored what I transcribe here. I will not repeat that I doubt it, that I do not believe it, because I have already said it, and because, in saying that I do not say it, I affirm it anyway.

Slosos keston de Hernando

---

8   In Spanish in the original. Estela's note.

EKFLOROS KESTON DE LEARO

Just when I was about to leave my room in L'Atlàntide to go down and pick up my transcription where I left off the day before, something happened that made me so angry that just seeing Hernando's words moments later caused me to experience it all over again. The paragraph in which Hernando discusses the possibility of understanding the stars and the difference "between reading them and understanding them" was tinged with something that seemed completely foreign to him. I decided to do a couple of things to rid myself of this bad feeling. One is that I'm going to skip that paragraph, and the other is that I'm going to write down what made me so angry so I can get the bad taste out of my mouth.

So what was it that made me so mad? At first it was nothing unusual. Rosete came to invite me to be a part of Team Save the Banana Leaf, whose objective is exactly what it sounds like: to save, recover, and recreate the banana leaf. Up until now, the banana plants in our gardens have been a kind of yellow tube whose upper part hangs from a green stalk, a banana-like caricature of those amazing trees.

Rosete wasn't looking for me in particular. From time to time, when people need help on some project or other, they try to recruit whomever's available, briefly explaining what the job entails. Rosete is our *correo vivo*, it's his job to convey messages. He's very slim, pale, and has a sweet angelic little face, but his soul is full of complicated folds with nooks and crannies of varying depths. He lives in a world where there is no room for "yes" or "no," where nothing is completely round or completely square. He's a master conversationalist (or at least he was), but he's incapable of being useful on any project because his thought processes do not lead to anything concrete, his thinking can't follow anything remotely resembling a straight line, so that's why, when we decided to ban conversation in L'Atlàntide, Rosete was the most affected. I didn't object to the prohibition of conversation inside our colony—not because I believed, like the majority, that conversing creates discomfort and disagreement, whereas the sight of others produces only pleasure, but because I was seduced by the idea of improving the conditions of silence. I do believe, like the rest of the members of my community, that silence is beautiful, that it's the best companion to both relaxation and work. Of course, Rosete didn't object to the ban on conversation either. I think that's also part of his nature. Being incapable of articulating a definite "yes" or "no," he doesn't know how to actively resist anything. Thus, conversation restricted, he was deprived of what was most important to him and before he could utter a complaint, before he could think of it himself, it occurred to the rest of us that he could be the *correo vivo*, which would be very useful because, since we don't converse within L'Atlàntide, we had to have some way to receive more detailed messages than the formulas transmitted by the Center for Research allowed. And so, Rosete comes and goes conveying messages. We communicate with each other through him. Besides having an incredible memory, he can perfectly imitate each person's particular gestures and manner of speaking, without parody, without caricature. More than the *correo*, Rosete is a living mirror, a mobile mirror that comes and goes.

Before giving me the message, Rosete told me (in French, since that's the language we used to converse in) that they were considering eliminating this type of mail:

—*Écoute!* They're not going to use words to send us messages anymore. It's part of the Language Reform. And since there won't be any more words, it doesn't make sense for me to come and just say a number, so then explain to me how…

His expression, one that was completely his own rather than someone else's, was so sad when he was telling me this that I felt sad for him. At the time, I only thought about how it affected him directly, I didn't think about how absurd it would be to yank the words we use to communicate out by their roots, even at the most basic level.

—So, what are you going to do? —I asked, more for my own information, so I could be his ally and console him.

—What am I going to do? Do? What to *do* isn't a problem, we don't always have to satisfy our own desires, or do we? What do you think? Look, I'm learning some quicks on the ones I've been working on; as I finish them, I'll come by to show them to you from time to time. They're not bad ideas. There's one in particular that's not going too bad. One day, the 16th, I was sitting on a boulder, thinking…

—Wait, hold on, don't tell me about it right now. —It wasn't the time to hear about one of his quicks. I was beginning to grasp what he had told me and my mind was reeling thinking about it, but since I didn't want to hurt him by cutting him off completely, I said:

—I don't want to see it at the halfway point; I want to see it when it's done, to enjoy it more. Will they be all right with your quicks?

—I haven't shown them any yet because I still don't have one finished, but in principle I don't think they should have a problem with the idea.

—Don't your quicks use words?

—Some of them do, when it's necessary...

—And do you think after the Language Reform you're going to be able to use words with your quicks?

—Well, that will be different. I'm going to use words, but...—he paused and added, in a defensive tone—I agree with the prohibition on the use of words. You see what's happening? We're not understanding each other.

—Of course we understand each other. I saw your sad expression and...

—Yes, my face was sad, but you don't understand my words. It should have been enough for you to just see my expression and we wouldn't have to fight.

—How can you believe that, Rosete? I couldn't possibly have known what was making you sad, don't be absurd.

—Absurd? Don't you see that words are the reason we misunderstand each other time and again? My expression already told you everything.

—Calm down, Rosete. Don't let yourself be fooled by the order that...

We felt the alarm—warning us against the excessive use of words—vibrate under our feet. Without realizing it, Rosete and I had been conversing. As I've already mentioned, we weren't supposed to converse inside the colony. But there we were again, Rosete and I, talking irresponsibly. How embarrassing! We quit talking as soon as we felt the warning alarm. The Center immediately and silently transmitted to each of us a string of pertinent notifications: N41, N42, N43, O87, and Y1.

I'll translate them here: N41 means that, "you are contaminating the air with unnecessary noise." This pertains to anyone who makes any kind of noise. N42, "verbal proximity produces unpleasant sensations and bad feelings." N43, "you make mistakes when you use words." O87 means, "be careful not to infringe on the space of those around you," and Y1 means that, "the number of notifications for the same infraction exceeds ten."

What could we do to soften the disapproving tone of the Y1? Without letting a moment pass, Rosete put his thin, warm hand on my neck, played with my hair and looked into my eyes; we smiled at each other and then began to make love. We took our time, as if we had met in my room expressly for that purpose, as if we had flirted precisely with the goal of being together. We spent all morning kissing, caressing, and cuddling in the darkness of silent lovemaking. When we were on the other side of the tunnel of kisses and penetration, it didn't take long for me to realize that a cloud of sadness had darkened Rosete's face and I tried to ask him silently, with my eyes, what had caused it.

He responded gruffly by breaking eye contact abruptly. He turned his head to one side and looking away, as if he were talking to someone else, said to me:

—Do you want to work on Team Save the Banana Leaf? — Though he wasn't imitating anyone in particular, his normal tone of voice changed and became exceedingly cold and severe. He didn't look at me again and instead directed his gaze toward some distant point. I was disconcerted. If I were to put it in human terms, I would say I was offended. Wasn't he kissing me just a moment ago? Didn't I kiss his entire body? Weren't we just partners in the pleasures of the flesh? Hadn't we both just let ourselves go, aroused by our marathon lovemaking? Hadn't we just entered each other's bodies like people desperately fleeing a fire, or boiling water, or a brandished knife? Weren't we both just humbled, and having abandoned our own consciousness, inhabited each other's skin more than our own, aroused by pursuing each other in an impossible chase? We started having sex to blot out the reproof of our behavior issued by the Center, but we really did make love— I was Rosete's and he was mine—and then, afterward, he rewarded me with distance and a wall of silence. I felt an overwhelming desire to distance myself from him, but I didn't have anything at hand to pierce him with except a few lines from my poet, not audibly, but silently, because a shred of sanity reminded me that they had just chastised me for conversing:

> Tonight rain returned to fall again on the coffee plantations.
> On the leaves of the bananas,
> on the upper branches of the *cámbulos*,
> rain returned again tonight, a rain so persistent
> and extensive
> fills acequias and swells rivers
> that groan with their nocturnal load of muddy plants

Rosete received the poem and first became even paler and then his skin flushed bright red. But he still didn't look me in the eye. I took his face in my hands and turned it toward me. He lowered his eyelids.

—What's wrong Rosete? —I asked him out loud.

Stammering, he repeated his earlier question:

—Do you want to join Team Save the Banana Leaf? Yes or no?

—No! I already have my banana—this too, silently—I have my banana, my leaf, and even my nightingale—I started reciting Quevedo's poem:

> Singing flower, flying flower,
> winged whistle, painted voice,
> lively feathered lyre
> tiny trilling bouquet;
> tell me, flying ounce,
> feather accented flower,
> lovely sum of
> beauty and delicacy,
> how does this harmonious sum
> fit inside one tiny bird?

Instead of spouting off and trying to pierce him with another poem, I should have backed up and explained to him what the verses I had recited just moments before evoked for me and then I should have continued with the next verse of the poem, "The rain on the zinc rooftops," but when he turned away from me and refused to look at me, I felt just awful, I lost patience. But still, I should have paused and spent some time on all the secrets of the poem. I should have shown him how it speaks of the banana plant and the neighboring vegetation, shown him how it contains the fibrous stalk, the leaf, the flower with its purple tip, the surprisingly white and tender flesh of the fruit, and the bright yellow fibrous peel. I should have made him, not just understand the poem, but feel it—hear the sound of a river running through the thick trees of the tropical forest, smell its perfumed aroma, and touch the dewy freshness of the predawn hours. I should have shared the feeling of the poem with him. How could they possibly want more bananas, coffee plantations, *cámbulos*, rivers, or nightingales?

But I didn't do it. By reciting my poems, I only irritated Rosete. In his eyes, the verses are nothing more than vile creations of the men from the time of History. I should have explained the lines to him because my own irritation didn't lead anywhere; it only distanced me from Rosete. And I don't want to do that; I don't have any reason to distance myself from him. Of course he started it, by looking at me the way he did he provoked me, but I (once the first impulse to respond to his aggression had passed), should have been kind to him to try to win him over to my side. Rosete is nothing without words. It's absurd not to share his gifts.

It's a miracle. After writing down the story of what happened with Rosete, the bad feelings completely vanished. I'm not upset anymore. I'm no longer ill at ease. I can continue with my Hernando.

Slosos keston de Learo

EKFLOROS KESTON DE HERNANDO

I cannot sing the soothing lullabies—such as *Rorro, a la meme, riquirranes, tintón, dame dame,* or *dulce bien*—from my childhood, not because I was deprived of them (Mama was always there to cuddle me), but because her murmurs were muffled by the cruel melody that had seized these lands during those years. Cortés' departure triggered fights to the death over the real and imagined riches of these lands—homes were violated, crosses cast a pall over the streets, people were tortured, there was an excessive buzzing of languages, hangings and dismemberments were carried out by the hand of justice, stones rained on the heads of respected men and their wives and children, and we Indians danced to the sound of the violence sown by the conflict.

Destiny did not spoil me because although it brought me into the world in the middle of a lavish fiesta, it left me among the shattered virtues. The inspector, the royal tax collector, the one who arbitrarily lost his encomienda, the treasurer, the attorney Suazo who was removed of his military and civil jurisdiction (simply because he obstructed them, he was falsely accused of not abiding by a cedula that did not even exist, was taken away in chains during the night, and shipped off to Medellín)—all of them (and I am not speaking of the Indians here, I will leave that story for another time if I live long enough) were performing a comedy of horrors.

When Cortés returned as a great Lord, with the title of Marqués del Valle—having been dispatched to New Spain as Captain General and granted the gift of a lordship over twenty-three thousand vassals; married to Doña Juana de Zúñiga, niece of the Duque of Béjar; and accompanied by an extensive retinue—those with bad memories of him were not soothed by his return and sent orders that the mayor should throw Cortés out of Veracruz, issued a proclamation that all who had gone to see him should return to their villages on pain of death, and forbade the Indians to give Cortés and his people anything to eat. And so the disputes continued, and I—endowed by the Creator with the gift of sight— was living there, suffering the spectacle of the atrocities even at that tender age.

No lesson, advantage, or benefit could be gained from witnessing the above, and there were even more interminable atrocities, to which there is no sense returning and wasting ink or wearing out my already old hand. But even if there was no advantage or benefit, I did win a jewel for myself, expurgating it from among the wreckage, disgrace, and unbridled greed. I managed to find a keepsake in a place where nothing good could be found, where people were forced to surrender and suppress the better part of their honor, if not of their spirit, to survive unscathed. There are many examples of this but I will offer Rodrigo de Paz as one: not even by proffering his ring as a sign of his unconditional allegiance did he avoid being tortured for information as to where Cortés had hidden his treasures.

They tortured him with water, rope, and fire until his toes fell off, and they took him to be hung, first walking him around the public plaza on the back of an ass, where he then stood naked with a dirty rag on his head for an entire day. Just two weeks prior he had marched with five halberdiers and twenty on horseback. And that is not counting what Rodrigo de Paz's soul had to suffer for obtaining the halberdiers and those twenty on horseback, which included wearing a dirty rag on his head while riding around on the back of an ass and being tortured with water, rope, and fire. And worse than the excoriations, gashes, bruises, and wounds they inflicted on him, were the ones he committed in order to get rich so quickly. Two quotes from Juvenal come to mind:

> Dare to be worthy of tiny Giano and of prison, if you want to be something. Integrity is praised, but tremulously. It is to crime we owe gardens, country houses, tables, antique silver platters, and wine glasses embossed with goats.

> And when was vice the greater? When was the bosom of greed opened widest? When were the games of chance most vigorous? ...Is it not sheer folly to lose one hundred thousand sesterces and deny a tunic to a shivering slave?

Not being an alchemist, magician, or evil warlock, I could not have found anything of value in the putrid slaughterhouse of virtues this land had become, but even though I was not Merlin or Titlacahuan (the sorcerer who tricked Quetzalcóatl), I did find, and steal, a jewel. And if it is true that stealing is never a good thing, it is also true that my act of stealing was not a bad thing, because even though I took what was not mine and did not ask permission, nobody would notice its absence. Because even though I stole it, I did not take it from anybody. And if it is also true that jewels are not good when they are mere vanity, when they satisfy greed and lust, it is also true that my jewel was not entirely reprobate and impious because it neither awakened ambition, nor was it taken out of meanness and covetousness. Mine was a pure jewel, even though it was a fruit reaped from where nothing good can come. Nothing good, and to complicate things, the court of the conquistador had arrived.

When Cortés was in Tlaxcala, en route to Mexico, after he and his company had starved due to the order given to the Indians that they should gather up all their food (so much starvation, according to the story, that some of the retinue died, among them Doña Catalina Pizarro, Cortés' mother), the Marqués del Valle received an order from the court that read like this:[9]

"For compliance in our service and the execution of our justice, we have decided to send provisions for our new president and judges of the Royal *Audiencia* of New Spain, and until they arrive your (and that of the Marquesa, your wife), entrance into Mexico might be inconvenienced; therefore, I order that in the meantime and for that reason, as has been said, that we have sent provisions to arrive in that land for our president and some of the judges, neither you nor the Marqueza, your wife, shall enter in the City of Mexico, you shall not travel within ten leagues of there, on pain of our mercy, and of ten thousand Castilian coins for our house and treasury."[10]

The order was sent on 22 March 1530 and was received on 9 August 1530. Cortés kissed it, held it over his head and obeyed,

---

9   In Spanish in the original from here. Estela's note.

10   The text in Spanish ends here and continues in Latin. Estela's note.

leaving Tlaxcala for Tezcoco. That is how he came to the village in which I had already learned to take my first steps, where I was living happily alone with my mother (but had not yet discovered playing with my friends), the same village where he left the brigantines with which he attacked Tenochtitlan by water.

Don Hernán's court was larger than the one in Mexico City, and the entire village was uneasy when they settled in Tezcoco. But it was not from that Court that I stole the above-mentioned jewel (though they certainly had plenty of gold, gems, beautiful clothing, and excellent horses), but rather from the situation I am about to recount right now. One day, when I was walking hand in hand with Mama, on our way back from some errand or other that I do not remember, we ran into some armed men from the *Audiencia*, or high court, who were taking a noble lord from one of the neighboring areas into custody with a lot of noise and ruckus. The noble lord was screaming at the top of his lungs in perfect Spanish, "It was not me," and then "I will not do it again," and then, "Let me go, let me go, let me free, by everything that is holy, for the love of God, my children and my village are waiting for me," pulling with all of his strength to free himself, crying an ocean of tears.

I quit squeezing Mama's hand. The noble lord's fear was contagious. I wanted to run, but I could not move because my eyes were glued to the man being taken prisoner. He was dressed in fine clothing, the fabric of which was the whitest white, and he maintained his elegance even while trying to escape from his captors. His refinement contrasted sharply with the coarseness of the armed men. If they were men, he was a swan and his robes were his wings.

If he was a man, the ones who held him captive were dogs, agitated hounds, smelly, muddy, growling threats while they held their crying white prey in their slobbery maws, a prey who even in such a difficult situation continued to shine with refinement and elegance.

One of the soldiers pulled at his victim's white robe with his paws, holding the front of the man's robe with his closed fist. Then he plunged a dagger into the fabric he clutched in his paw—slowly, tip first and then the blade—as if he were sticking it into something hard and solid, until the sharp tip emerged from underneath the cotton mantle. The noble lord appeared to be skewered in his clothes by the dagger. Not content with such boldness, the soldier pulled his arm back and in one swift motion stabbed his captive in the stomach. Without stopping, he pulled the knife back out, ripping the fabric of the robe and revealing a bloody wound. The time it took the weapon to enter and exit the fabric, wounding the body of the noble lord, was filled with a profound silence. The noble lord had remained immobile, like a statue impaled on the point of the dagger, and not a cry of pain escaped his lips when the blade wounded him in the stomach. The first sound we heard was the voice of the soldier who owned the weapon:

—No bawling, that's good; you surprise us, you stupid Indian.

They took him away, in silence, subdued, and crying again. The other soldiers who accompanied him did not know what to do, I saw them running in different directions, like ants scattering from a destroyed anthill. Then we heard that the principal lord had come to Tezcoco to greet Cortés and they took him prisoner because they were looking for a fight and wanted to irritate the Conquistador. We also heard that the armed men of the *Audiencia* were already on the outskirts of Tezcoco, supplied and ready to wage war on Cortés.

We never saw that noble lord again, perhaps because he did not want to return to a place that evoked such a horrific memory or because the cruel judges of the *Audiencia* took his life. Only God knows. But what I can say is that this is where I stole the jewel. If there had not been a dispute between the inspector and the royal tax collector on the one hand and the treasurer and the auditor on the other, and everyone against Zumárraga and Cortés, I would not have gotten it. I stole the dagger. The dagger was my jewel. From that time forward I could always see it in my imagination. That weapon became an important part of me that day. Not because I possessed it, but because I engraved it in my mind, stealing it so it would become part of my very being. I armed myself with it in hundreds of ways—I was a hero, a warrior, triumphant in thousands of righteous disputes; in my tireless private adventures I defended both Mama and myself (I cannot say I defended my people, because at the time my people were only myself and Mama) with that dagger.

Instead of taking something from the noble Indian, I stole something from the despicable soldier. Instead of taking the Indian's enviable elegance, or his fear that was not blind or naïve, I stole a prop from the scene. And not even the noblest one. The weapon was not white like the cloth was, the weapon was not fine like the linen was, and the dagger was not strong, only the noble lord's panic and cries were just. Even his tears seem to me to be a better keepsake, if I were to take something for my own use. Without minimizing the miserable quality of my spirit, I can say one thing in its defense: I corrected the destiny of the weapon, because in my imagination it was never again brandished against a defenseless person or anyone with a good heart.

I have said a little about the evil that was a matter of course at that time in New Spain, and I am sure that you all will hear much more about that, so it should be easy to imagine that I did not have to exert any effort at all in order to find evil adversaries against whom to brandish my dagger. In my childish imagination I saw myself fighting valiantly as a full-grown man armed with my brilliant, sharp-edged weapon. My weapon, and it was mine (even though the brute's dagger would never be mine), never left my sight. All I had to do was squint my eyes a little in order to see myself using it against this one or that one, always coming out victorious, because my private jewel was an infallible weapon of defense. I kept it with me, sheathed in the forefront of my memory. It was my closest companion and it never left me. There were times that it appeared in my dreams to save me; it was always at hand, held securely in my fingers, as faithful as a third leg (that is, those of my youth, since the two I have now do not even add up to one). My weapon was not kept in an isolated space, tucked safely away as my jewel, but was always with me everywhere I went.

It was around the same time I saw the principal lord detained with impunity by the soldiers who were enemies of Cortés (providing me with the most faithful companion, my jewel, my treasure, the dagger that they would never have imagined would have become an Indian boy's) that I first tasted *queso de tierra*, which is what the Spaniards called the blue-green algae we harvested from the shores of Lake Texcoco and formed into cakes, because the taste reminded them of cow's milk cheese. Even to this day I associate its taste with the arrest of the noble lord—the violence and elegance, the supplication and impiety mingle in my memory with the verdant succulence of the *queso de tierra*. The taste of the lime from the lake (this is what they used to make the exquisite *queso de tierra*) evokes the memory of the dagger cutting the fabric and the gush of blood running from the nobleman's stomach. I have not eaten it in years because it is a bodily pleasure, a call to gluttony. Because it is not corn, baked bread, minted coins, a book, a falcon or other game bird, something given for weddings, or possessions of the deceased that are distributed among the heirs, *queso de tierra* is exempt from taxation, as is everything sold by the Indians. And because it is a highly prized food, it is reserved for those who have a purse full of money. It is for all of the reasons listed above that I have not eaten it in years. But I have not forgotten the memory of it. The infamous arrest of the noble lord who was loyal to Cortés is also fixed in my memory in a strange way, and defending him in my imagination with my dagger reminds me of the pleasure of the taste of the *queso de tierra*.

Then Cortés left Tezcoco.

He is gone, even from my memory, and I have not even said anything about what my village was like at that time. Tezcoco was four or five leagues to the east, and on the opposite side of the salt-water lake, from Tenochtitlan-Mexico. It was the second principal city of this land, and the lord of Tezcoco was the second lord. It controlled fifteen provinces as far as Tuzpan on the coast of the North Sea. It is on an open plain between the lake and the mountain range and the big mountain called Tláloc. There is not a fast-flowing or primary river within the city, but there are many arroyos that run to the lake and almost disappear during the dry season. When I was a child, the water channels and irrigation canals that the two Nezahualcóyotl kings created to water their orchards and gardens were still well maintained, and I drank, as our grandfathers had done, the water from the wells. These kings constructed a system of waterworks—irrigation canals, wells, water channels—with so much knowledge of water management that they successfully diverted the course of one river, originating from the springs of Teotihuacan (that today is held in encomienda by don Antonio de Bezán, Chief Constable of the Holy Inquisition of New Spain), so that it would serve some of the houses of pleasure about a quarter of a league away from the city. But now the waterworks of the Nezahualcóyotls have been destroyed and the water courses in a disorderly fashion in different directions.

Because it was a rich and important city, Texcoco had many grand buildings, gracious houses, and its main temple was taller than the Templo Mayor of Tenochtitlan.

The palace of King Nezahualpilli was quite something to see. It was magnificent and could have housed an army. It was there that Ixtlilxóchitl, ally of the Spaniards and the first lord under their control in Tezcoco, lodged the three Flemish Franciscan friars—Fray Juan de Tecto, the Emperor's confessor, Fray Juan de Ayora, and Fray Pedro de Gante—who came to our city to learn the Mexican language. They say the house is devastated now.

The nearby orchard had more than a thousand incredibly beautiful cedar trees. There were also many gardens and an enormous pond, which could be reached by by way of flat-bottomed rafts through an underground canal.

Tezcoco was so large that it measured one league in width by six in length. It was a very large city. It was very beautiful. They did not neglect the lake, but rather protected it behind some enormous reed beds and very tall, cultivated trees.

According to Fray Andrés de Olmos, who said they showed him some paintings, the first man of Tezcoco[11] was born because they say that when the sun was at nine o'clock, it shot an arrow in that direction, making a hole from which emerged the first man, who had no more of a body than shoulders, arms, and hands and then a complete woman emerged, and when they were asked how the man could have procreated, since he did not have a whole body, they said some disgusting nonsense that is not for here, and that the man was called Aculmaitl, and that this is where the name of the village of Aculma came from, because *aculli* means shoulder, and *maitl* means hand or arm, since the man was no more than shoulders and arms, or he was all shoulders and arms, because as I said, according to this piece of fiction and falsehood, the first man had no more than shoulders and arms for a body.

—

Now I will return to my reliable and trustworthy Latin. Someone else was spying over my shoulder, as if I were the man made

---

11   In Spanish in the original from here. Estela's note.

only of shoulders, which did not stop him from making the woman his companion in such a dirty and unmentionable manner. As for me, they can spy on me; I will not put down my book, which does not arouse much curiosity in them because, after all, they are already convinced that I am foolishly obsessed with writing down the customs of the ancients, as I have told them I am doing whenever they have deigned to listen to me. I have explained: "I am writing because I want to leave a written account of the foolishness of those who did not know the light of God" and they do not bother to listen to me, because this has been heard quite a bit around here, and these days it is seen as a foolish and useless project. It was not like that in our better days.

I might be wasted, or only shoulders like the first man of Tezcoco, but I will recount the memory of the light that one day shone on the Colegio as it was, and not as it is today—the refuge of a poor useless man without legs and an old, bad wing under which they do a poor job of teaching students to read the ABCs and to repeat the Creed and the Our Father without understanding them.

Slosos keston de Hernando

Even though the dimensions of our colony are not extensive and despite the fact that there are no walls that allow us to be invisible from each other, or furniture to hide behind, or blankets to cover our faces with, or any kind of clothing, curtains, or rugs, we jealously guard our privacy.

Our customs are rich in the art of evasion and tricks of concealment. We respect the importance of silence, as I've said, and we also jealously guard our solitude. The Punto Calpe is our equivalent of the public plaza. That is where we drop our custom of "I'm not looking at you" and smile at one another, we catch up on each other's various activities (unfortunately, every day now we are using shorter and shorter utterances and filling our conversations with numbers and the names of letters), we exchange looks and gestures, we touch one another, we make dates to get together. This is where we weave the thin thread of our weak collective life.

Obviously if you don't want to interact with others, you don't go to the plaza. If I'm not in the mood to see anyone, I descend much earlier or later than the others so I don't run into anyone on the bridge, and if I do happen to meet someone during the off-hours, we just pretend not to see each other. If I really don't want to see anyone's face, I don't go by way of Punto Calpe and instead descend via another route and move around on my own. This is something I do from time to time.

That's why I was so surprised today when somebody grabbed

me by the arm while I was descending by way of the Punto Calpe during the antisocial hours. I was so completely focused on my own thoughts, so lost in thought, that for a second *I didn't recognize* the person who was holding on to me.

It's inconceivable to see a stranger in our community. Each one of us has distinct features. Of course these features change, because faces change, but not so much that they become unrecognizable. Since we've overcome the illness known as old age, each of our faces has had sufficient time to manifest the splendors and miseries of life. There are no strangers in L'Atlàntide. I have to add that since the founding of our colony, we have believed in the power of images and we were repeatedly and incessantly exposed to the image of each person's face. I'm getting off topic, but since I mentioned it, I'll spend a little time on the subject.

When they selected us, or better said, when they selected the egg and the sperm (after having examined the genes) that would become us, they opted for the greatest diversity of physiognomies. Our community is a sampler of what Mother Nature gave to human appearance. In our colony, "race" isn't important because each of us is our own distinct race and because the men who created us—the survivors—made each of us (aided by the Image Receptor) equally beautiful and equally worthy of respect. During the *Conformación*, they used the Image Receptor to transmit to us an infinite number of images of ourselves as we were at that time and how they could conjecture we would look as adults. The images were both still and moving, flat and three-dimensional. In these images, we saw ourselves in the most diverse of landscapes, visiting all the important places on Earth as they had been before the men from the time of History destroyed them. In these images we scale mountains, swim in oceans and white-water rivers, we dodge waterfalls and explore caves, we walk along many different paths, we plant trees and pick cherries and oranges, we cut sunflowers in vast fields covered with them. We made love, ate, laughed, we wore different kinds of clothing and sometimes nothing at all, and we were always beautiful. We ran through dense forests, stumbling in the semi-darkness; we dove into the translucent water of the Caribbean Sea and the reefs of the southern seas, we navigated the Amazon, traveled down the Nile, and jumped from rock to rock at the bottom of Sumidero Canyon. We saw ourselves controlling the flight of an eagle and racing an ostrich, and we rode camels, elephants, and horses. We skied the Alps, the Andes, and the Rockies. We climbed up to the crater of Popocatépetl and to the top of the Himalayas; we swam in the cenotes of Mexico; we flew above wetlands and prairies and saw rugged, unusually shaped cordilleras beneath our feet; we heard the cracking of the gigantic rocks of the desert and crossed the Sahara. We did everything that would have been possible to do if Mother Nature were still alive. But we didn't tame fire, slay a dragon, cut the head off a Gorgon, throw stones at Goliath, ride on the back of Pegasus, or create a fountain by stamping our feet—though we did, and I have no idea why, see ourselves being born from sea foam and sailing on an oyster shell toward the island of Cythera and the Peloponnese peninsula. Grass and flowers sprang up wherever we stepped and doves and sparrows accompanied us whenever we flew through the air.

I won't stop to write down all the images they transmitted to us with the Receptor because even though the images were of us, we never did any of those things. The images were created by the men who made us—the survivors—and have nothing to do with reality. I saw myself as an adult long before I actually became one; I saw myself at four, eight, and ten years old; I saw the Earth without a trace of the destruction we see today, when she was more than just a devastated wasteland covered with rubbish and battered by the dirty, irascible wind. Nobody would ever have guessed, without prior knowledge or an exhaustive investigation, that the globe below L'Atlàntide is the same planet that was lush and beautiful in the images. Who could have ever guessed that it would become a corpse? In the images there was no trace of humankind, its voracity and desire for self-destruction, or the stupidity that ultimately led to its annihilation and to the disaster that devastated the Earth. In the images you wouldn't know that man had abused Mother Nature or that the atmosphere had burned one day.

Once we were out of childhood, they stopped the continuous transmission of the images. It was no longer necessary. Each of our faces had been endowed with a soul. It was impossible to imagine that something could incite enmity, suspicion, or distrust in any of the inhabitants of L'Atlàntide because we all had the same roles to play.

So, you can imagine how terribly confused I was when I thought I saw a stranger. This thought lasted only a second, or even less than a second. My surprise immediately grabbed hold of something firmer. Of course it wasn't a stranger, simply because that just wasn't possible. I was distracted and I started to chide myself, thinking: "this is too much, I am too much." But when he saw my look of surprise, before I chided myself, Ramón asked me:

—24, is something wrong?

—Ramón—I replied—Ramoncito, forgive me. For a second, with the surprise of having someone take me by the arm at this time of day on the Punto Calpe, and with my thoughts somewhere else entirely, you won't believe it, but I didn't recognize you. I'm too much, what a bizarre feeling, Ramoncito. —I stroked his hair, fine and straight, like silk. —You look really good, Ramón.

—You didn't recognize me? Unbelievable…I would laugh, but it's too absurd. Come with me, 24, I want to talk to you.

Arms around each other, we walked down the stairs in silence. The ties that bind my community are very tight. We grew up together. We were educated together, we embarked on the road to survival, the founding of L'Atlàntide, and the creation of our way of life together. Not to mention that while we were growing up we saw each other starring in magnificent adventures on a splendid planet that our colony was trying to recover and maintain. We aren't independent and no one is considered to be better than anyone else. When we arrived at the Jardín de las Delicias, Ramón started explaining things to me as if *I were the stranger*, a foreigner.

—We're protective of our privacy and at the same time we enjoy our life together. You know that. Even though, and because, we think very differently, we've managed to create a communal life that protects us from each other, and that protects all of us from ourselves. Here, no man is a slave to another…

—Ramón, I already know all of this. Why do you feel the need to remind me when it's not necessary to do so? —I said, as soon as he paused.

—24, you can do whatever you want with your own time. And I don't need to tell you that it wouldn't hurt for you to also work for the good of the colony and the Earth, because you already know that too. And because at one time you worked very hard, you can enjoy a break if you want to take one. You can do what you want with your own time, but—here he paused and took a breath—*mais*—he emphasized the word, pronouncing it slowly, hitting each letter—but don't try to harm us, 24, this is not a game.

He looked me straight in the eye when he said, "This is not a game." Ramón is a wonderful person and he inspires an enormous amount of confidence, but I saw something deep in his eyes that I didn't like.

—What do you mean by saying that this isn't a game? I'm not playing around with the books. I take them very seriously.

—We're just about to finalize the Language Reform and are carefully considering the final details. You have to appreciate the importance of this, 24, understand that with this we will destroy everything that remains of the men from the time of History. This will separate us from evil forever.

—This belief that we have to forget the men from the time of History is absurd.

—It's not absurd, 24, not at all.

—Yes, it is.

—The only thing they managed to do was to annihilate themselves and destroy the natural world.

—They didn't mean to destroy the Earth. It didn't have to happen.

—But it did happen. And it didn't start out as a mistake, it began as a death wish. They were bent on destroying everything.

—That's true. But the men from the time of History were more than just that.

—Yes, they were also slaves to other men and to Evil.

—They were more than that.

—"There are two Gods: Ignorance and Oblivion."

—Rubén Darío.

—Let's get back to what we were talking about. You can do whatever you want with your own time, but you can't do whatever you want with our time. I don't authorize or forbid anything, as you well know. I'm not a censor. Like anyone in my position, I'm trying ensure that harmony and good reign in L'Atlàntide...

I interrupted him. After having seen that threat in his eyes, I wasn't in the mood for lectures.

—I already know all that, Ramón. I know it as well as you do, you don't need to say it again. You also know how I feel about memory and I'm not going to repeat it. And as far as books go...

—Stop, wait a second, 24. Listen: "learn, above all, to distrust memory. What we think we remember is completely alien to, and different from, what really occurred... To live without remembering is, perhaps, the secret of the gods."

—Mutis. Yes, but in context...

—No context. It's from "The Gaviero's Visit."

—I know. But books...

Then he interrupted me.

—Let's not ruin the morning arguing, Cordelia.

—My name is Lear now.

He roared with laughter.

—Your name is *not* Cordelia anymore? Now it's Lear? —He

laughed even harder. You can't be changing your name all the time, no way! The name loses its meaning. Am I still Ramón?

Yes, of course, I never change your names. The problem is that I need to escape from the names.

He started laughing again. It didn't matter; I laughed too. I realize it's ridiculous to be changing my name all the time, and even though I don't like being laughed at, I think it's better to laugh with them than to try to defend something that's indefensible. But however indefensible it is, I can't stop.

—You see? Oh, Cordelia, Lear, 24, or whatever you want to call yourself, let's not ruin the morning arguing. Keep your poets and your novelists; you can be all alone with them. You know they are the companions of death; man's disorder cloaked Mother Nature in death. And you also know that it upsets us as much as death and its primary agent, man, do. Why should we go back to them, 24? It's a one-way ticket to death. Man and his desire for death are dead, their books are meaningless, if we ever gave them any credence at all. But anyway, I don't control you. Do what you want, but don't be malicious.

—What do you mean, malicious? I don't call your ideas malicious.

—They're not just ideas. You've proposed another object for inclusion in the Menschen Museum. When the entire community is ready to take the final steps to eliminate, for all time, the danger of following in the footsteps of the heinous actions of men, you propose another *thing* for the museum. Understand that loving language also leads you back to the misguided and dangerous love of things. Loving language makes you kin to man. Let it go. Listen to our advice...

Ramón took my hand, helped me up from the rock I was sitting on, put my arm through his so that our arms were linked and started walking, taking me along with him. I was grateful for this because I was beginning to lose my patience.

—Do you remember when we rode down into the Grand Canyon on mules together?

—Yes, of course I do. There was a desert at the bottom and at the beginning of the desert there was an oasis, and in the oasis there was a camel stable. We swam in the pond because we were hot and dirty from the trip.

—Don't we have enough images to sustain us? In addition to this one there are thousands more to fuel us. You seem to want to defend memory. That's fine. Let's remember our images, but let's not preserve any trace of men. Words, to begin with…

—We didn't live it, Ramón, you and I didn't go to the Grand Canyon, we didn't see the camels. We have to keep in mind that those memories aren't real. The only thing we have, Ramón, whether we like it or not, are words:

> The singer wanders the world
> smiling or thoughtful
> ....
> On a palanquin and in fine silk,
> through the heart of China;
> in an automobile in Lutetia;
> in a black gondola in Venice;
> over the pampas and the plains
> on American colts;
> down the river in a canoe
> or he can be seen at the prow

> of a steamer on the vast ocean
> or in a sleeping-car of a train.
> ....
> With messages and mail-pouches,
> goes the singer for humanity.

I didn't continue with the poem because Ramón didn't hear it, he wasn't paying any attention to me at all. I quit talking, and by way of response he said:

—What a fool you are, 24, Cordelia, Lear, what a stupid fool... Come on, let's walk.

The Jardín de Delicias is beneath our colony, not too far from the Punto Calpe. It's a coral islet on which men never erected a single building and on which Mother Nature, for her part, permitted very little vegetation so that it still looks almost exactly as it did before, only slightly touched by the abundance of the natural world, hardly disturbed by man's persistent and destructive incursion on the land. The Jardín de Delicias possesses a rare beauty, as if it was always neglected by creation. We have almost managed to completely eliminate the radiation and because the waters that surround it are very shallow, the waves break only occasionally so that they don't shimmer or surge with black foam. If there isn't a storm traversing the sea, the glow of the dead ocean can be seen from a distance. But nothing is perfect.

We walked around the circumference of the islet in silence, appreciating its rare beauty. The second time around, we talked about the sandstone and the coralline material that surrounded it, we commented on the miracle that it didn't shatter at the time of the great explosion, and we squatted down to look at the colors of the sand. This is what everyone who visits the Jardín de Delicias does.

To our great surprise, we discovered a tiny little insect while we were squatting down. Yes, a living creature. It could be that one of the members of our colony had left some specimens as a wonderful gift for anyone who went down to the garden to talk, but the very idea of finding a free-ranging living thing gave us infinite joy. We both laughed, watching the tiny little creature jump, recording each of its actions in our memories. It scratched its head with its little foreleg, beat its wings, and we laughed even more. It shook its little head, as if severely reproving our laughter, and we laughed even harder. It hid between two pieces of white coral as if it were embarrassed that we were watching it.

—Isn't it amazing? —I said to Ramón.

—How fortunate to have seen it with you, Cordelia.

I stroked his soft hair again, fine and silky, looked into his eyes, this time I didn't see anything that bothered me.

We were so happy that we started dancing in the sunlight, shaking our heads like insects.

Afterward, I lay down on the light-colored sandstone and closed my eyes to remember the little insect and to enjoy the delight of watching it shaking itself. Then Ramón said to me:

—You need to realize that words are the problem. Forget them. Or ask yourself: "Why am I making such a fuss?" We only have six languages left now; fifty-four hundred had already disappeared in the last decade of the men from the time of History, before the final explosion.

—That's a bad argument. "Any language is a supreme achievement of a uniquely human collective genius, as divine and endless a mystery as a living organism." Nothing compares to the loss of language—I replied, without opening my eyes.

—Don't waste your time. I'm telling you, this isn't a game. Relax. Let go of words now. You need to understand the importance of the Language Reform. Understand that only without language, without grammar, can we create a new man: one that won't reference that dangerous creature, of the same name, who destroyed the Earth. Join Team Seafoam, or Team Orange Implantation, or Team Strawberry Re-Creation, or whichever you like, or research the reproduction of insects or the re-creation of the lizard's tail. And one day the bees and the flies will buzz and we'll forget we ever had words to eliminate.

I laughed. That really was an absurd idea.

—Don't laugh—he continued—wasps, bees, flies, and blowflies will buzz all around you.

I laughed even more.

—Little Minx. Lovely one. Let go of words, put them aside now. Remember your poet: "Two or three bestial cries, shrieking howls from the cave might more effectively express what I really feel and what I am."

He didn't say anything else. When I opened my eyes, he was gone. I headed off to my workplace alone to record what I wanted to preserve.

I'll continue with my Hernando, the wise man who wanted to document—using words—what his real life was like.

Slosos keston de Learo

EKFLOROS KESTON DE HERNANDO

There is much more waiting here at the threshold of my memory, many more details about my childhood years wanting to be recorded on these pages. All it took was conjuring the first memory for all the others to come rushing back to me. They are right here, murmuring. We have been sitting here a lot in my chair, my memories and I, fighting for the seat. They shove me over, they push the old man aside in order to take as much air as might be left to him. They suffocate me. They struggle to be relived slowly, one at a time, to live again for the eternity that memory generously bestows. But this old man cannot make space for all of them. I write one line and then dream of a hundred more, I write one word and, like birds to seed, I summon all of them near. I am the seed that invokes memories. I am the flesh that attracts those vultures. I will the seed to germinate, take root, and make itself inaccessible to the black birds. I wish that the almost-dead flesh of the old man would revive itself so the buzzards would take flight.

I need to keep to the story I have proposed to recount. I am very old, and even if I am not that old, I look it and, if appearances are true, I feel my age. My days are numbered. I cannot tarry with my own memories. I will quickly move on to the day my relationship with the Colegio de Santa Cruz de Tlatelolco began, and will remember it in detail.

That morning, I ran out of the house belonging to Don Hernando Pimental, the brother of King Cacama of Tezcoco, which was my house too and where we lived under the protection of one of my mother's cousins (who was one of the wives of this man, but not the one who was his wife in the eyes of the Church) after my father's disgrace, the deaths of my mother's parents and brothers, of all our kin; we had nowhere else to go, we had lost our noble status and position in society, we were practically servants, though we did not work for them or serve them. I was carrying a small basket in my hands. How old was I? Nine? I have become confused because of all the deceptions and lies. I remember the actual day of my birth because my community continues to commemorate the day they did not welcome me into this world; but I have become tangled up in all the webs of lies. So many lies in place of so many others they told me and asked me to tell that when I was ten years old they had me convinced I was twelve years old. That is why, even though I was ten years old on the inside, I said I was twelve that day.

I met my friends in front of the house of the *Juez de Plaza*, as usual and as was our custom, we did not say a word to each other. The only signal we needed was a glance toward the portico of the house of the *Juez*; we did not need to say a word or wait for anything. This gesture is the way we said hello and agreed on how to begin the day; convention and custom, it did not have any other meaning or enchantment. Instead of inventing a special way of greeting each other—shaking each other's arms, calling out, whistling, hitting each other on the back, wiggling our fingers, joining hands, or any other amusing or absurd signal—like other boys had, we simply glanced meaningfully at the portico of the house of the *Juez de Plaza*.

My friends were a little older than I was, but because we had

all studied together in the hall adjacent to the church that sometimes served as a classroom, they included me in their games. The
boys of my real age, the ones who were between eight and ten
years old, spent mornings and afternoons with the friars as we
had done before, but I had to pretend to be the eldest son of the
important noble lord that Mama and I lived with. My friends and
I had already learned what they taught there. The friars had already
taught us the Christian Doctrine "that speaks of the things that are
very important to learn and know and for Christians to perform in
order to achieve salvation and so that they know how to respond
whenever they might be asked something about Christianity."[41]
That is to say, we knew the Sign of the Cross, The Creed, the
Our Father, the Ave Maria, the Salve Regina, the fourteen Arti-
cles of Faith, the Ten Commandments, the Seven Catholic Sacra-
ments, the Confession of venial sin, the Confession of mortal sin,
the mortal sins and their contrary virtues, the three Theological
Virtues and the four Cardinal Virtues, the fourteen Acts of Mercy,
the seven gifts of the Holy Ghost; the Bodily Senses given us by
God, Our Father, so that we might praise and honor him and use
them in good and holy acts and works and not in evil ones, so that
we always perform good deeds with them; the three Powers of
the Soul, the three Enemies of the Soul, the eight Beatitudes, the
Gifts of the Glorified Body, General Confession, the blessing of
the table, the giving of thanks after a meal, and we also knew how
to read the words in a stumbling fashion, and answer several question in Latin, just like crows. This meager knowledge freed us to
roam around to no avail all morning and afternoon, even though
the friars thought they had released us to our homes to help our

fathers in the cultivation of the land or in whatever type of trade they did. But tell me—what could a father who had been a judge, or a governor, or a tax collector, a priest and teacher, a warrior, or an owner of vast expanses of land teach their sons of their trade, if the judges no longer judged, the governors no longer governed, the tax collectors no longer collected taxes, the landowners no longer owned land, and the priests no longer preached? How could I claim that what were once gods were now demons and everything was upside down and not wreak havoc? How can I say that? I cannot know the divine plan, I only know the light of the one true God and that Christ will return to reign over the Earth so that all mortals will believe; this is what the Franciscans proclaim and it is found in the words of the Bible. The Indian schools did not exist anymore, and given that most of the families had lost their haciendas, the most they could hope for, if they had not slid into poverty, was to save their sons from the Encomienda, since they no longer had anything to offer their sons in terms of wealth or increasing their properties. Martín and Nicolás, my childhood friends, were among these lost people. Neither of their families were *macehuales*, neither of their families cultivated their own lands with their own hands, or any had trade that they could pass on to their sons; both had seen better times and neither had managed to keep their properties intact. Thus demoralized in the confusion in which they now lived, those who had previously governed our world (those who were not *macehuales* or slaves) wandered about aimlessly, learning only to waste their energies, neglect good manners, and forget the greatness in which their people had once lived.

Mama was not thrilled that I was wandering around, dirtying

my feet in the streets all day like those other people who did not have any status. I was the only one left in her life to remind her of her former status and lineage and she treated me as if I were noble. She tried to educate me, but in those days I was released from her attentions and intentions by one of the women, or wives, of the man of the house because her son (the true first-born) and I were almost the same age and she did not want me around the house where he was (you will understand why momentarily), as if my rank were as high as theirs. Because of her, they had already sent me off to study with the friars, and an even greater surprise awaited me. But for now I was as free as a bird, just like the other boys who were a little older than I was and who had been my companions while we were studying with the friars.

As we did every morning, I roamed around with these boys and others who had already abandoned us to do something useful or to trifle their days away in worse ways. I set off walking arm in arm with Nicolás, whose father had been a judge among the Indians, and Martín, the grandson of a great warrior whose daring exploits the women of Tezcoco sang about at that time. We were walking close together, practically running, when we stopped because we saw Melchor Ixiptlatzin coming into the village. Melchor was one of our friends. Until recently he wore down the soles of his feet wandering along the shore of the lake with us. Now he wore them down in a different way. He was entrusted to bring three unburdened mules from a nearby village. He went back and forth on a daily basis, relying on the mules, who knew the way by instinct; he just had to be careful that the stupid animals did not die of thirst because if he let them go down to the lake for water, they ran the risk of drowning. He did such a bad job that one day a mule became ill because it was suffering from thirst and Mama told me later that Melchor Ixiptlatzin lost his job and got fifty lashes.

Melchor Ixiptlatzin was the son of the man who had once been the officiator of a *cú*, or temple. If I remember correctly, he was an *Ixiptla*, a devotee of *Nappatecutlí*, who was the "god of the makers of grass mats and *ecpales*, and is said to be the creator of this art, and who, through his virtue, made the bulrushes, sedges, and reeds sprout and grow. He was the god of all those—the *icpales* and *tlacuextes*—who worked with grass mats, and they had a feast day for him every year and killed slaves in his honor and made other offerings and performed ceremonies on his feast day. The priest of this god, whom they called *Ixiptla*, which means his image, would go house to house with a gourd of water in one hand and a willow branch in the other, and he would sprinkle the houses and the people with the branch, just like the man who sprinkles holy water, and everyone received it with great devotion."[12] Thus, though the father carried a gourd and a willow branch, the son now carries a flagon of water for the stupid mules and has one hand free, a waste of five fingers.

We stopped to look at Melchor's mules, who amused us so, and chat a bit with him, who, for his part, was not in any hurry.

Nicolás, the brute, said to him:

—Since you've been spending all your time with these animals, Melchor, you now have the face of a mule.

He did not find that joke very funny. At least he did not smile. Chewing on a twig, he drew a line with his bare foot, pushing

---

12   In Spanish in the original. Estela's note.

the ground forcefully and turning the dirt over with his big toe. We were there, making jokes, petting his mules, and I, at least, was envying him his contact with the animals (it would not have even bothered me to have the face of a mule if I could ride them from time to time; Melchor, braggart that he was, told us that was what he did when nobody was looking), when we saw some Franciscan friars coming down the road. The friars were all new to us, not one of them was from Tezcoco, and they were accompanied by a young man named Carlos Ometochtzin—who was from here, though I did not know him, and who had studied with them in Mexico City. I had only heard of him, he was older than I was and was also older than the older boys I was with. I did not pay any attention to the friars, but only looked at him; I doubt anyone could have resisted looking at him because he was so goodlooking and walked like a prince, without seeming petulant, but with a dignified elegance made more beautiful by a frank laugh and a bright gaze, which was lively and intelligent. We greeted the friars respectfully, Carlos stopped and greeted each of my companions very warmly, shaking hands and exchanging a few of words with each one. He greeted me with a gesture, since he did not know me, and as soon as they turned and went on their way Melchor said with a disdainful gesture, "Carlos Ometochtzin, you only wish you were a piece of shit, because that's better than what you really are." He spat on the ground as his final insult. What could we do but spit as well? But I spat without conviction because Carlos Ometochtzin was so handsome (as I already said) and when he spoke his seductive voice enchanted me. I could not spit at him, the son and grandson of Netzahualcóyotl. Instead I spat on top of my friend's spittle, which looked sad and ridiculous spewed there on the ground, just to add a bit of my own spittle to his to keep it company. Leaving his spit behind, Melchor continued down the road with his mules following in the steps of the Franciscans and we continued on our way toward the lake.

We children always tried to avoid the only road that led out of the village of Tezcoco. Instead, we usually left by the entrance, where the old, bald-headed woman spent the day sitting and peeling cacao, separating beans, washing kernels of corn, her face turned toward the village. Since she was now deaf and half-blind, she could only perceive what was right under her nose, so if you passed by on her side, she did not notice you. We would try to bypass her (by stepping off the road so that she would not see us crossing the short stretch that did not escape her poor vision) in order to escape being interrogated and forced into polite conversation. Unfortunately, just in front of her house, the basket slipped off my arm and fell two paces in front of me where the old lady could see me on the road. Since I did not want to go to the lake without a basket, I left the path of pariahs and lepers (who else except them—and us—walks on the side of the road) and went to pick it up. The old woman saw me, called to me, and asked who I was. My friends whistled and tossed their heads to let me know they would wait for me up ahead, at the usual place on the shore of the lake. With the basket in hand, or better said, with one hand in the basket, I started to toss it, making it spin around while I answered her, told her whose son I was, whose grandson I was, the names of my mother's brothers...

—*Child!*—she scolded—leave that basket in peace. Don't you

see I'm speaking to you? Now they don't even teach the children to listen respectfully to their elders.

I put the little basket on the ground next to my feet. And I kept it in place with my foot so it would not roll away.

—But what are you doing? Why are you stepping on it? Don't you see that that damages the weave? Let me see it, let's see, let's see…

I gave her the basket. She examined it thoroughly, inside, outside, the sides; she practically had her eyes glued to it to get a good look at it.

—It's nicely woven. Do you know if it holds water?

—I was just going to check…to test it at the lake.

—But putting it on the hard ground damages it and the water will leak out…

—I didn't know.

—No, you all don't know anything anymore, nobody tells you anything, nobody reprimands you, nobody tells you how to live or what the right way to live is. What will become of us?—she asked me in a mournful voice that she continued to use as she kept talking—what will become of us when those people from Castile get tired of stealing from us, when there's nothing else left to take and they leave? How will we pick ourselves back up if our own people don't know who we are, how we conduct ourselves, what we do, and how and how much? Listen…

She gave the basket back to me, as if it were too heavy for her, and began the usual lecture, this time without the mournful tone, but with a normal rhythm, as if she were praying. I respectfully let her finish a couple of sentences, looking at her without blinking. "The first is that you must be very careful to wake up and stay awake, and do not sleep all night long so that they will not say that you are idle and sleepy. Be sure to arise at midnight, to speak and sigh and pray to the gods. And be sure to carefully sweep the place where the idols are kept and offer them incense." As soon as I saw that she was absorbed in her recitation, I slowly started walking backward to see if she noticed I was leaving. I was trying to slip away and since it looked like she did not notice because she was intoxicated with her recitation of the words of the ancient fathers, I started to back away more decisively. "The second, is that you should be careful that when you are out on the street or road, that you walk calmly, do not walk too quickly or too slowly, but rather with modesty and maturity. Those who do not walk like that are *ixtotómac cuécuetz*, people who look around wildly like crazy people, the ones who go around without modesty and without seriousness, like flighty, boisterous people. And avoid the sluggishness of those who walk very slowly, the *huihuiláxpul*, *zocotézpul*, *eticápul*, those who go about dragging their feet, those who walk like heavy people and those who cannot walk because they are fat, or like pregnant women, or those who waddle and wiggle their bodies. Also do not walk along the road with your head bowed; or with your head inclined, to the side, or looking from side to side, so that they do not say that you are a silly or stupid and bad-mannered and undisciplined." Since I could tell she did not see me, though I did not know where her cloudy eyes were looking while she was lecturing me (maybe she was looking at other times) I started to run like the *ixtotómac cuécuetz*, like the flighty, boisterous people.

Some parts of the shoreline of the lake were bordered by tule,

a bulrush or sedge, that had been purposely planted there. I do not
think it was only to provide us with fiber (there was little ability
to work the fiber of the tule in Tezcoco and a great ability evident
in the baskets and mats that arrived at the mercados on Tuesdays),
but rather to hide the large expanse of the lake, because at a distance, the blue of the sky merged with the blue of the water, or
so it seemed, and if we did not adorn the shoreline with tule it
would seem that we lived at the edges of the earth, and we know,
because it has always been this way, that only savages live at the
ends of earth (over there, where they exiled Ovid), and Tezcoco
was far from being a village of savages. The green curtain of tule
connected Tezcoco to Tenochtitlan, to Tlatelolco, to Coyoacán, to
the various cities of the valley. It was a bridge to other people and
we turned our faces toward them. The lake transported us to the
sky and the clouds, to the lands beyond Nueva Galicia, beyond the
Chichimecas and the nomadic tribes, and beyond where the birds
that inhabit our sky for a few months come from, as a reminder
that the earth has no limits, and that this unending earth unites
with the blue of the lake that merges with the blue of the sky.
Today the curtain is not needed; I have heard that the lake has
receded away from Tezcoco, leaving it without a shore. But I have
not personally seen the cloud of dust left in its wake, the desert
that has opened up between the water and the sky.

We—Martín, Nicolás, and until recently Melchor too (all Christian names, because we had already been baptized and educated
by the friars, as I have already said)—we, as I said, played on the
side of the lake where there was not any tule growing, on what
was left of the shore, and our eyes and other senses were drawn

to the gentle waves, to the wet sand of the shore, to the insects, sticks, little pebbles, to everything that inhabited this stretch of shoreline that was neither solid nor liquid, but rather slick and bubbling, always on the verge of slipping away, and we hung onto the excitement of each wave, our backs to Tezcoco and the other villages, our backs to the savage and the civilized alike, we were one with the waves and the snails (waves do not exist anymore in any form, they have become water again; the snail, stuck to a tule leaf, like a hollow shell on a green balsa wood raft that successfully avoids capsizing with the movement of the wave does not lose its precious cargo, has put ashore, has left the leaf that served as its raft, taken its body out of the shell, it appears otherworldly, and walks naked over the muddy sand), the wave and the snail do not belong to the order of men, they do not speak their language, they have not been touched by the fire or the forge, or by the crucifix or the chisel, and in their short lives the only thing they came into contact with is a little feather of the dark gray bird that left Tezcoco weeks ago to return to the snow of the northern desert. Ah! If only we could have been like the wave and the snail snug in its shell! We knew too soon the crucifix and the fire, the chisel, and the gallows! Although one time…but I digress, remembering the mornings spent aimlessly watching the rolling waves, with my feet in the mud and the sun shining on the dark soil. If only I could go back there to see the tule, the jetty, and the road that led travelers away from Tezcoco!

My friends were closer than I had expected to find them and were so focused on what they were looking at that they did not even notice my arrival. They were looking at something that the waves had left on the ground overnight: a long, fat snake, drowned, bloated, about the width of a fist and as long as a stick.

What's that? —I asked, as if I did not see it.

They pointed at it with their stripped stalks from the canebrake. I saw the canes and ran to get one, I stripped it, and they continued looking at the snake in silence. I moved my cane closer so I could roll the reptile over onto its enlarged belly; I wanted to see its skin, but because it was lying on its front, we could only see its back.

—Don't touch it! —Nicolás said forcefully, somewhere between pleading with me and giving me an order.

—Look! —Martín added, pointing at the fat snake with his cane. —Its throat is open here (yes, the skin was open there), here's the mouth, the two eyes (it is true, you could see each of these painted on the skin of the snake, clearly marked on the back), the nose, the frown, the beard, and two ears…

—It's not a snake, it's…

I quit looking at the snake for an explanation and looked instead at my friends. They were serious; scared of the monster they imagined was taking shape before their eyes. Nicolás was blinking continuously, terrified. I do not think he was even capable of saying a single word. I was not in the mood for monsters, and not even when they said the word "Devil" could they infect me with their fear. I walked on and left them with their thoughts. Four steps away I saw an enormous fish, lying on the sand. It was bloated and black. Its two fins were extended like two arms and its tail was split like two legs. I called to my friends, "Come here!" and without saying anything I touched the two legs, both arms, and turned it over with my cane. "Don't touch it!" Nicolás and

Martín said in unison, but I had already touched it. On the belly of the fish we saw the same face, painted with such precision that all three of us squatted down, murmuring, to get a better look. Now I was afraid too and the three of us were pressed close together. A spider ran in front of us and stopped when it got close to the fish. It was a small spider, one of those that looks like a dark grain of sand running. It also had the features of a face on its tiny body. The three of us stood up. Refusing to accept that something strange was happening—because this was our territory and in it we, the collectors to whom the lake paid tribute, ruled absolutely—we left the spider and the fish and walked a few steps to find that a wave had receded and had left in its wake an expressive, painted face in the wet sand. It had eyes, its cheeks were slightly raised, its mouth looked annoyed, and in place of the nose there was a piece of driftwood that was polished smooth by the water. Exclaiming, scarcely saying a word, while letting out single syllables to release our excitement and fear, Nicolás and Martín jumped quickly away from the lake, while I moved closer to pick up the driftwood that served as the nose. I picked it up to look at it. The side that had served as the nose was curved; the other side was straight. When the wave wet my feet again, I noticed that the face was frowning on the smooth side, the mouth was closed tight, the eyes were half-shut, and each feature was precisely carved. When I say "precisely," I mean that even the lines of the forehead, the lips, the curve of the eyelids, and the ears were clearly carved on the driftwood. The wave receded and I took my eyes off the wooden face and looked for my companions. I saw them running away. I started to run after them. Without really realizing it, I was carrying the piece of lake-carved driftwood that served as the nose of the face in the sand and itself had a smooth side on which a face was carved.

I finally caught up with them farther ahead where there is a small hill in front of the dense growth of tule. Our grandfathers had built up a barrier of earth using mud from the lake to hide waste deposits. Time has covered the little hill with plants and we have shrouded it with stories: we said (just has they had told us) that on the nights of the full moon, witches, with their hair loose, meet at the foot of the hill to dig up and crush bones to make potions to control illness and to alter the course of the future. Between the tule and the little hill there is a dry, rocky hollow. They used to say, and we repeated, that those witches would bring a rag doll and a smaller one made of wax to practice their arts and magic. Now, I know that Horace, the son of a freed slave, a one-time military tribune, and friend of Virgil and of Maecenas also said the same about their witches. Theirs spoke Latin to summon the power to do evil and cast spells; our witches also wore their hair loose, but recited their incantations in Nahuatl. I do not know if God speaks Nahuatl, but the Devil speaks all languages. In that hollow between the whispering tule and the mossy green wall, they performed ceremonies that have traversed time, oceans, and languages to repeat the foolishness of fulfilling our wishes at all costs, even attempting to control the shape of the future (something that should remain exclusively in the hands of the Almighty).

When we were feeling adventurous, we used to go there to look for traces of the black rites such as the imprint of feet that had slid following a fearsome leap over the mossy wall, the residue of a bonfire, a length of thread. Now our fear had mounted. I was still carrying the driftwood I had picked up from the shore of the lake. When they saw what I was carrying, Martín shouted: "Why are you bringing that? Leave it!" I moved a few steps closer and put it down on the ground in front of them. Between the tule and the moss-and-mold-covered hillock, the driftwood rocked a little from side to side before settling into place. Once it stopped, once its curved back quit rocking, it made a sound, something like a growl. The three of us moved closer to it, holding hands, terrified. The driftwood opened its eyes and relaxed its mouth, we could see the line of its teeth. It smiled. The lines of the forehead were almost invisible and I could see the brightness of its eyes—playful, with a hint of something evil.

—Come on, let's go—I heard Nicolás say.

—Who could have carved it? And so well? —I asked. I was afraid like they were, but also amazed and curious.

—*Despisques!*—One of them said. That was the expression we used among ourselves to indicate that something was really good, that it was beautiful, that we liked it.

—The lake carved it, and it moves, it's alive—I said—back there I saw a frown on the face and here, well, you can see.

I had shaken off my fear. I moved beyond them and my audacity loosened the knot of their fear. They laughed at me. "Cuckoo, cuckoo!" they chanted, running around me like the witches did during their nocturnal circling of the dung hill, or the leg of a heron, or the smoke of their bonfire, or an egg rubbed over the body of a child, or whatever else…

I felt like crying, but I was not going to do that because they would make fun of me at the very least and because I might risk losing their friendship. If they left me, what would I do? My days would pass without rhyme or reason, I would wander aimlessly around the village. I quit looking at them and distracted myself, I do not remember how or with what, until they got tired of calling me crazy and stopped running in circles around me.

Four faces had appeared from the lake to forewarn me of what was about to happen. I had seen four faces: the one on the back of the snake, the one on the body of the fish, the one painted in the sand, and the animated face carved into the driftwood. Had these four faces appeared with their signs of warning to upset me, to mock me, or to calm me, like the waves? They frightened me, filled my soul with fear. They were definitely meant for me. They were not like the fiesta on the day of my birth, like my father paddling away to abandon me, like the Our Father I learned to replace other prayers, or like what was waiting for me that was *not meant for me* even though it fell on me. The faces had been brought forth by the faithful saltwater lake *for me.* The waters of the rivers fed into the lake whose waves arrived at my feet to warn me. But I did not have the ears, I did not understand the voice of warning, accustomed as I was to listening to what was not said for me to hear, already prepared to receive what was not mine or for me, but was given to me.

I could not continue participating in their games, because I was not at peace. I followed them like a little monkey, I do not know for how long, whether it was scarcely an hour or several full hours, imitating them so that I would not be left out, including finally following them back to Tezcoco. I do not know where the sun was in the sky when we returned to our village. Once we arrived, the first person who saw me told the second, the second told the third, the third told the fourth, faster than the wind, so that I had barely started walking along the first street into town when they came from the house to get me, to hurry me along, they were practically carrying me through the air with the urgency with which they were pushing me along. They brought me into the palace of my mother's relative (which was our home) by the little back door where the mongers come to sell their crockery and hens, ducks or sandpipers, tomatoes and tamales, bean tortas and pumpkin seed and chile salsas, and as soon as the darkness of the kitchen blinded me, Mama was cleaning me up, fixing my hair, and changing my clothes; other voices were talking to me, telling me things that I did not fully understand, while Mama was crying big heavy tears with her eyes wide open, not saying a word, just crying non-stop.

She did not say anything to me when they took me from the kitchen to the hall where the man of the house—the noble lord, son and grandson of noble lords—solemnly presented me to the friars, saying that he was offering me, his eldest son, for them to Christianize, to educate in the law of the Gospel and God. He spoke in both the local language and in the language of the friars, saying the same thing in Castilian for Bishop Zumárraga, the dignitary who had come in person for the impromptu welcome, with which the noble lords of Tezcoco celebrated the treaty with the friars for their mutual interests. The ceremony ended suddenly with the ceremonious presentation of the son, who was replacing Carlos Ometochtzin, as requested by the friars, to educate an heir of Tezcoco in the law of God, admitting him to the Colegio de Santa Cruz de Tlatelolco, which they would be inaugurating in two weeks time in a solemn and well-prepared celebration and to which they invited him (my false father), to seal, once again, their alliance and pact.

They were using me again to supplant his son. They did not want to make enemies of the friars by denying them what both valued the most, so they presented me in place of the grandson and great-grandson of one of the noble lords of Tezcoco, to instill in me the faith in the foreign god. That is the way the Franciscans and the Indians sealed pacts and they protected themselves by protecting each other. The friars requested the first-born sons from all the most powerful families, so I was not the only one they went looking for, though I was only a false son. They put us in Santiago Tlatelolco along with the students from San José, those who Gante had spent two or three years educating, and with those who were already being educated by Focher and Basacio, all prudently and carefully selected from the most powerful and well-known Indian families. For a reason that it did not take me long to figure out, they were bringing Carlos Ometochtzin, the first-born son of the stern and fair Netzahualpilli, noble Lord of Tezcoco, grandson of the sage and poet Netzahualcóyotl, back to Tezcoco, and they were returning him to his father (the brother of my false father), claiming that his education was complete, that there was nothing else they could teach him. They refrained from telling the truth, though anyone could have discovered it without much effort. I myself saw it that very day. They were bringing him back because his disposition and intellect did not conform to the Franciscan way.

To represent Tezcoco in his place, they sent me; or better said, they sent the one who should have gone who they said was me, who was not me, who I was supposed to be, the one I was forced into becoming in order to replace him. But if we tell the same story in a short amount of space, it was me, and only me, they took to replace Carlos. It was I who remained there forever living with the friars, just like the sons of the noble lords who came from the greatest Indian riches that the war with the Spaniards had not destroyed, from the enormous fortunes of those enriched since ancestral times by their own people, the cautious and the opportunistic, the clever and the liars, the enterprising and the underhanded, the spies and the traitors, those of misguided loyalties, those immensely rich Indians, who, although they did not enjoy their best moments, did not live like *macehuales* either. I, or the one I was supposed to have been, along with this elite class, like the sons of the Indians who, upon seeing Cortés and his people arrive, helped him for one reason or another, the enemies of the Nahuas, the resentful ones, those with traitorous hearts, those who were converted to the faith of Christ, those who were terrified and who knew how to make a fortune out of their terror like the sons of some of the new alliances that the friars or the conquistadors had been making. I will not name each one of those boys accustomed to opulence, those taught to abuse others ever since they were young, those who understood from the cradle the methods of betrayal in order to survive or those whose memory shrinks my heart. These vengeful boys who gained entrance into the Colegio by their own actions, like the infamous Agustín, who had lived with the friars since he was very young, who began his personal relationship with them by accompanying them to destroy some of the *cues* and then later accused some of his own family (his father and mother among them). Even though some of these boys were used to practicing idolatry themselves, some of which involved abuses that the Spanish law did not pardon, the friars took in this traitor to his family because he was left without anywhere to go or anyone to live with.

Before arriving at Tlatelolco, Agustín (along with some of his friends who were not students of the Colegio like he was, perhaps because they did not denounce their own fathers and mothers, and who, even if they were denouncers, lived in harmony among their own people) would spy on places where he might observe drunkenness or secret songs and dances, and then he would go back there with one or two friars, along with seventy to a hundred boys raised by the monks, and help them seize and tie up the heretics and take them to the monastery where they punished them by imposing penances on them, teaching them the Christian Doctrine, making the heretics go to matins in the middle of the night, and flogging them for a few weeks until they repented.

The heretical Indians left there catechized and punished.

Those boys, Agustín and his friends, created so much fear among their people that, in time, they no longer needed to be accompanied by the friars and began hunting alone, tying up the merrymakers or drunkards, even if there were one hundred or two hundred, taking them to the monastery to do penance.

Sometime later, the friars brought into the school another student, Esteban Bravo, from Tezcoco, though he was not actually from the town proper, but rather from S. Diego Tlailotlacan, which was half a league away. He would later help Fray Juan Bautista, as I did. Esteban Bravo became a good Latinist, though not stylistically because his translations were too Indian, he used too many words. Many admired this *and they paid him handsomely for it*, but I was never satisfied with copying and Juan Bautista allowed me to cut what seemed to me to be superfluous in the things I was translating from the Nahuatl; he was of the same opinion, because in the Nahuatl language we used many words to produce admiration and enchantment, which did not sound good in Castilian.

Among all the boys at the Colegio, I always believed that I was the only one who had arrived there by mistake. And if I could not get close to Agustín and his friends, neither could I get close to the rich boys, who were accustomed to a life that bore little resemblance to my own, even though my family was also noble and of the elite ruling class, as I've already explained, but I had already lost it all, beginning with my family. Nothing is left of that life, except my mother—beautiful, sad, alone, and, burdened by her sorrows and the years, not quite right in her head. It could be that I have protected my heart living so close to what I am recounting here. The time came that I could be close to them, precisely because I believed I was the only one who did not belong. But the story has brought us here and I will not continue with what I am not prepared to explain right now.

On the afternoon I was talking about earlier, they asked Carlos Ometochtzin to say a few words in front of my false father and his real one, as well as the friars and Bishop Zumárraga. He spoke first in Latin, making a joke that caused the Bishop to blush and produced discomfort or laughter among the friars.

Then, as if he did not notice the effect of his words, he spoke to me in the local language and, with the same fluency, he said: "You know nothing, you are empty-headed and you will see how small your brain is when you are with the friars, you will see its white cleft." He laughed at the end and he laughed so beautifully that I laughed with him. He went back to Latin and said things that flattered the friars and the Bishop and then said to my false father, in Nahuatl: "Fortune takes the path that fortune commands. Thank the friars for taking your son away from Tezcoco and placing him in the vessel of Latin knowledge."

Once the musicians hired by Don Carlos Ometochtzin's father had arrived to celebrate his homecoming and the Indian songs and dances began, the friars considered it prudent to leave. Without me, they would begin the celebration of Carlos's homecoming and of my leaving, or rather my impersonation. The party might have lasted all night long; Carlos would not lose his taste for joy and festivities until his sad end.

Waiting for us at the main door of Don Hernando's house (that was, until this day, my house) was a coach pulled by four horses, which belonged to the Bishop. We got into it and the first thing I experienced was the excitement of getting into a coach for the first time. The second was the realization that the coach was taking us far away, and I was sitting between two friars I did not know because neither Fray Juan Caro nor any of the others who had taught me the Creed and the Our Father were there, and before I could brandish my imaginary dagger at them to make them take me back to my mother's apron strings, I was harangued by Zumárraga: "The thing that my mind has been most preoccupied with for some time, and my will has been most inclined toward, and that I have fought for with the little strength I have, was that in Mexico City, and in each diocese, there would be a Colegio for Indian boys where they would at least learn grammar, and a large convent where there would be space enough to house a large number of young Indian daughters. Because the future of these lands lies in you—he continued saying—you have to work very hard and devote yourself to your studies and to the respect and diffusion of God's love. Do not disappoint us." He said something like that, without looking me in the eyes, as if I were not important.

Future, what future? Not even for half the world! At that moment I cared not a fig about any boys' school or convent. They had stolen me from my mother, from the town I considered to be my own (even though I lived in the house of others), and away from my friends. What else could possibly matter to me?

I did not hear the buzzing of the fat, ugly wasp (the horrendous wasp of interest) in Zumárraga's words, which had little to do with what he was saying about his mind, his will, and his "little" strength that had been devoted to the founding of the Colegio. I did not hear him simply because I was an unsuspecting child and because I was unaware of everything except my astonishment. If he had spent so much time and interest on our education, and if it (his interest) was as large as he said, why did he abandon the Colegio as soon as he smelled the skunk spray of inconvenience? He caught it (his interest) on the crest of the wave when he thought it could raise him up and let it go when he realized that he might crash into the ground along with it.

It was actually Don Sebastián Ramírez de Fuenleal who

conceived the idea of the Colegio de la Santa Cruz and who nurtured it from 1530 to 1535 without entrusting his dream to the crests of faraway waves. Fuenleal dreamt of it and Zumárraga used it for his own benefit, just as he let go of it when it was most convenient for him. And what else can you expect from someone who is seeking power? Is that the way to treat your own, is that what is best for your own? There is no good we survive. The bones of the saints—of those who lost everything because they thought with their hearts—are good. And the smell of their sanctity scarcely perfumes the harsh existence of the living.

I must quote Zumárraga again. In order to do that I will use what I remember having seen written in the hand of Francisco Gómez, the young man who met Zumárraga in Burgos, embarked for New Spain in 1533 against his will, and served as secretary to the Bishop for eight years: "If in just wars valiant soldiers confront clear risk of death and disregard it in order to obtain posthumous fame and glory, with how much more reason should we not enter ourselves, with souls determined to fight in the name of and for the glory of Jesus Christ in order to attain certain, not brief and mortal, fame, but rather eternal rest and immortality? But if we note our deliberation and idleness in completing what is given to us, when we see that so many people, who were strangers before, willingly receive the gentle yoke of Jesus Christ and are only waiting for teachers and masters, we undoubtedly recognize those guilty of betrayal and cowardice. It is true that if God had offered our patron saints Francis and Dominic such a great opportunity to save souls, they would have scorned the suffering of the martyrs in exchange for reducing the Savior's fold by so many sheep who had lost their ways and leave them to the positions that the fallen angels had left. For suffering is not awaiting us, nor pain, nor lashes, nor the rack, and we can even say that no work is awaiting us, so that it makes it unbearable to leave our country, family, and friends for the love of Jesus Christ, for whom we redeem ourselves and who did not leave the humble convent nor the life of poverty, but only heaven itself…" Waiting for them there were no lashes, pain, or the rack—other than the stretching that comes from convenient inconveniences and interests in this or that. But, as he saw for himself, even the branding iron arrived for the Indians, for on 24 August 1529 into his own hand was given one of the two keys with which to mark the Indian slaves so that no one else could mark captives without his intervention. Though I do have to mention that in 1530 the king decreed that Indians could not be enslaved and thus, with this order, the Bishop lost the key.

—

Caesar cut off the hands of Pompey's messengers when they mistakenly arrived in his camp and out of which he threw them, still bleeding. He cut both hands off each one for having mistaken the road, or because they had lost their orientation because they had been traveling all night and took the wrong road, or because they were afraid, or for whatever reason.

I know the painter who wanted to paint the dismembered hands thrown to the ground, severed from the body. He studied at the Colegio de Santa Cruz.

I know the painter who wanted to paint the blood running.

He studied at the Colegio de la Santa Cruz.

I know the one who wanted to paint the scene of Caesar giving the order. He studied at the Colegio de la Santa Cruz.

I know the poet who wanted to recreate the scene in a play. He studied at the Colegio de la Santa Cruz.

I know the writer who wanted to imagine the amputees leaving the camp, their discouragement and helplessness. He studied at the Colegio de la Santa Cruz.

But having known all of them at the Colegio de la Santa Cruz and having learned there of the existence of the Romans and their empire and the story of Caesar and Pompey's messengers, I can say that they chopped off my hands the day they took me to Tlatelolco. They amputated them. They separated them from my body. I was left without any way to scratch my head, without any way to feed myself, I was an invalid, incomplete.

Nurtured by the friars, other hands, new hands, grew out of my stumps. These are the ones with which I hold the barrel of the pen after I pick my teeth and scratch under my arm. Because hands communicate with the body itself, they allow one to touch and be touched. Without hands, the body is unable to touch and understand the world.

I was left without hands. But even though I did not lose them willingly, I can say that I do not regret it. Without hands, I touched and learned to sense and understand with a new tongue; I sensed and dreamt of contact with things in a new language. With my new tongue, I perceived the leaves of the trees and the wind that made them flutter. I heard the dog's bark of warning, I sensed the hop of the bird before it took flight, the stumbling footsteps of the other children. It was with this new language that I picked up my straw mat in the mornings, tied the tie of my robe, through a new language I brought food from the bowl to my mouth and learned to survive with something that I might dare to call happiness, because with this new tongue I also experienced unconsciousness: the protection and refuge of the imagination and memory.

Slosos keston de Hernando

EKFLOROS KESTON DE ESTELINO

Right now, I understand my passion for Hernando de Rivas, former student of the Colegio de la Santa Cruz Tlatelolco, less than ever. He was alive at one time, but he no longer exists. I've obliterated him with my liberal translation, I've erased his characteristics by imposing my own intentions and ideas upon him, my expectations of what he should say, what he should have said. Or if he did say them, have I lost track of what is his and what is not? I have made him experience things that he never articulated in his own words. I've made him so much my own that I have strangled him completely. Or has he strangled me, am I so much his voice that he is no longer outside of me, independent of me? Am I so confused that I've made myself believe that he lives in this love, that it's my consciousness that has died? Is he mine—as much as it is possible for him to be as a corpse—or does his heart beat on its own, of its own volition, and am I part of him? Oh no: I think I've erased him by writing my own version of him, adding this and deleting that, giving him strength where I found him weak or lacking vitality. Hernando: I can't understand how you can still light this foolish flame inside of me that keeps me from distinguishing myself from you. I am flesh of your flesh, slave to the mysterious union that consumes two bodies in a common fire.

But Hernando, listen: I don't know if your light continues to illuminate anything in the darkness we live in today. I don't know. I spent months worshipping you, searching for you and archiving you, paleographing your words, paleographing you, circling around you like a fly flying around a horse. During these months that I've been a fly hovering around your body, a wave of terror has silently descended over my country. Hernando: violence has infiltrated our daily life so much that it isn't even fodder for the tabloids or the pages of the bloody little periodicals anymore, but is instead part of daily gossip. The how-are-yous are followed, in the hurried conversations in the corridors, by strings of anecdotes: Do you know who they assaulted yesterday?...when I was driving in on the beltway...the daughter of a friend of my cousins...the neighbors who work out of their home...they killed him before they even got the ransom...they took everything, even his tennis shoes...they came in on the road and it was three o'clock in the afternoon... it was at a taxi stand, surely you don't think I would hail a taxi on the street...poor boy, he was the conductor of...And parallel to this outburst, a sick comedy is being played out on the front pages of the newspapers. There's one scandal after another. Who has stolen the most? Who has committed the worst fraud? Who has absconded with the country's resources? Who has usurped the citizens' tax revenue? Who has exploited his power? They don't skimp on the details either, they tell us everything in minute detail: how much they have in which bank, what they own, and what kind of fraud they've committed. We all know the magnitude of the abuse that has been committed against our nation, which has been stripped bare by its own people. But the legal system doesn't find them guilty. The judicial system mocks its citizens. It says, or so it appears: "Look, children, these gentlemen, who have stolen even your laughter, have, for the past fifteen years, robbed the equivalent of 400,000 dollars per capita, from each of the ninety million Mexicans. These gentlemen are *the leaders of your country.* Don't they remember the colonial era? We were born out of a colonial system and we still live in a colonial system. Our wealth goes to Switzerland, Luxembourg, to Fiji and the Cayman Islands, to Cuba (now there aren't even dreams for Cuba anymore)... Where else? In some cases, it's Citibank that knows, in others, it's the Bank of Mexico... We're a rich country, boys and girls, very rich and we have to continue to attract foreign capital by displaying our riches so they'll keep us from falling into barbarism."

The public thieves of the public goods go unconvicted. We all know they're guilty but that's not enough, nor is the proof of their theft. If one of them is imprisoned it will be for some other crime—something that can't be proven and with overtones of improbability. That's how Raúl, the ex-president's brother, will finally be put behind bars—for some crime he might have committed while infatuated with the star of a tragic telenovela, a crime of passion. But for clear cases of abuse of public goods, nobody will be imprisoned.

These two acts of violence are not simply crimes. They are political phenomena: models of unpunished larceny, committed by those in power.

The devils walk free because no one is in control of this chaos anymore. In addition to these two crimes, there are killings carried out in certain parts of the Republic that are "political" and are not (it goes without saying) punished either.

Nobody keeps up appearances, nobody bothers with appearances, nobody tries to, or even wants to, fix the evils that plague us.

"*Gobierno ratero*," they used to say when I was a young girl, now they should say, "*gobierno podrido*," except that they haven't lost the thieving component, or the *ratero*, of the "*Gobierno ratero*," they have simply perfected it to the point that it is completely rotten and corrupted, completely *podrido*.

Poverty is on the rise. (Yesterday I read in the newspaper that they found an infestation of fleas in Guadalajara and had to evacuate thirty-six homes in order to deal with the problem. And I'm forgetting the funniest detail: this infestation followed an earlier one of cockroaches. This is the story of a city fallen into poverty). There is overpopulation, a complete lack of opportunity for the younger generations, economic downturn, a decrease in production, etcetera, etcetera…None of the evils mentioned here can fully express the horror that the people of my generation feel. There hasn't been a coup d'état, instead we've suffered a blow dealt by the radicals. They have thrown us out of our own country without giving us another one in exchange. We're strangers in our own country. Unmanageable and wild, our faithful country prospers in the shadows.

Slosos keston de Estelino

EKFLOROS KESTON DE LEARO

My alarm rang more than five times during the night. I don't think this was just a stupid mistake, or to put it more graciously, the error of someone who was simply distracted. I was asleep, I didn't provoke the ringing by doing anything wrong, and I say this with absolute certainty because like everyone else, if I'm asleep, I'm not doing anything. At least right now, the alarm doesn't ring in my dreams. The bad thing was that it took me a long time to get back to sleep after being woken up by the ringing. It rang so much last night that I wasn't able to fall back to sleep between three of the times I heard it, even during the pauses that seemed interminable, time passed excruciatingly slowly. Every time I felt like I was finally about to fall into the deep well of sleep, the alarm started ringing again. This is bad enough, but the worst is that the musings that preoccupied me during my nighttime vigil, and that I wasn't able to let go of during the day, reminded me of the dark period when we tried to eradicate dreams. During that time, we rang the alarm to try to stop ourselves from dreaming.

It all started because there was some friction in L'Atlàntide and we decided to launch a serious and radical campaign in order to improve the quality of our life together. We attempted to do away with the intangible because when we analyzed the friction, it didn't seem to arise from anything concrete and the most obvious intangible thing was the dreamworld. I don't know whose idea it was (it might have even been mine, "That's my trouble. Dreaming").

That's why we decided to eradicate dreams. We didn't try to extract them once they were already in process, but instead we woke ourselves up when our brainwaves indicated that we were about to enter the dreamstate. It was a disaster. Not only were we not completely rested, but we were beyond irritable, we were all just bundles of nerves. The body, master of itself during sleep, seemed to be unable to slip into a completely relaxed state. While it's true that nobody actively performs in their sleep, it's also true that the body surrenders completely to restore itself during sleep. Tired of the pinch of the girdle of reason, at night the body is at ease. This is when the body rules.

During the prohibition against dreaming, our bodies were exhausted and something strange happened to our powers of reason. Some people swore to have seen things, which were normally part of their dreams, pass over the earth's crust and someone even had the audacity to say that he had seen them in L'Atlàntide proper, where there is not, couldn't be, and has never been anything other than air and our bodies. Of course we didn't give any credence to these things, but recognizing the disastrous effects, we ceased the campaign against dreams because our ability to reason was the most affected by their absence.

As mine definitely is today. The loud ringing of the alarm in the middle of the night has interfered with my ability to reason. I keep thinking the strangest things. Even though I'm thinking, or what you'd call thinking, I'm not thinking clearly. The first time the alarm woke me up and I couldn't go back to sleep, I tried to lull myself to sleep by playing around with rearranging some lines from various poems by Quevedo:

The soul is of the world of Love; Love is the mind
Among my crowned shadows.
He who does not fear attaining his desires
Gives haste to his sorrow and satiety.

I practiced that kind of mental gymnastics when the shadow that hovers over people who are awake during the night, when they should be sleeping, did not completely overtake me. As the hours passed, I did little things in my mind that became a bit more absurd. For example, when I no longer had any control over my "thoughts," I visited some of the people Mutis dedicated his literary texts to. Casimiro Eiger, the Polish Jew who helped the young Mutis revise his first poems, was conversing with Ernesto Volkening, a truly great man. They were discussing literature (in my imagination, that is), sometimes in Spanish, sometimes in French, seemingly without preference for either of the two languages. They also talked to me, but it wasn't quite clear if I answered them or if they attributed their arguments to me. For some reason they started to argue about Heinrich Heine, and Don Casimiro Eiger lost patience when Volkening told him that his opinion wasn't valid because it was only hearsay and that, because he must have read Heine in the bad translations done by Florentino Sanz, he had missed the essence and that by reading Heine that way he had read little more than a bad Gustavo Adolfo Bécquer.

—Yes, yes, that is what you must have read. How can you call someone—who writes in a poem *Wir haben viel für einander gefühlt, / Und dennoch uns gar vortrefflich vertragen / Wir haben of "Mann und Frau" gespielt / Und dennoch uns nicht gerauft und geschlagen*— "syrupy?" Only by having read that dreadful version that ignores the *dennoch* in order to make the poem lighter, more idiotic. Because Florentino translates it like this: Truly, we both felt it: / you for I, and me for you…and we lived / so well together!…And we played / husband and wife, without a scratch / we never even scuffled with each other…The *dennoch* doesn't mean *yes* even though you insist to the point of idiocy that it does. We have felt so much for each other, *despite which* we have gotten along very well. We have played husband and wife and *despite that* we have not scratched each other or beat each other…What wisdom in the "despite"! What a writer's eye! So if you dare call the great Heine "syrupy," forgive me, but in your reading there was not a single *dennoch*. Don Casimiro, you cannot express an opinion on this.

—Listen, you cannot—Don Casimiro replied to Volkening—you cannot talk to me like that. You do not have the right to call me an idiot because I have a different opinion, well for what…

Seeing how infuriated he was, I said "why would he need to read it in translation, if Heine writes in Don Casimiro's mother tongue?" They both looked at me with a deadly silence for a few seconds, continuing to regard me coldly before breaking the silence with: "And this one, tell me—said the deep voice of Volkening—who invited her to speak?" And then they continued talking as if they had never been on the verge of arguing. They walked away from me with quick steps so that I couldn't follow them. They left me sitting next to Carmen, Álvaro Mutis' Catalonian wife (of whom my poet said—and now I know that he was describing her perfectly—"her smile, with that slight sadness softens her") observing everything, with an expression that was neither warm nor cold, but rather something in between, and next to her I saw Jaramillo Escobar, who had an unusual grace, despite his extreme ugliness, arguing who knows what nonsense with Santiago Mutis, who was also there…

I looked back at Carmen, who was now talking to the Feduccis... All of this in their houses, with their things, next to the gardens or cafés or automobiles, their entire earthly lives, as they were before. They smoked and drank, one of them making noises while he sipped his cocktail. Such amazing visions! And there was El Gaviero talking to Gabo, Mutis with García Márquez. Both so magnificent!

We've lost all of that! We still have their books, but those have been rejected by the people of L'Atlàntide. The voices of El Gaviero and Gabo have been weakened to the point of becoming inaudible and their images have begun to dissolve before my eyes, as if they were made of a frozen substance that was melting in the heat. I wanted to go back and listen to them and watch them, but my imagination didn't provide me with a rope by which to hold onto them. They disappeared before my eyes. I saw them so clearly, I was there with them, I could even smell them, but then they vanished and I couldn't get them back.

Alone in the night of L'Atlàntide, I cried because I lost them; I was seized by feelings of misery and abandonment that now, by the light of day, seem illogical.

I'm not going to allow myself to be swept away by a melancholy that was provoked by a fantasy that came from being unable to sleep at night. I'll break away from my fantasies. I'll send a message asking the reasons for the alarms, I'll clear this situation up. Goodbye to Álvaro Mutis' navy blue blazer, goodbye to Carmen's white dress, goodbye Casimiro and Jaramillo Escobar and Volkening and Santiago Eiger. Goodbye Gabo, goodbye, I'm losing you but not entirely because I've got your books here with me. And so gentlemen, I return you to your tombs.

Slosos keston de Learo

EKFLOROS KESTON DE HERNANDO

I felt nothing for the first two weeks. I did not pay attention to the road that took me straight to the Colegio de la Santa Cruz de Santiago Tlatelolco (which had already been operating since the middle of 1535), or notice the building that received me, or how the students and the friars lived, or what my companions were like, or how many there were, or whether they noticed my arrival, or whether I was the only new one brought in for the inauguration because I was crying the entire time and, consumed by my tears, I did not pay attention to anyone or anything except my own misery. I cried at night, in the afternoon, off and on in the morning, and every time I looked at my disgusting bowl of revolting food, but nobody paid us (me or my tears) any attention because everyone, teachers and children alike, were working frantically on the preparations for the inaugural festivities. Two full weeks passed (time stretches out when it is submerged under water) during which time I observed myself being fit with a purple cassock, given a book, a trunk, and a pretty blanket—all paid for by my false father.

The cassock was put on my body. The trunk was put at the foot of the mat I would sleep on. The blanket was to cover me at night. And the book they put under my arm to indicate that I was a child of the Franciscans was, like the cassock, part of the outfit for the inaugural festivities. Which book was it that I carried so securely under my arm? I do not remember, and it is not that

I have forgotten, but rather plain and simple ignorance, because I never knew which book was traveling next to my chest. It was only mine to carry in the procession, along with the other students who were dressed as I was in cassocks and carrying books, toward the Colegio. The book later became part of the library collection. Though I did not give it a single glance or a single second of my attention, it had the character of my book, however briefly, as I read it with my blind arm. I had too many other things to focus on. First, as I have said, there were my tears, and when they left, there was an empty space, and then my sadness, and when my attention was tired of spending so much time on its sad preoccupation, it deigned to recognize one of the many new things around me that were demanding its attention. It is one of these I want to write about.

I had been at the Colegio de la Santa Cruz two or three days, or more, when they took me to one of the friars—brought in from who knows where to help organize the fiesta—who was to cut my hair as another part of the preparations for the inaugural ceremony. Up until this day, it had always been my mother who had cut my hair with great care. For years I wore the little tail down my back that in other times was the mark of the warrior who had not yet been taken prisoner or the young man being initiated into the art of war who had not yet met his fate even though he had already gone out to fight several times without dishonoring his people. My mother let me wear the little tail many years; even though we no longer had any wars to fight or honor to defend like we used to in the old days, we continued to uphold our traditions. When I went to the friars for the first time, she cut it off with a single stroke.

Since that time, I had worn my hair all one length. I am not saying that I especially liked my hair, but I had some attachment to that way of wearing it so when I saw the friar with the gleaming razor in one hand and the basin in the other, I started to cry even harder; I felt such panic and sadness and emotion. The friar barber said to me: "Shush, *muchacho*, shush. Be quiet. I may not be an expert in the art of the barber's razor and basin, but there are advantages. Look, *muchachito*, I do not know how to take blood. In my steady hands you will escape that. Let's see now…Have you never had your hair cut? It is quite obvious that you have because it is not very long. Why don't you come over here and let me cut it without drawing everyone's attention with your crying. Do you know what St. Francis used to say when they gave him a tonsure? Answer. Do you know?

I stopped crying to respond properly (like my mother taught me) that I did not know what St. Francis used to say when they gave him a tonsure and that I also did not know what the word tonsure meant.

"Tonsure, little one, means to shave the hair here, on the crown of the head, like mine is. Didn't anyone ever tell you what he said when it was his turn to approach the razor? Well, if he saw that they took care in cutting his hair, he would say: *Do not cut the fringe perfectly or precisely. I want my brothers to treat my head without any special consideration, without any kind of consideration at all.* And you, *muchacho*, you go around making such a fuss that not even the saint of all the saints did…Come here, *muchacho*, sit here in front of me, I have very little time to get all of the little boys' hair ready for the celebrations. Sixty heads are waiting for me and that is not even counting my own head. What with so much fuss and so many preparations, we look less like Franciscans and more like members of the Court who celebrate amid gold and..." He did not stop talking the entire time he was cutting my hair or when he was shaving the others, and I think that as much as people complained that the Franciscans were not as self-controlled or poor as the order demanded, the Order of the Friars Minor did not know how to observe the order regarding measuring their words. I never saw him again. It is possible that he might have left with the others who were preparing to go to the Philippines or that he was assigned to distant lands—to Guaxaca, or to Nueva Galicia with Fray Francisco de Lorenzo, and later he might have joined Fray Marcos de Niza on his expedition to Cíbola if he was a traveling friar, something I cannot confirm because I did not know anything about him, not even his name; my spirits were so low that I could not even ask.

Of those first days, just as I remember the friar barber, also engraved in my memory was the bad food, the sad bowls, and the place where we slept. When I saw the dormitory for the first time I cried even harder and the more I cried, the sadder it looked. I slept with all the other boys in a large room where the mats that served as our beds lined each side of the room and were placed on top of some wooden pallets because of the humidity. How sad was I when I saw the dormitory, when I first laid eyes on it? Did I realize from that first moment that Mama was not there for me to sleep next to? I did not think about anything, but I can still remember the disgust I felt, although now it is hard for me to connect that disgust to the place I have lived for so many years and that, in the end, was neither a nightmare nor a river of sorrows. The day set for the inauguration of the Colegio de la Santa Cruz arrived. We began our procession from the church of San Francisco in Mexico City, where Doctor Don Rafael de Cervantes, treasurer of the Church, preached. I will recount it as if it were happening right now:

The friars are in front, followed by the boys in their purple cassocks and the multitudes that crowded together on either side that could easily, given the slightest provocation, spill out into the street, seemingly both jubilant and somehow menacing at the same time. The Blessed Sacrament, many crosses, and palanquins on which the saints are carried are also in the procession. The arms of the crosses and the adornments of the palanquins are made of well-wrought gold leaf. Twelve friars are dressed as apostles with their insignias, and many who are accompanying the procession carry lit candles in their hands. When we pass in front of a chapel or a church we see well-adorned altars and altarpieces through the doors opened as if for a grand fiesta and people come out of each church or chapel, singing and dancing in front of the Blessed Sacrament. If the chapel is Franciscan, the singers are also wearing flowers. The entire street is covered with sedge and bulrush over which the procession joyfully dances, throwing roses and dianthus.

We pass ten triumphal arches en route, and each one has three parts like the naves of a church, like the church of Santiago that has three naves. The Blessed Sacrament, ministers, crosses, and palanquins pass under the ten triumphal arches, which are about twenty feet wide; all the people pass under the medium arches that are on both sides and are also made of flowers.

A thousand shields made of flowers are distributed among the arches, and there are large rosettes like onionskins, very round, very well made on the arches that do not have flowers.

At four of the corners, or turnabouts, that we have to make on the route, they have recreated real mountains. From each one of these arises a very tall rocky outcropping with tufts of grass and flowers and everything you normally find in a field, many trees (fruit trees, flowering trees, and trees with just leaves) and toadstools and mushrooms. The trees are so perfectly arranged and there are even some that are broken as if by time or the wind. There is moss growing on the trunks and at the top of the crown of the tree there are many large birds, falcons, crows, and owls. The mountains—sometimes sparse or bare of trees, and sometimes thick with them—are also populated by deer, hares, rabbits, jackals, and many snakes (with the fangs and teeth removed, because they were not insignificant little vipers but rather serpents as long as a man and as thick as an arm at the wrist). If you look closely you can see the hunters (who are so well camouflaged with twigs and moss and the leaves of trees that it is difficult to see them) with their bows and arrows.

In addition to the singers who join us, there is also a large choir in the procession and Indian music is being played continuously on both small and large flutes.

The procession passes a plaza where noble lords sit comfortably on a platform that has been prepared for the occasion and another enchanted mountain where Saint Francis is portrayed preaching to a great variety of birds (they are actually real birds, not fake ones) that sit all around the saint. Saint Francis starts to tell them (in Nahuatl) all the reasons that they should talk to and praise God: because he takes care of them and they do not have to work, sow and reap like men, and also for the plumage that God adorns them "with such a variety of feathers, that you do not have to spin and weave your own clothing, and for the space in the world He has given you: the air through which you fly."

Then the birds move closer to the saint to receive his blessing as he commands them again to praise and sing to God in the mornings and afternoons. And the birds are real, not tricks, but instead are perfectly trained by the men of these lands.

As the saint descends the mock mountain, a horrendous and ferocious beast comes running down from the mountain onto the road, startling us all even though we know this is a trick and part of the performance. The saint makes the sign of the cross toward him. "I recognize you as the beast that destroys the livestock and does evil things to the creatures made by God and attacks that which He has made for the good of man, I now reprimand you and invite you to submit yourself to the law of peace," to which the beast replies, between howls, "I repent and hope for forgiveness!"

The saint brings the beast close to the platform where the noble lords are and the beast indicates that he will obey and pledges that he will not do any more harm. He gives his paw to each of the noble lords who is willing to accept it, and that done he very peacefully goes back to the densest part of the mock mountains, having lost some of his frightful appearance.

The saint is left alone. He takes the opportunity to harangue us with a sermon on obedience, which is interrupted when someone dressed as a *macehual* pretending to be drunk, approaches singing,

or rather shouting, as drunkards do. The saint humbly asks him
to be quiet, while the rest of us do so loudly and make noises,
for which the saint quiets us as well and explains to the drunkard
that if he does not stop singing right now he will go to hell. But
because the drunkard does not pay any attention, two frightening
devils come from the side of the mountain to grab him and, even
though the drunkard resists, they take him to where the fires of
the mock hell are burning.

The saint wants to continue with his sermon, but then some
believable witches appear and dance provocatively around him,
and because they are disturbing the preaching and are not paying
attention to his pleas for them to leave, the devils return with the
mock inferno. They open the doors of hell and we can see the fire
they have lit, and the devils, evil women, and the drunkard shout
and scream as if they were really burning.

We get up and continue the procession with solemn music,
walking over flowers and surrounded by beautiful music until
we arrive at the church of Santiago where a stage has been prepared on which the Earthly Paradise has been reproduced. All is
completely silent, except for the music of the choir, as we look at
a scene depicting the tree of good and evil, the apple, the serpent,
the angel with his sword, and the fall of man.

Finally, we celebrate a mass to complete the formal inauguration
of the Colegio de la Santa Cruz, during which Fray Alfonso de Her-
rera preaches the second sermon in the great convent (which is what
we called the convent of Mexico City so as not to confuse it with that
of Tlatelolco). Fray Alfonso is originally from Castilla la Vieja, near
Burgos, and he studied law at Salamanca, where he took the habit.

His Sunday and Saints' Day sermons are much admired. His person is always praised in writing. It falls to Fray Pedro de Rivera to deliver the final sermon, which he preaches in the friar's refectory where food is served to Viceroy Mendoza, Bishop Zumárraga, President Fuenleal (who had not yet departed for Spain), the invited lords (among whom was my false father), and to the sixty original and founding students.

We all eat together at seven tables. The older students (the ones who came from the school of San José de Gante) converse with the dignitaries and the Bishop in Latin, and in Nahuatl and Castillian, as they are able.

During the meal they ask us to stand up and say our name and cite our lineage aloud and I almost make a mistake regarding "my" family. But one look, like a dagger, from my false father, makes me quickly correct it, and the fact that I initially said the first syllable of a name that was not mine merely makes everyone laugh.

The meal ends and the noble lords, the fathers of the students, take their leave. I pretend to say goodbye to mine, though we took our leave of each other long ago, and that night I pretend to sleep in the light of an eternally burning lamp until, by pretending so long, I truly am. For this one night we do not get up to sing the Angelus or the matins.

Slosos keston de Hernando

When we were children, the men from the time of History invented something for us they called skin... Wait a moment. Why am I starting there? I've gone back to a memory from my childhood because yesterday when I was coming back from work, I felt the need to move my legs and see the world, jumping from cloud to cloud:

> Sie schreiten von Berge
> Zu Bergen hinüber:
> Aus Schlünden der Tiefe
> Dampft ihnen der Atem
> Erstickter Titanen,
> Gleich Opfergerüchen,
> Ein leichtes Gewölke

That was when I saw Caspa playing around with something in such an odd way that I stopped to watch her more closely, ignoring my legs that were demanding to walk around after having spent the entire day inactive.

Caspa was holding a small object in her arms, next to her body. She was talking to it and rocking. It took me more than a couple of minutes to realize that what Caspa was rocking in her arms was a small, anthropomorphic living being—a human about the length of my arm. I was sure when Caspa quit holding it against her body for a moment and held it in her hands as she extended her arms to readjust and make it more comfortable before she resumed her rocking. The only thing visible, other than the blankets that covered it, was the little head of the baby that lolled from side to side as if it were lifeless. I could clearly see the slightly puffy face, the two red ears, and the bald head.

Caspa's rocking reminded me of the movement of the Cradle. It's not very easy to describe the Cradle because I've never seen it through adult eyes. The Cradle, as its name suggests, was a place to feel warmth and movement, though it didn't move from place to place; it embraced us, enveloped us, it almost swallowed us in its fake, doughy flesh, rocking us untiringly, lulling us to sleep. The men from the time of History devised it for our first years with the object of providing us with what they called skin. I remember the smell of the Cradle perfectly. It didn't only have a smell, it also made sounds—it made syllabic noises, hummed, laughed, hiccupped, cried, whistled melodies, and spoke to us. It was a great mother-like body, a body that enveloped each one of us, usually individually, but occasionally embracing several of us at once, playing with two or three at the same time.

And there was Caspa yesterday, in the middle of the sky, rocking from side to side like the Cradle, as if she was a living cradle for the child.

All of a sudden, Caspa hurriedly departed. Since there wasn't a storm clouding my vision, I could see that she disappeared through a crevice in the surface of the Earth. In a few minutes I saw her reappear without the live little bundle in her arms, and she headed toward L'Atlàntide. My curiosity got the best of me and I decided to investigate what was inside the crevice into which she had disappeared. The narrow opening in the rock led into a cement and asphalt vault, apparently made to house bombs (non-atomic ones).

The child was lying upon a marble and stone table, which was the topmost object of a pile of things. Lifting my feet off the ground, I flew closer. Wrapped up in blankets, making strange sounds, changing expressions from crying to laughing, making angry faces, puckering its lips, opening and closing its mouth, yawning and whimpering, the newborn changed expressions with a rapidity that suggested that there was no meaning behind those expressions, that the expressions weren't the expression of a feeling, but rather an exercise of unconscious gesticulation, reflex, and simple mimicry. It looked drowsy, as if it might fall asleep at any moment.

The vault looked like a grotesque, enormous temple erected to the art of war and the pile was its altar. The altar was stable, so there was not the slightest risk that it would fall. I sat on top of it next to the child and unwrapped the blankets in which Caspa had swaddled it in a kind of cocoon. I didn't dare pick it up. I had already seen how its head appeared to fall from its body. It put a chubby little finger to its lips and had fat little rosy-pink cheeks too. It breathed. It was warm. It had a peculiar smell. On its rosy-pink face there were some tiny round, white formations, like little drops of milk. Between its two eyebrows, a purple spot was just beginning to appear. As hard as it tried, the child couldn't manage to get its finger into its mouth. It searched for its finger with its mouth, but its hand took the finger to its eye, to its ear. It seemed to have all its parts—two eyes, two arms, ten fingers, two legs, two knees. It was a boy. I can't say anything else about it, I don't even know if his anatomy was even completely human, I just don't know.

I've never studied that branch of science; I've never worked with a living body. I am revolted by the mere thought of the organs, bones, and veins inside our skin. I worked with plants for one very simple reason: the inside of the body disgusts me. Dealing with organs, glands, and viscera is more than I can bear. Fortunately, not everyone in L'Atlàntide feels as I do. Carson, among others, has dedicated all of her energy to the study of, and surgical operations on, the internal organs and other things inside our bodies.

The baby was wearing clothes like the men from the time of History did. Seeing the diaper, I understood that along with it came urine and feces, that he would nurse, know illness, and, at some point, death. Before my very eyes he fell asleep, without taking his finger away from his lip, and moved his little mouth as if he were nursing. His little eyelashes were dark. He looked very much like Caspa. He was as beautiful as Caspa, and even more so. He was like the perfection of Caspa in a smaller version, but even more beautiful. I thought to myself: "And if that little boy urinates and nurses, Caspa menstruates. Her breasts fill with milk." The idea of menstruation and milk disgusted me; I put the blankets back on the baby's body and left him there.

But I didn't go back out into the open. I decided to conduct a thorough search of the vault. It appeared to be about the height of the dome of a cathedral, but it wasn't as long and it didn't have a nave. I saw the memory of man engraved inside. It was untouched by the final disaster; it didn't know the atmosphere had burned one day, scorching the plants, drying up the streams, roasting the bodies of every living thing. The vault didn't know that everything had been destroyed, that crystals, cement, and metal had all liquefied.

The vault didn't have any idea of this, because it had been created from an earlier death; in the same way that Goethe and Heine didn't know about the end of man because their works were written by the light of an earlier death, that of the gods. The vault, a ruin under the asphalt, still preserved traces of the men who had died in the explosion that had created it. One part of its curved walls was made of asphalt, and on this remained an imprint in the shape of a foot. Its owner must have exploded, bursting in the glycerin. I moved closer to get a better look. A fragment of the sole of a shoe was still stuck in the wall. Just beyond that, the rounded imprint of a head and two or three strands of hair bore witness, and a few centimeters away was a handful of splinters from a skull. The altar the child was lying on was made of parts of a chair, an intact table, along with cans, a cash register, metal shelves, and boxes with glass bottles, all absurdly arranged. In this tomb slept a newborn. Nothing protected him from the unhealthy air. How much longer could he live? Only a few short months before he would oxidize completely and then he would literally fall to pieces.

Two steps further on, I realized that Caspa wouldn't allow him such a horrific end. Some twisted rebar on one side of the vault formed a long, low chamber that I slipped into by crouching down. Under a protective air lock, lined up in front of me, were dozens of newborns piled up in an orderly fashion, in clear sight, in perfect condition, feet and more or less bald little heads. Rows of newborn corpses had been arranged in perfect order, the head of one on the feet of the other to make the best possible use of the space.

The vaulted crevice was a cellar of dead newborns. How many were there? A hundred? Yes, or at least more than double the population of L'Atlàntide. Caspa had put all of them to sleep for eternity before the unhealthy air devoured them, taking care that the corpses would not decay or deteriorate over time. Who knows with what terrible lullaby Caspa had transported them, in her own arms, to the arms of death. Once they were dead, she protected them from decay. That's what the cats the Egyptians embalmed must have looked like, arranged in interminable rows in the Vatican Museum, except that this new collection is much more horrific, harmonizing with the sinister environment of the vault that shelters them. That's how the heads of sacrificial victims must have been arranged in the Aztec *tzompantli*, the skull rack. That's how the piles of corpses from plagues, famines, and concentration camps must have been arranged too.

Looking at the row of those dead newborns, I thought: "And what if Caspa comes back and discovers that I have discovered her secret?" I left, practically running, without finishing my exploration of the vault. Seeing the piles of baby corpses produced less horror in me than the idea of Caspa discovering that I had discovered her. What would have happened then? Caspa's crime is unspeakable. It seems to me that it would be less so if she didn't kill the fruit of her sins; however, in the eyes of the people of L'Atlàntide what would be unpardonable would be to bring more members (or even one more being, one would be enough) to the Earth who would steal our energy and space, which has been so carefully calculated to conform to the exact number of members in our community. In my eyes, as I said, what is unpardonable is to kill the beings she created. It seems to me that it is unpardonable to create in order to destroy, to assassinate as a matter of course, to unthinkingly kill what you love. Because putting so much love and lullabies into those little bodies, the newborns had to have awakened something in her breast akin to love, some kind of attachment.

Her crime is so huge that if she had seen me witnessing it, I don't know what would have happened. If she kills what she loves, without it touching her heart, she would have wanted to kill me. But how could she kill me if I can't die?

Can I really not die? Or is it that I can't die of natural causes? Couldn't Caspa have manufactured an accident to do away with me? Couldn't she kill violently, like the men from the time of History used to do? Even though there aren't knives or swords in L'Atlàntide, she could pick up a stone, like Cain's, and smash me with it and hide my body so that nobody would be able to help me. But that's impossible, my vital alert would inform the Center for Research and they would find me and treat me immediately.

Caspa wouldn't be able to kill me. If she had discovered me discovering her unspeakable crime (that is what it seems to me to be), we would have been like two immortal gods in conflict, we would have performed the duel of the Titans. We would have jumped from peak to peak of the cordillera, drunk with rage, throwing our golden chairs and our tables across the abyss at each other in order to destroy each other's eternal celebration. No, I really don't know what would have happened. ("Nothing more sad than a titan who cries…victim of his own fatal martyrdom").

It was yesterday that I happened to see Caspa and discovered her vault as a result of my own curiosity. This morning I descended by way of the Punto Calpe during the plaza's social hours. The bright atmosphere of the stairway open to the sky is friendly and relaxing for people to exchange brief greetings. I was cordial and polite with everyone, greeting with a look, exchanging a few words, shaking hands here and there. I saw Caspa descend, rosy and smiling, radiating a serene vitality. Isn't the face the mirror of the soul? She had her hair knotted at the nape of her neck as if she wasn't afraid of exposing herself from pillar to post, as if she had nothing to hide. She is a beauty among beauties. Moreover, there is something in her face that invites confidence, something that no one else among us has, something I would dare to describe as maternal, even without being influenced in my word choice by my recent discovery of her secret. Caspa looks maternal and she radiates innocence. I would like someone to explain to me how someone with such a beautiful face, with such harmonious gestures, with such a graceful walk can kill—"*Si mata con una mirada amarga o mientras susurra halagos, si, como el cobarde, lo hace con un beso o, como el valiente, con su espada…*"

> For each man kills the thing he loves,
> Yet each man does not die

Or is her crime simply fruit of innocent oblivion? Yes, fruit of innocent oblivion, only conceivable in a member of our community. It was man who murdered what he loved and lost himself, and not because he eliminated pain and death. When we submitted, long ago, to the uncomfortable and primitive cleansing of our internal organs, we were unwittingly searching for the recovery that follows pain, but not the recovery of perfect health as we had said. No: we were looking to recover our center, the soul of man. But agreeing to the pain could not provide us with that, nor does death provide it to Caspa. It was the Earth that killed man when the Earth itself died. When Mother Nature departed, she took man along with her. Devastated, she left man without a soul. Man couldn't imagine this—he thought if we did our best to recover the fragments of Nature, we might be able to survive. We were all wrong.

> Ox I saw as a child giving off steam one day under
> the Nicaraguan sun of burnt golds, on the flourishing
> hacienda, full of the harmony of the tropics; dove of the
> forests resonant with wind, axes, wild birds and bulls,
> I greet you, for you are my soul.

Who is our soul? Without the wondrous Natural World, man is no longer human. He has even lost his language. Only we are left, but we're not human anymore. We are of another genus, one that doesn't have a name and doesn't want one because it rejects language.

> The earth is an open grave,
> …an open grave
> With yawning mouth the horrid hole
> Gaped for a living thing;
> The very mud cried out for blood
> To the thirsty asphalte ring.

Paz says, that death is the consummation of life, that without death there would be no life? Then Caspa could have life. But Paz would agree with me: life cannot be born out of absurd crimes.

At night the alarm keeps ringing. I need a good night's sleep. One night would relieve me of this feeling of fatigue. I haven't received an answer regarding the clarification I've asked for. And I've asked for it daily. It's also been three days since I asked Rosete to come so that I can send some mail, I want to send my complaint to Ramón about the issue of the alarms by him person-ally. "Take the bull," men used to say, "take the bull by the horns." I have to take this situation firmly by the horns, but I won't betray Caspa. Her crime doesn't affect the community. It doesn't rob us of our energies, it doesn't create us any problems, it only creates a problem for her. Yes, it is a crime and it concerns only her own conscience. She has to have a conscience. She has to realize what she's doing to her children.

Slosos keston de Learo

EKFLOROS KESTON DE HERNANDO

Despite the intense pain in my back that has kept me company in my chair for the past few days, I have continued to write as quickly as my old hand can make the pen flow. But the back pain is nothing compared to last night's terrible dream! Now that I have started to talk here about my time in this Paradise—for the friars wanted nothing more than for the first glorious years of the Colegio de la Santa Cruz in Tlatelolco to be Paradise, as Tula, Tlalocan, or Tamoanchan were for the ancient ones, a land of spiritual abundance, Eden—I should now describe from where these spiritual jadeites arose, but I feel I must write the dream down here because it is such an enormous torment that I cannot stop thinking about it.

I had been dead for a few days, laid out in an airy chamber filled with a sea of light. They had put a heavy piece of flagstone on my belly. I was wearing my purple cassock and had the body I had as a young man, not the ruin I live in these days. I had long hair. They had finished wetting me down with fresh water—I could even feel the water dripping on my skin, on my forehead, my chest, and my feet. Basacio, also young, as young as he was when I was his student, came close and was haranguing me in Nahuatl, telling me that it was a good thing I had died, because now I would leave behind the suffering of this world. I wanted to answer him, because it did not seem to me that was the best way to console me for having died. Basacio stayed by my side, holding my hand.

Miguel, our teacher, arrived and said more or less the same thing in a few short words. He took my other hand. My mood was getting worse and worse because, even though I was dead, I was not dead, and because the water had chilled my skin under the cassock and I was cold. I felt like I was about to start shivering any moment, but I was trying to control myself, to suppress the agitation that the cold had created in my limbs. I knew I was dead (even though I was not and my eyes could see) and like a good dead man I had to remain immobile and composed.

Fray Bernardino arrived and objected to the manner in which they had prepared me for the wake:

—What's this? The wet cassock, the stone on the chest? Is this some kind of bad joke?

—Fray Bernardino—Miguel said to him—How can you not remember if you yourself are our memory? This is the way we used to prepare our noble lords in ancient times. We dressed them in their best clothes and held a wake for them for four days. The stone on the chest is so that its coldness will slow the decay of the body and so that its weight will stop the bloating caused by death's putrefaction process. We've wet him down to cool him even more.

"To cool me down! —I thought to myself—They are killing me with the cold!" But I only said this to myself because I could not talk to them.

—Fray Bernardino, Fray Arnaldo—Miguel continued—we need to proceed with the ceremony. Now, to accompany him in his final resting place, we set fire to ourselves until we are ashes, just as the closest kin of the noble lords did.

—I will not object—Sahagún said, very solemnly.

—I, Fray Arnaldo Basacio, ask that you quickly set us on a fire, that you set fire to our clothes and our persons so that we can accompany Hernando de Rivas to his final resting place—and as he spoke, they showed no pain or desperation while flames appeared on their cassocks and advanced to their flesh.

—But it seems to me—Sahagún was saying, amid the flames— that if Hernando died because of the weakness of his flesh, for ignoring that chastity is the only virtue against lust...

—Ah! Too late you've said this! —Basacio answered, in flames.

—Late? There was no reason to say it, no reason at all. It is, with all due respect, a tall tale—Miguel said amid the flames, before disappearing in the smoke along with his words.

They were consumed in no time at all and I felt remorse for I knew that I could not accompany them, because nobody could take the stone off my chest so that my body could begin to decay, nobody would be able to bury me, they had gone ahead so as to accompany me but, once gone, they would go on without me because I would never be able to catch up with them because the stone kept me in place. The stone then turned into a huge woman who, pressing on my chest with her weight, brought heat into my body, but not the flames that would reunite me with them and that I continued to hope for—not flames and not death—instead the woman was a stone that held me inside my body.

I awoke quite shaken. The boys came to get me and brought me here, and here I have wasted time writing down what did not happen except in my dream, what nobody else saw, what the shadows of the night left in this old heart. The feeling the dream left in my fragile body is more painful than the sharp stabbing

EKFLOROS KESTON DE HERNANDO

pains in my back. Could it be that in this dream there was more of me that could suffer the pain, more than what is left of my old flesh today?

The afternoon is here. I have done my best for another day, but today the pain in my back has been in vain. I know I am not here to write down dreams or tall tales. That has been my approach from the beginning. Why let myself fall into this web of imaginary tribulations?

But not even after having written it down does the dream cease to have the effect of a blow to my weak old body, as if my poor old body had been in the jaws of someone who gnawed on it distractedly. Ah, the dream is gunpowder inside my chest. It is fire, a knife, a bullet, a blow, I don't know what it is. Well, if it is true that I was not dead in the dream and that I am not dead in waking (even though only a thin thread connects me to the living), the stone, the woman, it was all true one day. How much it came to weigh on my heart! How much it came to weigh on me, how much, how much! I hate to remember it.

Against lust—I read as a child in the primer with which they taught me to read and pray in Nahuatl and Latin—against lust, there is chastity. Lust is the third of the seven capital sins, the others of which are: pride, avarice, anger, gluttony, envy, and finally, sloth. Contrary to these seven vices are the seven virtues: humility is the contrary virtue against pride; liberality, the virtue against avarice; chastity, the virtue against lust; meekness, the virtue against anger; temperance, the virtue against gluttony; brotherly love, the virtue against envy; and diligence is the contrary virtue against sloth. Next in the primer came the five bodily senses: the first is sight, the opposite of which is contemplation; the second is hearing, the opposite of which is prayer; the third is taste, the opposite of which is abstinence; the fourth is smell, the opposite of which is to think about what you are made of; and the fifth is touch, the opposite of which is good works. Beyond these, there are the three enemies of the soul: the first is the world, the second is the devil, and the third is the flesh. The latter is the most important one because we cannot throw off the flesh as we can the world and the devil.

I remember the primer line by line because I learned it by heart, even though I memorized it in Tezcoco when I had a different lineage, when my mother was mine, when I belonged to my people. But the memory in which I kept it did not provide me with the gift of chastity against lust…Ah, take the bad taste of that dream, and the memory of what happened, out of my mouth. Lift my spirits. Maybe we should think of something that will scare death away from me, to lift the stone off of me, something that will bring me back to life and allow me to write down my memories. Let's begin with the example of Francisco de Alegrías, the friar who, taking advantage of his name and purse, which was much fatter when he departed than when he arrived,[13] took four young Indian girls dressed as boys to serve in his house and in his bed when he returned to Seville. They say that this Francisco de Alegrías was of the Moorish caste and that he was *extremely wrathful and wicked*.[14] They say that gambling cleric (whose name escapes me) escaped life in prison with the help of Pernía and is now a great gentleman in Guatemala who boasts about the fact that he said

---

13 In Spanish in the original. Estela's note.
14 In Spanish in the original. Estela's note.

and committed condemnable heresies. For example, he said that fornication was not a sin and he killed, with his own hands, the Indian who accused him in front of Zumárraga of having taken his wife as a lover and then the next day celebrated mass without absolution or dispensation. He also whipped an Indian woman to death, raped an underage girl, who later died as a result, and then did the same thing to his own daughter, the Archbishop saw him in his bed with his own eyes. After having escaped to Seville, he had permission to return to Nueva España before the Inquisition sent him back. Wolves and false prophets—those in whom lust is a virtue next to their many great sins...And what to say about that Juan Rebollo who always had a Rebolla in Mexico and wherever he was, who committed thousands of excesses; or Cristóbal de Torres, for whose dishonesties a husband stabbed and killed his own wife, whom the *Audiencia* found guilty of adultery with said cleric? Vicars, clerics, and friars went out into the streets at night *searching for idols*,[15] scandalizing everyone for they were careless about being seen entering *houses where public women were.*[16]

And what am I doing dreaming about a flagstone on my chest and suffering because I see that in the dream I am to blame for the cassocks of the friars being in flames and, even worse, why can I not let go of the uneasiness of the dream? I take the stone and the woman off my chest; the approach of my death should not be a burden for me. I deny the dream. I will avoid it in my soul and in my memory. Why have I wasted so many hours on this dream? Maybe because, for as much as the dream upsets me, it is

---

15   In Spanish in the original. Estela's note.

16   In Spanish in the original. Estela's note.

less difficult than remembering the Colegio's good years. Oh yes, that was paradise on earth, and it was lost too soon...!

I will not state the truth: that it opened a new world to us. We, the students of the Colegio de la Santa Cruz de Tlatelolco, were the Indian conquerors who traveled to a new land, but we did not injure anybody or carry swords, we did not steal anything or abuse anyone or sow death.

I will not even state what is known: that we learned grammar. That is not the story I am here to tell. You, reader, if you come to read this story, you will not be the teacher whose classes I might have taken in times past, nor will you be the student whom I might have taught what the Franciscans had taught me, what we would later teach to our own students who were white, not Indian, because the Indians had already been condemned to ignorance and eternal subjugation. That for which Rodrigo de Albornoz, the auditor from Spain, had petitioned the king—a general study of grammar, art, and theology to be taught to the natives of these lands—was accomplished with us and ended with us. It was not our Indian disciples Albornoz was dreaming of or who Fuenleal was thinking of. In us they educated teachers for their own, Hispanics who would aspire to the Franciscan habit.

We were all diligent students, we learned the trivium and the quadrivium in the blink of an eye, which would hopefully last a lifetime, during that time that seemed paradise. We devoured the books of the library as well as those the friars had in their trunks and some others that Fray Pedro de Gante or Zumárraga brought us on their visits. And then began the sad history that I will begin to tell tomorrow, nightmare or not; nothing should keep me from it, only the arrival of my death will interrupt that which I want to leave here, even though in order to do it I have lost time in introducing myself and my family, in talking a bit about Cortés and his group, in naming Albornoz, who was the first to dream about that which Fuenleal and Mendoza later supported, as did Sahagún for a long time. Tomorrow I will begin this history. Now all that is left of today is for me is to wait, dozing, until the boys come to pick me up: to take me, my cassock, and my two legs, back to the mat I sleep on, next to which are waiting the tamales and cup of chocolate that were left there for me to eat as night and the crust of stale sleep approach. Because that is how it is: I doze here, in my uncomfortable chair, as nightfall approaches and during the night, lying on my mat—with no writing or talking, having nothing and no one to have even the semblance of a conversation with—insomnia delights in tormenting my old bones. I wonder what is gnawing on me. What is it about me that you, insomnia, know so well that you come back to me night after night? It seems to me that what you seek from me, and my mat, is the death that consumes me day by day.

Slosos keston de Hernando

EKFLOROS KESTON DE LEARO

I haven't received a single response from the Center and the damned alarm continues to bother me at night. Every morning I find generic information about the Language Reform and its upcoming implementation in my mailbox. We all receive this on a daily basis along with some lessons in the new code they've just finished; it's basically just notification that the institution of the reform is approaching. It appears that some people are already using the new code among themselves to communicate and have eliminated the use of words entirely. I write, "it appears" because I don't know what they could possibly communicate with a "language" that is so terribly primitive. The gurglings of Caspa's newborns are richer, more expressive, and more precise than the new "code." They've done away with numbers too, arguing that a number is also a word. We'll no longer receive notifications in the form of numbers and letters that, until today, the Center has sent as a way to maintain order in L'Atlàntide. I'm not sure how far they'll go with this reform, but maybe it's best that they just get it over with and then, when they realize their error, they'll return like little lambs to the lap of language. It's obvious they'll need it.

Despite the fact that the Center seems to have become deaf to my petitions, Rosete appeared.

For a moment I thought he had been purposefully avoiding me, but I quickly realized that wasn't the case and that his bad mood didn't have anything to do with me, but was rather a result of the imminent discontinuation of his position of living mail. I had already been informed that the delivery of messages was going to change, that they were definitely going to implement the Language Reform. What an atrocious mistake. Rosete will no longer convey messages. The Punto Calpe will now be the only way for the people of L'Atlàntide to "communicate" with each other. But the Center will continue to operate—it is essential, it even controls our walls made of air—and we will continue to use sounds to request necessary services from it. We will have to say "G"—"G" to lower the covers and protections to the surface of the Earth. But they won't eliminate language from the Center entirely. They won't erase the *kestos*. I calmed myself with this thought. This stupidity will only be temporary.

Anyway, Rosete appeared. He arrived with a smile illuminating his face, a mischievous smile, like all of his were—animated, not by innocent joy, but rather by the spark of a joke.

—I have a message for you, Cordelia.

—Lear.

—Cordelia, Lear, 24, as you like.

—I've been calling you, Rosete, it's so nice you've come.

—Oh really? Me? First I've heard of it.

—I've called you repeatedly. The alarm is waking me up at night. I don't know why.

—Oh really? I'll check into it.

—I would appreciate it. I'm not sleeping at all well. And another thing, I want to see Ramón.

—Don't worry. I'll take care of it. The message was:

I was invited to the award ceremony for work done toward

the survival of our colony, which will be celebrated immediately. Rosete and I will go there together.

—Who will receive the awards this time? —I asked, just to say something. We had stopped awarding prizes long ago (170 years, which in theory we no longer count). I don't know why I asked, but a better question didn't occur to me.

—You're receiving one for "The Bond Between the Leaf and the Stem."

—Me? —I managed to say despite my surprise. The least I should have said was "again," or "why again?"

—Caspa is receiving one for "The Tip of Soothing Joy in Succulent Plants." This is the most recent achievement of all. This is what she has been devoted to most recently.

I raised my eyebrows. I opened my eyes wide in astonishment. If I could have, I would have put both my eyeballs in Rosete's hand to show him how surprised I was. "Soothing Joy?" The last two years? And her babies, aren't they a product of her work? He didn't give me time to formulate all the questions that Caspa's award raised for me before he said:

—You didn't know about this?

I shook my head "no." I was dumbstruck. I reviewed her work in my mind. It was eccentric, to say the least. I remembered seeing Caspa lying on the ground, completely stretched out. She was rubbing a cane of sugar at the point where the stalk meets the Earth, over and over on the same spot, rubbing it in a circular motion with her index finger. The cane was full of spikelets and its huge leaves radiated health. It was very tall and completely green. Caspa removed her finger from the spot she had been rubbing and revealed something that looked like a birthmark and that seemed completely *animal* in nature, if I can use that word in trying to describe it as precisely as possible, because I'm aware that a plant with a mammalian birthmark is ridiculous. But that's what it was like.

Before I could recover from the surprise, Rosete and I were already en route to the award ceremony.

I'm going to pause here to describe the place where we celebrate solemn ceremonies in L'Atlàntide. Our important community ceremonies are held a short distance from what was once the Mediterranean Sea, near the red salt flats and the white salt flats, where the sandy desert, that appears to have no end, begins; next to the Roman ruins of the Capitoline Triad constructed in honor of Jupiter, Juno, and Minerva with its magnificent, wide staircase. Behind the remains of the Capitoline are the ruins of the city wall of the medina, which is broken to pieces; its labyrinthine alleyways; the mosque, with its octagonal minaret. The columns of the slave market are still visible, its one hundred wells are still viable, and some of its doors are closed. L'Atlàntide celebrates its solemn ceremonies, in which all the members of the community participate, there, to one side of the Roman Capitoline atop a flying carpet decorated with this natural design floating above the sand near the Courtyard of the Rose on which Historical Men drew the outline of the eight-petaled rose of the desert.

We call this place La Arena.

Our flying carpet is firm, not soft like those of legend, and its purpose is to keep our footsteps from destroying the beautiful waves of sand on the desert's surface while we celebrate the ceremonies encapsulated in the temporary bubble we use to protect ourselves from the whims of the desert. Supported on only a few inches of sand, our invisible carpet demonstrates that our community is not insensitive to beauty. The people of L'Atlàntide fulfill our love of ornamentation without burdening the Earth, without leaving any marks or traces that we were there.

If, with the passage of time, we have children, anyone who wants to remember us will have to reconstruct our way of living without the use of things. If he opens our *Kestos*, he will know how we dominate the wind, how we work to reconstruct nature, and that will be all. Ah yes, and of course there will be these words. But most of them are not about the people of L'Atlàntide, but are rather pages I've managed to save from destruction—words about, or by, the men from the time of History, like Estela's translation of Hernando's memories. But there won't be any children or anyone who would try to understand what we were because we will always be, so we won't have any offspring, we won't produce descendants, nobody will follow us on this Earth.

I lingered here describing the place where we hold our ceremonies, but this time the awarding took place so quickly, without pause, or explanation, or temporal space for any logic whatsoever. Before I was fully aware that I was already there, they had given out the awards and Rosete and Ramón had disappeared. Although it appeared to be just exactly like all our previous ceremonies, everything took place at an *abnormal* speed. Or I was so far away that time felt different; I was so distracted that each sentence seemed to be missing something, as if some of the words had swallowed some syllables. But the people of L'Atlàntide seemed serene and nobody appeared to be in a hurry. I was trying to concentrate on what was taking place, but it was difficult to follow what was happening without losing the thread because some parts were missing. Everything was performed with a calm swiftness; it wasn't done hurriedly, but at the same time, it occurred or happened at an accelerated pace. I didn't see anyone run, or even turn quickly; in each gesture there was a ceremonious elegance, but quick, hurried, and seemingly incomplete, illogically truncated, divided, lacking continuity.

The ceremony took place in the blink of an eye. I didn't even have time to refuse the award (as was my intention); instead, I saw myself once again (as I had a thousand years ago) receiving an award for my work toward our survival, one that I had *previously, but not now*, deserved.

Now I'm reviewing the ceremony at a comprehensible pace. I've reviewed the visual reports of all the awards received and behind each one of them is a *monstrous, anomalous, absurd* type of work, like Caspa's that I've described here. That said, now mine is the one that seems to me to be the most deserved, given that it was for work that I did such a long time ago (and for the most dubious merit)—the conferring of these awards was an aberration.

Several times a day my mailbox urgently announces that the moment of the completed Language Reform is approaching. And at night the alarm rings...

Slosos keston de Learo

If they were able to, mothers, among the nobles and the plebeians alike, breastfed their children,[17] and if they were not able to, they looked for another woman to nurse their young. The mothers, or the wet nurses who provided milk, did not change the way they ate when they began to breastfeed; some ate meat and others ate healthy fruits, but none of them changed their diets. They nursed the children for four years, and they were so close to their children and raised them with such love, that the women excused themselves from lying with their husbands whenever possible while they were nursing in order to avoid getting pregnant. If they were widowed and left with a child they were still nursing, it would be unthinkable for them to remarry until they had finished nursing, and if a woman did otherwise it was considered a great betrayal. In order to determine whether the milk was good, they put a few drops on a fingernail, and if it was thick and did not run, they considered it to be good.[18]

—

Another boy was looking over my shoulder and he was very disposed to observe my work the entire morning according to what

17   The paragraph was illegible in the manuscript. I've taken it from Zurita's *Breve Sumaria y Relación*, but I had to change it around quite a bit because it was practically incomprehensible. Estela's note.

18   These last two lines are Hernando's (though they are identical to Zurita's). The Spanish text of the original ends here. Estela's note.

he said: "For I have so much admiration for you, maestro." He just now left me and could scarcely stop blushing. To make him go away I had to bring out the breasts of nursing women—having them pressing hard on the nipple to make the milk drop onto a fingernail caused him to blush. The next time someone wants to see what I am writing, I will start writing about urine-based cures, so that the stream of the Medes will make him go away (since my own would not be enough). It only alienates me from myself, or, to be precise, it alienates any little pleasure I still have in myself because the joy that should have flowered at seeing me, at my age, unable to walk supported by my own bones, turns to dust with the vapors of the urine that emanate from my poor, coarse robe.

If the Medes are not enough to make him go away, then I will turn to despicable customs that are attributed to my ancestors because there is no doubt they practiced them, but it seems there is no corner of the world that is not plagued by these evils, they have been in all latitudes since the most distant of times. Did you think Juvenal lied to us? And now that I have mentioned his name, it reminds me how, and how much, he ruminated and reflected on the fact that men would lie with other men. I do not deny that it is an evil practice, that it is a good way to scandalize people, and that it is convenient to warn against because it has been seen that whoever tries it finds it difficult to stop (from which it can be concluded that evil does not have to satisfy the body and that it is for this reason that no one should ever get close to this practice). But even so, I will not waste my pen complaining so much about this vice because envy, arrogance, killing or abusing your fellow men, and not respecting others are all far worse, but I will stop here with this list of the worst things because it will never be finished and that is not what I am endeavoring to write here and because the list of worsts in these lands would be interminably long.

In the history I have been writing, we had just inaugurated the Colegio de la Santa Cruz de Tlatelolco. If you, reader (in case you exist one day), have paid attention to what I wrote here about the celebration of the inauguration, you will realize that I am recounting it in full detail. However, many of these details do not come from my memory, but rather from what I heard said about this celebration, or what I saw with my own eyes of other celebrations throughout the years. Because at that time, as I have already written, my attention was not focused on anything happening around me.

Amid so much gold, so many garlands, so many triumphal arches, so many marvels and mountain dioramas, and songs and processions, only one thing shone through the watery curtain of my sad fantasies. It was the object I had carried with me since my Tezcocan fantasies, an object that I saw as the magical incarnation of something that has power over everything in the world. Not the rod of discipline, to which I had not paid the slightest attention; nor the Bishop's scepter, about which I could not care less; but rather the dagger, and not the inert dagger or the treacherous one, but rather mine, the one that was unhappy about being in the Colegio and was irritated by the monastic environment that surrounded us both. Only this dagger connected me to the world and the world to me, keeping me company in my sad solitude, promising to take me away from the Colegio, free me from the friars, and help me to escape the noble lord whose son

I supplanted, leaving the rule of his house in my hands, and from which I would evict all of the other ladies so that my mother would reign there. While the Franciscans told me about Christian virtues, the dagger managed to do what they were not able to do: it was able reach me, affect me, lodge itself in my mind and in my awareness and in my spirit. One time I paid attention to my dagger at the wrong moment.

Before getting to that, I should say that in my fantasies, in Tezcoco and in the Colegio, I dressed myself so as to honor the dagger, I dressed myself in such a way as to be ready to brandish it: I envisioned myself wearing metal armor, like those from Castile, but painted in our style and with feathers on the shoulders. I imagined my face painted in various colors, I envisioned myself holding my father's shield with feathers and precious gems, and the headdress of a tiger-knight on my head, my feet in gold-soled *cotaras*. This was in my imagination only (fortunately, because someone dressed in this way would provoke a great deal of laughter!) and, as I have already said, in the Colegio I did not have anything other than the cassock and dirt to cover my body because I did not have the opportunity of the regular bath to which my mother had accustomed me.

But it is not the bath that I miss most about her company... what am I doing? I have returned to Mama, or her absence, because, along with my dagger, she was the other element of the story I will recount here.

So, I went about unwashed, in my maroon robe, carrying my dagger. Nowhere else except our dormitory and the dining hall, or refectory, where we used to study with our teachers, the same one where we celebrated the first night of the inauguration with the Bishop and in which some one of us would read passages of Venegas, the Bible, Saint Jerome, Saint Basil's letters, one or another of the texts written by Fray Francisco de Osuna, the lives of the saints, such as Saint Francis or Saint Thomas, out loud for everyone. We did not dream of talking in the refectory while we ate, much less of making jokes or laughing!

I missed chatting. I was accustomed to spending a good part of the day in Tezcoco listening to stories here and there, taking part in the gossip and idle talk of my village, but in the Colegio there were no superfluous words. In order to teach us to refrain from talking too much, the Franciscans had us play a game. We had to count how many words we said during the day. I counted Valeriano's, Valeriano counted mine. Pedro de Gante (the student, not the teacher, but that little one picked up and taken in by the charity of Pedro de Gante, the Franciscan) counted Juan Bedardo's, Diego Adriano counted Martín de la Cruz's, etcetera. We counted each other's words and in that very difficult task we discovered how to have fun in concert with our forced silence.

It was because of this counting game that I first pulled out my dagger. Valeriano was a naughty little devil and he did anything he could so that I would say one word extra and surpass his word count, as if he would win something. We were in our dormitory. This was a large room, like they say the nuns' dormitories are (something I cannot verify). There were beds on wooden pallets (due to the humidity) on both sides and there was an aisle down in the middle. Each boy had a blanket and a mat, and each had his own chest with a key to keep his books and little bit of clothing. I do not remember why we were praying the *Te Deum Laudamus*—

"We praise thee, GOD! We acknowledge thee, the only Lord to be; And as Eternal Father, all the earth doth worship thee. To thee all Angels cry, the Heavens, and all the powers therein, the cherub and the seraphin, to cry they do not lin. O holy, holy, holy Lord! Of Sabbath Lord the God"—but just when I was on the word Sabbath, the naughty little devil Valeriano whispered in my ear: "Forty-seven."

What was I supposed to do with his forty-seven? Instead of ignoring him, I gave in to his provocation and got mad, but since I had to remain mute, I pulled out my imaginary dagger, vanquished the dragon that held me captive in this jail, and mounting my horse, I fled. Nothing more reasonable occurred to me. I was riding on my imaginary horse, dressed, as I have already described, in Spanish armor adorned with the peculiar Indian art of my imagination, when Miguel pulled my ear, obliging me to continue with the prayer ("We trust that thou shalt come our judge,"—this was where the others were with the *Te Deum Laudamus*, I remember clearly—"Lord, help thy servants, whom thou hast bought with thy precious blood"). Valeriano started laughing when he saw Miguel scold me for my foolish reaction to his naughty word counting, which gained him a nice good tug on the ear as well.

It was this same Miguel who told us on a daily basis: "In every word you exceed, sin finds an opportunity." He was one of our best teachers and guides.

Miguel, who was originally from Cuautitlán and was an Indian like us, had been an exceptional student of the Franciscans and was sometimes our guardian and teacher (it was he who also accompanied me in the story of the flagstone, the one where I was dead but alive and asleep, and that I wrote about here in one of my pseudo-histories). He fell ill in the great plague of 1545 and has been dead a long time now. I saw him leave this Earth with my own eyes. His last words were for Fray Francisco de Bustamante, who had come to hear his last confession. When Fray Francisco asked him for his sins, Miguel said to him (in Latin, of course, because that was the language he always spoke with the greatest fluency): "Oh, father, for this I am in great pain because I cannot repent for them as much as I would like."

Fray Francisco had scarcely finished the prayer ("May your portion this day be in peace, and your dwelling the heavenly Jerusalem. In the name of Jesus Christ our Lord, Amen") when, without a sound, Miguel offered his soul to Christ.

"In every word you exceed, sin finds an opportunity." And since I have already disregarded Miguel's counsel and have been excessive in my words in these pages, I will pause on another memory, which will explain the main reason for my sadness and bad behavior. Now that I have brought it up, I must tell the story because it is about my Mama.

Before I entered the Colegio, I had always slept next to Mama, in total darkness, of course, but still feeling her skin next to mine. I was used to her nearness, even while I slept. I was all she had, and she was everything to me. She was never hard on me. She never pierced my tongue with the spine of the nopal cactus so that a twig could be stuck through the open wound. She never raised her voice at me, or hit me with a stalk of tule. I was her jewel, and she was my treasure. Before she lay down to sleep next to me, instead of a lullaby she would comb her long hair, which was perfumed with flowers, and let it hang loose very close to my face.

Was it scented with basil? It seems to me that it was, that she scented her hair with the basil flower.

She was usually quiet and looked toward some undefined point while she combed her hair. I do not know what she was thinking about, whether she was thinking of my father or her family. Only occasionally would she say a few words to me, and it was always the same thing: that someone like me, of noble blood, would not live among the *macehuales* because the gods would not permit it, because sooner or later they would have to reestablish order in our land. Other times she would sing, she would repeat the melodies her mother used to sing to her. I adored the songs she would sing in a very low voice, scarcely moving her lips. But I could not bear what followed, what always came after the singing. If she sang for me, she would always cry afterward. Her songs always ended in tears. Then I would cry too, I would stroke her hair and would say to her in our language: "Mamita, do not cry, your son begs you. Mama, my lady, I promise that when I grow up and am as big as my father was, you will have everything you want, and you will not live isolated in this house, without dignity, because I will bring justice to your name and return you to the place you were born to. I promise, mother dear."

I did not intend to lie, I had confidence that my dagger could remove all obstacles and with it I could avoid any complications. One day, she told me between sobs: "It is not things or honor that I cry about. Everyone is dead. Everything has disappeared, my city, my men, my brothers, my army, the reasons for glory and happiness, everything is gone. That is something nobody can ever bring back to me. No one. No one."

I did not quite understand at the time. Now that I do understand, and if I had long hair to brush and her sweet voice, I too would sing the songs she heard as a child, and then burst into tears with the same intensity and for the same reasons. Like her, I too am a survivor. Everyone in my life has died as well and the dream I shared with the others—that of the greatness of the Colegio de la Santa Cruz (that I still have not managed to talk about)—has also died. Everything has died, everything has disappeared.

I think my legs refuse to carry me because they know where the soles of my feet want to go: to where the bones of my dead are hidden underneath a thin, soft layer of mud. My dead are so many that we cannot even take one step, my feet and I, without trampling on the bones of one of our own. Snap, each one I step on will make a sound because the bones will crack under our weight; snap, Fray Bernardino's rib; snap, Miguel's mandible; snap, one of my mother's little bones; snap, Fray Andrés de Olmos' knee. Snap, snap…And now that we are speaking of breaking the bones of the dead, what can I say about those of the children I never had? In some part of the underworld they must be wandering about and it could be that they come at the smell of my feet. Snap, I graze their skulls with my steps. Snap. I graze them with each step! This is why I cannot walk! My legs are wise…But I do not really have any reason to laugh. Beneath the soles of my feet, the flames of my dead burn furiously, the cold flame that dances at night, far away from me where I cannot see it, mocking me because it knows that during the day I will not move my weight over it. What am I? The survivor. What is that? One who has only half a life, or what is left of a real life. I have not lost only my faith.

The others died because they loved maize and could not live on corncobs and dry leaves. There in the underworld, where there is only pure grain, they play with the night maize.

But we were talking about her, about Mama. When I woke up, Mama was always already up, standing by, watching over my dreams, hoping I would remember. That was when she would talk nonstop, explaining to me what life was like before I was born, what her childhood was like, what my father was like, what my grandparents and my uncles were like, what our lineage was, which noble lords came from our family, which were dead, what they had lost, and explaining in full detail everything we used to have and what we should have again. All of this while she washed my face, dressed me, and fed me breakfast. She did not stop talking in the mornings, but this is also true: she spoke only to me. As soon as I left the house, she was silent. The other women who lived with us, told me: "Don't leave your Mama alone, when you're gone she doesn't say a word. As soon as you leave here, she is as silent as a stone."

Mama was very beautiful. I do not know how she managed to keep herself from someone who wanted to have her for himself. She must have been too foolish for anyone to want to have her, or too foolish to resist the offers, because she did not have anyone to protect her; she did not have parents or brothers, everyone was dead. A son was neither defense nor excuse, because the mothers of my friends often took up with men in order to have a house and food, or to provide their husbands with land and profitable alliances. I do not know how she managed to remain single. The fact is that this did not do her any good, she ended up losing everything, and not recovering even the tiniest corner of her dreams. Mama was not interested in anyone except her son, maybe it was due to this passion that she did not know how to make use of, or derive any benefit from, her beauty and become friendly with any of the Indian nobles.

For my part, and even though I was unfaithful to her by spending all my time with my friends, nothing made any sense without her. I was no fool. She was the prettiest woman on Earth, the one who lavished me with infinite care and affection, the one who brought light to my days with her chatting and cuddling.

When I was living apart from her, far away from Tezcoco where she lived, nothing was fun or easy. The friars did not have even the slightest idea of everything they had taken from me. The truth is that they did not make up for what I lost by not having my tongue pierced with the spine of the nopal cactus and then having the twig stuck through the open wound, which intensified the pain. I so feared those twigs from the earliest years of my childhood that I confess (though it might not be nice) that more than once I did not lament the absence of my father or the fall of my people, but instead I was happy, and thus exchanged, with infantile blindness, a father and a kingdom for the lack of a few small twigs stuck through open wounds in my tongue.

Some of my friends experienced the twigs through the tongue, like Nicolás, who described the tremendous torture with a terrifying intensity while he showed us his pierced tongue, still bleeding, that I was more than just afraid of them, I was terrified of them. Because Nicolás had a father who lived with him, I believed that, not having one, I would not suffer the torture. I was thankful then, as I said, not to have a father. Moreover, not having one, I was the only one among my friends who slept glued to his mother like a *macehual* and I would not have wanted to change that for any honor, land, or riches. For the child I was, there was no wealth comparable to sleeping next to her.

Having lost my wealth, although I would not experience the twig stuck through my pierced tongue or any other kind of wickedness because the Franciscan friars were extremely generous with me, my sadness isolated me, leaving me alone with my dagger and my fantasies. I did not make any effort at all to win my companions over, I was not pleasant to them, I did not make eye contact with them, or exchange even the minimum number of the words we were allowed. Separated from Mama, I was stuck inside myself.

One day, they assigned Agustín (the vengeful boy taken in by the friars when he lost his family because he had denounced them) to serve us our food in the refectory. It was like any other day, one student read, three others served, and we all ate in silence. Agustín put a big empty spoon above my bowl, off which nothing came, not even a drop of stew. He looked me in the eyes with a mocking expression that seemed to say, "I know you won't do anything, you chicken," and then he continued on to the next boy, serving him his portion, as he had done with all the others. He counted on the acceptance of the other students and was not at all worried that they had seen him deny me food, because I was not one of them, nor were my parents affluent or noble, nor my cousins their cousins, nor did my wealth (which was, in reality, nonexistent) compare to theirs, and he counted on the fact that the friars would not stop the reading for this lack and that my reticent nature would keep me from uttering even a peep, condemning me to not even the crumbs that the Franciscans had accustomed us to.

But I did do something because, even though we were not noble or rich, my mother had taught me to be proud of my family. Moreover, I had my dagger. Thus, brandishing it with a burning rage, I pushed back the bench on which we were sitting, almost tipping over my companions, and threw myself at Agustín, holding back none of my meager strength, which of course I did not need since I had the dagger (though nobody could have seen it except me because my dagger only materialized for my eyes).

The friars immediately separated me from him, asking me (in Latin, because we were only allowed to speak in Latin) what had happened. I told them the reason, though I could only do so poorly because my rage prevented me from speaking well ("He no serve Hernando food"). I uttered a clumsy, poorly strung together sentence that had not a single trace of elegance. I had to listen to quite a long sermon about the little importance of food, about the baseness of fighting for it, about the wrongfulness of trying to hurt a companion. Agustín also got their attention, but much more of it was focused on me because I had not only fallen to a lack of charity, but also to rage and violence.

You will remember that the cruel Agustín who denied me my plate of food, the one who left my plate empty, was one of those fearsome, vengeful boys, whose story I have already told. He was neither wise nor persuasive because he came not to spread the true faith and the word of Christ, but rather to punish his people. He scarcely comprehended even a trace of Christian wisdom and in all his actions he left a mark of vengeance that, for some reason unknown to me, he wanted to exercise against everything. Instead of the diaphanous light of the illuminated, of one inflamed by faith, he wore the dark cloak of the executioner.

Taunts and anger sang in his spirit daily. The harmonious song of the rooster did not wake him, but instead he awoke to the dark light of wrath.

My empty bowl was nothing compared to his infernal temperament.

Slosos keston de Hernando

EKFLOROS KESTON DE ESTELINO

As teenagers during the first two years of the heavenly seventies, we dreamt of sexual equality; we believed in the Cuban dream; we scribbled slogans against racism, our unconditional adoration for Martin Luther King, and abhorrence of the KKK on our school notebooks; and we wore scandalous miniskirts and took the contraceptive pill. The Indians were present for us at that time because their arts and crafts became part of our world, dressing us and decorating our rooms. We wore Oaxacan blouses from various regions, fabulous clothing embroidered in Chiapas, and necklaces and other things that our grandmas (and our moms who were devotees of Chanel, if their pocketbooks allowed) would never have imagined would be worn by young ladies of our social class. Instead of high-heeled shoes, it was more chic to wear plastic-soled huaraches (which were almost as uncomfortable as those spiked heels), and we were even brazen enough to wear the bright taffeta of the Mazahuan Indians instead of silk blouses. But the "Indian issue" wasn't a real concern, or at least not like the "Black issue" was—it was "Black is beautiful," but not "*Lo indio es lo bello.*"

A lot of embroidered blouses, a lot of dreams of sexual liberation, much reading of *One Hundred Years of Solitude* (which was the bible of our generation and a supreme outrage for our fathers), much Angela Davis and much Susan Sontag, and even more of the Boom— the Donoso Era, the Puig Era, the Fuentes Era...But I'll back up. I was fifteen when I read *One Hundred Years of Solitude* in my school

EKFLOROS KESTON DE ESTELINO

for young ladies from good families run by the Ursuline nuns. This was when and where the unholy airs began to blow, before the outbreak of the storm that brought the Jesuits and the Cuban dream, and that led to the unveiling of more than one nun and the drawing of more than one student off to incredible adventures... My best friend ended up as a guerrilla fighter in two different countries and two different wars before death took her from us forever, not to mention the adventures of other friends and those who went to live in the Colonia Martín Carrera (whose name we heard for the first time around then), or who spent some time with the Tarahumara Indians... *One Hundred Years of Solitude*—the fabric of the dreams of my generation—was part of this breath of fresh air, of these winds. I remember that a month before we read *One Hundred Years*, they forced Juan Rulfo's *Pedro Páramo* on us. I didn't dislike it, but I don't think I completely understood the power of the text (I did recognize the power of the printed word, but I wasn't captivated by the small-mindedness of the catchphrases). I saw in it the image of the parochial Catholic world whose sickly light made me nauseous. Little Pedrito Páramo sitting there by himself in the privy dreaming about Susana San Juan, hearing his mother's warnings: "a snake's going to bite you," "it's dangerous to spend so much time on the toilet." It seemed to me that he was the pet victim of Marian devotion. The mother, the grandmother, and the prayers built walls around the boy to protect him from his own body, from the development of his sexual, adult body.

As I've said, the miniskirt and the pill had arrived and we moved away from the veils and the mantillas that we wore to mass when we were little girls. *Pedro Páramo* represented a world we despised in our desire for liberation, despite the fact that it certainly represented freedom in literature. *One Hundred Years of Solitude* was something else. It wasn't just the way it was written, but rather what it had to say that made it representative (and I would go further and say: a banner) of the death of the repressive and oppressive provincial traditions. The Garcíamarquezian realm was our liberation from the Lópezvelardesque traditions. My reading of *One Hundred Years* was not a literary reading. I read *Pedro Páramo*, but *One Hundred Years* was inscribed on our skin. It's not that García Márquez wasn't a real writer, his novel *No One Writes to the Colonel* was a real book. But *One Hundred Years of Solitude* was the intimate wear and fancy carnival costume we wore to combat the Virgin Mary who we were afraid was trying to turn us into prudes. And at the same time, it was a chronicle and a condemnation, as well as a celebration, of an unusual freedom in tradition-bound Mexico. The south also brought us fresh, liberating air. Angela Davis was not the only one who opened the door for women to a world without mantillas and shawls; García Márquez' characters—lusty, naked, sensual—did as well.

We read the book in 1970, and we were unrestrainedly enthusiastic. Our fathers scheduled a special meeting to complain about the selection of school material because, in their opinion, that book should not be read by young girls from good families. And why was it a scandal, if the Mexican bourgeoisie tended to simply ignore books? Why did they place so much "importance" on one book? As part of our homework for our reading of *One Hundred Years of Solitude*, we made a fun little Super-Eight film that was the last straw for our fathers. It got all kinds of reactions. One father (a lawyer with Woodrich Euzkadi in Mexico, if I remember correctly)—undoubtedly a "sleight of hand lawyer," like the ones in Macondo who demonstrated "that the demands lacked all validity," and proclaimed that "the workers did not exist,"—invited us to his library to watch a professionally made film of him shooting a white bear (the same one he kept stuffed in his study). "This is what is important," he told us, "you all are wasting your time." His lecture was really more like a conversation among the deaf, because I never got the connection between our Super-Eight of *One Hundred Years* and the film of him shooting of the bear. (Of course, our little film participated in the same conversation among the deaf in that it didn't have anything to do with the novel either because it was basically a sequence of completely random "illustrations" of some brief passages of the novel.)

What was it about *One Hundred Years of Solitude* that made the hair of "good manners," of the "*establishment*," stand on end? The death of Rulfo's ghosts, dead through bodily desertion, prayers and scolding? The anger of the Fernanda del Carpios ("I married a sister of charity"). Were they offended? "Thifisif...isfisif onefos ofosif thofosif whosufu cantantant statantand thefesef smufumellu ofosif therisir owfisown shifisifit." The Fernanda del Carpios and the sleight of hand lawyers were not so wrong to be afraid of *One Hundred Years of Solitude*, given that it was inseparable from the dreams of my generation.

What scared the Fernanda del Carpios, the "goddaughters of the Duque of Alba"? ("A lady of such lineage that she made the liver of presidents' wives quiver, a noble dame of fine blood like her, who could claim eleven peninsular names...a lady in a palace or a pigsty, at the table or in bed, a lady of breeding, God-fearing, obeying His laws and submissive to His wishes…"). What scared them? The portrayal of Antilópezvelardianism? The Antirulfo-Sanmatean world in the lusty flesh "shamelessly" depicted in Macondo?

The world—as written in *One Hundred Years of Solitude*—was reborn for us. This was the new Caribbean and Latin American genesis, rewritten by García Márquez. In rewriting it, he improved it: evil was put in its place, in its proper place, and not in the flesh, not in the body, as it was protrayed very biblically in *Pedro Páramo*. Evil is not the snake that will appear in the bathroom, invoked by desire; instead it appears when a Buendía has public funds at his disposal: yes—that will be the shame of the family.

In *One Hundred Years of Solitude*, woman does not come from the rib of man, but neither does Fuensanta.

History can be re-written, roles can change meaning, and gypsies can become honest because reality is magnificent in and of itself, because we are reborn in the young patriarch, José Arcadio Buendía, who ensures the progress of the community; because our countries are not ruled by Pedro Páramos. *One Hundred Years of Solitude* is the jubilant acceptance that reality is magical, that the power of the imagination creates realities. The novel is filled with an incomparable energy and a promise of the possibility of happiness: the supernatural powers of science and observation. If Melquíades' gums can "magically" be filled with teeth, then there was hope for reality. *One Hundred Years* writes the past as a utopia, it re-writes our past because Latin America dreamed of following the Cuban model and "modernizing" through a socialist revolution.

The Cuban dream that preceded the Cuban failure. Macondo is "a happy village" that one reaches by following the song of birds. Macondo is José Arcadio Buendía's dream. He establishes a utopia by heading "toward the land that no one had promised them." My generation witnessed the birth of a New Adam, a New Eve, and a New Paradise. Adam is the one who eats of the apple (of knowledge). But the word is so powerful that it destroys him. The anecdotal lust in *One Hundred Years of Solitude* is shocking. There is so much narrative embroidery, such a compulsion to tell a story that it seems to be an irrational yearning, the author seems to be fleeing from silence, the silence of the dead ("there haven't been any dead here")—he has to denounce them in order not to become a cadaver himself. It is with this lustiness that the world reinvents itself and with which, in its haste, also seems to destroy itself. Its anecdotal lust, its cornucopia of anecdotes, doesn't protect Macondo from destruction. Eden falls. Everything seems to have been written already, and everything is condemned in the end. The liberals, creators of nonsense when it seems that they are winning the war against the conservatives, are "advancing in the opposite direction from reality," just like the Cuban dream.

"Look what we've come to," Eva-Úrsula said to José Arcadio-Adán. "Look at the empty house, our children scattered all over the world, and the two of us alone again, the same as in the beginning." Why does the Dream of Dreams die from the very beginning? What does *One Hundred Years of Solitude* strangle itself with? Sure, they can say I pull everything into my own wheelhouse, that I don't know the true measure, and that I see everything colored by my own obsessions, but what strikes me is that the Indians are not "actors" in the garcíamarquezian Eden, in this re-creation of reality. The great-great-grandson of the criollo marries the great-great-granddaughter of the Aragonese to found the Buendía lineage. The Indians don't participate in the re-creation of the world: they don't achieve legitimacy despite the many anecdotes, all that happens, and everything that spills out of that magic horn from which stories endlessly flow. And, as I said, we collaborated with García Márquez in this sin. We've paid dearly. We preserved the colonial and colonialist structure, we lost our own power in all the stories and so much history, and we have relegated ourselves to silence, and into the worst kind of silence, the kind that reeks even worse than dead bodies: the resounding silence of the death of the Dream. *One Hundred Years of Solitude,* our banner, was the first and the last of this kind of narrative. It redesigned our past, but it strangled our future. In its irrational, compulsive, unhealthy desire to narrate events, Macondo fails in miraculous prosperity and García Márquez redesigns the past and has the power to look into the future. García Márquez is the beginning and the end of the Macondian narrative. He sings the praises of the imagination, but ends up with a saturation of anecdotes. The world of *Pedro Páramo* was a world we wanted to end. *One Hundred Years of Solitude* was a profession of faith for my generation and a surprise for its premonitory and utopian qualities. But we didn't realize that we swallowed our own poison along with our banner. Many dreams died along with the big Dream. There is no utopia now. AIDS and disillusionment are here.

I'm not going to tell any more of my own story. I'm going to satisfy myself with the fragments of Hernando's story. I feel guilty, especially given my present reality. I feel guilty because I sinned in my dreams. Neither I, nor my generation, dreamt of anything that would erase the suicidal framework of our colonial past. So, I'll make amends for my shame in the best way I can: I'll dedicate myself and work hard to translate the text of an Indian from the Latin into Spanish, a text that should really be translated into Nahuatl if it was taught in school. We didn't get that lesson because we were content with dressing in Indian clothing and admiring their traditional arts and crafts. I would even say that, huaraches on the ground, we became more blind, more deaf, more guilty. I don't deserve to be heard. The author of *One Hundred Years of Solitude* had the right to the word because he spoke for thousands of dead bodies; moreover, he was a writer—that was his job. I'll keep quiet. I'm not a writer, and we, my generation and I, didn't earn the right to talk. I'll continue with my translation of Hernando; the most I'll dare to do is to repair what is illegible in the original and lie a little here and there to make his story more plausible.

Slosos keston de Estelino

EKFLOROS KESTON DE LEARO

The alarm rang last night. I know this is nothing new, but then it rang again later with an urgent message for me to communicate with the Center. I opened my inbox. I expected a visual message, but instead I found these lines written in luminous letters:

> Given that egalitarian tendencies prevail like a desideratum of the times in which we live, we accept the syllabic inequality of words without reservation even though they refer to things that should be as equal as everything else. Could the sun possibly be smaller than an orange? Does it not mask the elephantiasis of some words that are surely unpleasant or leave the bad aftertaste of linguistic monarchy in regard to others, and would that not represent another ill-fated survival of the old imperial orders that today we want so ardently to abolish? Old Marx was not reborn on the third day, we know that now; but if he had been, he would have devoted himself to selecting words of equal size, proclaiming the necessary precision of verbal communism, and today his sermons would doubtless be much more irrefutable.

I recognize these words, they're Eugenio Montejo's from *The Notebook of Blas Coll*. They quote them to convince me, as they are convinced, of the uselessness and danger of language because they don't know how to read this text, they don't understand it. That book is a love song to language, it's a humorous and delightful song, and after reading it, I turned into a bit of a *collística*, but not in the way they had hoped I would be.

Rosete came by first thing this morning. And because I was more asleep than awake and because it had something to do with the dream I was just coming out of, before he could say a word to me or ask about my issues, I asked him:

—How are your quicks going?

—What quicks?

—The ones you were telling me about, Rosete, the ones you were working on.

—When do I have time to work on anything? From the time I wake up until I go to sleep, I come and go delivering the mail.

—So, you're going to continue being the mail?

—Why not? —He looked at me strangely. —Why wouldn't I continue being the mail? Where did you come up with that? Are you trying to offend me?

He furrowed his brow and the smile disappeared from his lips.

—Forgive me, Rosete, please—I'm not trying to offend you, that's the last thing I want to do, I promise. I misunderstood everything then, about your role with the Center.

—There's nothing for you to understand, it's just that really...

—I'm sorry, Rosete, please, I gave him a kiss. He smiled at me, and for an instant there was a real smile on his lips, innocent and sure, then it was immediately replaced by one of his characteristic big mischievous smiles. He transmitted the message to me, keeping that smile all the while:

—Be ready first thing in the morning. We'll all go down the Punto Calpe together.

Without saying anything else, and without losing his composure or his big mischievous smile, he quickly left and I stayed in bed, still thinking and somewhat stunned. The Language Reform is ready to go into effect then. Is it possible that we really won't speak to each other anymore, that the people of L'Atlàntide will no longer exchange words? Nothing can be done. Is there anything that can be done?

I didn't ask Rosete about the ringing alarm. I looked back at the daily message sent from the Center. It said the same thing that he just told me: that the Language Reform was now in place, that the majority of the people in our community will not exchange words, but they still won't use the new code because they don't want to contaminate it with language. We'll begin to use the new code on the day of the implementation ceremony. After that, the Center will no longer send verbal messages; they will send images only. And on the same day, the Center will remove, from those who authorize it, the lower part of the frontal lobe of the left hemisphere of the brain, the area that controls a person's language capacity, causing in the people of L'Atlàntide what humans used to call Broca's Aphasia. Now, I'll continue with my Hernando.

Slosos keston de Learo

EKFLOROS KESTON DE HERNANDO

I missed Mama most at night when the light of the lamp kept me awake. The night, and everything in it, was illuminated with suffused light of the burning orange of the lamp Miguel kept going all night. Its light enveloped us in a hostile, flickering blanket. The shadows were the most tinged by it and were thus made darker, their shapes and sizes painted the walls of our room with monstrous leaping forms that made my young soul tremble. All night long I felt threatened by the light that glowed beyond my closed eyelids. Closing them did not protect me from the light, which intensely illuminated my sense of missing Mama's voice, her skin, her hair, her hugs. I missed everything about her, so much it hurt. That is why, and not for any other reason, and I swear again that I did not intend to sin, I somehow ended up putting my hands on my *pecker* to comfort myself. I did not rub it; I only held it, as if by mere contact it could heal the sharp stabbing pain of separation. It was more than just a sharp stabbing, what I felt was more like grief, a grief that pierced not only the skin of my spirit, but the skin of my body as well. I put both of my hands over my *pecker*, innocently, just like that—I placed them inside my underpants, it is true—but with all chastity and propriety. Not to do evil, but rather to try to hold onto a sense of well-being because, ever since I was a child, Mama was my well-being. I did not understand much about temptation, nor did I have any experience with it as it is described in Ecclesiastes. I can now say, with full knowledge of what I am talking about because I now know, that "the thirsty asp takes the form of carnal temptation and never says enough, but only more, more. It is the serpent that we all step on when we enter the world, for we were conceived by it, and it is this very serpent that we do not see or know how it has bitten us when we feel its rabid, thirsty bite and sharp stab of evil lust. Our mortal thirst is quenched and we do not die from it because God ordered the baptismal waters that somewhat suppress and temper our thirst for evil pleasure and change what was a sin into an opportunity for greater merit."[19] That is what Fray Francisco de Osuna said in *The Third Spiritual Alphabet*. Knowing of which I speak, I can say that it was not the asp that made me touch that part of my body; lust did not come from within or beyond me. "Let what I have said about the devil be enough because many other things that provoke and awake evil desires in us comes down to this as well; nonetheless, man is often tempted without any of this, because the thirst that remains with us from the serpent's bite awakens us to evil, as each of us is tempted, attracted, and ensnared by its evil desire."[20]

I know "our body is a brambly blackberry bush full of sharp thorns, which are the temptations that wound the soul: and even though the fire of the evil desire that tempts us burns within us, free will burns only if it consents to do evil or if God flees. He does not abhor nature but rather the sin and he dwells in the body that is subject to temptations even though he flees from the one

---

19   Quoted in Spanish in the original. Estela's note.
20   In Spanish in the original. Estela's note.

subject to sin."[21] I know very well what this blackberry bush is like and I will speak about its thorny nature when I come to that situation, but that is not the story I am telling now.

One night when I had a very hard time going to sleep because I was quite upset by the grief caused from not seeing Mama, the night I slept with my hands holding onto my *pecker* (something that must have comforted me, since I was able to sleep), I had a horrible dream during which I started to scream from the pain of it. I did not speak any words, but a cry came from my belly, something like "*Ay!*" but with some *h's* and *m's* too, I think I remember because I heard myself as I was coming out of the dream, I listened to myself. I was still asleep when Miguel rushed to my cry, and without knowing what to do, how to bring me back to myself so that I could escape the pain that was pursuing me in my dreams, and seeing that I did not wake up to his voice, but instead kept screaming the *ays* with the *m's* and *h's* from my dream, he pulled off my blanket and discovered my two hands holding my penis.

It was a terrible scene. When the friars came in response to what they referred to as my disturbance, I had not completely come out of the dream in which not only my life was in danger, but that of Mama's as well (I had gone to find her). We were lost out on the road and, because everything had changed, everything was different, and as we approached a tree to take some shade, some horrific animals that were men at first, but when they got close to us looked like a cross between cows and dogs that had a sticky kind of slobber coming from their mouths with which they started to cover our faces, keeping us from waking up…

---

21   Quoted in Spanish in the manuscript. Estela's note.

The worst of the dream is that they did not completely disgust me when I saw them as people because I think I thought they were friendly, I had even taken a step toward them. What was worse was that they turned into those monstrous animals before my eyes. Even though they were not monsters, they seemed that way to me because instead of greeting me warmly, which is why I had approached them, they covered us with that slobbery substance, with that sticky material that clouded our eyes, blocked our noses, filled our mouths, and seemed like it would choke us...I still had not managed to completely escape from my terrifying nightmare when Miguel was already hitting me with the same whipping rod with which they would soon be showing me how to beat myself in order to invoke the peace provoked by prayer, and while he was hitting me, he called me a "pig" and things like that, telling me that it was the devil himself who gave me those bad dreams and allowed them to get near to me before I fell asleep...

I was punished for three days for my non-sin. For three days they gave me nothing but water; I could not go outside to see the sun; for hours, I had to pray aloud whatever the voice ordered me to repeat and however many number of times...That was my punishment for trying to find some momentary relief from the pain that I did not know how to express and could not verbalize because, for them, my Mama was the other, my father was some-one else, and my name was something else...

The first year, Mama came to visit me every Sunday. The weeks were so long as I waited for the last day of the week to arrive. They allowed me to see her for only a few minutes after mass, as if they were getting me ready for the day they would deny me her visit. I stayed outside to talk to her because women were not allowed inside the courtyards of the Colegio. The Franciscans did not speak to women. When I did not know that they did not speak to them because they thought they were evil, I thought to myself "it seems that the Franciscans are afraid of women." Their law says: "Because we must keep ourselves not only from evil, but also from that which has the appearance of evil, we advise each and every one to carefully avoid the company of, and familiarity and conversation with, women." And not content with that: "He who might be persuaded by suspicious company or familiarities or imprudent conversations with women, and duly reprimanded, does not mend his ways, will be kept in the monastery for a period of time, will be temporarily prohibited from the exercise of his office by the Provincial Minister, or be removed from that monastery, or will be punished more seriously." And moreover: "everything that the Popes established religiously and prudently for women not to be admitted in the houses of the Regulars, is kept inviolably even with respect to young girls of any age...He who allows women to enter into our Hospices will also be punished with a grave penalty by the Provincial Minister." I do not want to make poor Carlos's (who, accused of sedition and heresy, was burned at the stake) arguments my own, but he spoke something of the truth when he said that the fear of women was a bit absurd. I am not saying anything against Christianity in defending him because those same Christians gave me knowledge, as Damián de Vegas did in a sonnet about a vision of the Apocalypse in Ch. XII of his book[22] *Poesía Cristiana, moral y divina, a la inmaculada concepción de nuestra señora: Mulier sole et luna sub pedibus ejus, et in capite ejus corona stellarum deducím*[23]:

> If she is clothed and adorned by the sun
> She who gave birth to the eternal sun,
> If her soles imprint the moon
> By the dapples with which she is marked;
> And if with stars she is crowned
> San Juan saw this beautiful damsel,
> With such a body, such a soul,
> Which no mortal could achieve.
> If angels have always been pure,
> And have always adored her as Queen with profound
> Respect, who in his determination,
> Of all men would be so daring,
> To blemish, as the world declares
> That under God none is equal in purity?

The Virgin was a woman and they would not have forbidden us to speak to her. Even though my mother was not a virgin, she was pure, she was beautiful. She did not use *axí*, the yellow cream made of earth that low women put on in order to have pretty, lustrous skin. She did not use colors or make-up on her face because she was not fallen or worldly. She did not dye her teeth deep red. She did not let her hair down (except in front of me) to be more attractive or leave some of her hair down with the rest over her ear or shoulder. She did not perfume herself with sweet-smelling

---

22 In Spanish in the manuscript from here until the end of the poem quoted by Hernando, with the exception of that which I left in Latin. Estela's note.

23 This was left in Latin by Estela, without translation into the Castilian, and I have left it in my version. Lear's note.

scents or rub *tzcitli* on her teeth to clean them. She did not walk around or spend time on the street or in the plaza. She did not go looking for vices or laugh like the low ones who never stop laughing. She was not in the habit of making suggestive expressions or gestures—making eyes at men, winking while talking, beckoning with her hand, or laughing for everyone. She did not choose whatever looked best on her, she did not want men to covet her. She did not act as a go-between for other women and men or sell other women. She did not strut around. Not all women are as corrosive as Soliman's water, not all women are poisonous tricks. I must write here about how a religious man met his death: burning with thirst, afflicted by a fever that kept him from boarding the boat that would carry him to Spain, he confused a jug of Soliman's water (that corrosive mercury sublimate used in the preparation of cosmetics) for a jug of water and died within a few hours of drinking it, victim of a poisonous cosmetic.

Moreover, my Mama was mine and even without taking into account what I have already said, she was upright and sensible and everything she said was that of a well-disposed, good and honorable woman. They kept me from seeing her because the Franciscans decided that mothers were the only women who could come to visit the students and that no aunt or other female relative could visit unless the mother or father were not alive. As far as they were concerned, my mother was not my mother, so, without thinking twice about it, without taking into account that she was the only person who visited me and that my false parents had not even set foot in Tlatelolco to see me the entire year I had been there, and that she, my non-Mama in their eyes, was my only visitor, they took her away from me. The Franciscans did not give much thought to those who had their real mothers either: those boys were lucky to have the chance to see their mothers just once a month, on the first Sunday. But what they did not cut out were the visits from the men, and they increased those of the fathers by quite a bit. My false father's visits gave me very little happiness, and I did not even dream that my false mother would take the time to come to see me, which did not bother me because I did not have any desire to see them myself, neither him nor her.

My Mama was so beautiful that I have no doubt that they gave this order so that they would not have to look at her, because it would hurt them to look at a woman so beautiful. But comparing our wounds side-by-side—that of the friars, in the flesh of lust and mine in the tender soul of a child—which should they have considered? Mine, without a doubt. For their wound, prayers and continence and nightly flagellation was enough because the Franciscan friars who lived in Tlatelolco were saintly; while for my wound, neither prayers, nor continence, nor the nightly flagellation brought me any peace. Moreover, my wound was born of separation, theirs was born before separating me from her. Theirs was a wound that did not deserve consideration or even discussion, given that its nature was of the same origin as sin. Mine, created by the absence of my Mama, was an innocent wound because the bond that binds a mother to her child is good. They will say that our bond was unusual, and this is true. Our love and the closeness of our relationship was annoying to some. It is possible that the people of Tezcoco—my relatives (whose son I was replacing)—sent me to the Franciscans not so much to keep their son close as to separate me from my Mama. Now that I think about it, it is possible. There is no way to know. I never really had a relationship with them.

Without comparing my mother to the holiest Virgin, as I am incapable of such heresy, I think they were wrong about everything because my Mama was incapable of invoking evil and she would have been embarrassed to know that she aroused the shadow of an evil thought in anyone. A song comes to mind:

> Surely, my muse,
> It must be for grand purpose
> that you take us by hand
> Through vain movement of the vain world.
> We might lose the allure
> For heavenly things,
> For it is eternal error
> To adore the things of Earth.[24]

In addition to my sorrow at experiencing Franciscan law in a chapter that was most painful to me, there were only a few weeks I was able see her on Sundays. Our weekly visits lasted only one year, one eternal year that congealed inside of me as the worst year of my life. After those awful 365 days had passed, I was not allowed to see her anymore. From then, until the Colegio was left in the hands of the Indians, I lost the good fortune of seeing Mama. When I got her back, during the time the Indians were the poor custodians of the Colegio de la Santa Cruz, she had only a short time left to live due to circumstances that I do not want recount here because it shames me now that I am unable to ever show her

---

24 According to what the translator tells us, this poem was in Spanish in the original and appears to be the *Canción a Nuestra Señora* by Damián de Vegas. Lear's note.

again the intense affection that—I do not want to repeat—bound me to her. Nevertheless, on the one hand, a black infantile anger made me blame her unjustly for our separation—since I had lost all closeness with her because she did not read or write and since she did not talk to anyone but me, as I said, I seldom knew much about Mama's life—and on the other, after hearing the Franciscans constantly saying that women were the seeds of evil, this is where I placed her. In light of the Franciscan's words, she seemed to me to be a strange being, foreign to me, and my life. When I saw her again, although my heart was, its own way, filled with joy to see her as much as it had been when I was a child, I did not show it and instead punished her for a crime that was not hers, overlaying my punishment with a false Franciscan purity believing that I was being faithful to the law by being short and stingy in expressing my love to her. At that time, she was no longer as beautiful as she had once been. She was sad and very sick. Her only joy, she told me herself, was in thinking that, educated by the friars and seeing how things were among the Indians, maybe her son might achieve some glory: a good position, something which justly should have belonged to me given the status of my family. Because I had been born noble, she told me once again, I should not die suffering the hardships of a *macehual*. When she died, she was worse off than a *macehual*, young and aged at the same time, deceived by the only thing that was important to her—by imagining that I would not end up being an Indian in these now unhealthy lands.

The only joy my Mama might have had at the end dissolved in light of my coldness. I did not want her near me, I did not want to look her in the eyes. I do not know if it hurt me to look at her or if I was angry, but my caprice removed her from my sight forever because I think she did not want to fight for her life when she saw that she no longer mattered to her son. She had lost him forever. In spite of this, knowing her nature as a dreamer, I know that she continued, until her last moment, dreaming of the good life she imagined for me.

Her dream did not seem so fantastic then, though it had something of fantasy. What should have happened was that, finding herself free of me, rather than surrendering to pain and illness, she should have found a man who would love her for her nobility and beauty. But that practice, and it was a practice, was outside of her nature as a dreamer. Instead, I know she would have recorded every detail of the dream she dreamt for me in her imagination. I do not think that she would have planned for her son what I ended up dreaming for myself sometime later—that I would dedicate myself with honor to the honest life of letters. "Ambition extinguishes curiosity, these two things are contrary to each other." In my fantasies, I put myself in the place of the curiosity, whereas my mother put me in the place where ambition is satisfied. They will say that place does not exist because "such are the ambition and arrogance that reign in the human heart that they are not satisfied with the whole world; instead they are enriched with longing and thirst for gold."[25]

Precisely what she might have imagined for me I do not know, although I can conjecture where it would lead—to honor, power,

---

25   In Spanish in the original. Estela's note. (*Editor's note:* These words are almost identical to those of Henrico Martínez in the "Prólogo al prudente y curioso lector" from his *Repertorio*.)

and wealth—but I will not deal with that here. I do, however, want talk to you about what I imagined for myself. I can even describe the routine I glimpsed in my dream: at six in the morning I would be in the chapel to attend daily mass. During the half hour that remained after mass, we would devour some bread for breakfast before we would need to be at the University at seven o'clock. From opposite sides of the city of Mexico (and us coming from Tlatelolco), students would depart in a plethora of colors of academic hoods and gowns. Those from the Colegio de San Pedro and San Pablo would come from farther away than we do and arrive wrapped in their dark brownish-gray gowns and wearing their long purple academic hoods. The students from the Colegio Real de San Ildefonso set off from the north side of the main plaza to the University and basically mark the path as they walk in the blue gowns and blue and purple hoods of grammar and art, respectively. Those from the Colegio de Cristo come from the Calle de Donceles in their purple gowns and green hoods. Those from the Seminary cross the intersection that separates the Catedral del Palacio de los Virreyes to continue on the sidewalk in their purple gowns and blue hoods, before arriving at the last corner and from there crossing Plaza del Volador diagonally, until they arrive at the University. From the opposite side and from the farthest distance south arrive the students from the Colegio de San Juan de Letrán wearing white hoods and purple gowns; the students of the Colegio Mayor de Santa María de todos los Santos come from the opposite corner behind the University dressed in a replica of the student habit of the Colegio de Santa Cruz de Vallodolid in Spain, which was a dark brownish-gray gown with a wheat colored hood.

Then when we are all very close to the University, just about to enter into it, we would join with those wearing civil robes, religious habits, and the vestments of doctors and teachers, walking two by two as we had on our way in. I direct myself toward the *Generales*, where I would have a reading of the *Decretales* with the chair of *Prima de Cánones* and a reading on something from either the *Digestos or the Esforzado* with the *Prima de Leyes*.

Once we finished our morning classes it would be time for us to return directly, since it would be prohibitive to stay longer at the University. The rest of the Colegios returned in the afternoon to take two more hours of lessons, but given the distance that separated us from the University, we would receive the last two lessons of the day from our teachers in our Colegio.

But my mother's dream (the one I did not share), as well as my own, would be denied in time, both turning into vain illusions. Mine became a false dream because when the Colegios were incorporated into the University, its doors were not open to the Colegio de Santa Cruz. There was no doubt that we were the best and most outstanding students, but since we were Indian…Was reality not enough to contradict their beliefs about our nature? The University did not accept the Colegio of the Indians even though we were nobles (as was later dictated by the orders of Palafox). In addition to their ideas about Indians, they had a good reason to close the doors of the University to us: we were better versed in the arts and grammar than others who had been accepted there. I am deducing this, even though it might seem to be senseless and foolish nonsense, because the Spaniards (the "Christians," as they are called in the surrounding lands, those outside of Tlatelolco and beyond of Mexico City) do not want the Indians to have any advantage over them. Whenever they can, they say that the Indians are less intelligent, that they are like children, but the reason they did not let us enter the University was because we were their betters, and these lands do not forgive those who are better. In these lands, those who serve the most are usually respected the least...If I were a poet I would say that this is the Heaven of Envy. Or is that the law across the entire world? Of course the world cannot be expected to lack the essence of evil because its very being is a river of sins. Even so, there is no reason to surrender to it, or to its pleasures, fame, or power, or to any of its deceptive enchantments. Moreover, the world does not forgive when it is not taken into consideration. It shows no mercy and avenges itself cruelly.

Since the world maintains a strange relationship with nature, it is crueler at certain points in the equinox, while in others it is more tolerant or punishes with less rigor; it has less of a taste for vengeance depending on the deeds of men and the times. I never left these lands but I can attest that none are crueler than these are today. Regarding the Hispanic, the exudations of his nature gives these lands an acidic bitterness. Two of my companions left here, and their lives were very different.

One was Pedro Juan Antonio, an Indian student of the Colegio de Tlatelolco who was especially well versed in the authors of the classics. Although he was younger than I, and therefore arrived at the Colegio at a time when the studies were less brilliant, he was attended to by the teachers as if it were the Colegio of better times. Due to his special assiduousness, he was educated by Fray Andrés de Olmos, who died in 1571; Fray Juan de Gaona, who died earlier, in 1560; Fray Francisco de Bustamante, a great preacher, who died in 1562; the wise Juan Foscher; and Sahagún, who died quite old, but still lucid, scarcely four years ago, in 1590. He had more teachers, but I am thinking about the most famous ones who were the most devoted to his education. Pedro Juan Antonio went to Spain in 1568, when he was 30 years old. At the University of Salamanca, he studied Civil and Canonical Law. In 1574 he published a Latin grammar in Barcelona titled *Arte de la lengua latina*, which we insisted that someone bring us a copy of; but it was all for naught, because though it was a book over there, here it was reduced to simply lines scribbled by an Indian.

The second one I am thinking about is my contemporary, Don Antonio Elejos, another author who wrote books about the brain itself. Thus, he helped not only the Franciscans, which is what we all did. I, myself, thanks to the facility that God gave me to translate anything from the Latin and the Spanish languages into the Mexican language, attending more to the meaning than the letter, wrote and translated a variety of things for Fray Juan Bautista, amounting to more than thirty quires of paper, and although it might be wrong of me to say (and I only dare to do so because others have already said it and because it is true), I assisted Fray Alonso de Molina in writing the *Arte y vocabulario mexicano* and Father Gaona in writing the *Diálogos de la paz y tranquilidad del alma*, and I was also the scribe for Fray Juan Bautista's *Vocabulario eclesiástico*, and for a large part of the *Vanidades of Estela*, the *Flos sanctorum* or *Vidas de santos*, the *Exposición del Decálogo*, in addition to other treatises and books, but I will not mention any more, although it would be closer to the truth.

But we were talking about Fray Elejos, who is more deserving than I, because in addition to having taught Theology, he wrote two works, as yet unpublished, each of which we have a copy of here at the Colegio: one volume of sermons, *Homilia sobre los Evangelios todo el año*, and the other a catechism in the Pima language titled *Doctrina Cristiana de la lengua pima*. He wrote the latter in the Pima language because he was taken very young to the province of Zacatecas, and those lands are not burdened by the hate of these lands, which are as abundant in bad feelings as in water. In Zacatecas, in addition to being an author, as I mentioned, he was received into the order of San Francisco despite the fact that he is an Indian.

Why was Elejos a priest, why was Pedro Juan Antonio the author of two long books, why were both professors of Theology, and recognized as such? (Why was I a teacher of Theology to many but never given the title of Professor of Theology?). Because Elejos and Pedro Juan Antonio fled from here, because they did not remain in the Valley of Anáhuac to feed the insatiable belly of this evil world, which is eager to feed on those who do not pay it even the slightest respect. Because although Zumárraga was humble and other Franciscans were devoted to the humble faith of those little brothers, they found a way to avoid injuring the world, they found a way to obey it, and when they did not (I saw it with my own eyes), they also lost and had to pay the World with their quota of pain at these terrible equinoxes.

What is left of me? What of Fray Melo? What of Fray Juan García? Of the latter there is more left than what I once was, for his intelligence, his fierce mind was something of which I have never seen the equal. Fray Juan García had the most brilliant mind (and still does, this he has not lost, in fact it appears it has become even more so), and his culture and knowledge are unmatched in these lands and are probably unrivaled in other less vengeful lands. What is left of him? His crazy brain, which by dint of working has managed to avoid the fetid emanations of these humid and cruel lands. As for the rest of his body, there is not a centimeter of healthy flesh, even if he is still beautiful. What I do not know is whether this is virtue, because part of the anger directed toward him was also because of his beauty. Why did he not leave here? Why did they stay? I do not know why the two friends stayed here, like holy Sebastians, allowing the weapons of envy and spiritual pestilence of these lands to pierce them and lodge in their flesh. Those who left here were saved, little by little, like Elejos and Pedro Juan Antonio.

As for the rest of us: intelligence, fidelity, and knowledge are not easily forgiven; and even less so if one does not surrender to the world its quota of veneration, if one is not a seeker of fame or foreign treasures, a desirer of riches, or a narrow-minded voluptuary. On the other hand, gossip, now that I remember, does not suffice as payment or satisfaction for the world, as if saying bad things about one's fellow man were a spiritual activity and not vile and mundane, for I never knew anyone to be more of a gossip than Fray Melo (forgive me if I offend his person in saying so). If you wanted to hear bad things said about your fellow man, no tongue could wag like his could. Oh, wicked Fray Melo, you have lost this too. The spark of your intelligence has faded with your corporeal suffering.

The Franciscans will put the two friars in their sack of saints. They will say that it was divine will that left them to the torment of their bodies. In my opinion, they lie in saying this. Those two friars are that way because the poison and envy do not allow the existence of their two great talents.

> In these lands, those who serve most are usually least respected and are the focus of more slander, or the indiscreet zeal of those who persecute them, or the false testimonies that raise them, they are like stones for the Royal Palace that God allows to be cut with the pick of slander...[26]

You all will ask: if, given that this Hernando de Rivas is not an imbecile (pardon my pride), and it is true, as he says, that these lands do not forgive the presence of something in them that might awake envy or burning hatred (what better pretext for both than intelligence?), why did the poison of these lands not do away with him before now? For two reasons I will give here: because my mother takes care of me from where she is because her love for me never ceased and there was no reason for it to cease upon her death, because her radiant kindness shines in my heart, illuminating the darkness, and (the second reason) because this poison is of recent minting and I am not of such recent minting, because this poison came to these lands with the Hispanics, not because they brought it, but rather because its presence here was brought to light with their presence here. Is this the way our land took revenge for our defeat? It seems to me rather that the poison arose because—just as my mother is still taking care of me after her death, just as my

---

26   In Spanish in the original. Estela's Note. (*Editor's note:* the words are practically identical to Vetancourt's in his *Menologium*, where he sketches Gante's biography.)

strength is my death, the one that accompanies me everywhere, just as her spirit accompanies and protects me and prevents them from tearing me to shreds—the dead of the Hispanics accompanied them as they entered this land, protecting them, but their dead do not coexist well with the dead of those who were already living here, and this clash brought about this exudation, this exuberant violence...The cohabitation of the dead of those who came from across the ocean with our dead generated this stubborn vileness and evilness, this poisoning exudation (as I have called it) that poisons every inhabitant of this land with ire and hatred.

It is true that my mother takes care of me, but it is also true that they have done much to hurt me—we would not say that I have survived completely whole. How is it possible that they might have succeeded in large and small ways to destroy me if Mama takes care of me with her ceaseless love? Because of her own nature. My story would be different if her nature had been like that of the mother of Francisco Bautista de Contreras (who is presently the governor of the city of Xochimilco), a son of the Colegio de Santa Cruz, and a native of the town of Quauhnáhuac (who is very adept, particularly with a pen in his hand, who has written well-structured letters to me in the Castilian language, helped to complete the *Contemptus Mundi*, and is, moreover, the author of the introduction to the book of *Las vanidades del mundo*)...the very same Francisco Bautista de Contreras remained whole, as if nothing happened here, as if the fat leg of envy could not trip him along his crooked path.

He lived as long as an oak and was always smiling and he managed it all because his dead mother, the one who protected his spirit, was a generous and good woman. If mine, instead of adoring me with such focused constancy, had loosened the knot that bound us, had looked around her and had been good to others, to her neighbors...if mine had had even an inch of the generous goodness of Francisco Bautista's mother, she would have had the substance to take better care of me and protect me better. My legs would be good, my breath would not have the penetrating, acidic odor of bitterness so reminiscent of these lands, and my story might have been different.

Francisco Bautista's mother was generous with everyone, for even though she lost him in giving him over to the Colegio and lost her husband, as my mother lost hers, in the war we had here when the Hispanics arrived, instead of doing what mine did (shutting her eyes to the world and running headlong toward death), she hardly had the life of a single woman being such a devout woman, conscientious of all things related to religion and service to God our Father, she became a benefactress of the Franciscan order. Because of the good industry and diligence of this Ana de la Cruz, native of Tlatelolco, the things of Christianity were carried out with much fervor in that village. Instead of surrendering to the egoism that consists of satisfying her own pain, she practiced spiritual works, as now none of the matrons do, *for the people who normally have done so have been much diminished and because they say they have plenty to do in looking for that which is necessary for their sustenance, and to pay their tributes and other taxes that are constantly being added*,[27] and also because goodness, it cannot be overstated, is not given in abundance.

---

27   This, which is in Spanish in the original, seems to be quoted from a text that I haven't managed to identify. Estela's note.

This Ana de la Cruz, mother of said Francisco Bautista de Contreras, helped greatly in teaching the Christian Doctrine and other prayers and devotions to the young ladies and other women who did not know them, she led the brotherhoods of the Holy Sacrament and of Our Lady, and constantly helped in the hospital, serving the sick.

They say that one time, when a priest did not want to accept the alms she gave because he knew that she was not a rich woman but rather a hard worker, that everything she had was extended to the four women with whom she lived in the same generous act toward her neighbors, as well as to the Church, she replied: "Father, what do I need it for? I do not have a husband or children since I gave my only son over to the care of the Church. Who do I need to give it to other than God who loaned it to me?"

When she died in holy peace, Francisco Bautista de Contreras had a kindhearted spirit to take care of him and protect him. Mine, the spirit who took care of me, is also good, but she did not know how to extend her goodness beyond me, so in that way she was egotistical and thus, her power to protect me was diminished. I do not blame her for anything; I simply observe the strength of the dead in the land of the living. And in doing so, I do not contradict the Christian Doctrine in any way. As for myself, I will have many to take care of and I am not sure that I know how to do it because I had so many students in the Colegio, not even counting my criollo students, whom I do not know if I will take care of from the place that awaits me in the near future because, though I was quite generous with them, I never received anything more than their ire as reward for my knowledge.

Who thrives in these lands? Who keeps their bodies from illness and strengthens their intellects? Only those who devour good reason or those who become enraged against intelligence? Not even them, if I remember one of those solicitors of evil who held the position of the same name. It is true that he is fat and healthy, which is a pleasure to see, but did he perhaps write a book for his people that might have appeared to be the work of Fray Melo? Perhaps he wrote what appeared to be a Mendieta, or perhaps a Zumárraga. Neither Mendieta, nor Zumárraga, nor Valeriano, nor de la Cruz, though I remember the bad jokes that he told us and that we praised him highly for it, but we cannot even compare those jokes with Fray Melo's unpublished work that was crucified by envy, or with that written by Pedro Juan Antonio, or with Fray Elejos' two widely unknown manuscripts, or Fray Juan García's innumerable works and thoughts; there is no comparison because they are nothing but bad jokes. So even though he delighted in tormenting others (helping, like everything in these lands, to destroy the good; in his case through mocking and coaching others to mock what was once healthy and once intelligent, favoring the pernicious power that these parts exude), it did nourish his own intelligence. He is fat and looks healthy, and survives where it is difficult to do so, but what is survival if we compare Fray Juan García's unhealthy body with his work and his writing? Or am I looking at it wrong? Am I also aiding the exudations that are trying to destroy everything good and fertile taken as intelligence in these lands? Am I confusing fat with good and he who has worked with the one who has done nothing good?

But why have I let myself fall into these useless ruminations? Remembering that these lands have a facility for destruction serves no purpose. Ah, headland of greedy people, army without weapons! Your jealousy destroyed the best of me, cut me at the root with allegory. Ah, bevy of envy that clouds the sun in the sky...And what if this is to be given into your hands? I might have muddied these pages with excrement, with nothing more than feces, rather than make a gift of my entire story, which is a flower and a bud—it is a flower that contains me, it is a bud because I was born from it—it is better than my old body, this sack of bones that the years and my pain have turned me into...

Slosos keston de Hernando

EKFLOROS KESTON DE LEARO

The men from the time of History would have said that I received a visit from Lilith. I was asleep and felt a tingling on the back of my neck, a feeling that was something between erotic and repulsive and which, upon seizing control of me, continued to move down to the level of my kidneys. It might have gone lower, I don't know, but when it arrived at that level, I woke up. The electric quality of the pain (if it was pain) was quite intense on my neck. I remembered Lilith and shook my head to scare her away, as if she were capable of sowing or spawning the seeds of one of her sons in me. I thought that if our living space was a house like the men from the time of History had, the curtains of my room, frightened by Lilith's breath, would have plastered themselves against the windows and the walls and danced a macabre dance of terror.

After I finished piecing together the details of the imagined visit from that evil spirit in my head, I realized it was probably the alarm that had snatched me from the arms of Morpheus and that the back of my neck was bothering me because of my exhaustion, which is a manifestation of sleep deprivation.

I got up, a bit agitated, and left to go to the Punto Calpe. I needed a change of scene to calm myself down. The discomfort in my neck kept me from going back to sleep. The night was unusually dark. The moon wasn't shining, and a widespread weather system had raised a dense dust storm that blocked out the glow of the Earth.

The winds blew with such force down there that you could hear them howl.

There weren't any clouds either. The stars were shining. The sky was dark blue. It would have been impossible for me to count all the stars.

I passed puddles without falling into them. At one point on the Punto Calpe I stopped and sat down on a step. I started to think about Lilith for a minute and felt that tingling on the back of my neck again.

I heard footsteps approaching me from behind.

—Who's there? —I called out as I stood up.

—It's me, Ramón.

—Ramón, what are you doing here at this hour? I see I'm not the only one who can't sleep. Let's sit here together, I've been looking for you for days.

—Lucky me. Why were you looking for me? —He replied, without sitting down.

—I wanted…—I faltered—I wanted to ask you why they've been ringing my alarm every night for days now.

—I don't know. I guess somebody wants to see you. I had hoped to find you here. I didn't expect to see you, but now that I found you, I realize that I didn't want anything more than this…Cordelia, look how beautiful the sky is, the stars…

—Lear.

He took me by the waist. He gave me a kiss. He gave me another. It took a couple of minutes for me to respond to his show of desire, but once those few moments passed I made myself his without reservation and we were expelled from the sensible world by the awful wind and the darkness, given over to the Levitical adventure of the flesh, aided by the floating stars. We seemed to be hovering above the earth. Me, Ramón, the stars, and L'Atlàntide seemed to be part of the same body, the same act. I would say the sex was perfect, but it would only be half true because something strange occurred during the act. The complete suspension I described was there, but, at the same time, we were distant from each other. Ramón and I observed one another with complete coldness. It wasn't happening simultaneously, but I would say that each tiny fraction of time had two parts and that in one we surrendered to lovemaking and in the other we were distant from each other, disconnected from what was happening. You would say that's impossible because moments do not have two parts and two people cannot have sex suspended in perfection unless they're not really doing it or unless they're intermittently distracted. It's not that we were distracting each other, it's more like in half of each moment we weren't doing it. In the half that we were doing it, the act was not only complete, but it was sublime, perfect, and my very soul, my mind, my memories, and even the memories I've made while reading—everything I'm made of—was completely given over to the act of lovemaking. In the other half of each moment, not even my hand was touching Ramón.

When we finished, Ramón hugged me and we went back to my room arm in arm. Once there, without saying another word to each other, we lay down and went to sleep in each other's arms. When I woke up, Ramón wasn't with me.

When I was just about to leave to go to my workplace, Rosete intercepted me:

—24…Ramón can't see you. He left three days ago to sleep temporarily at El Oasis.

—He left?

—He left, but he'll be back.

—Thanks, Rosete. —I don't know how I even managed to speak, and meanwhile I tried to think of something quick, something rational that would explain things to me. —Was there anything else?

—That's all.

—The alarms that ring at night.

—I don't have an answer.

He left. I came here. I did see Ramón last night, I'm sure of it. And the fact that we were and weren't there together has nothing to with what Rosete told me. Are they lying? Or is it that Ramón being there was here?

Slosos keston de Learo.

EKFLOROS KESTON DE HERNANDO

It might have taken longer for me to drop the cover concealing my non-crying, if it were not for the visit we made to the Church of San Francisco in Mexico City.

Now then, it will take some effort to explain the importance of that visit, which was not an effort in and of itself, but rather it served to sever me from the blindness of my crying. After that visit I was somehow able to settle myself into the Colegio, I managed to look around me, to go from mourning, or better said, from being a crier (since there is a big difference in consciousness between mourning and crying), to being student. I did not get used to not having my mother with me, but my crying stopped and I saw where I had landed, attached to a false name, noticed the people who had received me, learned what their names were, the story we were woven into, and the kinds of knots that were being tied to form and support us.

It turns out that in a little chest kept in the sanctuary of San Francisco, in nearby Mexico City, they kept the relics of the Church. One of the monks had the idea to take us to see them, I do not know if it was because they had recently arrived or for another reason; that being said, I was crying my eyes out and was out of sorts because not long before that they had completely prohibited my mother's visits and I could make very little sense of things so I do not have the faintest idea why they took us there, whether they gave us explanations as to where they were taking us, or if they lectured us before we left.

The fact is that a little more than a year after I entered the Colegio we went to the church of San Francisco to visit the relics. All the students chosen for the visit entered the sanctuary and squeezed close together so that everyone could fit inside. The sacristan of the church, whose own story I will leave for later because I learned it after that visit, raised his voice to silence us and then solemnly opened the little chest, telling us that it contained priceless treasures—bodily remains of holy beings who were deceased—and that the relics inside the chest instilled the place they occupied with holiness. Without taking anything out of the chest he explained to us what it contained in his friarly Nahuatl that was peppered with Latin and Castilian terms.

THE RELICS PRESENTED BY THE SACRISTAN

"First"—began the sacristan—"a bone of one of the eleven thousand virgins. Do you all know the story of the eleven thousand virgins? There is no reason you should know it since it occurred many years before you were born and in places very distant from here, farther away than where we—who came here to bring you the word of God—came from. The eleven thousand virgins received the palm of martyrdom for being the strangest army to ever walk the face of the Earth.

"Maurus, the king of Brittania, had a daughter named Ursula who was famous for her beauty and discretion. As luck would have it, Ethereus, the only son of the monarch of England, wanted to ask

Ursula to marry him—in part attracted by her famed beauty and in part by the interests of his father, who was an extremely powerful king who had subjugated many nations to his empire, skilled as he was at war and insatiably ambitious in his conquests. For this purpose, Ethereus' father sent a magnificent delegation to Britannia, with the charge of advising King Maurus of the intentions of the prince of England and the recommendation of bringing them to fruition, promising that if the King of Britannia complied he would be lavished with presents upon the return of the delegation, but that if he failed to comply he would be punished unmercifully.

"This petition would have greatly flattered every other European king. The English monarch was infamous for being a fierce man with an insatiable ambition, and marrying a daughter to his son would gain his alliance and protection from his endless appetites for his kingdom, binding him to a treaty of respect with the strength of blood. But, on the other hand, the Christian King Maurus was quite worried as he was sure that Ursula would refuse to marry a pagan prince, and if he did not accept the petition from the ferocious king of England, he would provoke the ire of this terrible man. And this he feared not because he was a coward, but rather because he was a sensible person, for he knew very well that he did not have any way to challenge the king of England in war and there was no way to get out of the tangle unscathed, or without losing his kingdom, his daughter, and his hide.

"Ursula, divinely inspired, said:

"'Father, tell him that we accept, but that I ask for four conditions to be met: first, I want him to provide me with ten very special virgins as companions; the second condition is that I and my ten companions will each have a thousand virgins for our personal service, with attention to the status we deserve; third, that he provide us with a fleet in which it would be possible for our eleven thousand virgins to travel for three years, for I have to preserve my virginity throughout this time; and fourth, that he use the time of my long voyage to instruct himself in the Christian doctrine and prepare himself to be baptized.'

"The delegation received the reply and conditions with sheer panic and tried to dissuade the king of Britannia from imposing these conditions, but Ursula was unyielding and explained at great length the advisability of each one. To everyone's surprise, Prince Ethereus, the only heir to the kingdom of England, accepted the conditions and pleaded with his father to accept them and moreover, excited by the idea of the cortege that would traverse land and sea accompanying his fiancée, he had himself baptized immediately. Why did the arrogant prince of England voluntarily submit to the foreigners? Because the divine will was weaving the story of the eleven thousand virgins for their praise and greater glory.

"When the news spread that they were looking for such a large number of virtuous virgins and an abundant battalion of male personnel to accompany and protect them, parades of applicants flocked into both royal courts either to offer themselves voluntarily or to witness the spectacle of the beginning of the voyage. Can you all imagine that?

"Saint Pantulus, the Bishop of Basel, was selected to participate in the voyage. Saint Gerasina, Queen of Sicily and the sister of Bishop Macirisus and of Daria, Ursula's mother, also heard the call of the divine will that she should join them and, delegating to her eldest son the rule of her kingdom, embarked toward Britannia with her daughters Babilla, Juliana, Victoria, and Aurea, and her young son, Hadrian. It was she who selected many of the virgins who came from many kingdoms to offer themselves and, as she was a queen and was used to governing with wisdom and good judgment, it was also she who made sure that the ships were well provisioned, and it was her idea that the virgins should be trained in the arts of war in order to be prepared for the voyage.

"Now ready to set sail, following the counsel of Saint Gerasina, Queen of Sicily, the thousands of virgins practiced mock battles. On hearing the agreed-upon signal, they lined up in military formation; upon hearing the sound of the bugle, they quickly scattered, some running as if they were fleeing, others as if they were pursuing. For days they devoted themselves to various exercises. That was when more men came to witness the spectacle of the training, sure, as I am, that it was God's direct mediation that gave them the power to do the training, for they were no more than women and, as such, if it were not for divine intervention, they would devote themselves to womanly occupations and since the young men could see the virgins ordered like men in war exercises, practicing war for the battles they were preparing for, without obligation and unafraid, of course they were thinking they would not fight a single battle, but rather travel in peace to spread the love of God across Europe by divine design.

"These women, working diligently in the training devised for them by Queen Gerasina, demonstrated such aggressiveness that those who came to see them, in addition to observing and admiring them, came to fear their fierce manner.

"When they embarked for Rome, all the women of the army had converted to Christianity, as demanded by Ursula, and enthusiastically embraced the vow of virginity.

"The details of their route and the time it took to get to Rome traveling over sea and land is not important. But what is important to note here is that as soon as he saw them arrive, the Pope—who was the nineteenth successor to Saint Peter and who had been governing the Holy Church for the past year and eleven weeks— was inspired by God to join them. Despite the fact that in order to do so it would be necessary for him abdicate his office, he decided it was unquestionably sweeter to follow the procession of women across inhospitable lands. Without saying anything to anyone, he immediately baptized those who had not yet received the sacrament, and thus, thousands received it at the same time in a lavish ceremony in Rome, which is a very wealthy city, none can compare with the grandeur of its buildings.

"After the magnificent baptism, during an exclusive meal to which he had invited Ursula, Gerasina, Bishop Pantulus, and the first ten companions in the cortege, the Pope made public his intention to abdicate. The Cardinals opposed his resignation and the mere idea seemed so foolish to them that they thought he had lost his mind, but Cyriacus remained firm in his decision to resign, and in the ten days that followed he named Ametos as his successor; that done, the Cardinals kept their objections to themselves and expressed their desire see Ametos named the new head of the Church.

"With this, Rome devoted itself to grand Christian festivities, because to the celebration of the presence of Ursula, fiancée of

Ethereus the only heir to the king of England, and the large cortege, they added the naming of the new pontiff. In the middle of the prolonged festivities, the generals of the imperial Roman army began to suspect that there could be a danger lurking in the female army because their presence provoked religious fervor and mass conversions that the nonbelievers in the Roman military did not look favorably upon.

"The men of Maximus and Africanus, generals of the imperial Roman army, infiltrated the troops that accompanied the women in order to discover their plans, and as soon as they knew them and received the order to do so, they quickly ran to advise Julian, the commander-in-chief of the troops of the Huns and a relative of both Maximus and Africanus, of the dates that the legion of Christian women would arrive at Cologne, and of the necessity to kill them.

"But then, an angel appeared to Ethereus, Ursula's prince fiancé, urging him to reunite immediately with the army of women en route to Cologne in order to receive martyrdom with them. Pope Cyriacus had received the same message from a different angel because, although there are no races or families among the angels, each angel is completely different from every other and so Ethereus' angel was as different from Cyriacus' angel as the wave the stone makes in falling into a pool is from the destructive violence of the stormy sea.

"It was precisely because of the angels that Cyriacus felt compelled to accompany the eleven thousand virgins. In the same moment that he received the angel's visit, many others received similar visits and set out to join the cortege of the eleven thousand, including the cardinal priest Vincent; Santiago, the archbishop of Antioch for the past seven years; Mauricio, bishop of Lavicana and uncle of Juliana and of Babilla; Follarius, bishop of Lucca; and Suplicius, bishop of Ravenna. They were not the only ones who had seen the prophesying angels: Marculus, the bishop of Greece, and his niece Constantia, the daughter of the king of Constantinople, also traveled from Greece to Rome desirous to join to the eleven thousand virgins. More people could have received angelic visits, because those celestial beings are innumerable, but only these few were selected. The stars that shine in the dark of night are only like a handful of precious gems compared to the number of angels. The prophet Daniel tells us: *Thousand of thousands ministered to him, and ten thousand times a hundred thousand stood before him.* And Dionysius wrote: *There are many armies blessed with divine intelligence that surpass the weak and limited assemblage of our material numbers.*

"The expedition left Rome. Upon arriving in Cologne, they discovered that the city was besieged by the Huns. The women and their companions had very little time to worry: 'What will become of us? What will we eat? Where will find lodging?' Because the occupiers quickly divided them and fell upon them uttering great riotous and ferocious shrieks and then mercilessly assassinated each and every one of the soldiers in the army of the eleven thousand virgins. All the excitement, status, and beauty were worthless, all were meat to feed the arrows and knives, all was blood to quench the ferocious thirst. The butcher-general in charge of the army was surprised at Ursula's beauty and proposed marriage to her, but when she immediately rejected him he mercilessly assassinated her with a single arrow.

"Even though it all happened so fast, there was more than enough time for them to use their weapons and strength. And the troops that accompanied them—why did they not fight either? If here in Mexico City, Cortés had conquered a fierce and valiant imperial army with fewer than two hundred men, why could the women over there, being so numerous and so well-trained in the martial arts, do nothing against the enemy? Those are the designs of God, whatever happens is governed and felt by his unknowable will. It is useless and foolish to fight against divine decisions. We must admire their glory.

"A certain abbot pleaded with the abbess of Cologne to donate one of the bodies of the virgins, promising that he would place it in a large silver casket and display it for public veneration on the main alter of his church, to which the abbess consented. But, overwhelmed by various duties, the abbot let more than a year pass without making the large silver casket or a place on the main altar for the body of the virgin, who continued patiently sleeping the sleep of the righteous in a wooden coffin on a table in one of the side altars of the temple. One night, during the singing of matins, the body of the martyred virgin left the coffin as if by enchantment, descended from the altar to the floor, approached the main altar, bowed reverently before it, entered the choir enclosure, and to the great surprise of the religious who were watching, silent and stupefied, unable even to breathe, passed in front of them and left the church, losing herself in the darkness of the moonless night.

"As soon as they finished their prayers, the abbot ran to open the lid of the coffin, but found it empty and so he quickly ran to tell the abbess the news. They went together to inspect the place where the virgin had been interred and found her stretched out there, her body whole and her flesh uncorrupted. The abbot renewed his pledge to make a large silver casket to display her in the temple, but the abbess, seeing what had occurred, roundly rejected him.

"Years later, when the abbot, who had continued to venerate the eleven thousand virgins, was near death and while he was repenting for his indolence, he received a visit from an incredibly beautiful virgin.

"—Do you know me? —she asked.

"—Well, no. —he replied.

"—I am one of those eleven thousand virgins to whom you are so devoted and I have come to tell you that if you recite the Lord's Prayer eleven thousand times in our honor, we will come to your side at the moment of your death.

"The abbot then began his prayers and when he was close to finishing the eleven thousand recitations of the Lord's Prayer, he asked to be anointed. In the moment they were anointing him, he said in a loud voice:

"—All of you depart now and make way, the eleven thousand virgins are coming.

"Then in a weak voice, he explained to them about the visitation he had received, after which they all left the cell of the dying man. Outside they heard female footsteps and voices, as well as songs and sounds of swords crossing, but when they reentered the room there was no trace of the visitation and they realized that the abbot had passed away and that his soul had risen to the house of the Lord.

"Here we also have—the Sacristan of San Francisco told us, pointing to the little chest that we had already forgotten about— a bone of Saint Martin of Tours, a piece of Saint Lucia's veil, a bone of Saint Pancratius, the child martyr who said to the emperor, when the latter tried to dissuade him from his faith in our Lord Jesus Christ and before being taken to be martyred on the Via Aureliana, where he was beheaded in the year 287 of our era:

"—It is true that, by my age, I am still a child, but I want you to know that I rely on the help of our Lord Jesus Christ, so the threats you so craftily just made scare me about as much as the paint of that painting on the wall. How can you possibly think that I am going to agree to worship your gods, knowing as I do that they were frauds, that they had incestuous relations with their sisters, that they assassinated their own parents, and that they lived abominable lives? If your slaves did today what your gods did, I am sure, and doubt it not for a single moment, that you would immediately condemn them to death. I am not surprised that you are unashamed to adore gods such as those.

"We also have two bones of the Theban Saints; parts of some bones of the Saints, wrapped in a paper without any other identifications than this; two other bones from the skulls of the heads of the eleven thousand virgins; a bone of Saint Christopher; a bone of Saint Alexander, *filius Sanctae Felicitatis, de pulvribus et ossibus multorun sanctorum*, wrapped in a paper with the same label; a bone of one of the eleven thousand martyrs, whose life I am not going to recount because we have already talked about one of the eleven thousand today. All of these relics have authenticated statements kept here with them as well.

"Without authenticated statements, though we hold them as true, we also have: half a shinbone of Saint Louis of Toulouse, one of our friars, and a piece of the tunic of the same saint; wrapped all together in one paper we have many bones of the companions of our father Saint Francis; as well as part of the jawbone of Saint Barnabas the Apostle (of whom chapter eleven of the book of the *Acts* says: '...they sent Barnabas as far as Antioch. Who, when he was come, and had seen the grace of God, rejoiced: and he exhorted them all with purpose of heart to continue in the Lord. For he was a good man, and full of the Holy Ghost and faith,' Saint Barnabas, the very same who, tied up with a rope around his neck, was dragged out of the city and burned alive behind the wall simply for temporarily blinding a sorcerer who well deserved it for treating with devils; that same Barnabas, now dead, whose bones the heathen Jews picked up and hid in a lead vessel only to throw them into the sea the next day, but his Christian friends managed to get hold of the venerable remains of the apostle and secretly interred them in a cellar until the year 500 of our era when the emperor Zeno, who later converted to Christianity and died a saint, of whom we also have a bone here, knew where the holy remains were because that very Barnabas appeared in his dreams to inform him.

"We also have here a tooth of Saint Lawrence of Rome, a Spaniard, deacon, and a martyr, who was martyred on the order of Decius.

"In the little chest that holds the relics, we also have that with which we honor our church of San Francisco—a piece of stone from the crèche, a bit of dirt that is almost like stone, from where

Christ's cross was raised when they crucified him, and another bit of dirt from the place where Christ was when Saint Peter denounced him. These relics are fundamental to the Church of San Francisco, 'He that shall overcome,'—these are the words of Saint John the Theologian—'I will make him a pillar in the temple of my God; and he shall go out no more, and I will write upon him the name of my God, and the name of the city of my God, the new Jerusalem, which cometh down out of heaven from my God, and my new name. He that hath an ear, let him hear what the Spirit saith to the churches.'

"And now, children, I will return the little chest to its place, to the custody of the Holy Sacrament, the time to pray the vespers has arrived and even here there may come a time when we remember their blessed stories offered to praise the grace of the faith and the generosity of the Lord Jesus Christ so that he will guide us with the light of his holy examples. Amen."

—

As soon as he finished his long story about the relics and the saints, the sacristan began the prayers without modifying the stirring tone of his soft voice and we, filled with the same fervor, repeated the prayers with him. It was here, with the words of the custodian of the relics, that I awoke in some way from my crying, to become, in my own way, part of the student body of Santa Cruz Tlatelolco. The stories of the saints received me. They gave birth to me. Wrapped up in the lives of the saints, as told by the warm voice of the sacristan, was one of my true births. I was born once right there—my birth as a student of the Colegio de Santa Cruz occurred in front of the relics and the sacristan. Received by the custodian of the relics, I entered into the Colegio de la Santa Cruz. I let go of the raft of my tears and sadness, on which I had climbed after leaving home, and I arrived at what I would be from there forward, and for many years. I arrived holding hands with the eleven thousand virgins, with Saint Lawrence and Saint Martin, with Saint Pancratius and Saint Sebastian. In their hands I entered into the Colegio de Santa Cruz when I was ten years old pretending to be twelve and desperately missing a mother, who was not mine in the eyes of others. My sadness changed course among the stigmata and the martyrdom of those men, I was born when I was received by them.

The bone of the eleven thousand entered my flesh to show me the pillar to which I could cling in order to understand my new story. Ursula and her whims, the son of the king of England vanquished before them, Pope Cyriacus renouncing his privileges, the queen of Sicily organizing the army of young women, the angels announcing the coming miracle and saying that it was no more than death, calling eleven thousand virgins to war, the city of Rome celebrating the visit of the legion of beauties, the Huns voraciously awaiting them in Cologne, like dogs hungry for female flesh, to deliver them quickly unto the belly of death, the already dead holy Virgin walking toward her tomb after waiting a year for them to give her body its promised place and later mercifully helping the neglectful abbot through the difficult passage toward death. Saint Martin wiping the shoes of his slave; Saint Sebastian persuading the brothers of the goodness of martyrdom, giving voice to the mute, reducing the pain of the old fathers and of their wives and of their children; in the long speech in which she praised death, Saint Lucia immobile, resisting the strength of oxen and men, even though she was fragile and had the constitution of a woman; and Pancratius, the child martyr—they all received me, they opened their arms to admit me to the Colegio de Santa Cruz, my new home. I exchanged the arms of Mama, and her cuddling and attentions, for the beheaded boy, for the Virgin whose eyes they gouged out, for the bodies oblivious to pain and the pain oblivious to the death of loved ones. In addition to replacing her embrace with this company, a change I scarcely understand as an old man because only a few days before I had brandished my dagger in all my fantasies in order to grow stronger against a fictitious enemy. I, who, in my dreams wore armor daubed with color and adorned with feathers and with my father's shield, upon hearing the stories of the saints, dropped the dagger, stripped my fragile body of the shield and armor, and joined the defenseless masses, the multitude of saints who found heroism in letting themselves be conquered, in receiving wounds, in the palm of martyrdom. In my dreams I had the makings of a hero if according to the code in the stories of the saints, a hero was one who chose torture and martyrdom rather than renouncing his Christian faith, so in my fantasies I was like a saint. From the moment we set off on the road back to the Colegio, returning from the church of San Francisco, I envisioned myself accompanying the eleven thousand virgins along strange roads, I saw large towns receiving us with celebrations, how we trained with our white weapons in beautiful meadows among flowers and stars that shone during the day while the hummingbirds were unafraid of the sound of our daggers and swords that clashed without piercing them in their graceful flight, and then I saw the savage Huns running grotesquely and clumsily toward us, I saw their vileness, I saw that they did not deserve to have us pull out our daggers and swords against them, I saw how they butchered us, how some of the saints did not touch the ground while they approached to stab them, levitating their incorporeal bodies full of so much holiness, I heard the celestial beings accompanying us in our death, wrapped in the music of horns and harps, of flutes and drums, while the Huns became more enraged upon understanding that nothing could hurt us, that killing us gave us pleasure and transported us to the land of well-being and joy...

My dreams changed, bringing me into the arms of the monks. Dreaming about the martyred saints, I could share my spirit with them. My dream, and that of the friars, brushed up against each other, they almost touched. I became one of their most loyal students.

Upon setting the dagger aside and opening the curtain of my tears, in addition to entering into the Colegio de la Santa Cruz and being able to see and understand where I was and what the teachers were teaching me, I had many revelations. It is difficult for me, now old and on the shore of death, to spend time on all of those revelations, some of them because simply remembering them hurts me more than I can bear, others because even though I clearly see the boy affected and touched by them, I do not understand them. I had one revelation that was pure foolishness and that I remember and can put into words: I believed I understood quite well what a sin was. It was not the same as doing something bad, like the Nahuatl word that means sin in that language. Sin was something more. Sin is something that does not necessarily accompany a verb. Sin was a sticky paste, something repugnant, always in pursuit of victims; a paste that absorbs, like the fable that runs through our pueblos says the caves of the serpent princesses do. There, where the serpent lives, the wind sucks at the passerby. There, where she lives with her court, she soaks up, absorbs anyone who goes by, taking him with her. That is the way sin works, it soaks up, absorbs. It is practically impossible not to fall victim.

He who is a victim of, or seized by, sin must repent in order not to be punished. But he cannot procrastinate in doing so; he must do it quickly. Swift horses are necessary to pull or draw it from his soul, so that he denounces the sin before he (who carries it adhered to his soul) receives the corresponding punishment. While it is true that Franciscans are forbidden from riding horses, it is also true that some must train their souls to cross the territory where sin lives, in order to save their souls from irremediable ruin if death strikes unexpectedly.

So, when I realized this, when the fervor was born in me, I saddled and harnessed one thousand horses to my soul. I made myself travel at a blurry, vertiginous pace upon them, simulating being in hurricane, a quick gust of wind that sweeps with it everything it encounters in its path.

The trot of the one thousand saddled horses was imprinted on the path of my soul, to avoid the punishment that the unavoidable arrival of sin invoked, caused my fervor to be only sporadic. For in order for the flashes of fervor to come to me, it was necessary to throw the swiftness of the saddled horses overboard, to move to one side and wrap myself in the serene peace of the illumination, of the nearness to God.

Now I do not advance or recede according to the dictates of my spirit—I am stranded in the immobile prison of my body. I am a prisoner of this bag of bones, of this handful of old flesh. Inside of me, complete immobility does not reign, my soul advances and recedes senselessly, coming and going, expressing its anger in tiny steps: it knows it is caged inside of me, in my body, in my bitter old age, in my imbecilic drooling passivity. When I close my eyes, tears fall that have nothing to do with pain or cold, but rather with my many years. Because I am old, tears run from my eyes, dribble drips from my mouth, I wet myself. I will not say any more, this is what I am: a prisoner in a pile of badly dressed bones, the quagmire in which dreams, faiths, horses, purities, punishments, and sins have stagnated.

Slosos keston de Hernando

The day of the abolition of words arrived. No, I'm not kidding, it arrived. Face it, Lear, it arrived! Today's ceremony made public and formalized the decree for the abolition of language.

Argh…I have to distract myself from my anger and anxiety with something in order to be able to talk about it…

I need to think about something that will distance me from these vile actions, in order to somehow look at them in a way that silent uneasiness and noisy rage won't overwhelm me. I'm looking for something, looking…Here:

Good thing I'm not a cartographer because my maps would turn the Earth into a labyrinth. "We'll take a route that will get us there more quickly," Rosete said as he led us upward, taking us to a high altitude where the atmosphere becomes thin and less resistant to travel. That way we could take bigger strides and move more quickly. Since going up is the quickest way to get somewhere faraway, I would draw the Earth as concave rather than convex. L'Atlàntide would be the heart, the atmosphere would be on the inside, and the surface of the earth would be at the base. Fortunately, I'm not a cartographer; but unfortunately, the way I imagine things is somewhat true. L'Atlàntide is inside the most indomitable, unmentionable, crude, immature, unstable, burning entrails of the Earth. In L'Atlàntide, the burning heat of the Earth turns into a liquidy ice, watery solidity. If what we have supposedly tried to do over the centuries has been to respect and reconstruct nature, in my cartography (as I'm calling it), we would be the monsters underneath the sea searching for the weak points in the continental masses to separate them with monumental sierras and provoke the uprising of the seas against the Earth, the revenge of water against solid, the reigning of shadow over light. L'Atlàntide would not only be the submerged continent, but its inhabitants would be the submergers of continents.

I'll explain everything about the trip with Rosete to La Arena and what happened there.

When we were about to complete our descent, we could see that chaotic winds were blowing across the desert, raising swirls of sand full of trash here and there. I descended toward the Earth in a prone position in order to get a better look. Because the bubble in which the people of L'Atlàntide gather impedes the entrance of the desert squalls, there, inside the bubble, sunlight sparkled on the sand. I saw a circle formed by all thirty-nine inhabitants of L'Atlàntide, minus three—one person, who was in the center, and the two of us were missing from the circle. When the one in the center moved, the others remained immobile; when those in the circle moved, the one in the center was as still as a statue.

Once we were inside the bubble, though Rosete was hurrying me, I stayed a moment longer to look at them from above. The one in the center was Ramón. I went toward the circle, to find a place next to Rosete, who had already found a spot, but Ramón gestured to me and I landed next to him.

—Lear, today is the ceremony for the abolition of language.

—Abolition?

—Most of the community already doesn't use language anymore, and now you won't use it anymore either, or at least not with any of us, because nothing can oblige you...

I interrupted him:

—Ramón, this is too awful. You shouldn't do this—I repeated, facing the circle, looking from one side to the other—you shouldn't do this!

—It's already been decided—added Ramón.

—Maybe, but you shouldn't do it. Don't do it. I beg you. Language...

A booing drowned out my words. A booing, which was accompanied by the most obscene, frightening, imbecilic, and abominable movements of their new communication code.

—Enough! —Ramón yelled, accompanying the word with a kind of movement. The "Enough" was for me, the movement was directed at the others. He didn't even have to turn around to be "understood," because the gestures of their code are so moronic that they look the same from the front as from the back, there is no front or back, or top or bottom to them. The final words he added for me were: "I concede that the gods have been just and that everything is, finally, in order."

"Mutis," I thought, "now they're quoting Mutis," and then I said angrily to myself, "How dare they use my Mutis like that!" I moved away from the center, but didn't quite join the circle. In the saddest and most absolute silence, the people of L'Atlàntide went over all the gestures of their new communication code, which was made up of movements and gesticulations that I describe, impartially, as horrific, completely foolish, and totally meaningless. "Oh divine sound! /

Oh sonorous sound!" Where have you gone, joyful noise, voice, song, ringing of words?

That was the ceremony. Goodbye to those magnificent beings who one day celebrated L'Atlàntide! Now there was nothing but ugliness and the ridiculous, stupidity and obscenity, foolishness and absurdity, idiocy and nonsense. Those quasi-divine beings have become dimwits, dolts, good-for-nothings, simpletons, slow, worthless, idiots, losers, useless, jerks. I want to believe that better times will return someday, just as the famed swallows returned year after year in earlier centuries.

As soon as the review of their code was complete (it didn't take them long to finish on account of its poverty), Ramón gesticulated the grotesque movement that meant "done" or "that's it" in their new code, an obscene movement that lacks grammar. Everyone present, all the people of L'Atlàntide, repeated the gesticulation that didn't exclude any part of the body, in which the mouth, foot, buttocks, hand, and backside are indistinguishable from each other and, overtaken by an inebriated euphoria, they repeated it and repeated it (that's it, that's it), as if abolishing language provoked a joyful intoxication in them.

I didn't move a muscle, of course. I prepared to leave La Arena with my heart constricted with sadness and my body shaking with fear. I didn't want to allow a stupid feeling like panic to grow inside of me as a result of their demonstration of uncontrollable and enormous collective enthusiasm.

As I was leaving, I happened to notice Rosete. While he continued to make the same gesture as everyone else, he did his best to do it with beauty, exchanging some part of their moronic gestures for a certain corporeal harmony. Like when his right hand touched behind his left ear while he opened his legs to do that little jump with his eyes wide open, the determined elegance that was imprinted on all his movements until then only managed to magnify the grotesque absurdity. Rosete only succeeded in making himself more pitiful, and the pain of seeing him like that increased my terror. I quickened my step.

From the corner of his eye, Rosete noticed me watching him and then anxiously hurry away. Because he was calmer than I, he quickly intercepted me and made another gesticulation in my direction:

"Wait,"

and immediately the sign that means

"come,"

followed by

"bath,"

and finally

"oblivion."

Bath of oblivion? This was too much for me. I declined with a slight movement of my head, refusing to repeat the equivalent of their NO that Rosete insisted I imitate after him. Are they going to obliterate Broca's Area now, damaging their brains in order to prevent them from speaking? Will they go further than that, completely altering the structure of their brains, and in doing so eliminating even the slightest possibility that they would have the opportunity to take refuge in language?

I left them to their anomalous ceremony at the point of bathing themselves in oblivion, entering into the most profound darkness of the soul and of the intelligence.

I'll continue with the transcription of Hernando's words. I'm not sure the most appropriate thing to do at a moment like this, but fate put this manuscript in my hands just when the saddest chapter in the life of the people of L'Atlàntide was about to begin. I'm writing and if I stop, the horrible tide of idiocy that is flooding the colony might end with me. I will cling to Hernando.

Slosos keston de Learo

EKFLOROS KESTON DE HERNANDO

We never went back to see the relics kept in the Sanctuary of the Temple of San Francisco in Mexico City. Other relics arrived for this church as well as others, and at all the churches they were received with a pomp and celebration that I do not want to recount here because they have been written about more than once and because they are not relevant to my story. However, I cannot omit the arrival, somewhat recent, of the *Lignum Crucis* that was brought, along with other relics, by Fray Alonso de la Vera Cruz, as recently as 1573, when, after a long stay in Madrid, he arrived with the title of Visitador, a title that he never abused or even used because he did not consider the dispatching of visitadores to be advisable. He had accepted his powerful position so that it would not be given to another who would come to disrupt the province. They gave one part of the relic of the Lignum Crucis to the Cathedral and distributed the other parts to Augustinian temples.

Of course, Fray Alonso de la Vera Cruz, founder of the Colegio de San Pablo, upon which he bestowed a collection of globes, maps, scientific instruments, and a magnificent library, was an avid reader. Every page of each one of the books in the four libraries he founded (the one mentioned here, along with those in the Augustinian convents in Mexico City, Tiripitío, and Tacámbaro) was underlined and annotated by his hand, as he had the habit of examining all the new books that arrived. They say that when the tribunal of the Holy Inquisition had taken Fray Luis de León into custody for some proposals that sounded so bad in Spain, Fray Alonso brought all the weight and deliberation and feeling that the case warranted; and regarding the case of Fray León, Fray Alonso de la Vera Cruz said calmly, *Well truth be told, they can just burn me if they burn him, because I feel the same way.*[28] And now that we have paused on Fray Alonso de la Vera Cruz, I remember with absolute clarity the volumes written in his own hand, and printed by others, that we had in the library of the Colegio: *Speculum Coniugiorum* and *Resolutio dialectica cum textu Aristotelis*, the latter coming from Salamanca and the former from Mexico; but we did not have a copy of the one imprinted by Juan Pablos in 1554, and instead had the imprint of the same, signed by Ioannis Pauli Brissensis in 1556. Nor did we have a copy of his *Recognitio, summularu*, from Juan Pablos in 1554, nor of his *Phisica, speculatio*, also published by Juan Pablos in 1557.

When Fray Alonso de la Vera Cruz left Europe for the first time, he had already been ordained to give mass and his last name was Rodríguez. He had graduated in theology and arts from the University of Salamanca, and in 1535 was the teacher to two sons of the Duque del Infantado and had a decent salary. Fray Francisco de la Cruz selected him, as a cleric and scholar, to teach arts and theology to the religious, and upon arriving in these lands he received the habit in Vera Cruz, from where he took his name, abandoning the Rodríguez of his crib: *Truth be told, they can just burn me if they burn him, because I feel the same way.*

---

28 Hernando put this in quotation marks and is quoting from some document. Estela's note. (Icazbalceta quotes these same words in his *Bibliografía mexicana del siglo XVI*, attributing them to Grijalva, the Augustinian friar chronicler; it might be a line inserted by Estela, rather than something originally written by Hernando. Lear's note).

Speaking of burning, I could do that to these pages of mine. How long has it been since I proposed to tell the history of the Colegio de Santa Cruz? The days pass and pass and turn into months, and I, with my loose tongue, go jumping from line to line without fully entering into my story, without touching the line I am trying to leave here, hidden in a chair, kept safely in Latin so that it will resist time with ink and paper.

Yes, I have already said a couple of words about our daily routine: that I learned Latin correctly, that I received various lessons in Christianity like all my friends, that I studied the trivium (grammar, rhetoric, logic) and the quadrivium with the additional branches of study (the four mathematical arts: arithmetic, geometry, astronomy, and music), and, when they thought they were preparing us to live the lives of friars, I received lectures in the Holy Scriptures and certain advanced courses in religion.

But writing those few lines is the same as saying nothing. In them one does not read what kind of student I was, or that my intelligence and my spirit received a certain kind of training, or that they turned me into a wiser Hernando. These few lines are too far away from me, just as the high white clouds of this windy day are far above my head. I am going to approach the writing of those days with something that they cannot claim did not touch me—the longed-for cilice.

When I heard the gleaming word "cilice" the first few times, it evoked nothing of pain, nothing of the penance that humiliates human pride and purges the body of worldly trappings. I will say that it even gave rise to the opposite. The word "cilice" had a special brilliance that turned the object with its name into something desired by us boys. The first who was selected to use the exalted object was Martín Jacobita, of whom I will speak more later because in addition to the fact that he was my friend for many years, and that we experienced many things together, and that the very sound of his name touches my heart, he was also the rector of the Colegio for a time. Martín Jacobita, native of Tlatelolco, the Barrio of Santa Ana to be precise, was chosen for the cilice—according to my understanding, and I believe that of the others as well—as a reward. Fray Alonso de Molina, our teacher and composer of sermons, called him aside, and, taking him by the shoulder, as if to tell him something very important and very private between the two of them, told Martín that he deserved something for being such a good student and then disappeared with him in the middle of the night, taking him to the friars' apartment to make him the first of the students to learn the secret of the cilice. Much later, Martín Jacobita reappeared with a face that one could say practically glowed. His eyes shined (because he had cried?), his cheeks were flushed bright red, his mouth was half open, and his breathing was abnormal. He was like a fish that was taken out of the water and restrained from wiggling, having been given in exchange for his restraint the promise that he would escape death. Martín did not know how to face us after that important experience, and, running the risk of damaging the prestige earned by his impeccable humility, I will say that he was filled with pride, he boasted, he showed off because he now knew the cilice, while we were nothing but little boys, kids, young ones of little courage, not the least bit brave.

Martín Jacobita had been the chosen one, he was the first of us to use it…What was it? —the rest of us silently wondered, not daring to ask each other…The cilice was a wide belt of bristly hair or an iron chain with sharp spikes that is worn tight on the body and right against the flesh for purposes of mortification. It was used on the waist or arm to lacerate the flesh in order to cultivate the spirit.

Martín Jacobita wore it during the hours of sleep. On waking to sing the matins he disappeared again in the darkness of night, accompanied by Fray Alonso de Molina, to the friars' room above the Church of Santiago, next to the Colegio, where he was stripped of the cilice, although only temporarily: it had already begun to bind with him. Martín now belonged to the "torment," and this lent him an aura of importance, the glow of the chosen one.

The following morning after coming back to sleep and having woken up again for morning prayers, we were sent to the friars' vegetable garden to harvest some necessary items for the meal when Martín Jacobita, without saying a word to me and giving himself some ceremonious importance, showed me the red mark that was similar to a scrape on the elbow or the knee that children get when they are playing with their friends. Though it was beautifully distinct, it was made more beautiful by the knowledge that it had left him *that*, the magnificent and brutal object that the friars had put on *him*, choosing on him out of all of us, because his prayers and studies were exemplary. All of us wanted to have the good fortune to get close to the cruel and holy object, to the cilice. It was like a finger beckoning, it was the mark, the dream, the aspiration…

When it was finally my turn to use the cilice, I was disillusioned.

In spite of all of my hopes, it only provoked a bit of physical pain for me, not so much as to be unbearable, not so little as to be unnoticeable, but its use was not accompanied by any spiritual exaltation, it did not touch me personally, it brought me no closer to the divine Word. Instead, I can say that the effect of the cilice was the opposite, that in no way did its effect resemble what the friars hoped it would provoke, which is what I saw when my companions were wearing it. What did I think the cilice would be? What type of initiation ceremony could I have imagined I would find within its little iron chain links or with its sharp spikes tight against my flesh for mortification purposes that made me yearn so much for this thing that was so perfect and so mundanely covetable?

It never occurred to me that the cilice around my waist or arm would have produced a pain similar to the nopal spine inserted through my tongue, which was something that I feared so much that I renounced the father that I did not have anyway. Was it because I did not have a teacher to show me the benefits of the needle-like spine for my character? At the side of the Franciscans I learned the words of the Saint:

> Know that there are things great and sublime in the
> sight of God, which are often considered vile and
> despicable by men, and there are others considered by
> men as very precious and important, but which God
> looks upon as worthless and contemptible.[29]

---

29 Hernando quotes from Saint Francis of Assisi's *The Admonitions of the Spiritual Exhortations*. Lear's note.

I will respond honestly and say no, in my imagination there was not the slightest bit of wisdom in the cilice, but rather only spiritual abjectness instead. Even in our childish innocence and grace, the coveted cilice was an object of infatuation, of arrogance, or at the very least of immodesty, as the nopal spine piercing the tongue never would have been. With the nopal spine, it was clear that it was a punishment, and nobody, prior to understanding the Christian value of penance, would wish for a punishment. However, in the cilice we did not look for penance because it was an undergarment to make us more important in the eyes of others, so that they would hold us in higher esteem. A misguided value that led us in the wrong direction by infatuating us! Now, I have said that Martín Jacobita was the first chosen, and that I believe I saw something of vanity in the gesture he made in showing me his flesh marked by the cilice, but with the minimum respect to his inestimable person, I have to make clear that he was not to blame for the *passive scandal* that ensued. Martín Jacobita did not bring about the spiritual ruin with his deed or action; we could not blame him for anything he said or did. By coveting it and giving it a mundane value that it completely lacked, we all used the cilice in a way that reduced it and changed its significance. Even though we were children, we did not lack human nature. The Saint said it well:

> The devils did not crucify Him, but you, incited
> by them, have crucified Him, and still crucify Him
> when you delight in vice and sin. Of what then
> can you glory?

And also:

> For if you were so wise and clever that you knew all
> things, and could interpret all languages, and penetrate
> all heavenly mysteries with the greatest clearness, you
> could not glorify in all this, for one demon knows
> more of heavenly, and even of earthly, things than all
> men put together...Again, if you were richer and more
> beautiful than all others, nay, even if you could work
> miracles and put the devils to flight, still all these things
> are contrary to your nature, and in no way belong to
> you. In all this you cannot glorify...[30]

But, I repeat, I never want to speak ill of Martín Jacobita, and
now even less than ever (if that is possible). The only one I want
to bury is myself: I was the one who committed the sin of pride
in using the cilice. It is only in my imagination that I see my
companions as being prideful of the cilice, because I know very
well that it was me. Saying that they demonstrated pride before
penance, I interpret as a sin, but I should not pay attention to
myself. My judgment of them is unreasonable, who am I to judge
souls, especially when they are exquisite souls like Martín Jacobita.
Of my own I can say that I sinned *ab solam voluptatem* (though
it sounds absurd to say that here) with the cilice by egotistically
seeking pleasure rather than penance, which is the natural out-
growth of such a practice. In me, it was an approach to sin even
though I could not recognize it as such as the time because I did
not have the spirit of the Lord:

---

30   In both cases Hernando quotes from Saint Francis of Assisi, again one of
the "Admonitions of his Spiritual Exhortations." Lear's note.

The servant of God may know whether he has the spirit of God, if, when the Lord works some good through him, he is not puffed up in body or mind, knowing that in himself he is contrary to all good, but rather appears viler in his own eyes, and esteems himself more miserable than other men.[31]

Neither the cilice nor the lives of the saints put me on path of true faith. Neither did rhetoric, nor dialectics (*What else is dialectics* —said Saint Augustine—*but skill and expertise in arguing?*), nor mathematics, nor astronomy, nor the prayers. All of this used to help me connect my story to that of the Colegio's, but not my spirit to a real, firm path that would lead me somewhere else that is not this wreck of a legless body. My still-nascent religious fervor needed nourishment that my clumsy spirit could not manage to provide. This was not the fault of the wise Franciscan teachers, but was rather due to my own nature.

Time has almost completely gotten away from me today in quoting of the words of Saint Francis. The cilice could not have been as bad as I have depicted it if evoking it brought the words of Saint Francis to me. I demonstrate every day in the slow manner I narrate my story that my firm legs (yes, they are firmly attached to the floor, I cannot lift them up) do not permit me to keep up with my memories. My mind carries the burden of my body, and it is with the mind that my hand writes. My words lack the spark of faith, as I have said from the beginning; if they came from the voice, they would be written from the depths of the soul, from the deepest part, from the eye of the soul, and my hand would fly, free of my firm legs and completely separate from my body

---

31   Hernando quotes Saint Francis again. Lear's note.

and the bad memories, the rancor, the sacrileges, the jealousies, which I will recount from here on. What I need now are horses that might quicken my mind and hand, pulling us along without driving back the disgraceful condition of the land, so that the heat will not tire them and they will not sink into a deep, dark layer of mud. These horses, and the whips I will have to use to make them run as quickly as my thoughts (my mind is the only part of me that still runs, I feel that even my blood stagnates, gets tired of circulating through this old body), will save quill, paper, and ink once I finish using them for my purposes here. I do not have recourse to the eye of the soul because the cilice was the door through which to enter the bad memories.

I will jump from one to the other until the weight of the years summons the end of my life. But before falling into bad memories, I will note one good one. It was not a beatific state. Since I do not belong to the perfect ones, I will say that my soul, stripped of its will, took the unitive path. Once again, what at first glance does not have the appearance of truth really was true.

Slosos keston de Hernando

EKFLOROS KESTON DE LEARO

When, one afternoon, I saw a member of my community crouching on all fours drinking murky water from a stagnant pond in a desolate spot on the surface of the earth, I decided not to write one more word about L'Atlàntide until they abandon their foolishness. I made the decision sadly, and with a feeling of defeat, of helplessness. I said to myself: "I won't write about what happens here and we'll pretend it's not happening. I'll keep acting like everyone from L'Atlàntide drinks the pure water that falls from our colony's walls of air into babbling brooks." But I can't stop writing. I must do it. I can't avoid it.

I had been working on the transcription of Hernando for a bit (I'm having difficulty and making slow progress) when I heard a commotion in the distance that seemed strange to me. I closed the *kesto* and went to see where the unidentifiable noises were coming from.

I approached. What seemed to me from a distance to be a commotion were sounds similar to those I believe a herd of pigs would make: nasal and chest sounds, sounds that don't come from the palate, the teeth, or the tongue. On a barren, sandy mountaintop was a cross, and on the cross a man, and at his feet a group of my people were cursing him. I moved closer. The one on the cross was the one I once christened Ulises. Some of them were whipping him with a rope, others were spitting at him, all of them were shouting at him, if I can call that abominable screeching shouting. There were fourteen or fifteen playing that "game."

Suddenly, they all burst out laughing. They took him down from the cross on which they had tied him, someone massaged his legs, another his arms, and all of them kept laughing, laughing their heads off. Caspa threw herself on the ground because she couldn't control her body for laughing. The very same Ulises joined her. In a few seconds everyone was on the ground on their backs, with their hands on their bellies, laughing so hard they were crying.

I dropped down to where they were and asked in their stupid code something more or less the equivalent of "What's going on?" or "What are you all up to?" to which Jeremías answered with the equivalent of "Nothing."

—What were you doing?

This he couldn't understand.

—And the cross? —I made myself understood by pointing to where it had been and making the shape with my fingers.

They stopped laughing and looked over there and I did the same. There wasn't anything there. The cross wasn't there anymore. They got up and left me, walking along the paths of the unfinished flower garden that was just on the other side of the barren hill.

I stayed on the mountain. I looked for traces of the cross. There were clear marks in the sand. Someone had planted a post there. I searched for the cross with my eyes, but there was nothing left of it, not a splinter. And I mean not even splinter.

I looked some more. I couldn't find it anywhere. I walked in the garden, looking for it, but there was nothing there except their artificial flowers—flowers with symmetrical petals on top of a stem coming out of the ground—and orderly paths. They had made the cross disappear with their laughter.

I came back here. I'm writing this without commentary. Tomorrow I'll go back to my Hernando and Estela. I have to forget what's happening in L'Atlàntide.

Slosos keston de Learo

The celebration on the day of my birth was not for me. My father was not mine. I got my dagger by stealing it, and though it is more mine and more of a dagger because I could see it with the eyes of my imagination, nobody else would ever have been able to see it with their physical eyes. My Tezcoco was not mine because I was Tlatelolca. Tlatelolco, my homeland, did not belong to me. I became one of the students of the Colegio with a name that was not mine; another—who was not me—had been selected for that spot, I took the place of someone who had nothing to do with me. My Mama was taken away from me entirely; they did not know that the one they believed to be my mother was not mine. My first memorable sin among the Franciscans was not committed by my body, even though the gesture might have made it appear that I deserved the punishment. My first corporeal penance was nothing more than an act of arrogance and conceit. What a succession of "not mines" were assigned to my awkward life in those first years! I've enumerated them to clear them from this space if only momentarily, since unfortunately we will eventually come across more "not mines."

One night, the flickering light of the lamp that Miguel, our guardian, never extinguished, the one that was always—as I have said—the companion to our sleep, and the one that it took me a long time to get used to and be able to fall asleep with, was agitated by a moving body. Like that flickering flame, in my sleep

I felt the subtle movement of the air caused by someone who displaced it and I woke up not understanding what was happening. My sleep has always been fragile; it scampers about instead of resting on warm sand like most mortals' sleep. I sleep fitfully, unable to find an even rhythm. During the night, I am a dog chasing prey. If I could remember my dreams, I would say that, as a dog, I chase what I fear as a person.

The flame moved. The change in the lamplight alerted me, abruptly bringing me out of sleep, and I opened my eyes. Fray Pedro was walking toward me. He was carrying the Vulgate in his hands, opened wide, and he was crying. He moved his lips, but I could not hear what he was saying. He was reciting the passages from memory and his eyes did not see the lines he fervently held in his palms.

Noticing me watch him, he spoke to me. His voice made its way to his lips.

—The kingdom of God cometh not with observation. Neither shall they say: Behold here, or behold there. For lo, the kingdom of God is within you.

He stopped speaking, came to me, and knelt by the side of my mat where he began to speak again.

—For as the lightening that lighteneth from under heaven, shineth unto the parts that are under heaven, so shall the Son of man be in his day.

He paused briefly to shake me benevolently by the shoulders, as if to shake me completely from my sleep, or my ignorance, and he continued:

—And the seventh angel sounded the trumpet: and there were

great voices in heaven, saying: "The kingdom of this world is become our Lord's and his Christ's, and he shall reign for ever and ever."

That said, he put his index finger on my nose and looked me in the eyes. His own eyes shone with the radiance of candles. I perceived with complete clarity that something—something that was not him—was burning inside of him. An otherworldly fire inhabited his body.

I did not dare move my nose away from his exalted finger because it seemed even his finger was lit by whatever was hiding inside of him. He seemed hot; I could feel the heat against my skin as he fervently continued reading the pages of the book. He pinched my nose so hard that the pulsating blood I felt could have been his or mine.

At that moment, Miguel rang the bell to wake us up for matins. That is the only thing that could explain his absence, because he was always there, close to us, a protective guard watching over our sleep and our chastity. At the sound of the bell, Fray Pedro let go of me, and repeating the *genus angelicum* several times, took two hops away from my little mat. From that position, he urged my companions to get up promptly. And that is what we did, all of us. While we were singing the matins, I could not shake the feeling of his finger on my nose, or seeing him gazing into my eyes, or hearing the sound of his voice in my ears, and those three sensations guided me along a path, where I seemed to weigh nothing, a dark path that conformed to the direction I was going, that took shape as the prayer advanced—it became brighter and brighter until it blinded me. Near the end, I lost consciousness, I was not aware of myself.

I could hear my voice off in the distance, singing, but I did not know where I was. The perfect and powerful light to which I had arrived kept me from seeing. It seemed I had reached the point at which one arrives without oneself, and a profound joyful peace ran through my spirit as I was singing the matins. Nevertheless, even though I was completely given over to that singular sensation that had left me blind and self-less, I perceived a certain complicity in my singing companions' tone, and though for a moment I sensed a cowardly fear approaching me from a few steps away, the feeling completely disappeared. As we were finishing the prayers, I began to leave the unitive path to follow the illuminative way. When I saw Fray Pedro's face, I was able to ascertain that I was flying (in a manner of speaking), that we were all flying, that even when I was in the most complete solitude, or in the most perfect form of solitude, I was also part of everyone and everyone was part of me (I am not sure how to explain this), and we shared a spiritual closeness in the absolute dissolution of our bodies. And if I could see it in Fray Pedro's face—in his eyes, in his features, in his entire face—it is because that is the one place the footprint of mystery leaves its mark. Imprinted on his face was the truth that walking in faith led to the possibility of bodiless flight.

I could keep writing about this here, but anyone who has not previously experienced what I am talking about will not be able to comprehend it. Time, which will accompany the archiving of these pages, will add its own explanations, in its own language. By then perhaps everyone will have seen the invisible bodies of the angels and will have conversed with them, by then perhaps there will be no one left who does not know faith in the Lord Jesus Christ.

But they will be unable to explain it in Latin, or in Nahuatl, or in Castilian, or in Portuguese and I fear that time will not be able to express what I am writing here either and that the angels will continue on their ethereal path without stopping to speak to humans.

I did not open my eyes solely with the object of gazing into his face. I felt as if the floor was falling out from under me, and I confirmed that fact when I saw it beneath my feet. Martín Jacobita was beside me and I touched his hand to get his attention and feel some sense of relief in the delicate flame that enveloped me, burning me, and painfully turning me into exquisite smoke. As soon as I touched his hand, I knew that it was not his skin that I was touching, that it was not dust or flesh, but rather the spirit flowering, being delivered to me. And when Martín turned his eyes (in which I was trying to find some relief) to me, although I did find both his eyes and relief, in the refreshing sense, they inflamed me, they stirred up more smoke, they were air that enhanced the painful and exquisite, the fearsome and comforting certainty that even though we were of the world, we had cut all ties with the things of this century.

That was what it was to attain death, the perfection of death. I went through the door. I went further, beyond myself. I quit being who I had been, who I was, who I am.

How did I fall back into the incomplete and blind death of life? How did I return from the paradise of the intuitive and illuminative path, to the blind eyes of mortals? Who was the traitor bringing me back to myself? The cell of life extended its bars in front of us and the rapture, the exposure, the nakedness, the swoon, the exaltation—*all that we had experienced*—disappeared.

And for the first time in many days, upon finding myself returned to myself, imprisoned, I slept like a log the entire night.

During that first transcendence (how long it might have lasted, I do not know, we did not have clocks there), I did not sleep at all. We did not sleep and there were only sacred foods to eat. No cornflour, potatoes, *chiles mosquito*, onions, or tomatoes passed our lips, but instead a balm made of something outside of the spirit nourished us, and that, upon passing our lips, awoke the hummingbird that had approached its flower, the bee, the earthworm, the ant, and the mystery of life and the Word. The foods were also impregnated with the flowing drop of life. In one moment (though there was no time where we were, there is in my memories), Fray Pedro, exalted, took the corn tortilla and made it fly from one hand to the other and then, looking toward heaven, put it on his face, and then holding it like a veil over his face, he started to eat it from its center, in small bites, laughing softly.

My feet did not touch the floor; I was flying without wings, floating. My body—while it was in flames—was as cold as a cloud and thin as vapor. Vapor, it was vapor and made of vapor, I looked into the eyes of Fray Pedro, who no longer had the veil of corn on his face, and I saw that he too was floating, liberated from the weight of his flesh, and realized his body was also vapor, and he saw that mine was as well. A strange wave of joy flooded us at the same time. I do not remember exactly what terms I used to ask him if he felt the same thing I did. He answered me in the infinite purity of his shining gaze (his eyes were like those of someone who had been asleep, then opened his eyelids and recounted, for a companion watching over him, the details of his dream). His voice and his eyes were one:

—That is what it is like, Hernando; that is what it is like to experience divine love.

Were the others feeling the same thing? It seems to me they were. The branch of an old tree creaked repeatedly in the wind, it sounded like a door opening, closing, opening…It was the door to heaven that was opening for us, that had opened. We were, in fact, on that side. Without leaving this one, we had left it.

The fervor that we—Martín Jacobita and I—manifested convinced the friars that we were the two chosen to follow in their footsteps. They chose Martín Jacobita and me to take the path to ordination. We shared most of the lessons with our companions in the Colegio, but we stopped sleeping with them. We were taken to the friars' rooms. We slept with them above the church and we helped them with the work that friars do, like seeing to the construction of the convent, taking care of the books in the library, accompanying them to special events. Having abandoned my body and my intellect to devote myself to the contemplation of the supreme good, having completely put myself aside so that I might be consumed and made vapor of the divine good, allowed me to reconcile that part of my own life with the one that capricious fate had chosen for me. I did not impersonate anyone when I dressed in the habit of the Franciscans. But this exact point of unique congruence, this one in which I was the same as my story, this one that defeated the destiny of impersonations and the "not-mines" to which I seemed to be condemned, this one was impossible.

We should have realized from the beginning that the dream of ordination was not possible. We did not. We did not think badly of anyone. We ignored envy; we did not want to admit man's enslavement of others. We plugged our ears with wax to avoid hearing the chant of a few horrific, ghastly creatures telling us the truth:

> "This will not be possible."
> "This will not be possible."
> "Cursed be the man that trusteth in man," in the words of Jeremiah.

Slosos keston de Hernando

EKFLOROS KESTON DE LEARO

I was in the midst of transcribing Hernando when, out of nowhere, Ramón suddenly appeared next to me as if he had come out of a hole in the earth. He was different from the last time I saw him, so different that he didn't seem to be himself, not only because he arrived wrapped in a grayish, stiff cloth that formed rough folds around his body, distorting him at each fold, but also because everything on his face, which was uncovered, seemed to be in a different place. I didn't understand what was happening to him. I had time to observe him carefully, though, because he was mimicking me; he was doing what I was doing, but more. I was looking at him and he was devouring me. I was visually examining him and he was consuming me. I was analyzing him and he was cutting me into pieces. Before the people of L'Atlàntide abandoned language, this would have been enough for me scream to high heaven and take off—insulted, humiliated, infuriated. But under current circumstances, his gaze (an atrocious, unbearable, disgusting thing) was the least of it.

While he was doing that to me with his eyes, I examined him carefully with my own eyes. What appeared to be so different about him? A mass protruded farther than all the other folds on his belly. Since there was no distance between us at all while he performed that horrific exercise with his eyes, I had the audacity to touch him, to see what he had under the largest bulge of cloth over his belly. It was just him. I discovered what had changed so much—he had fleshed out, his body was *fat*.

What had he done to himself? I'm not going to say yet what he did when I touched him, because before he did it (slowly, like a heavy bundle), a light bulb went off in my head. "Ramón eats flesh," I thought. "That's why he's fat, that's why his skin looks like that—he eats flesh." The idea disgusted me, of course, and what I didn't have time to do was to measure the consequences, or of what he *did* in response to my examination. But what I did do in that instant was perceive his odor, and he smelled completely different than normal. The disgusting thing he did—in response to my audacity to touch his belly (yes, a member of our community has a potbelly, a real paunch)—was that he (or what was left of Ramón) stuck out his mouth (he doesn't actually have lips anymore) and shook it in front of my mouth, trying to give me an artful kiss, one I didn't want to receive. After looking at me with the idiotic aggression of his poor imitation of amorous desire, Ramón tried to kiss me by force. Although force, or what we consider to be force, is an exaggeration, because he didn't have any strength left. Paunchy, bloated from eating an excess of who knows what strange things (I have no evidence that he eats flesh), Ramón had much less strength. He was like an animal at risk of extinction, debilitated, diminished, giving his last and feeble fight to stick his dick into a female. But the comparison isn't valid because an animal wouldn't be capable of that despicable, offensive, abusive look.

Of course I didn't let myself be kissed, or touched, by Ramón. I blew at him with all the force in my lungs and that was enough to push him backward, tumble him to the floor, and, as if he had forgotten that he had seen me and thought he desired me, he picked himself up with difficulty, wrapped himself back up in the cloth and started walking off somewhere else.

I don't think my intuition that he eats flesh was wrong. I think he does eat flesh. What flesh is out there that someone might eat? Obviously not any of the people of our colony, that doesn't even seem possible. But I do know what flesh is out there—the flesh of Caspa's children. They are eating children. How horrible, they're a bunch of pigs. My divine companions—who achieved a state of perfection that exceeded the human dream—who, upon erasing words from their lives, have turned into pigs that consume the flesh of dead babies.

Slosos keston de Learo

EKFLOROS KESTON DE HERNANDO

How is it that I landed here—where the fire of faith does not burn—if I was already a burning ember on the illuminative path? And, if it was already written that I was going to fall, how is it that I would not remain on the purgative path of novices? Who was any more deserving of the tireless yearning for God? Why are my words those of regret and demonstrative of loss, rather than ones that dream of recovering that magnificent vision, of reaching even for just one moment that beatific state?

Because all the rage of these latitudes was unleashed against us. We climbed Jacob's ladder in the opposite direction—we descended to the things of the world when a brutal attack against the Franciscans and their work disrupted the order of the Colegio de la Santa Cruz.

The Colegio de Santa Cruz had been operating officially for three years, and the Franciscans had been teaching there almost four years, when Carlos Ometochtzin (called Yoyontzin y Mendoza in the Castilian language)—el Chichimecatécotl, which is the title given to the lords of Tezcoco, the grandson of the sage and poet Netzahualcóyotl, son of the severe and prudent Netzahualpilli, and nephew of Talchachi—was accused of heresy, among other things. His accusation was like a ball of dry grass burning in the courtyard of the Colegio and in the center of my heart for two different reasons. The first, which has to do with the Colegio, was because none among our enemies forgot that Don Carlos had been educated by the Franciscans and, in their eyes, accusing him turned that malicious warning—"It is very good for them to know the doctrine, but reading and writing is as dangerous as the devil"—into wisdom. And in my heart because they will remember that I replaced the accused, Don Carlos, at the Colegio de Tlatelolco in the name of my village, Tezcoco, and in the name of the son of the other "Don" Hernando. It is true that he did not take as good care of their language as he should have, and maybe that is why they launched their savage attack against him, or maybe it was because of a woman he took who belonged to another, or because he carefully managed what belonged to him, or because (and this is what I believe) he was good, wise, prudent (less so in his words), and a jokester. Moreover, the matter, which smelled of the devil's smoke, upset the order in my heart because I thought: "They brought one Tezcocan here to replace another Tezcocan, and even though I am not the one who should have been the student of these Franciscans, with my luck it would fall to me to replace the first in whatever happens next." But I will set aside my own fears to recount the sad business of Carlos Ometochtzin.

Even though from a distance, and at first glance, it might seem absurd, the accusation was a pretext to launch an attack against Bishop Zumárraga. Accusing Don Carlos, who had been a student of the Franciscans, meant accusing Fray Juan Zumárraga. To blame a former student of his order—when he had insisted on the harmlessness of educating the Indians, when he had said himself that he was in favor of Indian studies and especially of the maintenance and improvement of the level of education at the Colegio de Santa Cruz—was to attack him. It was for this reason that Bishop Zumárraga decided to listen to the recriminations without defending

Don Carlos before he took the enemies' side completely and cruelly attacked Don Carlos himself while pretending to pursue fairness and justice, loyalty to the Crown, and fidelity to the word of Christ. What he was trying to do was to save the work of the Franciscans from attack and save his own skin. By turning himself into an accuser, he was evading the accusation that was directed against him, the Franciscans, and their work. Poor Don Carlos Ometochtzin was martyred to save the Franciscans from this attack. Though Don Carlos cannot be called "poor" because it does not fit his temperament, his intelligence, his beauty, or his charm. Allied with those envious of him, those opposed to the Franciscans, and the haters of the Indians, Zumárraga launched a cruel attack on Don Carlos, who was then a lord of Tezcoco.

Those who testified against Don Carlos might have spoken some truths, but there is no doubt that they told some lies, like the one about the son they attributed to him. They said that Don Carlos's "son" was between ten and eleven years old and that he did not know how to make the sign of the cross or know anything of the Christian Doctrine because the accused had been opposed to teaching him. But this child could not be his son because of simple common sense—at the time of trial, Don Carlos was little more than twenty years old, and this is an exaggeration because I cannot even prove twenty. As much as he might have been in a hurry, I do not believe that Mother Nature would have permitted him to father a child at seven years of age.

During Lent, someone accused the good and wise Don Carlos of digging up the remains of terrible practices from the base of one of the crosses in the pueblo of Chiautla in Tezcoco.

The authorities had the bases of the crosses dug up and found things related to sacrifices: papers with blood, flint in the shape of sacrificial knives for extracting hearts, little pebbles and different kinds of beads, including some copal, and three or four paper mats and other kinds of mantillas, as well as figures of idols carved in the rocks. If they were there under the crosses or whether they were put there when they dug around the bases of the crosses, this we will never know, but their discovery, whether it was real or fake, led to the trial against Don Carlos Ometochtzin, el Chichimecatécotl.

Since I had set aside my fears to explain what this situation was about, I am going to return to them. It is not at all pleasant to remember the injustice of so many people launching a savage attack against the good and wise Don Carlos Ometochtzin simply because they hated him. It is true that a cowardly fear caused me to practically feel the flames of their cruel bonfire, but it was a brave fear when I saw the face of their viciousness against the Indians and against whatever was wholesome and good in them. In a way, I identified with him; I was him. In a way, I achieved martyrdom through his punishment, but it was a martyrdom that went against martyrological rhetoric, one that shattered the principles because it was not burnt at the stake or allowed to fall from everything the Christians—not the heretics—had built. The angels did not come to see him die, nor did he levitate before being burned. He was tortured, beaten, and abused, and his torturers, batterers, and abusers had holy words on their lips. Inasmuch as I saw this and knew it, something I could not completely accept galled me, and my child's soul did not know that I was tasting, for the first time, the revenge and envy that are so abundant in these lands.

I will recount what they said against him to convince Archbishop Zumárraga to take him to the bonfire. Gerónimo de Pomar testified that there were idols in a house called Tecuancale (that nobody was living in), and that Talchachi, Don Carlos's uncle, had put them there and that they made up part of the very walls, and that the vacant house was furnished with mats and wicker and leather chairs, and that there was a fire in there every night because some people met there to worship their idols or *chalchuyes*.

Lorenzo Mixcoatlaylotla testified that it was seventeen years ago that Tlachachi, Don Carlos's uncle, had put the idols in the house, but that he only put them there as a joke and he used them only because they were stone. No one paid any attention to him, but at the end of the trial they made him walk through the procession of flagellants, hitting himself, not for reasons of faith and in order to achieve a true purity in his spirit, but instead to make him punish himself for having taken the wrong side.

Doña María, widow of Don Pedro, former governor of Tezcoco, testified that one night when she was sleeping with the other women, she heard footsteps in the bedroom, and that she ordered one of the Indian women who was next to her to light an ocote pine torch because she heard footsteps. As soon as there was light, she saw Don Carlos. No one knows how he got in there unless he was helped by the devil. And it was not the first time that Don Carlos had bothered her even though she was his niece, because he wanted to make her his wife even though he already had one. That time, they removed him from her room by pushing and shoving him.

There were two or three testimonies that destroyed him. One of those was that of Melchor Ixiptlatzin, that childhood friend of mine who was taking such poor care of the mules the day the Franciscans came to Tezcoco to pick up the one they thought I was, the one whose place I took. Melchor Ixiptlatzin testified out of hate and malice and enmity. If, on the day the Franciscans took me from Tezcoco, Melchor had said, "Carlos Ometochtzin, you only wish you were a piece of shit, because that's better than what you really are," now he smeared him with shit by the handful. I later discovered that his contempt for Ometochtzin came from his family, because years ago his mother had taken Don Carlos's father to court—I am not sure for what household affairs, what she wanted that he did not want to give her—though nobody testified to this at the time of the trial. I did let Sahagún know, though not in front of the other boys. Don Carlos's situation was so delicate that it even gave pause to a Tezcocan. I told him when we were alone and he looked at me with such sadness in his eyes and said: "Nothing can be done, nothing can be done, what a shame, it is human nature." Then, days later, when I insisted that we had to do something, that we could not let someone so envious cruelly attack him, Fray Bernardino said to me:

—Hijo, you are too young to understand, but it is more complicated than you imagine. Maybe it is entirely true that this boy Melchor testified against him because he does not like him, but maybe it is not. How can we know? What I do know is true, because I witnessed it with my own eyes and cannot deny it, is that the one time that the Franciscan brothers, finding ourselves in a predicament, appealed to his generosity so that he might help us with some small thing, given that he was the brother of the lord of Tezcoco and because he had been educated by those of our order, his only response to us was mockery and that he did not have the heart to convey our message, though I do not know precisely what that might be. I do not think Carlos has an evil heart. Why would I need to go around saying that he does if I cannot prove it? But what I do know is that he does not have much respect for the Franciscans who educated him; that we are not worthy of his respect does not have to matter to us, but considering that he paid us with such poor currency, what can you expect from a young man like that? We can expect that his impetuous actions have caused him to make more enemies than those he could have earned by being more prudent, cautious, or generous.

I do not know if, over the years, Carlos was generous or cautious or prudent, but he was a handsome and arrogant young man of seventeen, protected by his parents, educated by the Franciscans, who had not thought, at that point, of malice or of the foolish powers of envy and vengeance.

Melchor was the one who testified that when Don Carlos went to visit his sister in the pueblo of Chiconabtla—also in Tezcoco, where she is the wife of the cacique of the pueblo—he observed the proceedings ordered by the provincial padre because many people had died because there was no water due to a lack of rain. After the proceedings, Don Carlos said, in front of Don Alonso, his brother-in-law, and Don Cristóbal and two other noblemen of Tezcoco:

"You will be sorry. What are you doing with these Indians, what are you doing, do you think you are doing something...do you want to make these people believe what the padres preach and say? You are being deceived; what the friars do, it is their job to do, but it is meaningless. What are the things of God?

They are nothing: fortunately we discovered what we have, what was written by our ancestors: I will have you know that my father and my grandfather were great prophets, and they said many things of the past and for the future, and neither one said anything of this, and if any of this were true, what you and others say of this doctrine, they would have said it, as they said many other things, and this Christian Doctrine is nothing, and what the friars say is not perfect: there is more than what the Viceroy and the Bishop and the friars say, all of it matters little and it is nothing, except that you and others praise it and authorize it and build it up with so many words, and what I am saying I know better than you because you are a boy; this is why you should let go of those things that are in vain, and do not continue with this, I tell you as an uncle to his nephew, or make the Indians believe what the friars say, they are doing their job, but not because what they say is true, that is why you should stop and not continue with it, instead see to your house and take care of your hacienda."[32]

Even his own wife, Doña María, testified against him. According her, Don Carlos had a mistress named Doña Inés, and some one hundred and forty days ago, more or less, Don Carlos, finding himself ill, had this Doña Inés brought to his house, and he had her in his bedroom with him some days, and Doña Inés was forced to make them food and to serve them, and when he was better he took her back to her house, and, to make him look worse in the eyes of the judge, she said that Doña Inés was Don Carlos's niece, although, again, these stories do not sit well with me, because Doña Inés was the same age as the accused.

---

32   In Spanish in the original. Estela's note.

When they asked Doña María if her marriage to Don Carlos had been good, she replied that they had been happily married for the first two years, but that from then until now she said Don Carlos had been abusive to her; that she did not know anything about idols, or that he sacrificed to them, or that he venerated them.

The false Franciscan priest, Francisco, the man to whom his mother had been married by the Franciscans, Don Francisco Maldonado, native of Chiconabtal, returned to testify against him and said—among many other things, all to make him look bad—that Don Carlos had said: "Notice that the friars and clerics all have their own way of penance: the friars of San Francisco have one form of doctrine and way of life, and manner of dress, and form of prayer; and those of Saint Augustine have another way; and those of Saint Dominic have another; and the priests have another, as we all see, and likewise among those who took care of our gods: those from Mexico had a manner of dress, and a form of praying, and offering, and that is the way the friars and the clerics do it, none of them agree with the other; we follow what our ancestors followed, and in the way they lived, we live, and this has to be understood like this…each one willingly follows the law they want and the customs and the ceremonies…

Do not do what the Viceroy and the Bishop or the Provincial tell you to do, or continue to name them, I too was raised in the church and the house of God like you, but I do not live and do like you: what more do you want? Do you not fear and obey those of Chiconabtla? Do you not have food and drink? What more do you want? Why do you go around saying what you are saying?…

Brother, what do women and wine do to men? Is it by chance the Christians do not have many women and they get inebriated and the religious fathers cannot prevent it? We eat and drink and enjoy ourselves, and become inebriated like we used to. See what you are, sir; and you, nephew Francisco, see that you receive and obey my words...the land is ours and belongs to us...None of those liars have reached our heights, nor are they with us, nor do they join with those who obey and follow our enemies..." [33] Needless to say or imagine how these words fell on the ears of the judge, because it appears to be seditious, an insurrection against the king. This is what the real or fake idols found at the foot of the crosses led to.

The men who worked for him, those who were in his service, those who owed him loyalty also testified against him. With each testimony they invented more sins, with a speed that no soul, not even the most sinful, could have committed in real life. They made Don Carlos an assassin, they said he carried out human sacrifices, they made him irritable when he was not, they filled him with vices and sins of the flesh and the spirit; people who in other times called themselves his friends and in-laws, the noble lords of his kingdom, were testifying against him...And for what? That spittle that the Indian Melchor spat on the ground upon seeing him when we were children and we ran into him makes me question whether there was an inch of truth in all he spat then. Cristóbal, resident of Chicnautla, said that Don Carlos said: "I am lord of Tezcoco, and there is Yoanizi, lord of Mexico, and there is my nephew Tezapili, who is lord of Tacuba; and we have not allowed

---

33   In Spanish in the original. Estela's Note.

anyone to come between us or be our equals. After we are dead it
might well be, but right now we are here and this land is ours and
our grandfathers and our ancestors left it to us: brother Francisco,
what are you doing, what do you want to do, do you perchance
want to be a priest? Are those priests our relatives or were they
born among us? If I saw that my fathers and ancestors were in
agreement with this law of God, perchance I would keep it and
respect it. But, brothers, we keep and hold what our ancestors held
and kept, and we give ourselves to pleasure and have our women
as our fathers had them..."[34]

If he said it like that, he had more than one reason to say it,
and his words do not sound foolish, but the Indian in front of the
judge of the Inquisition does sound foolish in repeating them.
Why would they go in front of the judges and say that? Were they
perhaps afraid that the judges would also accuse them of the sins
mounted against Don Carlos? Did they want to obtain some favor
from the Bishop, and in attacking Don Carlos were they hoping
to please him? Some were forced to testify by the firm persuasion
of the Viceroy's guards, others were pushed by their wives, some
had other motives to testify, others had been given money to
testify; the teeth of one were chattering out of fear while he was
talking; another did not show it, except that in squinting his little
eyes between sentences he seemed about to laugh at the slightest
provocation and said, by the way, that he did not find it easy...
They testified without understanding that their words, instead of
saving them, would come back against them over time. They were
Indians, and their blows would come back against the Indians.

---

34   In Spanish in the original. Estela's note.

They wanted to protect themselves from the Hispanics by striking at each other. Envy, that dark bird that likes to live in these lands, persuaded them, with soft words, to serve her.

Carlos Ometochtzin was condemned to be burned at the stake. Contrary to what Zumárraga hoped to achieve with his sacrifice, the enemies of the Colegio de Santa Cruz grew stronger. They sharpened the claws of their souls. The Franciscans also lost. It is true that nobody accused Fray Juan of being millenarian or seditious again, but instead they went at the Indians harder, and due to having gone too far in their punishment, a short time later the order to stop judging the Indians in the Inquisition arrived, in the fear that if an Indian burning were carried out it would make even Emperor Charles feel guilty during his long meditations on death.

Slosos keston de Hernando

EKFLOROS KESTON DE LEARO

Even though I didn't sleep well at all again last night, I was able to sleep deeply this morning. I was already late when I found Rosete at the entrance to my room, turning slowly around in circles like a demented person. What was he doing?

—Why are you turning around in circles, Rosete?

He didn't answer me, but I answered myself. I remembered that in their code this movement, the one that repeatedly turns slowly around, means: "I came to tell you."

But who came? Rosete hadn't come in to see me. He was stranded there where nobody would have found him and where I came across him by chance because I was leaving so much later than usual. And to say what? Even though I almost bumped into him, he didn't say anything when he saw me, aside from stupidly turning around and around in circles, his body bent to one side, his hand hanging, and the other one half bent, as if he was afflicted by some kind of awful muscular disease.

His repetitive motion exasperated me. I tried to stop him, first with my voice ("Stop it, Rosete, stand still!"), then I used all of my strength—both of my arms, my core, my legs, my whole body— to keep him still so that he would stop because the inertia of his stupidity had trapped him in the movement.

—What did you come to tell me?

Nothing. He didn't say anything. I looked into his eyes.

That beautiful pair of sparkling and teasing eyes looked dull, dead.

There used to be so much life in his eyes, just like his words used to create waves in the air.

—What's wrong, Rosete? Are you sad?

Once again he didn't answer. He had remained just as I had left him, suspended in his stupid movement. The once-animated Rosete had turned into a mannequin, but not in a way that had preserved his radiant appearance. My graceful Rosete was no more than a preternatural mannequin. His skin looked dried out, and here and there he had some pinkish spots that seemed to be caused by irritation or neglect. I opened his mouth without any resistance from him. Not like he was a slave (he couldn't understand my words because he couldn't hear them), it was more like he had just turned into a puppet. The mucous membrane inside his mouth was split in countless places. On the inside wall of the right cheek (the one with the biggest red spot) was a huge, open sore that had almost perforated the flesh.

I became enraged. Why was he hurting himself like this? Yes, this really was my business, it concerned me, why injure something that I love, something that also belongs to me? Yes, Rosete is mine; he is part of me. I've known him all my life, he's part of my childhood, my being, my personal memory, in a way that the mother and father I don't have could be only artificially. And furthermore Rosete is handsome. Or he *was* handsome.

—You haven't used substance 234 to absorb the radiation. You go out, go down to the Earth, and you don't protect yourself. What are you thinking? —Again, no response.

I shook him forcefully, roughly pulling each arm, to the point that I could have even hurt him. Nothing. He didn't react.

He didn't hear, didn't feel, didn't notice me, didn't know I was right beside him. He probably wasn't even there, he was someplace else, maybe…

I set aside my unproductive rage.

—Doesn't it hurt, Rosete? —I asked, softening the tone of my voice. But, to whom was I speaking? Rosete seemed to be incapable of understanding me.

He started turning around and around in circles again, resuming his mindless motion, brainless, lifeless…What other words can I use to describe the expression of their code? "I came to tell you, I came to tell you, I came to tell you…"

I hurried away from there to get back to my workplace. I'll immerse myself in my books. If Rosete could speak, if he could remember language, he might cite Catherine Linton-Earnshaw-Brontë:

"What in the name of all that feels, has he to do with books, when I am dying?"

Slosos keston de Learo

EKFLOROS KESTON DE HERNANDO

The year 1539 was beginning to fly by. The Lady Constable, wife of Chief Constable Joan de Sámano, invited the brightest students from the Colegio de Santa Cruz, among whom I was undeservedly considered, to a gathering. Fray Arnaldo Basacio and Fray Bernardino de Sahagún (who was with us then) considered it appropriate to prepare, along with Fray Juan Foscher, a presentation for us to perform as a gesture to thank her. Though the Viceroy was not in attendance, and others of importance absent along with him, the crème de la crème of the city were gathered, and that is why they decided to bring the attendees together with the Colegio.

At that time, as he was doing his utmost to spend much of his own wealth, along with others' wealth as well, the Viceroy was going by way of Nueva Granada looking for a port of entry for his return from the expedition to Cíbola.

Fray Andrés de Olmos, Fray Bernardino, Fray Juan de Gaona went to work on the presentation, along with Fray Juan Foscher, of course, and we students suggested a word or two. We rehearsed several days. It was an allegory about the education of the Indians and the Christianization of the lands—ours—that King Carlos had gained for his Crown and that had recently been revealed to Europe. As it was only a game, we did not wear costumes, or disguises, or use axes, or lights; we wore only our purple cassocks and two little-friar habits.

The presentation we rehearsed alluded to the number nine—in the sense of the meaning that nine had among their ancestors and among the Náhuas and the appearance of nine in the nomenclature of the year that might herald the coming together of the two sides of thought from the two sides of the ocean. We would recite our speech in Latin and one of us would translate into Spanish if necessary. We would sing the presentation to a tune that Fray Juan Foscher had composed especially for the occasion, and that he would later prepare and adapt slightly to transform into music for prayer.

The verses for a single voice would feature Juan Berardo, a great singer, and in time a very good Latinist who had his own style, though it was plain. Juan Berardo died scarcely two years ago, in the year fifteen hundred and ninety-four. He had an extraordinary sounding voice even as a child, an exceptional voice. They said that his entire family had been famous for their voices, but I always suspected that they had invented (for some foolishness I do not understand) a tradition that had not existed in reality.

We arrived at the gathering after the attendees had already eaten. Fray Arnaldo, Fray Foscher, and Fray Bernardino greeted the Lady Constable with "Peace be to this house," as the Franciscans always do upon arrival, to which the person in question responded:

—But why so late? We invited you to dinner; it was the little Indian friars who were to arrive at this hour.

—Where our children eat, we eat. As for the rest, the rule of the Order, you must know my dear lady, is strict. There is no place in our bodies for the *primuras* with which you surely flattered your distinguished guests.

The Lady Constable laughed to hide the fact that she did not understand; the poor woman was so stupid it was embarrassing.

—And what do you bring before us? —she said, referring to us but not looking at us. She did not have the courtesy to greet us, to glance at us, or to say: "You are welcome here," or any other semblance of courtesy.

We Tezcocans must have something in common with Carlos because I could not stop myself from saying in Latin:

—First of all, according to wise customs, we have what you do not have for us: a greeting.

My companions laughed, Fray Foscher and Fray Arnaldo looked at me severely and I closed my mouth.

I was embarrassed, it is true, but I could not repress it. Lord help me, although I was not the son of a nobleman, like those who were with me, but instead a false one, a fake, my blood boiled from the so-called Lady Constable's lack of basic courtesy; if I had been equally rude, it was because of her own bad manners.

The lady grew uncomfortable in light of my comments, though she did not understand a single syllable of what I said. Her husband, Don Joan de Sámano, asked the friars what I had said because he did not follow the letter of the Latin language either.

—He quoted—Sahagún said—Horace, the ancient sage, who said: "The supreme pleasure is not in expensive foods, but rather in you yourself." And he added a phrase from Seneca: "Of what external thing does he need, he who has gathered all his things unto himself?" And I add to his words these of Horace: "Mentior al siquid, merdis caput inquiner albis corvorum atque in me veniat mictum atque cactum Iulius et fragilis Pediatia furque Voranus."[35]

---

35 I kept the Latin so one can understand the flow of the dialogue. Estela's note.

—And what did you say? —asked the uneducated lady.

I hastened to translate this myself into Castilian:

—Fray Bernardino added a quotation from Horace: "And if I am a liar, may the ravens foul my head with their white droppings and let Julio, slender Pediacio, and the thief Vorano come to relieve themselves on me."

The words were not at all well received, neither because I said them, nor for their meaning. She looked at me as if she did not see me, completely denying my existence with her eyes.

A general discomfort seized the entire gathering, set off by the friars' tardiness, sharpened by their justification for it, and made so much worse by my two clumsy interferences and the false translation unfortunately first given by the beautiful Fray Bernardino (whom the ladies loved so, even though he was no longer as lovely as he had been in his earliest youth).

In attendance, invited by the Lady Constable, were City Magistrate Don Gerónimo Ruiz de la Mota, Royal Tax Collector Hernando de Salazar, Gonzalo Ruis, Don Luis de Castro, Harbor Master Bernardino de Albornoz, and Gonzalo de Salazar, as well as judges, councilmen, and other members of the municipal council. It was for this audience—who had turned cold as stone—that we did our sweet performance, which was received with enormous disgust. While we were speaking the parts that the friars wrote for each of us individually, they were talking among themselves, I will not say that they were watching us with contempt because that would say too much. They were actually watching us without seeing us, as if we, the students of the Colegio, had studied to make ourselves invisible and our words were simply the sound of the wind.

Upon finishing the piece, the tax collector exclaimed:

—They are like magpies or crows; they have memorized a speech written by the friars!

That was all, they did not need to utter any other commentary. Plainly ignoring us, they proceeded to speak of other things, in the face of which Fray Bernardino and Fray Arnaldo proceeded to say their goodbyes. Even though we had not received any semblance of a greeting, we did the same. As I gave my hand to the Lady Constable—who had the face of a crawfish and a hand like the claw of a bird of prey—I said to her:

"Of what external thing does he need, he who has gathered all his things unto himself?" I am translating the words of Seneca for your Excellency. The Lord be with you, madam. Thank you for having received us into your house, we are undeserving of such a great honor.

She opened her bulging eyes as wide as possible in response to my impudence of having addressed her. She did not respond. But there was no need, because I could read quite well in her look:

—Why are you speaking to me? You are not even of the same species as I; you are a much lower one.

How she tried to humiliate me with her gaze! I bore it unblinkingly and in my own way I too spoke to her with my eyes, replying:

—It is true what you think, madam—I did not say it in the guise of a Latinist, but rather in pure Castilian—we are not equals. You are not even a magpie and your soul does not even resemble a crow's.

Then she responded. Without concealing her unhappiness with my double impudence (having addressed her and having born up

under her gaze), she hastily removed herself from my presence—
with an abrupt movement she emptied her nearly scarlet cup of
alcohol all over my habit and haughtily said in a loud voice:

—The friars do not even teach them where to put their feet
so that we will not trip over them!

No apology, of course. Not even a gesture that might express
"Oh no! The contents of my glass spilled on this boy." She com-
pensated me for her accident, if indeed it was an accident, with
silence; and it was her silence, counseled by envy, and not, as it
seemed to me, the eloquence of desiring to pour, not just her
glass, but her very own urine on me. ("Never get upset, counseled
Saint Bernard, by the good that comes to others; so their health
may not be the disease of your soul and may not their words be
your infernal hell.")

Fray Bernardino, Fray Foscher, and Fray Arnaldo did not say
a word. They lowered their gaze to the floor. Imitating them, I did
the same, as if my foot had, in effect, made the obstinate monster
trip. If by her we judge the rest of her sex, the Franciscans would
be short in their disdain of women. The only thing clean about
the nasty Lady Constable was her blood.

We were barely away from that bad situation when Fray Arnaldo
turned to me harshly:

—Hernando: you must learn to be more prudent. These
people are looking for ways to do harm: to you, to us, and to
the school. We came here to soften their positions, and you—he
wanted to go on, but in truth he just looked at me severely and
his lips tight with anger, quoted the following words from the
wise Francis:

"The true servant of God is not troubled or angry about anything; he lives justly and seeks not himself." We must remember the words of Saint Francis at all times and keep ourselves under his illumination in order to not commit acts of arrogance and anger. Hernando remember: "Those truly are peacemakers, who in all the sufferings of this life keep their body and soul in peace for the love of Our Lord Jesus Christ."

—Please calm yourself, Fray Arnaldo—said Fray Bernardino.

—These people were going to be upset in any event. We should not have accepted their invitation…They had us come out here with the simple objective of finding a way to attack our boys.

And because at that time I did not know how to hold my peace, I in turn quoted Saint Francis to them ("Therefore whoever envies his Brother for the good that God says or does in him, commits a sin like unto blasphemy, for he envies the Most High Himself, Who is the Author of all good words and works)," but these words did not fall on anyone's ears because from then until the time we arrived at Tlatelolco, Fray Arnaldo Basacio and Fray Bernardino de Sahagún did not stop talking, which was quite unusual and exceptional, as it was not their habit to engage in conversation about the things of the world in front of others. "Indeed, I counsel, warn and exhort my friars in the Lord Jesus Christ, that when they go through the world, they not quarrel nor contend in words, nor judge others, but be mild, peaceable and modest, meek and humble, speaking uprightly to all, as is fitting."[x] We students followed two steps behind them and Fray Juan Foscher, walking with notable lethargy and muttering something to himself with a sad expression, was two steps behind us.

At that gathering, the Christians arrived at a definitive ruling regarding the Colegio de la Santa Cruz, and their pronouncement spread like wildfire. It did not take us long to realize this. The next morning, when I arrived to carry out an errand that Fray Juan Basacio had entrusted me with (I think to remove me from his sight completely for having angered him), I observed an acrid discussion in the vestibule of the church of Tlatelolco among a group of people who were talking so harshly to each other that before I heard their voices I was able to recognize their persons. One of the two dressed as a Franciscan was that very same Fray Juan Basacio. It seemed that he had found others on whom to discharge his unusually bad mood. Another Franciscan and two priests were embroiled in an argument with him, all speaking extremely loudly. It caught my attention to see Fray Basacio, with his unusually bad mood exploding (he was always so calm) in the middle of that angry discussion, and perhaps that was why I approached to see if I could serve him in some way.

The other Franciscan, Fray Mateo by name, was the one who had come to inspect the construction of the convent of Tlatelolco; he had been with us more than a week examining as many of the walls of the convent under construction as he could, because his job was to go from one part of New Spain to another discussing the workmanship of the friars, suggesting and criticizing; this is why they had sent him, it was not to teach grammar, of which he had no knowledge. He was an expert master-builder and an intuitive engineer who had seen the work done by so many others on the convents and the churches of New Spain. The previous afternoon I had heard him in the refectory talking about how the

Indians who had raised the first vaulted structure in New Spain, that of San Francisco, had run away upon removing the wooden falsework, fearing that it would come down because they were convinced that there was no way to support it. When he recounted this anecdote, he emphasized the stupidity that he attributed to the innocent Indian builders, mocking them in a way that he would not do to the Franciscan builders.

I moved closer, my curiosity piqued; I was interested to know what it was that they were discussing. I was dressed in a poor, rough sackcloth robe that one of the Franciscans had put on me while they were drying my wine-stained clothes, since it would not be proper for a little Indian friar to be wearing clothes that smelled of a drunkard.

The other one who was there was Diego López de Agurto. He was a native of Mexico City and was the son of Sancho López, a public scribe, and many years later he was a prebendary and then a canon and a chaplain of the *Real Audiencia*. And though he had served in the church of San Francisco since childhood and prided himself on being a master of ceremony and ecclesiastics, he was still an unlettered man. He scarcely knew how to read and, in addition to demonstrating little knowledge and poor judgment, he is restless and vain, and distracted by affairs with women. But because he was a Hispanic of pure blood, he became a canon and a chaplain. Diego López de Agurto argued heatedly, while Fray Mateo, the wall-looker, supported him with a thousand words for his every claim and Fray Basacio argued back whenever he could chop a word in against their mounting anger.

—It is not possible that they can speak or understand Latin, they are only Indians—the wall-looker said.

—But Fray Mateo, what we are saying here is not just conjecture. We have seen that the Indians are capable of learning grammar perfectly and even some basics of theology—my friar was saying, trying to reason with idiots.

—Theology! Theology you said! How can you possibly believe that? Let us leave that out of the discussion. There is no Indian good enough even to learn grammar well and Latin requires a refinement of the mind and a sound judgment that the natives do not have a place to pull from—Diego López hastened to respond, practically jumping up and down with anger.

—Diego, I am telling you…

—With my own eyes—interrupted Fray Mateo—I have seen them suffer under the simplest problems of construction, and there is an abyss between building and understanding and speaking the Latin language. Look, Basacio, to say the very least, if you do not treat these poor wretches with the rod and the whip, they are not even capable of putting a couple of stones in the right place. So do not try to convince me that they can learn Latin, that is nonsense…

—Let us try. Ask some of these boys yourself…

—Let us see, you—Fray Mateo said to me—you, *chico*, do you know your prayers in Latin?

As I have said, I was not wearing a habit or a cassock, and he might have chosen me to ask his stupid questions because he thought I was not a student of the Colegio de Santa Cruz, much less one of those chosen by the friars to lead a religious life.

He had simply missed the opportunity to avoid this error because, though he might have seen me in the refectory, he had never laid eyes on us, the Indian students. For him we were lost souls wandering across the earth, just as we were for those at the gathering the night before.

—Me?

—You: do you know the Christian prayers in Latin?—Wall-looker then asked me.

—Yes, I do know them, the Franciscans taught me.

—And which ones do you know?

—Which one would your graces like me to recite for you?

—The Pater Noster.

I said the Pater Noster, oh, and with such fervor, as if My Lord might appear with its recitation.

—Well done, *muchacho*. I do not doubt—he said to Fray Basacio—that these natives have a memory. I do not question that, why should I? Any child in Castile can repeat the Pater Noster. All right now, *chico*, the Ave María…

I recited the Ave María for them, again carefully pronouncing my words.

—Good, as I have already said: memory is a faculty of crows.

—Would you like the Regina Coeli?

—Well, go on then! I think that would be more interesting, the Regina and the Coeli together…ha ha (the idiot laughed in my face), or do you know that it is one prayer, even though it is always said with two words?

I decided not to bother reciting the Regina to the fool, I did not have faith that my celestial Mother would reappear before my eyes with this prayer, nor am I confident that in her infinite piety she would have the will to come expressly to tolerate the company of this big an idiot. It would be easier for my father to appear from the depths of the ocean or for my poor mother to be granted permission to visit me even though she lives as close as Tezcoco! But I decided not to hold my tongue and I began to recite for him some of the Justinian Institutions:

—*Lustitia es constans et perpetua voluntas tus suum cuique tribuendi.*

—Don't give me this nonsense, you foolish and braggartry boy; you are smug about something I don't understand. Is that really part of the Regina, go ahead, tell me—but Fray Mateo interrupted me as soon as I began.

—All right now, Indian, leave aside your Regina Coeli, as that is too easy, and better yet recite the Creed.

And I set myself to doing so. Arriving at the phrase *Natus ex Maria Virgine*, he interrupted me, correcting me erroneously:

—*Nato ex Maria Virgine.*

—*Natus ex Maria Virgine*—I repeated, quite sure of being correct.

—Repeat "*nato*," do not be foolish, you have made a mistake— he claimed, convinced of the inconvincible.

—*Natus ex…*—I repeated, as I did not have any reason to make his stupid errors.

—"Nato," I said it is "nato"—he interrupted, now very annoyed.

—*Reverende Pater, nato, cujus casus est?*

Insulted and confused, not knowing how to respond, and getting angrier, he glared at us without saying a word. Fray Mateo knew a lot about stones and vaults, but nothing of Latin grammar.

"It is logical that each one works to know his job, and being ignorant, does not want others to be as well."

Needless to say that for the uneducated Diego López de Agurto the natus and the nato were the same thing, that is why it was not him I looked in the eyes when I said: "*Dubitatis quin vidicetis? Cave ignoscas?*" ("Do you doubt vengeance?" "Do not pardon"), phrases that infuriated Fray Mateo to the point of exasperation, not because their meaning was so contrary to the Franciscan sense, but because he did not understand them, and without even saying goodbye, he turned his back on us and left, muttering who knows what to the ignorant Diego López. Birds of a feather will flock together.

Fray Mateo might have understood his gypsum and his stones and his arches and his vaults and his chisel, but he had no understanding of grammar. The first time I realized this was days earlier when he corrected what an Indian had carved into a wall while showing the man how he should hold the chisel to use it more effectively, and the second I saw at that moment—in the color of his skin, his anger, and his confusion. But while I could appreciate the goodness of his person and that he was knowledgeable about stones and mortars, he was incapable of appreciating what was good in me, or admit that I understood Latin grammar even though I might not know how to carry stones or how to use a chisel.

Fray Arnaldo put his arm around my shoulders and we walked back chatting in Latin. I said to him:

—Now they will not bother us anymore Fray Arnaldo, now they have entered into reason, they have seen…

But he did not let me finish:

—The have seen nothing. They lost their eyes a long time ago, *Hannibale vivo.*[36]

—Their eyes will reappear…

And for my witty remark about eyes reappearing in the empty sockets of envy, Fray Arnaldo smiled, and said in a low voice:

—*Deo favente.*[37]

A few days later, maybe two or three after the scene I recounted with Fray Mateo, Francisco Sánchez, a cook and lay brother, came from the convent of San Francisco with the story that there was a scandal in Mexico City because Fray Mateo and Diego López and his brother Sancho López, secretary of the *Real Audiencia*, were saying that it is was wrong for them to teach us Latin—that it could be very bad for the Indians, that it will turn us into heretics, that we made poor use of everything. Because we Indians were nothing but children, we needed to be treated as such, which meant keeping us away from the knowledge of Latin. The cook heard about this in the convent, but he also said that the same sentiment was swiftly spreading among the lay Christians, that a resounding NO, regarding the little Indian friars, was hovering on everyone's lips and that the worst reason for the scandal was that, not content with giving us weapons to become heretics, they had given religious habits to two of us. What did they think we could do sheathed in them but introduce Hispanics and Indians to unspeakable sins?

---

36   "Meanwhile Hannibal lives." Estela leaves this phrase in Latin in her manuscript. Lear's note.

37   "God willing." Estela left this in Latin in her manuscript. Lear's note.

If it is true that we Indians are, as they say, like children, if that is true (and I will not spend any time on that bit about magpies and crows, a stupid claim that does not deserve to be heard), if it is true that we are like children, they cannot believe us to be manageable or innocent. To say that we are like children is to forget human nature. One cannot trust the nature of the children either, or depend on their innocence, subjugation, and docility.

Slosos keston de Hernando

EKFLOROS KESTON DE LEARO

I slept in fits and starts. Not because the Center was waking me up, but because they have stopped waking me up. It's been a while now since I've received any communication from them. No messages, no instructions, nothing. Maybe I should ask them to tell me something so that I might be able to rid myself of a bit of the massive uneasiness I feel. It was this uneasiness that woke me up. The pain in my soul was so intense that for a moment I cursed the fact that I did not participate in the bath of oblivion. But then I immediately rejected that crazy idea. I am the only one who speaks. Lear is the only being who talks to herself. I don't have anyone to talk to. They have people with whom they can speak their minds in their stupid code, on whom to unload their obscene gestures. That does not mean that their "language" is more speech than mine, because theirs is not a language, it's an aberration. If I quit speaking and understanding, language and grammar will be lost forever. It will be the end of man; it will achieve what my people are trying to do. I would fulfill their horrible desire.

Last night the Center did not wake me up, it was only my heart roiling in the rough waters of its solitary anxiety. Ah, but solitary is an inadequate word to describe it. My anxiety has been left infinitely alone because there's no one to keep it company, not even I can help it because I've lost my brothers, they're all gone. All gone. I'm the last human being left on the Earth. The people of L'Atlàntide are no longer the children of men and women.

Now they are what they wanted to be—their own children. They are godless beings—they don't have parents, language, land, or Nature; they are timeless, pain-free, and senseless.

Since I had woken up (I want to talk about this, Lear, don't get distracted), I was able to confirm that silence no longer reigns absolutely in the night of L'Atlàntide. They sleep in short stretches like animals sleep, but darkness makes them take shelter in L'Atlàntide and they remain there at night, lying on their backs like cats and dogs do, not making much noise. Then suddenly one of them will drink some water, another simulates copulation, another scratches his belly like an imbecile. Just as they are not asleep, neither are they completely silent, but their babbling doesn't make enough noise to wake me up. I say they were "babbling" because they weren't talking. They were trying to talk. One of them repeated the sound "gle" in her sleep, another something that sounded like "hm," another, writhing in his sleep, produces "pes." Their bodies command them "Talk!" but they can't do it, their brains won't let them.

I've tried to see in their eyes if their spirits also demand words. There is nothing in their eyes that seems to suggest such a desire. I do, though, I ask them for words. Speak, people of L'Atlàntide. Exchange two, three, a few words with me. Or understand the words I say. But they don't understand what I say to them. They did something to their ears, something that breaks down the words I articulate. I know this because Rosete imitates what I say to him:

If Lear says: "Rosete, stop for a moment, I want to tell you something. Pay attention, Rosete. Do you understand me?" Rosete, mimicking me, acting like he's my mirror, answers: "pit-pot-pot, mch mch, pit-pot-pot, mch mch," repeating my intonation with astonishing precision, but mixing up the sounds of my words, babbling them.

What did the people of L'Atlàntide do to their ears to disarticulate the sounds that make up words? What did they damage to make words sound different, to make them lose their rich sound, their nuanced notes?

I need to stop complaining in order to write down what I want to record here. Since I slept so poorly, I lingered longer than usual when I awoke, letting fantasy, instead of my uneasiness, completely overtake me. In a very bad state, seized by a profound unhappiness, I got up, took a bath, but took in almost nothing of the waters that are our fluid and nutrition. My stomach was upset and I didn't want to drink or eat anything. I even thought of going back to sleep, but force of habit took me toward the Punto Calpe; however, I abandoned the bridge and thus, was defenseless when I took a route that I had never taken before. *I started wandering.* I didn't have the strength to work on my Hernando and I hadn't been able to rid myself of the uneasiness. And I did not want to take the gigantic steps of my people, though it would be more precise to say that I didn't know what I wanted, maybe sleep, but I was sure that I wouldn't be able to sleep and the idea of going back to my fantasies in my room in L'Atlàntide terrified me. I was like a lost soul. I could have pleaded for what Fortunata did in Santa: "I pray that God might give me the most horrible of the diseases," because that would weigh less on me than not having god, or not being able to get sick, or not having anyone in L'Atlàntide who might have made me wish for an illness.

This was the state I was in when I realized I was walking down the middle of a cobblestoned street (but I can't give the details of my route, because I wasn't paying any attention). The first thing I saw were the cobblestones themselves: round stones that had been placed with meticulous care and precision made up the surface of the street. The buildings on both sides of the street, also made of stone, were still intact. I kept walking. The city opened up with my steps, as if the men who lived there had just abandoned it. A window was broken here and there, but the walls and the roofs were still in place. I arrived at the remains of the wall that surrounded the city, then at the bridge, and the river. The river wasn't colored, like all the others I had seen with my eyes, nor was it full of scum and debris, rather it was like those rivers I had learned of through the Image Receptor during my time in the *Conformación*—it was a river of clean water.

From the jaws of two shining metal grapnels came the tensors that supported the bridge. I stood on one of these to watch the river run. On my left, the water was the color of mud, and on the other side it was a clearer blue, as if there were two separate currents that circulated in the same riverbed. I heard the river run. The nearly intact city wall rose above, and bordered, the river. Behind it, inside the city limits, I thought I saw something that made me quite uneasy—a living thing disturbed by the soft breeze. I went back into the city and followed the streets along the city wall. I was able to open a massive door by simply turning the latch. The entryway of the house was dark and dank and the closed-up smell turned my already upset stomach. At the back I could see a light. I walked toward it. I found the interior courtyard of the large house.

In the center of the courtyard was a tree. It was the swaying crown of the tree I had seen from the bridge that crossed the river. A tree. Alive? Dead? A tree!

An immense panic seized me. Was I delirious? Were the city, the river, and the tree the fruit of delirium? Had I (alone, alone!) lost my head, like all of the people of L'Atlàntide had? Was I taking the painful route toward madness, instead of taking, as the others had, the road to stupidity? I couldn't trust my eyes, or my ears. Just as I had heard the river, I heard the leaves of the tree rustling.

I ran out of the house and kept running until the city was well behind me. Once I was sure I was outside of it, I took the giant steps my people take and left the surface of the Earth with my head absolutely spinning. Once above, I ran like crazy until I ran into L'Atlàntide. I threw myself into the bath like a crazy person, unsettled and terrified. I stayed in the water for a long time. I drank until I was full. I don't know how I managed to calm myself down, setting all reason aside. For a moment everything I thought I had seen in my entire life, with my own eyes, seemed to have been equally fantastic, but I pushed this thought away from me with all my strength as I rejected all other kinds of speculations. I questioned my own existence. I questioned the Earth, I questioned the destruction, I questioned Mother Nature. I questioned language.

I came back here to write these notes. Since I saw, or thought I saw, the thing that I must call a tree, words are ricocheting around in my head, deafening my thoughts with their meaning. They're from Mutis, my poet, from "The Dream of the Prince Elector":

I've never seen a similar being...No, Your Most Serene Highness, that flesh you now appear to have in your arms is not for you. Return, sir, to your path and try if you can to forget this moment that was not destined for you. This memory threatens to undermine the substance of your years and you will not end without this: the impossible memory of a pleasure born in regions that you have been forbidden from.

Although I have little strength, I have to work on my Hernando and on future occasions write notes about everything that I can't explain to myself. But above all I must write what Hernando wrote one day. I have to do it because I am beholden to him. Hold onto me, Indian, hold onto me, give me meaning, don't abandon me, don't let me be abandoned like the dust in the air. Only you, Hernando, can keep me from falling apart, or I will end up worse than the rest of the people of L'Atlàntide, I might lose my body, reason for being, and heart, in this whirlwind.

Slosos keston de Learo

EKFLOROS KESTON DE HERNANDO

I remember a simple triviality that I cannot get out of my head: when I was young and urinating into the dormitory's chamber pot, I would sometimes hear a sharp little sound, like a high-pitched cry that was almost obscured by my healthy stream. A mournful, continuous, irritating sound that resonated after the falling stream, which I repeatedly and mistakenly interpreted as someone's cry, and which left me full of compassion and moved by the cry that I know was not a cry because when I stopped urinating I was surprised to hear silence, surprised to see that, after my urine fell, no part of the sound remained; it left me surprised and not knowing what to do with the remnant of sadness that the little sound attached to the urine had provoked in me. Because while I heard the urine fall, in those long precious moments that did not respect the law of time, I did not think, held as I was by the repeated mistake that I seemed unable to avoid, that it was the urine that made the noise that sounded like a cry and the idea that someone suffered intensely in that moment left me ruled by an uncontrollable sadness, and there seemed to be no way to stop it. I would say I even thought—though it was more of a notion because I was overwhelmed by the effect of a sound that did not correspond to that which had caused it—I even thought it was a trick. Because of that simple trick I embarked on a journey of uncontrollable sadness that made me cry. And while I was crying, I imagined (because I had to justify my crying somehow) that something horrible had happened to hurt a child or an elderly person, and to feed my tears I remembered the tattooed faces of the slaves, a whizzing arrow flying to pierce a mother's breast, a sick child, a cripple. When the stream stopped ringing in the chamber pot, leaving behind the empty sound of the cry I had imagined, I was unable to immediately halt the sad and tearful journey I had embarked on. If someone had surprised me while I was crying and offered me consolation or asked for an explanation, I would tell him that the tears had come over me when I was praying for the unfortunate ones of my imagination (the cripples, the ill, the widows, the injured, those unjustly stripped of their lands, orphans), and would never confess to the urinary origin of my crying because by this time I myself would have already forgotten it.

I am recounting this because it occurred to me that I am trapped again by the same old mistake, though in a different way today. I am talking about it because I am afraid that everything I have been writing here did not happen that way, I am afraid that the shining facts came into my consciousness because I made myself believe them to be true. That all of this came from urine falling into a chamber pot; that I embroider, interpret, explain something that did not happen, that the reflection of something I did not understand correctly left its mark in my imagination, as if it were something real that moved me to compassion and to tears.

Slosos keston de Hernando

EKFLOROS KESTON DE LEARO

There's no way to understand them now. Without words, without grammar, their code is more incomprehensible every day. Today I saw a group of ten descending in silence during the off-hours on the Punto Calpe. I took one of them, Jeremías, by the arm and followed along. They were going toward the Jardín de Delicias.

When we arrived, we found Ramón, Italia, Ulises, and a young girl, who was at most eleven years old—a young girl who was Lilia. Lilia at age eleven. Our Lilia, but at age eleven. Lilia, our companion, the one who grew up with us, but Lilia turned back into a young girl.

Everyone surrounded the girl. Lilia had fistfuls of dark sand in her hands and she was letting it fall artfully and carefully over the light-colored sand. We watched her do this in silence. She was outlining (drawing with the dark-colored sand) a beautiful and touching figure that non-figuratively represented a destroyed figure, or, better said, a figure of destruction and its casualties. The figure Lilia outlined with the light-colored sand over the dark sand was one there are no words for; however, that fact doesn't match the stupidity of those who have renounced language.

Everyone who was present looked at it and understood it. When she finished, Ramón repeatedly made a string of snorting sounds, raising and lowering his "voice," blowing through his nose with greater and lesser force. Though it was nothing like a melody and was really just the repetition of unpleasant noises, he was so inspired in repeatedly making them that you could say that Ramón was singing, in a grotesque and ridiculous way, but singing nonetheless. At the sound of the noise, the image we created by looking at the image drawn by the young Lilia (that is, the impossible Lilia)—the representation of the destruction—as I was saying, the image that we created started to dissolve. I'm going to repeat it, but I'm going to repeat it very clearly. The image we created by looking at it, as well as the bi-colored sand, the light-colored sand that fell from her fists, and the dark sand that came from her little hands, the island, and each one of us, dissolved.

For me it was not at all pleasant. When I came to, I was back in my room in L'Atlàntide, lying down, resting, not thinking about anything.

I wondered if it was a dream. But that's stupid because it had to be a dream, there is no other explanation. It had to be a dream—one dreamt with such intensity that it seemed real, like the one with Mutis' friends.

I went back down to the Jardín de Delicias on my way here and found Lilia's sand painting. It's a perfect representation of the destruction. If they can still express it, maybe they haven't lost their souls. Are they conscious of their expression, or do they draw like a bird flies, like a fish swims, like a tiger leaps? In the end do they obey a superior grammar? Am I the only reader?

A rare calm reigned over the atmosphere. Far in the distance you could see a huge dust storm slowly advancing, moving across the sea like someone who walks with a lame step.

Slosos keston de Learo

The Franciscans left the Colegio de Santa Cruz. They walked out and left the Indians under the protection of the Indians. Their departure had been partially to defend us from the grumbling, because they naively believed that the attack on the Colegio de Santa Cruz was meant to hurt the Franciscans and their work in these lands. I say naively because there were many more reasons behind the anger against the Colegio. With the intention of saving us, they left us to our own mercy and even more defenseless. When the Franciscans departed, they decided to move us—Martín Jacobita and me—from their two rooms back to the dormitory of the Colegio, leaving us to live among the rest of the students. They thought we would be a good influence on our companions and that the other students would have the utmost respect for the discipline the friars themselves had taught us, so that they would follow us. *Perinde ac cadaver.*[38]

Zumárraga withdrew all economic support from the Colegio and petitioned the king to revoke its status as an Imperial Colegio and have it converted into a hospital, all, it seems to me, to protect himself against the accusations and avoid more attacks against the Franciscans. The king temporarily suspended the income he sent us and instead the Viceroy paid what would have been a small,

---

38   Estela quotes the phrase "in the manner of a corpse" in Latin. They are the words of Saint Francis of Assisi that prescribe discipline and obedience to superiors. Saint Ignatius of Loyola also used them in the same sense in his Constitutions. Lear's note.

although useful and generous, amount for each one of the students, which would have been enough, and we would not have found ourselves begging to support ourselves if it had been better managed by the majordomo and if he had used less of it for his own benefit.

As for Zumárraga, it was not because he did not respect the work of the Colegio, but rather because they had used it to attack him: by using the Colegio as an argument, they had branded him a millenarian, and with that, disloyal to the Spanish Crown and His Holiness, because they said that the Franciscans wanted to use us to create an Indian Church that would separate from the one run by the Pope, that ours was the seedbed for the new Church, and that Zumárraga spoke continuously about Babylon...

The financial problems had a solution: the matrons generously provided food, bringing us tortillas made with their own hands, boiled beans, and salsas to season whatever we harvested from what we had sown in our vegetable garden. And, needless to say, we already had books, so we desired nothing more from the world. In the case that we came across something unexpected, we would ask and that was all.

But our danger was something else entirely. The village of Mexico had decided to do away with the Colegio de Santa Cruz, as if our knowledge exacerbated their uncontrollable desire to destroy. We whetted their appetite for evil and sharpened their bad temperament.

One Thursday afternoon, as part of their plan to do us harm, they organized a visit from prostitutes, which had terrible consequences for two of us. They brought them, according to what

I heard a little later and as I will explain here, from the famous house of Tezcoco and they left them in front of the Colegio, instructing them that they should say that they were a present sent by some friends. Without knocking on the door, they entered directly into the central courtyard and one of them began to sing, which brought us out of our rooms. They sang with such beautiful voices that we came out to see where the singing was coming from. There they were—five beautiful prostitutes, painted and bedecked to seduce even the most chaste of young men. There they were—one of them was singing, the others were gesturing for us to come down and join them. None of us took the first step because we did not understand what this visit meant or why they wanted us to come closer. We students, who were practically children, watched them with fear and fascination. Agustín began speaking, interrupting the prostitutes' singing, telling us loudly that they were strumpets and that we should go down and enjoy ourselves, that he had already done it several times and that there was nothing better than to touch the flesh between their legs. Then we started to say among ourselves that if that is what they were, we should not go down. We should throw them out. That was when they called us by name, Martín Jacobita and myself, saying sweetly: "Martín Jacobita, come closer. Come here, come close, Hernando de Rivas, we have messages we need to give you, we are not strumpets, we are baptized women, converted to Christianity by the Franciscan fathers."

I asked them then:

—So, you are not strumpets, messengers of wickedness and lasciviousness?

—We are Christian woman and that should be enough. If you want to know more, come closer...

—I am Hernando de Rivas. Is it true that you have a message for us?

—Yes, we do have a message and it is very important that we deliver it so that we remain in good stead with those to whom we owe our loyalty.

The fact that it was the two of us they called by name should have made us suspicious, but we were not in the least; we were naive like the Franciscan brothers who never taught us to acquire even the shadow of evil, and since they had called us, and we were well-mannered, we approached the center of the courtyard where they were sitting on the ground, to hear what they wanted with us, how we could serve those beauties, and not because they were beautiful, but rather because we were so naive, as I said.

But those prostitutes were beautiful. Beautiful as only the famous ones are, the ones you have to pay in order to obtain their favors, who are not modest about revealing their charms, who make themselves beautiful to call upon the desires of young men, to awaken lust and lasciviousness. But we did not even think of lust or frivolities, only of being all ears to hear their messages. Moreover, we had never seen anything like them before and we did not know how to determine whether they were prostitutes, women of easy virtue, lewd instigators of lasciviousness, so that is why both of us, whom they had called by name, approached them and were in turn approached by them in the way they do (it is not words they normally use to talk to young men). It was just at the moment when one of them, undoubtedly the most beautiful, was doing a dance to arouse us, playing with us to make us want her, making Martín Jacobita and me blush, and causing wicked thoughts to course through us, that the Franciscans arrived after having been called by the tricksters who had thrown the prostitutes at us, and who had told the friars that we had invited these fine ladies to spend the night at the Colegio to enjoy ourselves, and who, fearing that we would throw the girls out before anything happened, had rushed to call the Franciscans, not allowing the sin time to advance too far.

Upon seeing the beauty dancing in front of us and Martín Jacobita and me so close to her, Fray Bernardino roared with rage, cursing them with vile words I had never heard him say, and they were saying that he should not to say those things to them, that he should not treat them disrespectfully, that they had come because they had been called, that they were only doing their job, and Fray Bernardino was telling them that they were not working but rather sowing evil in the world, and they burst out laughing, and I, with the arousal their dances had awoken in me, did not know what to do or what not to do.

Neither Fray Bernardino nor the other Franciscans wanted to hear my explanation, nor the one that my companion Martín Jacobita tried to give them. The Franciscans were more than furious with us. They decided to take back our Franciscan habits in a very sad ceremony that I will not describe because I find it completely lacking in grace and not worth remembering.

The letter Archbishop Zumárraga sent to his Majesty the King of Spain referred to this time:

"I ask that H.M. make known whether the hospital will have

a space and which part of the church will be the hospital...and that H.M. have the mercy to allow me to leave the bell house, which is now the printing press and the prison, that I am now building, because what was a prison will now be a hospital. It seems that the religious would be better employed in the hospital than in the Colegio de Santiago since we do not know whether it will survive because the best Indian students *tendunt ad nuptias potius quam ad continentiam*. And if it would please H.M. to grant me the same two houses that had been mercifully given to the students of the Colegio to be part of this hospital for people ill with venereal disease. I think they would be better applied to the hospital and I think they are finished, though they know how to beg, as is usual for my order."

And while he was thinking about begging, which we had to do from time to time, the dreams for my life—those of my mother, my own, those of the friars—rolled around on the floor, broken.

Slosos keston de Hernando

EKFLOROS KESTON DE LEARO

I followed them for days whenever they descended by way of the Punto Calpe. They never went back to draw anything, but several times one of them has appeared in his child form. The next day, the same one might appear in his adult form.

None of them remembers anything. The right hand doesn't know what the left hand is doing. This illness began before the decree abolishing language because they were already abandoning it. Nothing has any consequences.

I went back into the vault (which was the tomb of her children) that I discovered when I followed Caspa. The vault was different. It seemed to be more like a cave, a hollow between the rocks— I say "it seems" because in seeing a difference, it seems I was losing my powers of observation. The surprise kept me from concentrating. The bubble that had been burst open by the bombs, the walls of asphalt and cement with the altar in the middle, it was different, it was different…Piled up at one end of this geologic formation that replaced the vault I had seen in this same spot lay (like those poor children) an uncountable pile of sugarcanes. I picked one up to be sure that was what it was. At the thinnest end of the stalk there was an animal-like black bump. I picked up another stalk and it also had a bump. I picked up another. In addition to the bump, there was a little piece of fiber, like the ones that covered Caspa's babies, hanging from its tip. I moved more stalks but I didn't see any more marks. Putting the stalks back in their place was no problem simply because there had been no order before. I can't put them in order because the order to which they should have belonged no longer exists.

There's no connecting thread at all. Things happen, but don't remain, they're not fixed, they don't keep still. They aren't entirely real. They can be erased in a single stroke.

Any possibility of interrelation has slipped away among the holes that have been forming on the surface of our reality, the reality of all the members of my community. We can't communicate with each other because we don't belong to the same time. The tight mesh of reality that the men from the time of History enjoyed, and across which they began dialogues and had misunderstandings, performed actions and deeds, has broken, it has split open. Nothing I do can be perceived by another member of my community unless it's outside of the time in which I live. We've already lost common time. I think we've lost it completely. Their language reform, the insistence on oblivion, has erased us. Now we are nothing. I've lost all hope that we'll return to the time of Time.

We can't die.

What I had believed to have been dreams are not, because we can't dream either. The veil between sleep and wakefulness has ripped.

How can I explain what's happening here if it's completely beyond words? What tool can I use to describe it? And what can I compare it to? There is not a single sign nearby on which we can see the absence of a syllable.

Where would I find the word GOD cut in half so I could prove to them that this is what's happening?

Has the tape, on which time is recorded, finished? Are we now repeating the present by using segments recorded at other times?

This is exactly what was happening when Ramón and I were having sex. I was living what had already been lived, by me or by someone else, and that incomplete connection left me outside, I was only attached to the present in certain instances. It's not that we were distracted because we no longer have the tape for the luxury of distraction. To distract oneself is to squander the temporal-spatial film.

I could say, "This is not happening now in this instant," because between one word and the other I hear the ever-increasing crackling of absurdity.

Nothing has consequences. It comes from nothing and it goes away. The most basic measure of history has dissolved.

Their dream—the dream of my community—has been realized. In their dream there is no past and it's not important to them in the least that the cost of the disappearance of the past is the loss of the future. In their memories they can't converse with the past. I detailed the importance of memory in this very archive, but I didn't imagine that its complete loss would have this repercussion: now nothing has any repercussions. My brothers, the beings who live with me in L'Atlàntide, have escaped time completely.

I go down with them to the Punto Calpe; they're punctual. Nothing they say or do will have any consequences. But now they don't say anything. Now they don't use words. They make their grim gestures. Now they aren't Mother Nature's helpers. Now they don't clean up the debris from the great explosion. I'm not the only one who has abandoned that work.

I quit to devote myself to the memory of time. They quit to abandon all types of memory. The Earth has been left alone again.

I'm the only inhabitant of time.

And at night, the alarm rings, and rings, and rings...

Slosos keston de Learo

EKFLOROS KESTON DE HERNANDO

Three weeks—which were terrible for me because I did not have the words to convince Sahagún or Basacio of our innocence—at most had passed since the incident, when one day while I was at the market in Mexico City to pick up the woolen cloth for the cassocks of the new students at the Colegio (we had received five, along with a providential donation from the mother of one of them who had given it to us asking only that we would receive and educate the new ones), and just as I was making my transaction, the face of one of those prostitutes, who was almost unrecognizable because she did not have a drop of paint on her face, approached to greet me. My first reaction was not to have anything to do with her. She was more beautiful than the sun. She radiated an aura of innocence. "Don Hernando"—she said to me—"how good to run into you, I wanted to ask for your forgiveness and give you an explanation that might in some way help you…"

—We Franciscans do not speak to women—I managed to reply, gathering strength from who knows where, because I did not know what to do when I looked at her.

—But Hernando, you are not dressed as a Franciscan anymore, and I heard…

—I continue to be in spirit—I interrupted her, full of shame.

—In spirit? How would I know? But what I need to tell you is of the utmost importance for you—and suddenly, adjusting the

tone of her voice and raising it louder, she took my side against
the vendor and obtained the woolen cloth for the cassocks practically as a gift, arguing that it was not very good, that it was for
the Franciscans, that it was for children, weigh and consider the
Colegio de la Santa Cruz. Each one of her gestures, each of her
inflections, all of the features of her face and body spoke of an
innocence that disarmed me. Was she the one who danced that
lascivious dance, inciting me to wickedness and moral corruption?
Could it be? Her body, her face, her beautiful hair radiated purity
and serenity. I remembered what that dance had been like and
I did not find anything dirty about it. Watching her talking to, and
arguing prices with, the vendor, it seemed to me that her dance
was just that, a dance, one that was animated by the lewd voices
of the others (who were undoubtedly public women, though at
that moment I was doubting everything), and I didn't know if
they were angels or spirits or simply voices emitted by the stones,
but it seemed lewd to us. I was so convinced of her innocence
while she was talking calmly and gently, even managing to reduce
the price to such a ridiculous sum that I felt a terrible shame for
having been aroused by an innocent dance.

While they cut the piece of woolen cloth that I would take
from the roll (I could have taken the whole thing for the price
she negotiated) she started chatting with me, talking, not like she
had with the vendor with pauses and silences and with a clear and
strong voice, but rapidly and in a very low voice, sweeter and still
more innocent, saying to me:

—Don Hernando, what I am saying is true—I am very dis-
tressed by the problems I have caused you. Look, I am not, like

Father Sahagún shouted, a public woman. The other women I entered the courtyard of the Colegio with were, and I did wrong by going with them, but I have to feed my daughter somehow. There is no reason for me to lie to you, it is not the first time they have paid me to go some place with the others. I sing and dance, they sin. I do not want to do anything except practice my art and I do it because I believe in the beauty and the grace of our dances and in the beauty of the music of our ancestors, and I do not believe it is evil to do that, and it is not bad for them to pay me for it either. If our noble lords no longer have the goods or money to pay for dances and songs, I have to dance for the Spaniards and, because they do not have our wisdom, if they have me accompany those ladies, well, I cannot refuse...I hope you understand. I never imagined what would happen. Look—she continued, taking the piece of woolen cloth they gave us—I will walk with you, they know who I am here, it will not damage your reputation. What happened that day—she continued talking, without waiting for me to say yes or no—what happened was that some of Jerónimo López's people paid us to go to the Colegio and we never imagined they would immediately notify the friars of our visit...You all did nothing wrong, nor did I. I only did what I was told to do, and very wrongly for just a few coins. The public women did not have time to do their things with the boys, and I assure you that you would not have done them because I was there to protect your chastity. Will you let me go and explain this to Father Sahagún?

Terrible idea! How could this woman believe that Fray Bernardino would let her get near him? Not even if he were not a Franciscan...

How could I come up with a pretext for her to see him? He only had men as advisors, so I could not even imagine that he would be willing to see her.

—Try to figure out a way to tell him, Don Hernando, I know very well the harm my behavior has done to those men. I am very ashamed…

If it was true that she was angel, for her beauty and the illusion of purity that she radiated made her seem angelic, it was also true that she was a fallen angel because when I was walking by her side I was very well aware that her feet made a sound when they touched the ground. Guiding me by the hand through the streets of the City of Mexico, in less time than it takes to say "time" (or so it seemed to me since I did not even have time to realize it), I found myself beside her in the room she lived in. Carrying the piece of woolen cloth, I was flying with the angel who dazzled me. When I found myself inside her room, I did not have time (again time), not even for a minute, to fear any wicked intent on her part, and I did not believe that it was in her flesh that she was the fallen angel. In front of us, lying on the floor, was a little girl, a living doll lying on her back on the mat, playing with her own little hands and making some sweet little sounds with her fat cheeks.

—See—she said, returning to the conversation she had started to engage me in just moments ago—see Mama came back with a friend to bless you. —She spoke to her as if to introduce me to her, but she did not stop, or go to her, or touch her. The little one turned her little head anxiously toward her Mama. She was another little angel, except that this one was a little chubby. I stopped gazing at the first angel to focus on the second.

The bigger angel did not go to her, and the little one followed her with her head, calling her with those little sounds she knew how to make.

—Can I hold her? —I asked her.

—No, no, don't pick her up, she'll get urine on you.

The little one was about to start crying.

—Tears again—said the heartless bigger one. —Don't screech at me.

—Let me hold her—I said in my best voice. —I don't care if she pees on me.

—Well, if you want to…

I did want to. I took her in my arms, reeking of pee, dirty not from dirt but from several days of filth, or that is the way it looked, as if she had never even been near water. She became happy, if you can say it that way, because she was saddest being I had ever seen. I do not know if her urine dirtied me or not but her dirty sadness penetrated me.

Not even when I picked her up did the Mama turn around to look at her. No telling what she was doing where there was nothing to do, but she was not preparing to greet her daughter. She came and went through the empty room, taking graceful little steps, quickly, as if she were in a hurry to get someplace. The little doll settled herself in my arms and made sweet expressions at me with her dirty little face.

—Listen—I said to her, because it was true—I have to go now, they are about to recite the Nones.

—Wait for me a moment, I'm leaving now, I'll accompany you a little bit longer. Leave the baby in her place and let's go.

No, for that I did not have the heart, to leave her there all alone.

—Can't we take her?

—Why do you want to take her?

—So that she won't be here alone. —I said, seeing that her place was just a single dark room in which there was nothing more than the mat where the mother and daughter must have slept. There was nothing else. Not even a table, nothing.

—Leave her alone, nothing will happen.

—Happen, nothing can happen, there is nothing she can hurt herself with. But she'll be sad.

—She's going to be sad…She'll cry for a bit, because she's fussy, but then she'll be all right.

—Will you come right back?

—I don't think so. I won't come back until tonight.

—Aren't you going to give her something to eat?

—When I come back with something to give her.

—Won't she be hungry?

—Of course she will, she's alive.

—Come, let's take her, I don't have the heart to leave her.

—How silly you are…

—I'll carry her.

—You've got your woolen cloth.

—I can carry both.

—No you can't, you're a friar, not a *tameme*—you're not an Indian porter. And anyway, who will carry her back? Tell me that. I'll come back with her by myself.

—Your arms won't fall off…

—No they won't, but I don't want to take her. Leave her there.

—Stay with her.

—What am I going to do here, sit around? I don't have anything to keep me here, there's nothing to do here…Let's go.

At least let me give her a little bit of water or *atole* to drink if you have it…

All they had was water. I gave the sweet thing a few little sips of water, and left her, in her dark corner, the poor little girl, brooding in her daily sadness. I wondered silently how such a lovely angel, who appeared to be so pure, could have a heart so hardened against her own daughter.

—I know what we'll do—she said to me, as soon as we left, not even in her mind had she given any attention to the little one—I'll write a note to Father Sahagún and leave it at the Colegio, I can just go to Tlatelolco and I'll explain to him.

It seemed like a very good idea to me.

—It's just that I don't have even a single cent to buy paper or to pay the scribe. Give me one of the coins I saved you, and as soon as I can I'll pay you back. I'm only asking you so as to not lose any time. I don't want you to misunderstand.

This she said as she had said everything earlier, gracefully, each of her sentences accompanied by an angelic movement of her head, occasionally raising her little hands to emphasize something she said. But even after she said it like that I did not believe it a bit, I might have been an innocent Franciscan but I was not an idiot, and I had already seen that my angel was not so good, she was horrible with her daughter. I gave her a coin that would pay for more than one round-trip between Tlatelolco and Mexico in a six-horse carriage. She did not even thank me. She disappeared among the people, practically flying, and I did not have the slightest doubt that she would not run off to spend the money while carrying her sad little girl in her arms, much less worry about me. I imagined she would spend the money on bows and petticoats to dress more prettily.

I returned to the Colegio convinced that the angel would not do anything for me, that everything she had done—tell me the story of Jerónimo López and lower the price on the woolen cloth—had been to get that money, so it took me by surprise when the friars called me the next day.

They were all there and in front of them was a piece of paper. Fray Bernardino, who was the one the letter was addressed to, spoke first.

—Hernando, we received this letter today. Read it and tell us if it is true.

The letter, which I was unable to read all at once due to emotion, went more or less like this:

"Dear Franciscan Friars: I am a woman obliged by the necessities of life to dance to give pleasure to men and women, to children and the elderly, for I am a widow and must support my daughter. Three weeks ago I was paid in cash to go to the Colegio de Santa Cruz, along with some prostitutes. I went there to dance for the students; the others were there to offer their flesh to the students for sinful purposes. The person (one of Jerónimo López' men) paid us in hard cash and in advance. If he had not paid us in advance, we would never have been able to collect because your students were chaste and did not yield to any of the dirty provocations of the prostitutes I was forced to accompany out of necessity.

I beg forgiveness before God for the harm we caused you. I also beg God to forgive me if I somehow contributed to marking your pure souls with the stain of sin. Dance is an art and I am devoted to it, and if I find myself obliged to accept unholy company to feed my little daughter, I ask your Excellencies' forgiveness. Dear fathers, forgive me. Pray for me before God."

Her scrawled signature was illegible. It was clear that the hand in which the rest of the letter was written was not the same.

—What can you tell us about this? —Fray Bernardino asked.

—That it is not a lie. —That was the only thing I managed to say because I started to cry. The friars did not say anything else. My tears displeased them.

They called Martín Jacobita, gave him the letter to read and asked him for an explanation; he explained to them in every way he could what had happened that night, which of the students had called them strumpets, why he and I had approached them, how they, the friars, had arrived, etcetera.

She, who was not a harlot, but rather a singer and dancer, had reconciled us with the friars. They did not put the Franciscan habit back on us, the law did not allow it. Fray Bernardino explained that this did not mean we had lost the robes and said as soon as the occasion arose, we would wear them again.

We never did have the occasion to wear the habit again and it would not have happened anyway, even though I might have worked hard to invoke it, because the friars never knew about what I am going to recount from here forward. The occasion never arrived, nor were the habits returned to Martín or to Hernando. Years later I wrote this with my own hand for Fray Bernardino:

"The habits of Saint Francis were given to two Indian youths, the most adept and reserved that there were, who testified the things of our Catholic Faith to the natives with great fervor… They had the habit and they might have been trained for the things of this Holy Religion, but we found through experience that they were not suited to such a state, and thus we took away their habits, and never again have we received an Indian into the religion, nor do we consider them to be qualified for the priesthood." I spoke to Fray Bernardino a lot about this passage and we thought about writing it in several different ways. We ultimately agreed not to mention Elejos, because we did not need to glorify him in order to avoid greater violence.

I was also the hand of Daciano, when Fray Juan Gaona convinced him of his error in a public dispute and forced him to do penance:

"Come here, brother, you say that the Indians generally possess many talents and natural inclinations very suitable to helping them to be good Christians, and you have brought particular examples of Indians to whom God communicated his spirit, who have had the desire to serve him, renouncing the world and following the evangelical life. What then is the reason that you do not give them the habit of the religion, not just for laymen, but better yet to be priests, as in the early Church they chose heathens and Jews newly converted to the Faith to be priests and bishops?…And that is to say, that they are not for masters but rather for disciples, nor for prelates but rather for subjects, and for the best in the world…To some of the Indians raised and indoctrinated by your hand, and appearing to be well inclined, they gave them the habit of the

order to test them and then in the novitiate year clearly understood that it was not for them, and that is why they let them go,
and made the statute that they would not be received."

Slosos keston de Hernando

EKFLOROS KESTON DE LEARO

Feeling the need to stretch my legs around mid-morning, I abandoned, halfway through, the work I had set for myself for this session. My ability to concentrate is diminishing because I sleep so poorly with all the ringing of the alarms. So I went out to stretch my legs when I realized that my concentration was so bad that I was only wandering through Hernando's text, unable to translate Estela's lines into my *cesto*.

I headed south.

A meeting was being conducted on one of the high peaks of the once-snow-covered cordilleras of the Andes. I drew near. They were all communicating in their new code—they were writhing around in their grotesque contortions, gesticulating obscenely. In a silence colder than the snow that should have been there, they writhed around like earthworms in salt, like the slugs the children from the time of History used to torture for fun. They really did look like slugs because their heads were no longer heads when they writhed around like that and their rear ends were no longer their bottoms. Headless, bottomless, their faces faceless, their hands handless...

What were they saying?

Nothing. With that stupid code they didn't communicate anything. Each one repeated what they had learned through memorization, but they didn't say anything to one another, simply nothing.

Nothing.

There were Rosete and Ramón, and Caspa, and Ezequiel and Jeremías, Italia and Lilia, now an adult.

They had already forgotten everything.

They had reached the heaven they were searching for. This is what man has evolved into—this idiotic dance where they put one hand on their buttocks while they stick their face to their knee and lift one foot…bending over and writhing and flinging themselves down and getting up, as if they were tired of their bodies.

I wanted to talk to them, but what good would that have done? This gave me a lump in my throat. They wouldn't have been able to understand me anyway, they wouldn't have comprehended me. They've already forgotten language and their power, they weren't capable of understanding a single one of my words. They've already forgotten everything.

Is this really the end of man, as I've just described it—this succession of spastic movements, this disarticulation of the body?

It was enough to see them and feel the horror that their gestures produced to comprehend that what was breaking apart was more than language. Or maybe in breaking with language they broke with everything man was or could be.

In this they've made a mistake. Because they can no longer appreciate the beauty of the shining moon, the roar of a breaking wave, or the strange beauty of a mollusk, or the sunset…

They didn't imitate animals or things. They were…they were imbeciles, atrocities…Ghastly…They were soulless beings; they were not even imitations of apes or stones.

Slosos keston de Learo

EKFLOROS KESTON DE HERNANDO

Another two weeks would pass before I saw my angel again, exactly one month from the first time I had seen her. I had gone to Mexico to pick up some paper for the Colegio, which had been ordered by the Franciscans quite some time earlier for our printing press. I had to complete the transaction, take care of the payment (with Franciscan money), find a porter to help me, and take it back before night fell and, with it, the rain. That is what I was doing (the paper had been paid for) when I saw her—she was more beautiful and had the same aura of purity. She smiled when she saw me.

—How are you Don Hernando? Better, I hope.

—Yes, better, I want to thank you…

—There is nothing to thank me for. Nothing. Why should you thank me? I did not do anything, I only undid a bit of the damage I had done. And I have some of the money left from what you gave me, only I do not have it with me right now…How will I get it to you? Should I stop by to give it to you or would the other Franciscans look poorly on that? I should not even ask, should I? I saw it in your face. Do not worry, I will not go to see you, the last thing I want to do is cause problems for you. Where are you going?

I told her what I was doing.

—What a coincidence. I have a friend who would be happy to take your load of paper at no charge because he has to go to

Tlatelolco today, and he will not mind taking it for you, I promise. And do not worry, I will not ask for the money I saved you for transporting the paper, like I did last time to pay for the scribe. But I do want to ask you for something in return. Look, let us arrange the transport of the paper first (hopefully it will not rain) and I will explain.

I walked along behind her to arrange for the transport of the paper. I felt like I was running, though she seemed to be walking so calmly, so full of grace. She was so beautiful, even more so than last time. We arranged for the paper to be picked up and delivered to the Colegio for a ridiculously small amount of money.

—You see? Spend more time with me, Don Hernando, and the Colegio de Santa Cruz will overflow with blessings…Now, as I already told you, I wanted to ask you something for myself…— she looked at me so naughtily. Her look embarrassed me so much that I wondered if it were not a sin of the worst kind just to allow myself to be looked at that way. —I wanted to ask you a favor. A tiny little favor. A little nothing. May I?

Since I did not respond to her "may I?" she asked again:

—Well, may I?

—What? —I managed to reply, coming out of my surprise.

—May I ask you…a favor?

—As I owe you so much, I have no wish other than to quickly repay you if it is something that the Christian law allows. Since I am still a Franciscan to all intents, if it has anything to do with sin, even though all of my will is to obey you, I cannot.

—Do you think I would ask something sinful of you?—she asked with an angelic face. Then I would have bet my soul that she was incapable of sin, with that beautiful, innocent face.

—No, no, no—I was embarrassed—it is just a manner of speaking.

—What I want to ask you is in accordance with Christianity, but I want to talk to you calmly, and it makes me nervous that we are being observed. Will you come home with me?

The last thing I thought prudent (I had had time to think about what I had done the last time I saw her) would be to go with her to the room she called a home.

—I prefer not to do that, they will see us go inside and…

—Nothing will happen. My neighbors know perfectly well that I am not a strumpet and that I never dance or sing at home, but, in order not to arouse the least suspicion, we will leave the door open, and I will explain everything to you there…

—No…

—Besides—she used this as a pretext and I am aware she brought this up because she knew that this would touch my heart—my daughter is alone and I have not seen her since this morning, and she might be hungry, poor little thing…

I did not say anything else. I walked behind her. That day I did pay attention to the route. Mexico was not a city I was very familiar with. I had jumped straight from Tezcoco to Tlatelolco, and even though we often came here to run errands, and I usually did them alone since the friars left the Colegio, it was not a town I managed very well. I needed to pay attention to where I was going; I needed to exercise my powers of reason to understand it. In Tlatelolco, on the other hand, I could walk with my eyes closed and know where I was. It was like the palm of my hand. This city was not. I knew it, but I had not lived there long enough to have it engraved in my brain. So I was walking behind her, paying attention to the route she took to what she called a home. We arrived. It did not manage to be outside of the Spaniard's blueprint where the streets were not yet cobblestoned and where circumstances dictated disorder, instead it was practically next to the Salto del Agua, the public fountain. I had walked a good distance last time and had not even realized it, as I was focused only on her graceful step. We were at the other end of the city, next to a church. Hers might be the priest's house; in fact, it seemed to be part of it because it was right beside it.

We went inside. The other angel—the little one—cried weakly on her mat. When the ray of light came in through the open door, she did not make the slightest effort to increase the volume of her cry, or to stop it. Just like last time, the Mama—my beauty—did not pay her any attention. I did not ask, I went to the little one and picked her up. She quit crying immediately. She was even dirtier and sadder than the last time, now the dirt extended to her limbs. The angel said:

—I forgot something. I will leave you this for the girl—she gave me a tortilla she had hidden in her hand—break it into little pieces so she does not choke. I will be right back, I won't be long.

She left. There I was, in an empty room that belonged to a woman who made her living by dancing and singing in the fiestas, and not necessarily the sacred ones, taking care of her daughter. I decided to bathe the girl. I took an empty container that was on the floor and, with the little one in my arms, went to the Salto del Agua. The women there helped me fill the jug. I went back to the house, which as I have already said, was only a few steps from there, and began to bathe the little girl there, in front of the door. She stood up between my legs, holding tightly to my thighs and knees. She was very small in size, but maybe not so young if her legs could already support her. She very happily let herself be bathed; everything amused her, and my clumsiness, since I was anything but an expert in bathing children, did not seem to bother her. I left her there, cleanly bathed, and went inside to find a change of clothes on the mat that was not too dirty, and then dressed her. Seated in the doorway, I started to give her the little pieces of tortilla, breaking off bits of the cooked corn masa with my fingers. She devoured it. She was happy, and even so, one could feel her profound sadness, forged perhaps by so many hours spent alone.

Her Mama—my earthly angel—returned, more lovely even than when she left. As soon as she saw me, I started making excuses:

—I am just now giving her something to eat because I bathed her first. I put a change of clothes on her that I found on the mat.

The little girl made as much of a fuss over her Mama as I did.

—But why did you bother, Don Hernando, I do not know what to say—she said to me, returning to the more formal form of address, as if I were older than she.

She took the girl from my arms, or better said from between my legs since she was leaning against them, and gave me an order.

—Come inside—she said, jumping directly back to the familiar form of speech.

We went inside and she closed the door behind her, breaking the promise she had made me. She lay down on the mat, with the girl in her arms, raised her torso to take her blouse completely off, and lay back down, and then, twisting and wiggling around to get comfortable, she began to nurse her little girl. The little bit of light in the room illuminated her body, which was practically naked since, in settling herself to get comfortable, her skirt had slid up her thighs.

I had never seen a body stretched out like that, practically uncovered, and even if I had seen it before, it would not have had the same savage beauty. As the minutes passed and my eyes became more accustomed to the darkness, I found her more beautiful each moment, more complete, more naked. Unclothed like that, she lost nothing of her innocence or virginal appearance; but even though she retained that air of purity, it awoke something in me I did not recognize. The two bare breasts, the bare belly, the bare legs—the folds of the skirt on her lower belly and the little one were the only things that were covered because the little girl was lying on the mat, instead of on her mother's body, and the skirt had inched up with her wiggling movements, so there was practically nothing covering her. I knew I should go, but I could not move. Her beauty had me fixed to the dirt floor, as if I were made of a hard stone.

The little girl nursed, ceaselessly and motionlessly. The Mama turned over to nurse her on the other breast without moving her. In doing so, she turned her beautiful bare back and buttocks (which were nearly revealed by the raised skirt) to me, leaving her long legs stretched out and exposed before me.

What was I doing there? I momentarily gathered my strength and said:

—I'm going now.

—What are you going to do? —She turned her lovely little face toward me, giving a face to her savagely beautiful back, making her even more cruelly beautiful. —The paper still hasn't been delivered; he said he would leave in two hours, which have not passed yet. It makes sense that his trip would be slower than yours, because he's carrying a load and you're not, and anyway, I don't know if he is going directly to the Colegio, he might have other errands…Don't go.

Her "don't go" was enough for me to abandon my good intentions of leaving.

—Come here, sit here beside me. Let's talk. There's another mat rolled up over there—she said pointing to one side of the door. —Unroll it and let's talk. Remember, there was something that I wanted to ask you.

I obeyed. I took the mat and unrolled it, my eyes had gotten used to the darkness and I did not need the light of day to see well. The little baby slept, but continued nursing. As soon as I was seated, the beautiful angel looked straight into my eyes.

Thank you for keeping me company—she said—since I don't have a husband, only a Franciscan would be able to keep me company while I feed my little one. I always do this alone. I don't like it.

The little girl, asleep, nursed more slowly. With one slight movement of her torso, without touching her (which she had hardly done, lying down as she had with the baby at her side), the Mama took her nipple out of the little one's mouth. And that's how she remained, nude before me, staring straight at me. Getting up from the mat, without saying a single word, she took her skirt off too, she rolled the little one onto her back, and sat there in front of me, so close I could touch her because I had recklessly placed my mat very close to hers. She smiled at me with her usual innocent expression.

—What I wanted to ask you, Franciscan brother, is if you would give me a kiss. But I didn't dare. Franciscans don't...

Without saying anything more, she threw herself into my arms. She kissed me. She put my hand on her breast. She raised my cassock. With one hand she grabbed my lustful member. She did not give me time to think, to say yes or no, or do anything.

I sinned. I sinned some more. I kept on sinning. God forgive me, I would do it again today if I could—in the half-light of that very room where desire illuminated my eyes with the clarity of the sun, I would keep on sinning.

I left her house when the little girl's babbling woke me up, because I had inexplicably fallen asleep. Her body had something that put the people who were close to her to sleep: she put the little girl to sleep by nursing her, she put me to sleep by possessing me—she possessed me by playing with me as if the day would never end, and then she put me to sleep when neither my spirit nor my body could satiate her. She slept too. I did not say goodbye to her or to her little one. I practically ran out of the room.

That long day was not over. I started to run toward the Colegio, far enough away to distance me from her, from my angel, and I might have arrived at the Colegio by the skin of my teeth, if the smell of the girl had not stopped me. I do not know why, but while I was running I raised my hand and when it passed in front of my face the smell of her stopped me short. In that moment I did not feel any remorse for having sinned. But what I noticed, with astonishing force, was the stench of my cassock. Touching her had given me back my hands, the ones I had lost as a child when I entered the Colegio de la Santa Cruz, and along with them, my sense of smell. The cassock stank. Inside of it I smelled like friars smell—of filth, of confinement, of books, of cooking smells—and all of this was accumulated along with many days worth of the sour sweat of chastity because the routine of the Colegio did not allow us the bath except very occasionally, and since we wore the same cassock every day I do not think it would surprise anyone that we would smell so horribly bad.

The Indian boys called us stinkards, in Nahuatl they called us stinkards, that is what they called the little Indian friars. But even though I had heard the word they used to refer to us thousands of times, even though in my first years I had been clean like all Indians, even though my clothes had smelled of flowers and herbs, even though that is what my life had been like before, I never thought I was a stinkard. The odor became part of everything else—the way of life was inseparable from it. It did not bother me as something apart, because it was not separate. It was (like the robe, the book, the ink, the little trunk at my feet that kept me company) the life to which they had brought me.

When I quit bathing, what hurt me was not to lose cleanliness, because I was quite carefree, but rather something that was associated with the bath. Not the water and the herbs with which I was scrubbed, but rather the brilliant pure light, those sheets of horizontal light that enveloped me, that did not come from the sun or the sky, but radiated from the body that leaned over to wash my body, and that, once the bath was finished, governed and protected my naked body with the rule of her love. In that moment I was not little or big; a boy or a girl; or Indian or white, but rather a perfect being. The aura of her love filled me with radiance and the two of us illuminated each other like two celestial bodies in their private heaven.

It is hard to imagine that I could have lost this paradise by not bathing, that not bathing made me *dirty*. Like one plus one equals two, not having Mama with me left me without the sense of touch that the heavenly moment of the bath gave me, but it did not add up to the two of filth and the odor of dirtiness. Moreover, when my backside was chafed for lack of cleanliness, when I had irritated and open wounds, it did not occur to me that a bath would remove that discomfort. Why would I think that being scrubbed with water and herbs would not have any other effect than of taking me to love's paradise, to the paradise of Mama's pure and chaste love? She did not touch my body to arouse sin or lust, and scrubbed me only to intensify the spark of her luminous love.

How could I think that not bathing would not make me a stinkard? Even worse: I did not notice the disgrace of my odor until the smell of another person brought to life what I had been carrying around for years. The source of this smell was not the heavenly power of water and herbs, but rather the flame of lust. It was the smell of a woman mixed with the smell of my body, which was inflamed by her. The two created an unknown, but familiar, smell. It struck me like a blow—it entered into my olfactory awareness with a single blow—and I was suddenly weak. My legs refused to keep walking and threatened to refuse to support me. I sat on a polished stone on the side of the road that I do not know how I, or which part of my body, discovered, since I could not see through my blurred vision, and my sense of smell was otherwise occupied and so could not be of any service even if stones had a smell, and my sense of touch was also impaired by the blow of the odor.

My position, seated as I was on the stone, made the odor even stronger and kept me from seeing anything at all. It was as if my eyes were tracking the back of a horse that was spinning around wildly, drunk or crazed. My eyes stopped for a moment and I saw a child with his mother at bath time and I felt the weight of her hands on me and my heart fell and broke into a million pieces on the ground. I burst out crying. At that moment I could finally reconcile with Mama. I forgave her for having abandoned me on Sundays because even though the prohibition against seeing me was not hers, my heart had experienced it as if it had been hers. And more than forgiving her for nothing, I felt again what it was like to be with her and again the pain of losing her.

The odor was still on me, or the two odors—the stench of the stinkard, the odor of intercourse—and my eyes once again tracked the back of the drunk and crazy horse and I cried some more and my motionless knees, though bent, trembled. The horse started to kick, but did not spin around anymore. As if they were riding on a pendulum, my eyes revisited the familiar odor of intercourse. I knew men and women who were anointed by that odor when I was a boy. And from the weight, or bob, of the pendulum on which my eyes rose and fell I saw them again, one-two, one-two, their eyes glowing with lust, their mouths stamped with kisses, their rumpled clothing impregnated with that odor, and of nothing else, one-two, but they did not come in even numbers. The vanquished and the widows consoled themselves for their losses—the dead, poverty, lost land, and men taken as the property of others and subjugated—fornicating untiringly, inflamed by that light that does not envelop, like that of my childhood bath, but rather blinds. Better to enjoy themselves blindly than to see themselves enslaved. And that is how the Indians continued, in desperate fornication, searching for the blindfold, the momentary oblivion, the fire that would consume them once and for all, turning them into ash that the air would take away, free in the winds and the heavens. I saw all of this from the throne my dizziness had converted that stone into. And I heard a man and a woman moaning, as I heard them one time as a child, when I did not understand the source of their black moaning. And I heard her, the one I had just finished having, and I heard myself in her, having her, and I felt my wretched intestines start to rise again even though they did not surpass either the dizziness or the spinning.

The horse suddenly stopped, tossing back to me the eyes that had been tracking his back. Here. There you are. There I was. I had just finished committing the sin that the friars said I did before I actually did. At that moment I deservedly lost the habit that I had already lost, and I lost it by my own merit. I was now expelled from the Franciscans, finally legitimately thrown out. I was no longer one of them, nor did I belong to my own skin. I was returned to myself, to my people, to those with whom I had passed the first years of my life. Except that they were already gone. Mama was dead. The copulators were now surely no more than ash ruled by the mistress of the winds, finished off by pain and loss.

To what could I return? If I paid attention to what I had between my legs, I could only go back to the heartless woman who had snatched me from the Franciscan friars.

But she was not a person who would take care of anyone. Not even her own daughter received any succor from her bosom. She was a selfish and cruel angel.

I felt I would gain little by returning to the Colegio, and I knew that I did not have anywhere else to go. How would my false father receive me?

So I went directly to the river to wash my filthy clothes and wash away the odor that upset my intestines, which made them feel like they were little living creatures in the bottom of the river.

I still do not understand why, if the Franciscans had taught me to distinguish good from evil and to fear punishment, and in spite of having committed an ugly sin, I do not understand, I say again, why I did not feel remorse on the way to the river. It did not even occur to me that bathing myself would wash away the odor in which others might be able to read my sin. On the one hand I wanted to rid myself of the stench, and on the other to settle my little animal, which was uneasy again, by soothing it with water. Not for one instant did I think about reprimanding it or myself. Remorse did not enter into my heart. The sweet, selfish angel had poisoned me completely.

I reached the river. I pulled the filthy clothes over my head, I folded them in my arms and, holding them, I went into the water naked with them. It was cool, almost cold. It was just what my body needed. At its contact, my blood revived, and a jolt of happiness hit me. I tied the purple cassock to a submerged trunk so that the flowing water would cleanse it. I could not do anything else for it, since I had never washed a single piece of clothing with my own hands.

I walked along the riverbed, feeling the water wash over my skin, caressing it. What happiness I felt. Living in the friars' world had cheated me into an old age that was not mine. The water's touch purified me of them. Hernando could run, shout, dance, and fly from time to time. I reclined in the water and began to swim like I did when I was a child. I quit thinking. I was a fish, I used to be a fish, my gills had inflated and I did not want to return to the frying pan. The selfish angel had inadvertently been generous to me. She had taken me out of the frying pan and I was back in the water. Angel, little angel, I will turn around and come back to put my penis inside your little body. Now I will be the child who sucks on your nipples. I quit swimming. I walked on the sandy bottom. On your nipples, I repeated, and I imagined them between my fingers and in my mouth. I put my hand on my penis, and this time not because I was afraid. It was hard, standing erect in front of me. I moved my closed hand up its shaft, I moved it down, up, down. I opened my eyes. A few meters away by some giant reeds, waist deep in water, like I was, a couple was wrapped around each other. How did I not hear them? She was moaning and gasping. Her beautiful unbraided hair bobbed, the ends dipping in the water. I saw them in profile, I could see one of his hands across both of her breasts. I saw their open mouths, saw them swaying, her fingers searching for his hand and my enormous penis, between them and me, blessing us. Were they two demons, these copulators?

Were they merely a mirror reflecting my lustful thoughts? After emptying it, I let go of my penis, and along with it, my moorings. I swam back, retracing my steps. I untied my cassock. I got out of the water.

Miserably naked on the bank of the river, I felt cold. I recognized my smallness in the weariness of my flesh. But I did not have a single regret. A pompous and arrogant silence settled in the core of my soul.

I wrung out my cassock as best I could, twisting it with my hands. I hung it over the giant reeds and sat next to it. The couple kept moaning. They were certainly demons because time did not pass for them. Maybe they had been wrapped around each other for a hundred years. Maybe more, and they did not know that the Aztecs had won the islet on which they raised their empire. Maybe more, and they did not even know about the arrival of man in these lands. Maybe even more, and they fished for the serpent in these waters, and they were urging it toward the earthly paradise, pulling it along with a little stick or calling it with whispers and whistles.

But, no. I saw them get out on the other side of the river. First him, he got his clothes and started dressing. Then she got out and quickly put her clothes on and started to braid her long hair.

"It is quite a long trek that awaits me to reach the Colegio—I must have thought—and I'm as hungry as a bear."

I slipped the still-wet cassock over my body and set off, walking barefoot. If I had invoked that couple with my erect animal, how many more couples might I have seen along the way? Every fifty steps I could have stopped and undressed, I could have called the copulators and they might have converged. Before my eyes might have passed a woman and her husband, a brother-in-law and a wife, a girlfriend and boyfriend, an aunt with her nephew, a niece and her uncle, a maid and her master, a mistress with her servant boy, and I might also have seen one man sodomizing another, a boy penetrating the ass of a dog, and dogs and birds copulating with each other, as if my own lust would fully awaken spring.

But in these lands there is no spring to awaken because here nothing overcomes the winter. Behind the branches of the weeping willows, by the protected walls, hidden among shrubs and giant reeds, there, on the limestone that scratches buttocks and legs, my people, the Indians, lament their defeat with sweet moans. Steps farther beyond, in the white streets, behind the balconies—on top of the soft cushions or leaning against a table or stretched out on beds, or hiding in the stables on the straw, or even against the doorjamb (in order to keep watch), or on top of a bench, or in the garden like toads—the Spaniards, the conquerors of these lands, celebrate their victory in twos, moaning as well, the wives feigning disgust to assure their husbands of their chastity, little whores letting out fake little screams to please the ones who are paying for their pleasure.

How many might be enjoying themselves and how many demons might be stroking the tip of the flesh with their repugnant tails? Lilith will go from neck to neck, entering and leaving to ignite the desire of the idle or the sleepers, and all the children conceived will be her children.

But I will not dawdle anymore. I was not thinking about children, or Lilith, or demons, or the hundreds of sinners who might be celebrating at this moment in that new Gomorrah, triumphant or defeated. My head was cleared by an animalistic burst of laughter.

Slosos keston de Hernando

EKFLOROS KESTON DE LEARO

Now they imitate vegetables—just as the sun guides the movement of the leaf and the flower, the sun guides them to the Punto
Calpe. At the time of day that the sunlight leads the people of
L'Atlàntide to the Punto Calpe, Carson dislocated her right arm,
ripping it out of her torso with her left hand, right there for
everyone to see.

That really happened. Carson disarticulated her own arm, she
ripped it off her body.

When I saw her do this, my first reaction was to run away.
I thought she would bleed, that the bones and the muscles would
be exposed. I felt an infinite revulsion. But the people of L'Atlàntide
move more quickly than I do, they accelerate time, and that's what
Carson did. Before I could hightail it out of there to avoid seeing
the blood and open flesh, Carson flipped her arm around, shook it,
not spurting any blood at all, and raised it to her eyes. I managed
to see her hollow bones. She immediately put it back inside her
body, putting her arm in her torso, hand-first into the shoulder joint.

I suddenly saw one finger coming out of her ear and the tip of
another one poking out of her nose. Carson opened her mouth:
the rest of her hand was behind her tongue.

The people of L'Atlàntide kept on gesticulating their stupid
messages, not paying the slightest attention to Carson. I was the
only witness, and what she did struck me as so atrociously repugnant (worse than the blood and viscera I had been afraid of) that

I moved in close so that she would see me watching her and stop doing such disgusting things.

But it didn't matter to her that I was watching. She wasn't in the least bit embarrassed, and before my very eyes she opened her mouth wider, and even wider, dislocating her jaw, and with the left hand she ripped her jaw off and tore a strip of skin from her body. She peeled away a strip of skin that went from her jaw to her neck, continuing between her breasts and down both sides of her belly button, and then down to her pubis where she let the strip dangle between her legs.

She didn't even bleed. She just blinked once. My eyes were wide open in astonishment and horror. The opening exposed by the strip of skin that now hung from her like a frontal tail allowed me to see the arm that had entered through its hole, plus an infinite number of things. Not viscera, but *things*, things of different colors and shapes, things arranged in strict order and the economy of space inside her body.

Carson manipulated some of these things with her left hand. Suddenly one of the objects fell to the ground. She pulled out her right arm and reattached it to its normal place. With both hands she picked up the thing that had fallen (a triangular-shaped form) and kept on touching the other things. I did manage to see some viscera behind them.

Have we lied to ourselves? Who made these things? Are we all filled with things, or just Carson, the anatomy specialist? What is this? It wasn't like this before they abandoned language, was it? Or does this aberration precede the Reform?

Carson picked up the strip of dangling skin and started to put it back in place. It was obvious that its edges were not sticking together, and you could still see a gap between her arm and her torso. She raised both of her hands above her head and clapped them once. This got the attention of the others. They drew near. I moved away from them. They formed a ball and, as if they had perceived the similarity I had observed, they "organized" and started making a droning sound.

Droning. They were droning. Without separating from the honeycomb, Ulises and Lilia performed one of those horrendous simulations of copulation that they have taken to doing. He stuck his penis in her while she was perched on all fours, not aroused in the least. He did show some signs of pleasure—he shivered two or three times—and with one sharp moan he completed the farce. She got up as if nothing had happened.

Caspa raced up the steps of the Punto Calpe carrying a bundle in her arms. The drones separated from Carson to open the way for Caspa.

Carson still had the two open gashes in her skin, but now she also had more wounds on her skin—scratches, bruises, and she was bleeding here and there. The drones had been beating her while they droned.

Caspa handed the bundle to Carson. Carson took it in her arms, unwrapped the cloth that covered it, and started to rub it over her body. It was one of Caspa's newborns. She slid the baby over her enormous breasts, over her round and ample belly, across her broad hips, she smeared him, rubbed him. The baby cried. I would say that he melted, like soap (but I've never seen a cake of soap, I've only read about it). The drones no longer droned, but they were surrounding her again. One moment they were honeycombed against each other and then they quickly separated. There were no signs of the newborn. There were no marks on Carson's skin.

In seconds nobody was left on the Punto Calpe. I slowly went down to write these notes.

I'll go back to my Hernando. But first I have to end with these verses from Brontë:

> Few hearts to mortals given
> On earth so wildly pine
> yet none would ask a Heaven
> More like the Earth than thine.

Slosos keston de Learo

EKFLOROS KESTON DE HERNANDO

I would like to be able to raise my head to look at the sky. I should hold something in my hands that would reflect it because I want to see it, to know what is moving in it, what swishes across its blue body, though its movement might not be quite a swish, but rather the smooth elegance of an enormous body that quickly passes over the dauntless smell. The cloud does not walk or fly—it seems to glide, as if through water. Its movement is an action devoid of all feeling. For the cloud, traveling is not displacement. Its movement contains something as inescapable as death, something of a violent peace. And even though it does not release any emotions traveling like that—so slowly and so quickly at the same time, ripping without tearing, detachment without attachment—the cloud's movement without movement, beautiful, white, almost corporeal, persistent and willful, constant, headstrong—it moves me to tears to remember it. I wanted to see it, and they will say I mourned. But it is not because I mourned that I want to see the cloud cross the sky, but rather because I miss its soft beauty. It never retraces its path. It does not change its route. It moves forward, passes over me, covers a good part of the blue sky and continues, moving forward. There it goes. Forward on its way.

If only my life had been like the passing of the cloud, beautiful, harmonious and moving, steadfast—and not that fluttering snap, not that successive leaping and all those hurdles—because (and this is what moves me most about the movement of the cloud) in its path there is not a single hurdle. Nothing stops it, the wind carries it, its body carries it, it seems that it was born to move inexorably forward, traveling without moving, flying without flying, made of the same material as the movement, pure progress, progression, movement…On the other hand, my body—the soil watered by my life, in which my life was created—is not like that; my body is earthenware and stone. My earthenware body is fragile, brittle; my stone body is heavy and slow, it tumbles down the backside of the slope in fits and starts, and when it reaches the bottom it breaks into twelve pieces. My entire body is carved on one of the twelve fragments, which is how they put me back together. And the other eleven will remain there, as if they had not been mine, and the piece on which my torso is carved begins to grow into an arrogant trick-ster, confident in the image carved on it, and it does not remem-ber that it was one of the twelve, that it is not my entire body.

It is from that fragment that I tell you my story: that is what I am, that is what is left of me. The cloud…I wanted to at least see the cloud, feel it fly, hear it move along, but my body of stone cannot figure out how to turn to look enough above me and the pages I write on do not reflect the sky, and there is not a good soul around here who would take me to the shore of the lake to see the body of the passing white cloud reflected in it. Now that the light of the sun is dimming because a cloud is passing overhead, now would be when, if they took me to the shore of the lake, I would see the passage of the cloud reflected in it. But I do not know if the lake is even capable of reflecting the blue of the sky and the passing clouds. I do not know if trash and disorder have damaged it to the point that it has turned into a twelfth of what it was, like my body, and a trick makes it believe that it is still the entire lake. In that case, if I would not be able to see the sky reflected, I would not want to go to its shore. I prefer to imagine the cloud that has just passed. The cloudless sky shines a perfect—I would almost say immortal—light on the flagstone floor.

The next day, I woke up to sing matins with the backs of my knees hurting and a kind of burning sensation coursing down into my belly. My arms hurt too, but it was not pain exactly that extended throughout the rest of my body, stabbing more in the backs of my knees and arms and increasing greatly throughout the rest of my muscles and bones. Before I had time, a minute at least, to remember what I had done, the memory slipped from my body. I sang with greater fervor than other times. I did not quite know if I was profoundly joyful or desperately sad. Sad and joyful in extreme degrees, my consciousness dazed, and a cloying taste turning, by the second, into an appetite that until that moment was completely unknown to me. It was Friday, the day of flagellation. The whip was already inside me. Not in the pain, or almost pain, that penetrated my muscles, but in the appetite it awoke in me like a wave that came from afar, commanded by a distant star over which I was powerless. I was not the same for weeks after that. I knew, as the Franciscans had said, that I had committed a terrible sin, but had not yet reached the confessional. I also knew that this terrible sin was the whip of my days and that it was a strangely sweet whip.

Slosos keston de Hernando

Is my body full of things too? I'm sure it is not. I'm not full of things. I breathe. I'm alive. My body is made of flesh and not of hard artificial material. I think I'm filled with viscera. I have desires. It fills my heart with horror to know that I can never again exchange another word with anyone, that I can never again converse, but worse still is knowing that I can never make love again. Never again, Lear, get it through your head. The people of L'Atlàntide are now poor imitations of flesh; they are pieces of furniture full of things. You are the only one made of flesh and the only one who still has desires. They can never make love again; they mate, they imitate dogs in heat. They've lost their connection to the flesh. With words dead, there isn't a tree that would welcome them, give them shade, fill them with Mother Nature's spirit. I'm not a lion or tiger to supply them with meat. There isn't a why or how to avoid the things. But they're worse than things. They're alive only because of them—the things. Without them they wouldn't breathe, the blood wouldn't flow through their veins.

I was mistaken when I compared them to vegetables. They're not like Caspa's sugarcanes, which are plants with animal-like marks. They have no relation to plants. They don't come close to being plants with their diligent and painstaking lack of consciousness. Though they're beasts, they don't come close to being animals. And they're much less like stones, because they don't stop doing for even a second. They are doing something all the time.

In front of Ulises' room I found Jeremías squatting down, pushing. He got up when he heard my footsteps. In the exact spot where he had been, he left a thing, a red cube. It was warm. It was covered with a slimy substance that could have been semen or phlegm, and it was probably neither of these two things, but when I touched it I thought that whatever was covering it was a secretion from Jeremías' body and this produced an uncontrollable repugnance in me. I dropped the red cube and wiped my hands off as best I could. That fluid, the cube, Jeremías, the others, and those who are not in front of me in this very instant—they all disgust me.

I remembered Carson peeling the skin from her body. I remembered the couples I had seen, one of them sticking his penis in the other like dogs and horses do. I remembered their droning, their tendency to dissolve, their stupid code—it all made me sick.

They are repugnant, repulsive. Am I equally repugnant and repulsive to them? I don't recognize my brothers and my friends in their faces and bodies. I don't see in them the people I grew up with, my companions in the adventure of survival, the founders of the Age of Air and the repudiation of things. They are no longer what they were. Their perpetual present doesn't understand their past. They are not the same as those beauties who ran through the forests, petted zebras, rode ostriches, and scaled the Rockies. These beings are something else because they don't remember anything, because they don't speak, because they don't inhabit time.

The people of L'Atlàntide are now an extinct species. I'm the only survivor. The ones I say don't exist anymore are always doing something; they are compulsive doers.

If I wanted to describe everything they do, how they don't stop making things and don't desist from doing and doing and doing at lightning speed, in less than the blink of an eye, I would have to follow them without taking my eyes off them, record them from the Center. Follow them while I write here. Words are slower than their vertiginous movements, but I could summarize their actions. To become their chronicler, I would have to work only on them. They invent stories all day long. Goethe said that we invent stories to escape our memories.

Today, in the human equivalent of ten minutes, they congregated on the Punto Calpe and, mimicking speech, they pretended to argue. They divided into two angry and infuriated gangs, cursing each other with poor imitations of curse words. Then I saw them descend like a flash of lightning and pick things up from the surface of the earth. Some of them carried construction beams, others carried cement blocks, or sheets of corrugated metal, or fuselages, or tubes, and all displayed an astonishing amount of strength.

They used these things to hit each other, one gang against the other, and when they lost their weapons in the heat of battle, they used their fists and teeth or other body parts to hurt each other. I saw Ulises, who had disarticulated his own leg, hold it with both hands and furiously beat Lilia with it—he turned his leg into a club to use it as a torture device. Since he only had one leg, Ulises leaned on Jeremías, who in turn was biting Lilia's ankles and toes. I think he was even eating her toes, or that's the way looked to me. Lilia bleated like a sacrificial lamb. She didn't do anything to defend herself. I didn't do anything to try to make them see reason and stop their idiotic simulation of war either. I watched them with a heavy heart. My beautiful Lilia was not only left without some of her toes, she had also lost an eye, and one of her breasts was bleeding profusely.

With pieces of plastic taken from a trash heap, someone made a strip that served as a ludicrous banner for one of the gangs, which at times also was used to beat someone like a stupid bullwhip. Someone else tossed around an enormous rubber tire. They nailed sheets of aluminum to a stick. Another person had a net full of glass shards and was beating his enemies with it.

They have become ghastly beings. The atmosphere has corroded their mucous membranes so much that some of them can't close their eyes because they don't have eyelids anymore. Their teeth are visible behind their translucent lips. Others have fallen to such a degree of neglect that they are missing one limb or another. When I was going back to my room the other afternoon I found an abandoned penis on the steps of the Punto Calpe; it seemed to have been left there out of carelessness. Most of them go around dirty, and they are always carrying things with them. The last time I saw Rosete he was walking around wrapped in a Persian rug, his hair a mess, crying out in an incomprehensible mumbo-jumbo, dragging his feet, and his face and hands showed similar signs of deterioration that reminded me of leprosy.

Ah, my beauties. We've lost everything. In the ultimate community of men and women, we were all equals, no one thought less of another because of race, sex, or appearance. Nobody was rich or poor, powerful or enslaved. We lived in harmony; we overcame disease, old age, and death. In that idyllic community that could have been eternal, our fear of the past resulted in the destruction of the species.

But let's write a human end to L'Atlàntide, and not the abominable one to which we have fallen, perhaps until the end of time. Let's say that Time ultimately defeated L'Atlàntide. Let's say that God abandoned it and ordered seven plagues to fall on it when he saw that nobody remembered him. Let's say that the ambition to perfect the species made it embrace a suicidal cause. "O memory, wake!"

None of this will be true. L'Atlàntide doesn't accept the end man had imagined for it. The shining silk of the spider—sparkling in the sun, oscillating beautifully in the wind—is more like the people of L'Atlàntide are today than the men from the time of History.

And what if I don't understand anything? What if, free of words and time, stripped of all reality, they have found paradise?

> to live without remembering might be the
> secret of the gods.

Slosos keston de Learo

EKFLOROS KESTON DE HERNANDO

I've written here, and hidden in my chair, how I sinned in the arms and between the legs of an evil angel—one of the *diablomes* who walks the Earth on two feet, incarnated in the body of a woman. But this was not what darkened my soul, what made my spirit go from bad to evil, from what one should do to what one should not do, from disappointment to mockery and contempt. An abyss separates that child who understood the grace and divine words found in the stories of the saints, the one who flew on the wings of faith, and me—the legless one.

I am a person who lacks illumination, distant from the light of faith, lost in the darkness of detachment, disillusionment, and disinterest. I do not belong to anything. I am not from that time unfamiliar with the lock and key, I am not from those magnificent cities where the houses were always open, where the *quequezalcoa*, *tlenamacac*, and *tlamacazqui*—which were the three levels of priests (the first, "feathered serpents," devoted to Huitzilopochtli and Tláloc, the second, "merchants of fire," and the third, "servants")— ruled these lands with wisdom, nor am I from over there, from the fog and heavenly clouds where my people believed they saw the first twelve Franciscans descend, nor from the cruel European lands. I do not belong to China or to the lands of the blacks.

The years, baring their horrible fangs, expelled me from the warm bodies that my own body believed it belonged to. My dear mother: I, Hernando, your son, did not recognize the words of the ancient gods.

Did I not understand the divine words that are everywhere, that all things see and all things know, and that it is so wonderful that the Earth has its kingdom here, which began at the beginning of the world and which one day wanted to bring us into its faith because we needed to be blessed? What did I have faith in? Which world did I belong to?

One day I want to leave written here that I, Hernando, lost everything that gives a man pleasure and joy, that my life forever lost whatever meaning a man's life has. At night, I raise my prayers so that God's light might again envelop with light the darkness I live in. Do our lives not mean anything anymore? Will we be flung into the final river that will carry us to death, with our eyes blinded in the thief's sack of lies? Together, inside that sack, like good stewards of the Colegio de la Santa Cruz, we will steal to see how we can profit from our victims. "If we will die, we will die: if we will perish, we will perish; the truth is that the gods die too." But, apart from this useless sack, this not-life-not-death, nothing is allowed. "*Nec vivere nec mori volumus: vitae nos odium tenet timor mortis:* We do not want to live or die. We are possessed by the hatred of life and by the fear of death."[39]

Slosos keston de Hernando

---

39   This sounds like a Nahua song to me. Lear's note.

EKFLOROS KESTON DE ESTELINO

The following appears at the end of Hernando's words, in a different hand:

"Here end the writings of Hernando de Rivas, one of the first boys of the Colegio Real de Santa Cruz, native of Tetzcuco, an excellent Latinist who translated anything whatsoever from Latin and Romance into the Mexican language with great facility; attending more to the meaning than to the letter, he wrote and translated a variety of things—more than thirty quires of paper for Fray Juan Bautista. He died in the year ninety-seven [1597], on the eleventh of September, and I believe Our Lord paid him for his faithful labor because he was a very good Christian Indian, loved the things of our holy Catholic faith very much and taught the Mexican language to the religious for the honor and service of Our Lord. With his help P. Fr. Alonso de Molina composed *Arte y Vocabulario mexicano*, P. Fr. Juan de Gaona composed *Diálogos de la paz y tranquilidad del alma*, P. Fr. Juan Bautista el *Vocabulario Eclesiástico* (a very important work for priests), and a large part of P. Estela's *las Vanidades del mundo,* the *Flos Sanctorum* or *Vidas de Santos*, the *Exposición del Decálogo, a*nd many other treatises and books that I will try to bring to light, if the Majesty of God would be served in giving me life to do it, non *recuso laborem*.[40]

---

40   These words almost coincide with those of Fray Juan Bautista in the Pro-logue to his Sermonario, reproduced by García Icazbalceta in his *Bibliografía Mexicana del siglo XVI.* Editor's note.

These quires, which I have not read, will continue to be guarded in the hidden compartment of the chair, according to Hernando's last wishes, which I thereby respect. R.I.P."

I'm not sure what to say. I knew from the beginning that these pages would end at some point, and I had prolonged the arrival of the end for the sake of the story. This note, written by a man who is completely unknown to me, robs me of my Hernando (where was the end of Agustín that you promised to tell us, what is the story that made you loathsome? What happened in your life to make you lose your faith?) and forces me to live immersed in an atrocious reality, no better than Hernando's, "where envy and lies imprisoned me." Would it occur to you to recite these verses of Fray Luis de León?:

> Oh, now safe harbor
> for my long error!
> Oh, so desired
> for certain repair
> of my heavy, dark past,
> joyful repose, sweet, restful!

Slosos keston de Estelino

EKFLOROS KESTON DE LEARO

Last night, between alarms (which I now understand don't ring for me, but are rather a result of the reigning disorder), I saw Estela, I saw Hernando, and the three of us saw each other.

Though his eyes were open, Hernando denied seeing me. But he did hear me and he laughed when I told him who I was. Estela looked at me, eyes bulging, and said:

—What a priest, what a priest!—She was as excited as a gas bubble in water.

Today I'm going to try to go back to be with them, I'll go back in time and revive them. I want to go into the *cestos* to live with them.

I can't stay with my community anymore. I'm going to try to transform myself into words and jump into the realm I can share with Estela and Hernando. I think I can do it. The realm that books inhabit is a real place. The one I'm in no longer is. If we have lived in a fantasy—a fantasy in which there was no feces, or trees, or death—from the beginning (as I suspected in the end), misled and immersed in a virtual reality that didn't coincide with our actions, then in breaking with grammar, the community has also broken with the version of reality imposed on us. They've left me alone "with my feet on the ground," and yet floating among the clouds, on the verge of disintegrating like they are.

I will be with Estela and Hernando until the end of time. I'll erase the announcement of Hernando's death, I'll take out the paragraph in which it is mentioned, I won't let him meet his end. Nor will I allow Estela to meet her death either, the one that she would have experienced in the great explosion. I'll bring both of them to me, we'll share a common *kesto* that nobody will be able to lock. The three of us will inhabit in the same realm. The three of us will belong to three distinct times, our memories will be of three distinct ages, but I will know Hernando's, and Hernando will know mine, and we'll share a common space where we can look each other in the eyes and we'll establish a new community.

Ours will be the Heavens on Earth. L'Atlàntide will belong to the past, like ancient Tenochtitlan, like Hernando's Mexico, and Estela's country.

The three of us will devote ourselves to remembering. That's how we'll establish the beginning of time. Christ will not awaken in our shared dream, but Mohammed and Buddha, Tezcatlipócatl and the poet Nezahualcóyotl will shake hands. We'll live our lives remembering. Our future will be spent remembering. But we won't dissolve, we won't fall into the trap of idiocy my community has plunged into.

We'll save language and the memory of man, and one day we'll shape the hand that will tell our story, and we'll wonder about the mystery of death, the foolish absurdity of men and women. We will feel horror, even though our bodies will experience neither cold nor pain.

An abyss will open at our feet. Those will be the Heavens on Earth.

Slosos keston de Learo

TRANSLATOR'S NOTE

Carmen Boullosa originally published *Cielos de la Tierra* in 1997, five years after the quincentenary of the so-called "discovery" of the "New World." This was a time when many Latin American writers were reflecting on and writing about the significance of this 500th anniversary. What is so interesting is that this novel is as relevant, or perhaps even more so, now than when it was published twenty years ago, especially given the current political and cultural climate around the world where we find a resurgence of racism, intolerance, and discrimination, not to mention the damage we are doing to the environment of our earth.

I was introduced to this novel through a presentation given by Charles Hatfield, who would soon after suggest I translate it. After reading *Cielos de la Tierra*, I knew it was the perfect project for me to embark on because of the subject matter and themes Boullosa treats in the novel. Little did I understand on that first quick reading the profound complexity and the great challenges I would face in bringing it into English. This was a fascinating novel to translate and I'm privileged and honored to have had the opportunity.

The novel, whose title I've translated as *Heavens on Earth*, tells of worlds where language and speech, and consequently agency, are denied, suppressed, or obliterated and is deeply concerned with translation, literature, language, and the (re)telling of history. This is most obvious in the fact that the three main characters are all translators. However, the depth of Boullosa's preoccupation with translation here is illustrated by the fact that all three translator-narrators work with, and leave their mark on, the same text: a history of the Colegio de la Santa Cruz de Santiago Tlatelolco written by a sixteenth-century Aztec native who was educated by the Franciscans at the Colegio. Hernando, the translator-narrator from early sixteenth-century Mexico, translates the history and memories of the ancient Aztecs, which he incorporates into the history he sets out to write on the Colegio; Estela, the translator-narrator from late twentieth-century Mexico, translates Hernando's manuscript from Latin into Spanish, incorporating her own memories and stories; and finally, the translator-narrator who is writing from the post-apocalyptic future, Lear, translates her own experiences into Spanish and transcribes Estela's Spanish translation of Hernando's Latin manuscript using the writing technique of her futuristic community.

To create this novel, Boullosa makes heavy use of both attributed and unattributed quotations, which she excerpts (or paraphrases) from poetry, novels, essays, biblical stories, religious writings, Aztec legends and poetry, historical narratives, and archival documents. For example, Boullosa interweaves excerpts of poetry and prose from Álvaro Mutis, as well as excerpts taken from the poetry of Emily Brontë, Oscar Wilde, Rubén Darío, and Ramón López Velarde; excerpts of novels written by Gabriel García Márquez and Federico Gamboa; excerpts of essays written by Emilio Pacheco and Michael Krauss; excerpts from the writings of Saint Francis, Bernardino Sahagún's *Historia general de las cosas de la Nueva España*, Fray Juan Bautista's *Sermonario*; historical works written by Joaquín García Icazbalceta; Gerónimo de Mendieta's *Historia eclesiástica indiana*; Motolinía's *Historia de los indios de la Nueva España*; and Torquemada's

Monarquía indiana, among many more. In Lear's sections alone, there are excerpts from twenty-eight poems by ten different poets, which range in length from just one or two lines to several stanzas.

Given all these layers, this novel might be best understood as sort of palimpsest whereon the traces left by others show through a parchment that has been overwritten many times. Here the three narrators become the mediators, or intermediaries, through which we hear these other voices, through which the other stories are told—each one leaving a trace on the parchment.

All the translations of Spanish-language literary quotations and paraphrases in Lear's section, most of which have not been translated before, are my own, with the exception of one biblical paraphrase. Though literary references are not predominant in Estela's narrative, in one section Boullosa quotes extensively from Gabriel García Márquez's *Cien años de soledad*, a classic work of Latin American fiction. Given that this text had already been so masterfully translated by Gregory Rabassa, one of the most iconic twentieth-century translators, I decided it would be best to use Rabassa's translations of the quoted passages rather than to create my own. In the sections narrated by Hernando, Boullosa also quotes and paraphrases rather extensively from the Bible. Rather than translate the passages taken from the Bible in Hernando's sections myself, I decided to use the *Douay-Rheims Bible* (DRB) version, which is the English translation of the Latin Vulgate Bible, which itself was translated by St. Jerome into Latin from the Greek and Hebrew texts between 382 and 405 AD. Saint Jerome's Latin Vulgate was the version sanctified by the Roman Catholic Church in 1546 to be the authentic and official version of the Bible.

I would expect that the Latin Vulgate would be the Bible that Hernando would have read and quoted from, and so I chose the DRB as the English version most contemporary to his time. The DRB New Testament was published in 1582 by the English College at Rheims, and the DRB Old Testament was published in 1609 by the English College at Douay.

My strategy in translating this text was to foreignize the translation enough to allow the reader to not only be aware of, but also experience and appreciate, the linguistic and cultural differences of a text originally written in another language and cultural context. To this end, I decided to use the original Spanish-language terms in the following instances: proper names, place names, loan words, and culinary terms.

Regarding proper names, I have kept these in Spanish unless they belong to historical figures outside of the Hispanic world and for whom there are accepted English-language versions. Related to this decision of using the original Spanish for proper names is the one to retain diminutive forms, familial names, and terms of endearment in Spanish, rather than translating or Anglicizing them. I have also kept place names in Mexico in the Spanish. However, for any other locations around the globe referred to in the novel, I have used the more familiar and commonly accepted English forms as recognized in North America.

In addition, I did not translate Spanish words that have been borrowed into the English language and can be found in the dictionary, even though they might be unfamiliar to the general English-language reader. Examples of some of these words are: acequia, cacique, cedula, cenote, comal, criollo, encomienda, mestizo, and quetzal.

I made a similar decision with regard to leaving many culinary terms (food or kitchen items) that are specific to the Mexican or Pre-Columbian context in their original form either because Boullosa had already provided an explication in the text or because I added a bit of explication myself. An example of how I might explicate for the English language reader is this one from Hernando's first section: "As soon as they entered Acallan they were given the <u>hot, thick, sweetened cornflour drink known as</u> *atole* and the <u>sweet roasted blue cornflour drink called</u> *pinole*." Here, the underlined text represents the explication. In addition, because I explicated the term *atole* in this instance, when it appears later in the book I simply use the Spanish term. This, then, is the strategy I employ throughout the translation: I use a foreign-language word or phrase accompanied by an explication on the first appearance in the text, and thereafter I simply use the term in the original language.

Some of the challenges related to translating this novel in particular arise from trying to capture the narrative voice and style of the three narrators, one man and two women, each of whom is writing from his or her own perspective and living in a different time period. The eras in which two of the narrators live are so "foreign"—one being the science-fiction world of a post-apocalyptic future and the other being sixteenth-century Colonial Mexico—that they have distinct languages associated with them, namely, the futuristic science-fiction terminology, as well as the Esperanto, French, and German languages associated with the futuristic world and the now archaic languages of both the civil and religious worlds of early colonial Mexico, which includes Latin, Spanish, and Nahuatl.

The first "foreign world" terminology the reader encounters in the novel proper is a phrase in Esperanto: *Ekfloros keston de Learo*. In Esperanto, the word *ekflori* means "to bloom or flower" and thus suggests an opening, in this case the opening of a section narrated by a Learo (a.k.a. Lear). *Kesto* in Esperanto means a "box, chest, or coffer," which might suggest a box such as those found in the archives, or in this case perhaps an archived document, as in an entry, report, or manuscript. The ending of the section is indicated by the Esperanto phrase *Slosos keston de Learo*. In Esperanto, the word *slosi* means, "to lock," suggesting the closing or ending of the section. Each "chapter," or section, opens and closes with the phrases *Ekfloros keston de* and *Slosos keston de*, followed by the Esperanto version of the narrator's name.

There is another term that comes up several times in relation to some work that one of Lear's companions in L'Atlàntide is doing with "quicks." The word "quick" is recognizable as an English word, but it is also an Esperanto word, and in both languages it can mean "alive" or "living." From the context, it would seem that the character is doing some type of experiments with live animal matter. Because this is a science-fiction world, the term "quicks" does not make any more logical sense in the original Spanish text than in English translation and the meaning of the word is left up to the interpretation of the reader in both languages.

The greatest challenge in translating the sections narrated by Hernando stems from the fact that his sections reflect not just one foreign world, but rather three. There is of course the early colonial world in which he lives, but there are also enough references to the Pre-Columbian world that it is very much present in the novel.

Moreover, the early colonial world in which Hernando lives is inhabited and governed, by the religious of the Franciscan order on the one hand, and the colonial government on the other. Challenges also arose from the fact that Boullosa incorporates pieces of text taken from historical narratives and archival documents, the latter of which are characterized by both high formal and colloquial registers, a circuitous writing style, archaic language, and non-standardized spelling.

Throughout the sections narrated by Hernando, I have tried wherever possible to translate using language that coincides with the outside sources Boullosa uses so as to reflect the time in which he was living. In order to do this, I turned to the historical thesaurus of the Oxford English Dictionary, especially when it came to finding the right idiomatic expression that would coincide best with the early sixteenth century. What was most interesting about attempting to use words, phrases, and expressions that would have been contemporary to Hernando's time was discovering that so many of the phrases and expressions we use today actually date back to the fifteenth and sixteenth centuries. This reminds me of something Umberto Eco wrote in the "Postscript" to *The Name of the Rose*, where he mentions the feedback he received from readers and critics who complained that sometimes one character or another sounded too modern, and Eco writes that "in every one of these instances, and only in these instances, I was actually quoting fourteenth-century texts." So, despite the fact that we know that languages change over time, perhaps some aspects evolve much more slowly than we think.

Traveling through space and time with Lear, Estela, and Hernando while I translated their lives was a remarkable journey. It was a thrill to jump back and forth among their realms—from L'Atlàntide in the post-apocalyptic future, to Mexico City of the 1990s, back into early colonial New Spain, and forward again into the future. Throughout the process I endeavored to balance my fidelity to the author and the original text while translating the stories of the novel in a way that is readable, if not entirely comfortable, for an English-language audience. My goal was to translate in a reasonably faithful and clear prose that does not domesticate Boullosa's novel, but would allow the English-language reader to experience the foreign in *Heavens on Earth* and, moreover, to appreciate the foreignness on the many levels—language, culture, time periods, settings—present in the novel.

I would like to thank Carmen Boullosa, first and foremost, for giving me permission to translate this fascinating text; Charles Hatfield for introducing me to the novel; Lourdes Molina and Lilly Albritton for being there throughout; Rainer Schulte for being my mentor for more than a decade; Benjamin, always; George Henson for introducing me to Will Evans, and finally Will himself along with the staff at Deep Vellum for their commitment to publishing this novel for the English language readers.

SHELBY VINCENT
Dallas, TX, 2017

SHELBY VINCENT is the managing editor of *Translation Review* and a lecturer and research associate at the University of Texas at Dallas, where she earned her PhD in the Humanities with a focus on literary translation studies. In her free time, she is a literary translator, and has contributed to the translation of *Woman Street Artists of Latin America* (Manic D Press), as well as translating Carmen Boullosa's *Heavens on Earth*. She is currently translating another book by Carmen Boullosa, *La virgin y el violin* (*The Virgin and the Violin*).

Thank you all
for your support.
We do this for you,
and could not do
it without you.

DEEP
VELLUM

LIGA DE ORO ($5,000+)

Anonymous (2)

LIGA DEL SIGLO ($1,000+)

Allred Capital Management
Ben & Sharon Fountain
David Tomlinson & Kathryn Berry
Judy Pollock
Life in Deep Ellum
Loretta Siciliano
Lori Feathers
Mary Ann Thompson-Frenk
& Joshua Frenk
Matthew Rittmayer
Meriwether Evans
Pixel and Texel
Nick Storch
Social Venture Partners Dallas
Stephen Bullock

DONORS

Adam Rekerdres
Alan Shockley
Amrit Dhir
Anonymous (4)
Andrew Yorke
Anthony Messenger
Bob Appel
Bob & Katherine Penn
Brandon Childress
Brandon Kennedy
Caitlin Baker
Caroline Casey
Charles Dee Mitchell

Charley Mitcherson
Cheryl Thompson
Christie Tull
CS Maynard
Cullen Schaar
Daniel J. Hale
Deborah Johnson
Dori Boone-Costantino
Ed Nawotka
Elizabeth Gillette
Rev. Elizabeth
   & Neil Moseley
Ester & Matt Harrison

Farley Houston
Garth Hallberg
Grace Kenney
Greg McConeghy
Jeff Waxman
JJ Italiano
Justin Childress
Kay Cattarulla
Kelly Falconer
Lea Courington
Leigh Ann Pike
Linda Nell Evans
Lissa Dunlay

Maaza Mengiste
Marian Schwartz
& Reid Minot
Mark Haber
Marlo D. Cruz Pagan
Mary Cline
Maynard Thomson
Michael Reklis
Mike Kaminsky

Mokhtar Ramadan
Nikki & Dennis
Gibson
Olga Kislova
Patrick Kukucka
Patrick Kutcher
Richard Meyer
Sherry Perry
Steve Bullock

Suejean Kim
Susan Carp
Susan Ernst
Stephen Harding
Symphonic Source
Theater Jones
Thomas DiPiero
Tim Perttula
Tony Thomson

SUBSCRIBERS

Ali Bolcakan
Andre Habet
Andrew Bowles
Anita Tarar
Anonymous
Ben Fountain
Ben Nichols
Blair Bullock
Cameron Leader-Picone
Charles Dee Mitchell
Chris Sweet
Christie Tull
Courtney Sheedy
Daniel Galindo
David Tomlinson & Kathryn
Berry
David Travis
David Weinberger
Dawn Wilburn-Saboe

Elaine Corwin
Elizabeth Johnson
Geoffrey Young
Holly LaFon
Horatiu Matei
James Tierney
Jeffrey Collins
Jill Kelly
Joe Milazzo
John Schmerein
John Winkelman
Kevin Winter
Kimberly Alexander
Lesley Conzelman
M.J. Malooly
Margaret Terwey
Martha Gifford
Mary Brockson
Michael Elliott

Michael Filippone
Mies de Vries
Neal Chuang
Nhan Ho
Nicholas R. Theis
Patrick Shirak
Peter McCambridge
Rainer Schulte
Robert Keefe
Ronald Morton
Shelby Vincent
Steven Kornajcik
Suzanne Fischer
Tim Kindseth
Todd Jailer
Tom Bowden
Tracy Shapley
William Fletcher
William Pate

AVAILABLE NOW FROM DEEP VELLUM

MICHÈLE AUDIN · *One Hundred Twenty-One Days*
translated by Christiana Hills · FRANCE

CARMEN BOULLOSA · *Texas: The Great Theft* · *Before* · *Heavens on Earth*
translated by Samantha Schnee · Peter Bush · Shelby Vincent · MEXICO

LEILA S. CHUDORI · *Home*
translated by John H. McGlynn · INDONESIA

ANANDA DEVI · *Eve Out of Her Ruins*
translated by Jeffrey Zuckerman · MAURITIUS

ALISA GANIEVA · *The Mountain and the Wall*
translated by Carol Apollonio · RUSSIA

ANNE GARRÉTA · *Sphinx* · *Not One Day*
translated by Emma Ramadan · FRANCE

JÓN GNARR · *The Indian* · *The Pirate* · *The Outlaw*
translated by Lytton Smith · ICELAND

NOEMI JAFFE · *What are the Blind Men Dreaming?*
translated by Julia Sanches & Ellen Elias-Bursac · BRAZIL

CLAUDIA SALAZAR JIMÉNEZ · *Blood of the Dawn*
translated by Elizabeth Bryer · PERU

JOSEFINE KLOUGART · *Of Darkness*
translated by Martin Aitken · DENMARK

YANICK LAHENS · *Moonbath*
translated by Emily Gogolak · HAITI

JUNG YOUNG MOON · *Vaseline Buddha*
translated by Yewon Jung · SOUTH KOREA

FOUAD LAROUI · *The Curious Case of Dassoukine's Trousers*
translated by Emma Ramadan · MOROCCO

LINA MERUANE · *Seeing Red*
translated by Megan McDowell · CHILE

FISTON MWANZA MUJILA · *Tram 83*
translated by Roland Glasser · DEMOCRATIC REPUBLIC OF CONGO

ILJA LEONARD PFEIJFFER · *La Superba*
translated by Michele Hutchison · NETHERLANDS

FORTHCOMING FROM DEEP VELLUM

EDUARDO BERTI · *The Imagined Land*
translated by Charlotte Coombe · ARGENTINA

ALISA GANIEVA · *Bride & Groom*
translated by Carol Apollonio · RUSSIA

FOUAD LAROUI · *The Tribulations of the Last Sjilmassi*
translated by Emma Ramadan · MOROCCO

MARIA GABRIELA LLANSOL · *The Geography of Rebels Trilogy: The Book of Communities; The Remaining Life; In the House of July & August*
translated by Audrey Young · PORTUGAL

PABLO MARTÍN SÁNCHEZ · *The Anarchist Who Shared My Name*
translated by Jeff Diteman · SPAIN

BRICE MATTHIEUSSENT · *Revenge of the Translator*
translated by Emma Ramadan · FRANCE

SERGIO PITOL · *Mephisto's Waltz: Selected Short Stories*
translated by George Henson · MEXICO

SERGIO PITOL · *Carnival Triptych: The Love Parade; Taming the Divine Heron; Married Life*
translated by George Henson · MEXICO

ÓFEIGUR SIGURÐSSON · *Öræfi: The Wasteland*
translated by Lytton Smith · ICELAND

DEEP
VELLUM